NORTH OF MONTANA

NORTH OF MONTANA

A NOVEL BY

APRIL SMITH

ALFRED A. KNOPF •
NEW YORK • 1994

Grateful acknowledgment is made to Bourne Co. Music
Publishers and Hal Leonard Corporation for permission to
reprint an excerpt from "In the Wee Small Hours of the
Morning," words by Bob Hilliard, music by David Mann,
copyright © 1955 by Better Half Music and Redd Evans Music
Co., copyright renewed 1983 by Better Half Music and Rytvoc,
Inc. This arrangement copyright © 1993 by Better Half Music
and Rytvoc Music. All rights reserved. International copyright
secured. Used by permission.

This is a work of fiction. Characters, organizations, and events
are the product of the author's imagination or, if real, used
fictitiously. Any resemblance to actual people, living or dead,
organizations, or events is entirely coincidental.

Library of Congress Cataloging-in-Publication Data
Smith, April
North of Montana : a novel / by April Smith. — 1st ed.
p.   cm.
ISBN 0-679-43197-7
1. Government investigators—California—Los Angeles—Fiction.
2. Women detectives—California—Los Angeles—Fiction.
3. Los Angeles (Calif.)—Fiction. I. Title.
PS3569.M467N67   1994
813'.54—dc20   94-12311   CIP

Manufactured in the United States of America

First Edition

FOR DOUGLAS

LOS ANGELES, 1990

PART ONE
PURE SEX

ONE

IT WAS PURE SEX.

Opening day at Dodger Stadium and all I had to do was stop at California First Bank on Pico to pick up some surveillance film, then off to the cool breezes of Chavez Ravine, a pitching battle between Martinez and Drabek, a Dodger Dog, and definitely one of those malted ice milks in the giant cup that make you feel all bloated and content like a fat stupid balloon.

I am having the obligatory chat with the manager of the bank that was robbed the day before. We have already been there of course and done our initial investigation, but the manager is still in shock and needs to talk. He is about fifty, a marathon runner with pale hair, stoop-shouldered, wearing a blue madras jacket with nice deep purples in it and gray slacks. He keeps a laminated plaque of The Objectives of Kiwanis International on the wall above his desk.

In fact he runs a spotless organization. It is a brand-new branch with shiny oak floors and large watercolors of fields of flowers in brass frames. The girl tellers wear pretty dresses and costume pearls, the boys have slick haircuts and wide-shouldered suits, although I can't figure out how they can afford to look that way on their dog-meat salaries. Along with brochures for savings plans and loans there is even a pot of coffee and a plate of mini chocolate chip cookies on a table near the back door where the robber exited with $734 in cash.

The manager is touching my arm with bony, trembling fingertips. It is the sixth robbery of his banking career and after each one he gets an incapacitating migraine headache. It's seeing that gun, he tells me, starting to flush pink, so I give what support I can muster (while arguing with myself whether Juan Samuel or Brett Butler should be the lead-off batter), reminding him that we are living in the bank robbery capital of the United States, that at the Los Angeles field office of the Federal Bureau of Investigation we work maybe ten robberies a day, so especially if your branch happens to be situated near two freeway off-ramps the odds are good that it will happen to you—but the odds are also that nobody will get hurt, that's why the bad guys take up this line of work, it is so astonishingly low risk.

I am wasting time and not making a dent in his anxiety; his spick-and-span little Swiss clock of a world has been skewed so dreadfully out of shape by the violent invasion of the barrel of a gun that it can no longer be trusted to tick along reliably. The FBI comes along after the fact, and now here is this five-foot, four-inch female agent, who on opening day is not even wearing the authoritative gray suit that falls to the knee but a T-shirt and jeans, and, I am sorry to say, a pair of pink high-top Keds. She is a long way from being a solid brother of the Kiwanis Club, and her petite frame and impatient attitude present not the slightest assurance that the whole damn thing won't happen to him all over again.

I have to get up on a ladder to remove the surveillance film. Half the time there isn't any film because the bozos have forgotten to reload the camera, but today is my lucky day. Also I am usually being harassed by my partner, Mike Donnato, who loves to make me go up on the ladder so he can allegedly look at my rear end, but it is just a joke because he is married and we have been together three years and once when I changed my hair from black to red it took him a week to notice. Today Donnato is on vacation and I am alone.

I have noticed that nothing good happens to you when you are alone.

I get the film, put a new roll in the camera, leave the manager at his desk unhappily pouring herbal tea from a thermos into a mug that says Captain, and go out and sit in my car, which I have parked in the shade. I am listening to the AM radio for a report on the traffic going to Dodger Stadium when I see a man get out of a car, put on sunglasses, and tug a baseball cap way down over his eyes, acting real hinky. He buttons a short-sleeved shirt over the one he's already wearing. And there is a bulge under the shirt.

I am trying to rationalize that he is probably an undercover cop assigned to the bank after the robbery when he looks dead at me. I stay neutral, not smiling. We hold eye contact until finally he looks down, shakes his head once, and gets back in his car.

All I know at this point is that the man is about six feet tall and white. I don't know if he got back into the car because he took me for some kind of a cop or if he just forgot his passbook—if that's a Walkman under his shirt or a Browning pistol. I decide to get his license number.

So I roll the Ford behind his car just as he's backing out and we almost crash. I get the number, put on my turn signal, and move slowly out of the parking lot like I'm going to go left and be gone, watching all the while in the rearview mirror without moving my head, just the eyes.

As soon as he sees me turn, he zips back into the parking space, cuts the engine, gets out of the car, and heads for the bank on the run.

This is when I get seriously annoyed with Donnato for being in Catalina with his wife while I am confronting a robbery suspect alone. In seven years as a street agent I have had to draw my weapon maybe a dozen times, always with a partner or heavy-duty backup. We are not local cops. We cannot arrest someone on suspicion. We have to present evidence to the Assistant U. S. Attorney before we then make the bust unless it is a felony in progress. Our operations are carefully controlled. I have never been in a free-floating situation like this in my life. As if words of wisdom from Mom and Dad, two principles from training school flash repeatedly in my mind: Keep a clear head . . . and go by the rules.

If I call in a "211 in progress request assistance," LAPD will pick it up and send in six screaming cruisers while the radio room at the Bureau contacts the bank to verify that a robbery is happening. If I am right and it is a robbery, springing all that firepower on the man inside could precipitate a bloody disaster. If I'm wrong and he's just another slob in a baseball cap, the rest of my squad will be royally pissed for having been called back from a relaxing afternoon at Dodger Stadium.

I wheel back into the lot, park the G-ride behind a dumpster, and try for that clear head: my job at this moment is to make sure nothing goes wrong inside the bank. I am going to let him rob it and let him come out. That way everyone will be happy, except the bank manager, who is probably dead of a heart attack by now despite his undoubtedly low cholesterol. The bank will be insured, the customers safe, and when I do call it in, I'll know I have probable cause.

I am listening to the police scanner in my car, waiting to hear the LAPD dispatcher say, "211 silent, California First, 11712 Pico," which would mean one of those well-groomed, well-trained young tellers had tripped the silent alarm, but all I am hearing is the sharp squawk of routine police business over the roar of two nearby freeways and meanwhile my anxiety level is going sky-high. What do I do when the dirtbag comes out? He's probably on dope and can run faster than I can—then a new flush of dread as it dawns on me that my bulletproof vest and shotgun are in the trunk.

Incidentally, real time elapsed since the guy went into the bank is probably less than ninety seconds, but by now I am frankly scared, convinced that something went horribly wrong inside, that the nice new oak flooring is splattered with civilian blood—and just as I am finally reaching for the radio here he comes, running with a fistful of cash, looking around, throwing away his baseball hat and tearing off the second shirt.

I still haven't actually seen a gun, nor have I been alerted to any crime, but a reasonable and prudent person does not race out of a bank discarding clothing, which seems to me at that moment of hyperreality to be a legal principle of exceptional solidity and more than enough justification to roll my car in front of his, block his exit as soon as he has closed his door, draw down on him, and ascertain if he would like to meet God.

I am carrying a .357 Magnum which I point against the driver's window inches from the guy's ear.

"Freeze—or I'll blow your head off like a ripe watermelon."

He stops trying to jam the keys into the ignition and stares up at me with runny eyes.

"I'm really nervous right now, so don't make me use this because I probably won't kill you, I'll just maim you for life."

The old clichés really work when you want someone to get a very clear, very quick picture of the consequences of his actions.

He seems hypnotized by the barrel of the gun, which must look like a cannon from his point of view, with a blurry, indistinct but clearly assertive person at arm's length behind it.

"I want both hands on the windshield, real, real, slow."

He puts the palms out and they cleave against the glass with a moist suction. Graying hair flies around his head in sweaty wisps. A soft belly presses up against the wheel. Somewhere it registers that the subject seems down. Irritated. Sad.

"Don't move or I'll blow your face right off." He doesn't move. "Now open the door and back out."

As soon as the door is opened I jam the gun into the base of the skull and remove the bulge from his belt. It is a starter pistol.

"On the ground. Hands behind your back."

Now he's proned out on the concrete and I get the handcuffs on him.

"Back into the car. On the front seat. Face down."

He's in. He's down. And the adrenaline rush sweeps through. Suddenly I'm becoming sensory perceptive, feeling things I wasn't feeling before, like the intense heat of the noon sun, the fact that I can't catch my breath, sweat coursing under my arms and between my breasts.

And I still haven't called the damn thing in.

Someone's loping through the parking lot, past people who have frozen in place like odd statues all facing the same way.

"I can't believe you're still here." It's the bank manager, also breathing hard. "We've just been robbed again . . . and"—then, in-credulously—"you got him!"

"That's why they pay me the big bucks."

I pick up the radio. At this moment I want to be very cool: "This is signal 345. A good 211 just occurred at California First Bank, 11712 Pico. I am 10-15 with one male subject. Would appreciate assistance to handle additional inside investigation."

There is silence on the other end. "Say again?"

Well, that's about as cool as I get. *"I got the sucker coming out of the bank!"*

Another pause. Then: "You gotta be shitting me."

I hear the information echoed on the police scanner as the emboldened bank manager, my deputy and new best friend, rescued from despair after seven robberies and bursting now with hope for civilization, scurries around the parking lot telling people to "stand away" from the crime scene and suddenly here comes the chopper and all faces turn toward the sky.

An LAPD officer hovering above us bellows through a bull-horn, "Are you okay?"

I give him the international okay sign—a tap to the top of the head—and he banks away as the crazy Latvian cop who has this beat skids through the parking lot with sirens screaming, along with about a dozen other boys from the Wilshire Division who want to see how their brakes and tires really work. It was beautiful.

■   ■   ■

The next morning is party time. My squad has a tradition of coffee and donuts at eight a.m. and they are ready for me when I drag my-self in after staying at the office until almost midnight the night be-fore pushing the paperwork through.

I get a round of applause and one of those three-foot-long green foam-rubber hands with the fingers forming "number one" and another thoughtful souvenir from the ballpark: a cardboard tray with a Dodger Dog still wrapped in the authentic aluminum foil bag, a double sack of peanuts, and my favorite malted ice milk melted to a fine lukewarm puree.

"We thought about you all nine innings," says Kyle Vernon. "Of course, damned if we were gonna leave!"

The others laugh. They didn't have to leave because I had it all tied down.

"Our supervisor's out jerking them off in Washington, why should we miss Sciosca's dramatic run in the bottom of the ninth?" says Frank Chang with a sly smile.

"His what? Oh *shit!*"

Meanwhile Mike Donnato has been lying back in a chair, with tasseled loafers crossed up on his desk, and stroking his blond beard, which is on the way to gray. It is natural to be gathered around him; ten years older than me, he is the senior squad member and spiritual leader.

"So, Donnato," I smirk, "how was Catalina Island? Nice and peaceful? Go scuba diving?"

He wrinkles his nose. "You got lucky."

"You're jealous!"

"You wait your whole career for a break like that. There is no justice."

"But you and Pumpkin got to see some really neat fish."

"If you don't buzz off I'll make you drive," Donnato threatens lazily.

"Hey, I'm out of here."

"You think this bust is your ticket to the C-1 squad?"

"I'm writing my request for transfer today."

"Get in line, baby. Duane Carter's really pushing for that transfer to headquarters," says Kyle.

Duane Carter is the squad supervisor and not much liked.

"Carter's pissed too many people off," says Barbara Sullivan, our robbery coordinator, aka The Human Computer. "They'll never assign him to headquarters, they'll leave him here to rot."

"You wish."

"No, I don't wish," says Barbara, whipping the pearl she always wears back and forth on its gold chain. "If he's going to rot, let him rot in hell."

"Either way, Duane won't make it easy," says Kyle. "He likes torturing you slits."

Barbara makes a face.

"His word, not mine," Kyle shrugs.

"As an Afro-American, I would think you'd be especially aware of offensive stereotyping."

"Forgive me." Kyle matches her arch tone. "I have misplaced my gender sensitivity manual and I am at a loss as to how to reply."

"Try this: 'Yo! Honky bitch!' " says Frank, and we all laugh because we have just been through a multicultural awareness workshop that was one big snore.

"Carter won't have a choice." Donnato swings his feet to the floor and breaks off a piece of sugar donut in a matter-of-fact way. "It was the perfect bust."

I am thrilled. "Thanks."

His eyes are full of warmth. "You just earned your spurs."

Rosalind, an administrative assistant who's worked in this field office twenty years, comes up to our group.

"Ana? Can I talk to you?"

"Join the party."

"Did you hear about Ana's perfect bust?" Donnato calls. "If you haven't, she'll tell you."

"Ana," she repeats impatiently, "I have to talk to you."

"You better mind." Kyle smiles toward Rosalind, who is old enough to be his mother, but today she doesn't want to play. Planted there in the middle of the room, I notice she has a peculiar look.

"What's the matter?"

She leads me away. Her voice is low.

"A message came for you. It's bad news, Ana."

Something went wrong on a case. Which one? My brain is not functioning yet this morning. I'm still back in the parking lot playing Sheena, Queen of the Jungle.

We step into a doorway for a shred of privacy. We face each other. She is even smaller than I am. She has to look up.

"Violeta Alvarado was killed."

I must have stared like an idiot.

She gives me a yellow Post-it telephone message slip that says "While you were out . . ." with a Spanish name and phone number. I look at it but it makes no sense.

"Violeta Alvarado?"

Rosalind nods. Her eyes are moist and round with sadness, anybody's sadness. Her eyebrows pinch together with sympathy that comes from having lost who knows how much in her lifetime.

She gives a little shrug. She understands my confusion. It is natural when you hear something like this. She takes my hand in both of hers.

"They said she's your cousin."

She watches me, patient, present, waiting for me to comprehend.

TWO

MY DESK is among twenty others lined up in pairs in a big open room called the bullpen. The light is fluorescent yellow and you can only see the outside world if the door to Duane Carter's office is open and you can angle a view through his window of Westwood looking south.

But from where I sit all I get is a vista of a long metal coatrack against an anonymous beige wall. The single item hanging on the rack is an old tan sport jacket. Written across the back in black marker are the words Bank Dick's Undercover Disguise. The front of the jacket has been decorated by generations of agents with medals, advice, maps, and obscenities in everything from green ink to real blood (gleaned from a nasty run-in Special Agent Frank Chang once had with a stapler).

Since I look at it all day, I have come to think of the Bank Dick's Undercover Disguise as a partner—a veteran who has been through it all, who knows our secrets and knows the answers but is bound to silence by the poignant dumb invisibility of a ghost. Who suffers more in his isolation? Him or us?

I phone the number on the yellow Post-it and get a loud Latino television station in the background and the voice of an older woman: *"Bueno?"*

"Mrs. Gutiérrez? This is Special Agent Ana Grey with the FBI."

She immediately begins talking with great urgency in Spanish.

"I'm sorry. I don't speak Spanish."

"No?" Surprised. "No problem. I can speak in English. I am very sorry about your cousin."

If my instincts were right about the dirtbag at the bank I am probably right again that this is some sort of a scam.

"Just a minute, ma'am. I don't have a cousin named Violeta Alvarado."

"Yes, she talked about you. You are the big cousin who works for the United States government."

I blush at the thought of being anybody's "big cousin who works for the government."

"I'm sorry, but I have never met Ms. Alvarado."

"I know you are the one. And right now, your family needs your help."

She is so fierce, so absurd, that it makes me laugh. "It's not my family! Look, I was born in Santa Monica, California—"

"And your father's people come from El Salvador."

Suddenly I am very uneasy. Nobody has mentioned my father in years. He was allegedly from Central America but I never even knew which country, since he abandoned us when I was a tiny child and was always a taboo subject in our home. My mother and I lived with her father, a police officer, and I was raised Protestant and white; you couldn't get more white, all the way back to the curl in the horns on the headgear of our Viking ancestors. I happen to have thick wavy black hair but that's as Mediterranean as I get. Hispanics are simply another race to me.

Colder now, "Why are you calling, Mrs. Gutiérrez? What do you want?"

"It's not for me, it's for Violeta's children. They have nobody in this country to take care of them."

Part of me is working hard to believe this is all a fake. Already

I have come up with a scenario for how the scam must work: they find some indigent who dies. Call a relative (real or imagined) who has never met the person. Hit them up for "money to take care of the children." Sooner or later somebody will send a check out of guilt. I start to take notes. Maybe this will warrant opening a case.

"Really?" Writing now, "And what are the children's names?"

"Cristóbal and Teresa."

"What is your relationship to the children?"

"I live in the building. I become very close with Violeta because we are both from El Salvador. I baby-sit for her children while she works. Only now there is no one because she is dead."

"How was she killed?"

"She was shot down in the street, on Santa Monica Boulevard only two blocks from here. She was shot up so bad that her hands were gone. When they laid her in her coffin they had to put white gloves on the end of the arms."

"What did the police say?"

"They don't know anything."

There is a breath or a sob and the woman's tone becomes desperate: "Who will take care of the children?"

The professional response comes easiest: "I will put you in touch with a city agency—"

She interrupts: "The last lady Violeta worked for still owes her money. If you can get the money, I will take care of the children until they find a home not with strangers . . . but with family."

The way she says "family"—with intimacy and conviction, the way religious people speak effortlessly of God—is embarrassing. My only living family is my grandfather and my lifestyle is aggressively without God: the furnished one-bedroom in Marina Del Ray. My 1970 Plymouth Barracuda convertible. Sixty, a hundred hours a week at the Bureau, a diet shake for lunch, and a mile in the pool every day. A career timetable so tight you could plot it on graph paper—a straight line to Assistant Special Agent in Charge or even the first female Special Agent in Charge of a cherry field office like Denver, which, because I am a woman, will require at least five more years of crossing each square perfectly, never one millimeter off; no messiness, no mistakes, no fat.

Reaching for my Rolodex, "I'm going to refer you to a social worker."

"No," insists this stranger with absolute authority, "it is not right. These children are of your blood."

"That's ridiculous."

"Violeta and your father came from the same village."

"Which village?"

"La Palma."

"Never heard of it."

"She told me it is a small place, maybe one hundred miles from San Salvador, with a black sand beach."

Of the few fragments remaining of my father there is a relic as real yet mysterious as a shard of wave-polished glass: *When your father was a boy, he played on a black sand beach.*

It shakes me.

"Mrs. Gutiérrez—I'm sorry, but I have to take another call. Good luck to you."

I hang up and stare at the Bank Dick's Undercover Disguise. The sleeves are empty. The heart, weightless.

After a moment I realize the intercom is in fact buzzing. Barbara Sullivan has something for me on the bank robbery.

THREE

ONE ENTIRE WALL of Barbara Sullivan's office is covered with still photographs taken by surveillance cameras of bank robberies in progress. To the untrained eye, except for gross differences in gender and race and type of weapon, they all look pretty much the same and walking in there can actually make you feel nauseated, overwhelmed by the tang of film developer, confronted by a floor-to-ceiling sea of gray images, most so grainy and out of focus you need a magnifying glass to get any detail.

But to the Human Computer the surveillance photos are daily bread, to be carefully chewed, swallowed, digested, and turned into masses of information stored in the brain for instantaneous retrieval. The Human Computer forgets nothing, including the minutiae of one's personal life. Before she got married to another agent, Barbara and I used to pal around police bars together and she can still repeat the time and place that I met every one of my liaisons. She even remembers their ranks and names.

The job of the bank robbery coordinator is to find connections between the more than two thousand bank robberies committed each year in Los Angeles County. Most individual robbers will repeat ten or fifteen times for less than a thousand dollars a take, easily losing themselves in a tangle of freeways or a robber-friendly matrix of underinformed and understaffed law enforcement. Now that gangs have become involved, resources are stretched even thinner. Our conviction rate is not great. Often it is the Human Computer, meditating alone before this sorry montage, who provides a clue that leads to an arrest.

When I walk into her office, Barbara is reading *People* magazine with Jayne Mason on the cover and eating birthday cake from a big slab someone left in the lunchroom, deep chocolate with raspberry in the middle. She pushes a slice on a Mickey Mouse paper plate toward me along with a folded napkin and red plastic fork. I have brought my mug, knowing she always has fresh brew flavored with cinnamon perking along in her personal coffeemaker.

"I am absolutely devastated about Jayne Mason," she says, not taking her eyes from the magazine. "My whole world just went up in smoke."

I look at the upside-down photos, familiar as a family album. Even now in her fifties or sixties or who knows what, Jayne Mason remains one of our truly enduring movie stars.

"She's a drug addict." Barbara slaps her hand down and looks up with real hurt as if she's been personally betrayed.

I sip the coffee. "Why is that a surprise? She's an actress. Of course she's on drugs."

"Oh, come on! *Jayne Mason?* Every American girl's prefeminist dream? You have to admit she's exquisite."

She flips the magazine around so I can see the famous black and white portrait of Jayne Mason taken when she was barely twenty, the amazing cheekbones then described as: "Pure as the curves of a Stradivarius . . . heartbreaking as the Mozart played thereon."

Barbara is going on impatiently, "Don't you remember those wonderful old sentimental musicals?"

"I hate musicals."

"She was *angelic.* She always played the good-hearted farm girl whose pa just passed away or the poor street urchin who gets the swell idea of putting on a musical production, then finds out she has tuberculosis. But don't worry—the handsome young doctor saves her life and she becomes a big Broadway star."

I say nothing. Barbara glowers at me with frustration. "Your idea of a tearjerker is *Terminator.*"

"That's right. The robot dies and it's sad."

"She turned down the title role in *Gigi*—big mistake—because she was having a tumultuous affair with Louis Jourdan at the time." The Human Computer cannot be shut down: "Her first dramatic role was *Bad Men,* a famous western with John Wayne."

"Even I remember that. They were making love on the tallest butte in Arizona and supposedly they really screwed."

"Look at this!" Barbara picks up the magazine and throttles it. "She's an addict! Like every other sleazeball on the street."

I swipe it from her and examine a photo of Jayne Mason taken just last week. She is getting into a limousine wearing dark glasses and a tailored white linen suit, clutching a bouquet of yellow roses, looking like she's running for a plane to Rome rather than dodging reporters on the way to the Betty Ford Center.

Barbara sighs. "I used to wear a full slip underneath my Catholic school uniform because Jayne Mason looked so sexy and romantic in them. The first time I saw her on the Academy Awards I was three years old and watched every year since, hoping she'd be on. She was the queen of queens in the prom gown of all prom gowns. God, I wanted to be beautiful."

But I am fussing over something else: "You can't remember anything when you're three."

"I can."

"I remember nothing before the age of five. The whole time we lived with my grandfather in Santa Monica is a blank."

Barbara gives a wry look over her coffee cup. "Have you spoken to your therapist about this?"

"Why? That's normal."

But Barbara's attention has returned wistfully to the magazine.

"I was so sorry when Jayne didn't marry President Kennedy. They would have made the sexorama couple of the century. Nobody wears full slips anymore." Then, without a pause, "When does Duane get back?"

"Day after tomorrow."

"We're going to have something very special waiting for him."

Barbara smiles. Small-boned, with curly reddish hair down to her shoulders, a pert nose, and wide-set blue eyes, she has an advanced degree in biology and looks about as much like an FBI agent as I do, especially with a Mickey Mouse napkin tucked into the neck of her yellow wool suit.

She places one of the surveillance photographs in front of me.

"Here's your guy."

There's my guy in the baseball hat and two shirts standing in front of a teller's window in California First Bank. He isn't pointing a gun or doing anything even slightly dramatic. The photo is stamped UNSUB. Unknown Subject.

"And here's your guy again."

In a second photograph he is wearing different shirts, a different baseball hat, with the same puffy face and sagging eyes.

"Same M.O.," Barbara continues, pointing with her fork. "The gun, the baseball hat, same instructions: 'Give me your hundreds and no dye packs.' "

The second photo is stamped UNSUB, Bank of the West, Culver City Branch, 1984. I am astonished.

"How do you do that?"

"Vitamin A."

"How do you remember? Is there some kind of trick?"

"Sure there's a trick."

She stands abruptly, dumps our plates in the trash, and turns to me, arms folded.

"When I was a new agent, Duane Carter used to routinely get me up against a filing cabinet and suggest how we might spend the rest of the afternoon. I would laugh him off, being cute and 'not wanting to hurt his feelings'—then one day he pulled me down on his lap on top of his hard-on and slipped his hand under my skirt."

"Barbara!"

"Yeah, well, I should have shot the sucker between the eyes but instead . . . I didn't handle it very well. I cried. Told him I had a boyfriend. Some damn lie or other. This was before sexual harassment cases."

She whips the pearl back and forth.

"He would take me to lunch when we were supposed to be discussing a case and talk about how we should get the penthouse suite at the Beverlywood Hotel, how Mormon males are great in bed, they have some super sexual secret, that's why they have so many wives and children . . . when the truth is, he hates women."

I look again at the little Catholic schoolgirl from Chicago in the yellow suit and pearl necklace, still so ladylike in her obsessive rage. "I am so sorry you had to put up with that shit."

"After I got married I deliberately transferred back to Duane Carter's squad. For years he thought he had this dirty little secret on me. But times have changed and I've got it on him."

"How? It's too late for legal action."

"I'm watching him and he knows it. Why do you think I've hung in as robbery coordinator so long? It's the perfect position to keep sticking it to him. Like right now—you're going to bust this guy for *two* robberies and get your transfer to C-1 and it will drive Duane Carter absolutely nuts because you're a woman and you did it, and he ain't getting transferred nowhere."

I put my arm around her shoulder. She is my friend. "Don't spend your life on Duane Carter."

"It makes me happy." Her thin rosy lips compress into a tight smile.

"Someday," I tell her, "you're coming with me over the wall."

"Go with God."

■ ■ ■

Three hours later I am in a stuffy interrogation room at the Metropolitan Detention Center with my guy, whose name is Dennis Hill. I had interviewed him when I gave him his rights and had him sign the FD395 form, but he had refused to talk. He's wearing orange overalls with MDC on the back and looks just as sullen as he did yesterday, when I busted him—a jowly unshaven face and unkempt gray hair matting and merging with curls growing up the back of the neck.

"You're a pretty good bank robber, Dennis."

His eyes watch me. I see intelligence there.

"This is not your first job. You've just never been caught before. Am I right?"

He doesn't answer.

"That makes you pretty good. Not great. But good."

I show him the two surveillance photos, one from his most recent work, the other stretching back into history.

"We pulled down these photos. That's you. Both times."

He looks at the photos and back at me with heavy eyes.

"It's okay, Dennis. You don't have to say anything. We've got you on two."

I slip the photos back into the envelope.

"You've got me on dick."

His first words. How charming.

"Is that so?"

"You don't know the half of it."

"Why don't you tell me?"

He puts both hands on the table and pushes his chair back. I tense involuntarily, even though there is a six-foot-four cop standing at the door.

Dennis runs a hand through his greasy hair.

"You know where I used to live?"

"Paris."

"Palos Verdes. In a house that was worth at the time . . . maybe half a million dollars."

"You must be a better robber than I thought."

He shakes his head. "I was an executive sales director at Hughes Aero-Space. Made two hundred thousand dollars a year."

He is quiet, as if waiting for me to put the pieces together. I remember my first impression when I confronted him in his car in the parking lot. He didn't resist. He seemed edgy . . . down . . . on the down side of a high.

"Who got you into the powder?" I ask gently.

"Nobody but myself. High roller. Big deal with women. Nice car. Liked the ponies. Big shit, you know?"

I nod. "You got in over your head. Started selling your assets to pay for the habit. And when you lost it all you got desperate and robbed a bank. It was easy. So you did it again."

A tremble goes through him. "I've got a son. He came to see me this morning. He still loves me."

He bites a corner off the nail on his thumb.

"You're a smart, educated guy, Dennis. Why didn't you go for help?"

"Because I happen to love cocaine."

We sit in silence for a while. He loves cocaine. I have never heard it said more clearly or more completely without apology. He loves cocaine more than he loves his own son.

I believe I can smell the sweat on him and the sweat on the cop and the rancid layers of sweat on the grimy tile walls of a thousand other murderers, pederasts, rapists, junkies, movie stars, and thieves who will tell you with the same unself-conscious certainty that they did it, whatever it was, because they were in love. And being in love absolves them and makes them innocent.

I stand up. "Let's get a stenographer in here and get your statement."

"Statement on what?"

"The other robbery."

Of course he hasn't actually admitted to the Culver City job. I'm angling. I'm hoping.

"I didn't do another robbery."

I wait it out a moment, thinking, I'm getting somewhere with this guy. We have a rapport. I'll come back—

Then he says, "I did six."

■　■　■

Donnato treats me to lunch the next day at Bora-Bora, a collegiate hangout where the waitresses wear skimpy little shorts and Hawaiian shirts and everything is served in plastic baskets and it is so noisy we can hardly hear each other.

"This is the one that's going to do it for you," he says. "Get you above the crowd."

"I'll miss you, Donnato."

He shrugs and takes a bite of a chicken burrito. "You've got to move on. I told you: seven years. That's the time most agents light their blue flame."

"You think the Kidnapping and Extortion Squad is the right move?"

I have asked him this before but for some reason I want to prolong the moment.

"I told you: less pressure. More involved cases. You can take some in-service courses, and the supervisor is a nice guy."

I reach over and smooth some tortilla flakes from his beard.

"What are you going to do without me?"

"Drive some other split-tail crazy with lust."

"Is that what you think?"

"Ana, I can read you like a book."

"You are so full of it," I tell him. "You are the most married man I know."

"Luckily for you."

I am dying for a beer but when the waitress comes I order another iced tea.

"Look at you," I tell my partner. "Can't take your eyes off her Lycra bicycle shorts."

"Is that what they're made of? I thought it was the foreskin of a whale."

Giggling, "So don't pretend I'm anything special to you. Just because I'm leaving you forever."

Suddenly Donnato seems to tire of our little flirtation. He gets that way. He says being a street agent is a young person's game, although he's got the tight, honed body of a thirty-year-old. But he has three kids and his heart lies with them. Somewhere along the line being an involved father gained an edge over being an agent, although he still performs both roles with a dedication and intensity most people barely muster for one. You can see the exhaustion come over him like a shade.

"Ana, you're a terrific agent. I'm really proud of you."

"Hey . . ." I am choking with awkwardness, but it has to be said: "You taught me everything I know. I guess this is the time to thank you for it."

We both look away, embarrassed, catch CNN going on the television set above the bar, and stare at it until the bill arrives; he pays it, and we leave. Back at the office I get the forms from Rosalind and spend the rest of the afternoon composing an eloquent statement on why I should be transferred to C-1, Kidnapping and Extortion.

Just as I am about to leave for a 6:30 p.m. swim workout I get a call from LAPD Detective Sergeant Roth.

"Ana? It's John."

He waits. So do I.

Cautiously, "Where are you these days, John?"

"Wilshire Division, crash unit."

Another silence. I listen to his tense breathing, not knowing what to say.

"You must be a busy boy."

"I was thinking about you."

"Only good thoughts, I hope."

I've been standing with the strap of the swimming bag over my shoulder, poised to go, as far from the desk as possible, the curly cord of the telephone receiver stretched taut. They teach you in the academy that anxiety is the same physical response as the body's flight-or-fight reflex: hearing John Roth's voice again is producing the exact chemical reaction I would have, to use their example, if a man wearing a ski mask had stepped out of my shower stall.

"I've been working a homicide that took place about two weeks ago on Santa Monica Boulevard. A female Hispanic named Violeta Alvarado. No next of kin except for two minors, but a neighbor says the victim was related to an FBI agent named Ana Grey." He adds, singsong: "It had to be you."

Tense: "Must be."

"So then this is a condolence call. I'm sorry."

"Don't be sorry. I didn't even know the deceased."

I give in to the pull of the telephone. The cord slackens as I sit back down and allow the bag to slump to the floor.

"This is too weird, John. That you would get this case."

"I know it."

When John Roth and I first started having sex we used to marvel at how powerful and instantaneous our connection was, as if we were riding a secret current that swept past ordinary pleasures to a lagoon of desire known only to us. We thought we were so inventive and unique and amazing that we used to joke about making an instructional video or posing coupled for an artist; we used to watch ourselves in a mirror and tease each other with pet names, "John" and "Yoko."

So now, a year or so after the crash and burn, maybe we're both thinking—me with cold dread—that our connection is somehow still in force; that the universe has brought us together again in a strange and unexpected way.

"We probably have a lot of dead people in common," John says.

I laugh nervously. He seems encouraged.

"I was calling outside of channels because I thought you'd want to check this thing out."

"It has nothing to do with me."

"The lady was insistent—"

Suddenly the flight part of the flight-or-fight reflex clicks in and my foot is tapping up and down as if it had a mind of its own.

"Look, John. It's weird, it's funky, it's whatever, but it's over. I never even heard of Violeta Alvarado and I really don't give a rat's ass, so please don't call me again. I've got to go. I've got a meeting."

I hang up and grip the familiar nylon handles of the bag, heavy with rubber fins and hand paddles, a folding hair dryer, and a mesh sack containing slippery old bottles of shampoo and moisturizer with the writing rubbed off. Crossing the bullpen, I try to concentrate on how good it will feel to hit the water and stretch it out for that first fifty yards. As the workout builds, the fear will dissipate; by the end of the hour I'll forget about John Roth.

FOUR

FRIDAY NIGHT and I have big plans: grocery shopping and a hot bath. Barbara lent me the hardcover edition of *Clear and Present Danger* by Tom Clancy and I am looking forward to reading it in bed with a cup of raspberry tea. There is a lot to be said for the monastic life.

Ocean View Estates is one of the oldest apartment complexes in Marina Del Ray. It was world famous for a brief moment during the quaint psychedelic era of 1970, when I was ten years old. At one of their notorious swinging singles parties, somebody sprinkled LSD over the potato chips and three people boiled to death while tripping out in the Jacuzzi.

Afterward they changed the name from South Sea Villas to Ocean View Estates, but the singles and transients and corporately owned condominiums remain. Friday nights they still have a "social barbecue" where everyone's supposed to come out of their huts and gather around some greasy old grills, but dragging my briefcase and four plastic bags of groceries past the pool area, all I see this Friday night is an extended Middle Eastern family right off the boat, women in black veils unpacking bright yellow boxes of take-out chicken, tortillas, rice and beans from El Pollo Loco. My brand-new multicultural training tells me they haven't got a clue.

My place is located in a cul-de-sac of two-story brown stucco apartment buildings still absurdly called Tahiti Gardens. It is a long way from the parking garage but it's home. I have lived in these three furnished rooms for seven years. The good part is I have never had to buy a couch.

The mailbox is filled with catalogues and one large brown manila envelope with no return address. I might have gotten to the envelope earlier if I weren't fumbling with the groceries and desperate to pee. Instead it lies on the counter.

The air is stagnant and laced with the smell of carpet shampoo and Formica scrubbed with scouring powder; I guess latex wallpaper over wallboard over cinder block doesn't breathe. Shoving the heavy glass doors open, I step onto a balcony to a nice view of the largest manmade marina in the world, six thousand boats moored at neatly laid out docks, a shifting forest of white masts. I enjoy looking at the boats even though I've never been on one, letting my eyes wander the riggings and blue sail bags and pleasantly swelled white hulls glazed with golden light. Someday I will learn to sail.

Forty-five minutes later the groceries are put away and I am sorting through the catalogues to decide who to spend dinner with, Eddie Bauer or J. Peterman. The timer goes off and I pull chicken cordon bleu prepared by Boy's Market—my little indulgence—out of the microwave and settle on a stool at the counter, cozying up to a warm cloud of steam scented with toasted bread crumbs and Gorgonzola cheese.

I open an Amstel Light.

And the envelope.

Inside is a series of photographs of an autopsy taken by the Los Angeles County Coroner's Office.

I stare at the glossy images in a state of numb disbelief. They are eight-by-tens, in color, and more pornographic than anything I have ever seen or could imagine. The victim is identified by a plate reproduced in the bottom right corner of each as V. ALVARADO.

There is no cover letter, there doesn't have to be: the angry marks of the sender are all over the photographs like fingerprints.

First there are aerial shots of an intersection with an arrow drawn in grease pencil to show the probable route taken by the car.

Next, overall streets: bars, warehouses, street corners, alleys.

Orientation view of the crime scene: The body as it lay face down on the sidewalk. White triangular markers set next to a purse thrown five feet away and more markers where the bullets hit a bus-stop bench and a wall.

Closer on the body: She had tiny bare feet. God knows what happened to her shoes. The tight jeans with zippers at the ankles have white embroidered flowers over the pockets. The shirt is still tucked in neatly but the entire back is blackened with blood and a tangle of dark hair that blends into the sharp shadow cast by the flash.

Her face, on its side looking at the camera, is heart shaped, jaws apart, tongue swollen and protruding in the classic configuration of a choking victim. The eyes are half closed and that is what draws you to the picture, those dark glinting slices of obsidian beneath lids set halfway between anguish and nothingness.

The pictures of the actual autopsy, showing the progression of the body from when it was brought in fully clothed through every step of the procedure, are grisly as hell.

But the worst—as I sit frozen on my kitchen stool—is not the surgical blood and gore but the initial shot of the naked body lying on its back on the gurney after it has been undressed and still looks like a person. It is shameful to look so frankly at someone no longer able to defend herself, spread in death with blood smeared all over, rudely exposed with no secrets left. The magnitude of the violence that it takes to shatter a human body to this degree is deeply sobering. I think, my God, somebody take care of this woman, pull the sheet back over her, do whatever it takes to restore her dignity.

The rest of the photos document the probing of the wounds to remove the .45s. The Y incision down the abdomen to the pubic bone. The removal of the rib cage, which I have been told they do with a pair of pruning shears. The examination of internal organs.

Until all that is left of the victim, the violence, and the scientific examination of that violence is a scraped-out carcass. A bit of nonliving refuse and on to the next. The packet is minus any medical dictation except a form stamped M.E. REPORT PENDING.

I slip the photos back into the envelope, shaken by the impact and outraged that John Roth would send them to me. But why should I be surprised? He's always favored shock tactics—the midnight phone call, the drunken appearance from behind a pillar in the garage. Six months ago I heard he received a thirty-day suspension for firing a handgun into the pitcher's mound of a public park while doing some righteous partying with a bunch of other officers. I jump off the stool and stalk into the bedroom. The smell of congealed Gorgonzola cheese is making me sick.

Punching his number without even thinking about it, "Stop pulling this shit."

"Cool out, Ana. You're way over the top."

He sounds stoned. I got him in his apartment in Redondo Beach, where I can easily picture him sitting on the seat of a rowing machine—because the only other furniture is a NordicTrack—wearing nothing but a pair of sweatpants and smoking a joint. Young to be a detective sergeant, he has built himself one of the world-class torsos, but still wears that sort of Tom Selleck moustache that went out in the seventies, maybe to distract from rivulets of acne scars that run across his cheeks.

"Ana . . . what are you so afraid of?"

He used to whisper that in bed, challenging me to take it farther until we passed some very distant boundaries. When I told him I'd had enough, his bombardment of flowers, phone messages, faxes, cute little trolls with open arms took on the same aggression as his sex, infuriating me to the point where I once threw a punch and cracked him on the lower jaw. The more I pulled away the harder he came on, relentless and increasingly irrational, until I took to carrying a weapon at all times.

"What is the point, John?"

"Thought you'd be interested in a last look at your cousin."

"Fuck you."

"Fuck *me*?" He laughs. "Miss Señorita Alvarado was a fucking dope dealer."

Mrs. Gutiérrez described Miss Señorita Alvarado as a long suffering mother of two.

"What makes you say she was dealing dope?"

"It was a hit."

I am interested. "Were there witnesses?"

"A street kid named Rat called it in to 911 but—no surprise—later told the investigating officer he didn't see a thing. Doesn't matter. It was a drive-by. The weapon was a forty-five-caliber Mac-10, fully automatic, good for nothing but killing people. Fifteen shots were fired. The victim was hit by seven."

"Could have been random."

"Take a look at picture number five."

I walk back into the kitchen with the phone to my ear and pick up number five, the one where the body was washed to show the wounds. Half-inch bullets do not make neat pinholes. They break bones. They rip out the windpipe and cause hemorrhaging in the thorax.

"That's a lot of destruction."

"You know what it feels like to get an injection. Imagine something the size of a pencil being shoved through your body."

"How do you die?"

"Blood fills the chest cavity until you can't breathe."

"How long do you think it takes to drown in your own blood, John?"

"Couple of minutes," he answers matter-of-factly. "You lay there thinking about it. Look at the hands."

No hands, just two bloody stumps.

"They blew off her hands," he instructs. "As punishment for taking what didn't belong to her. Dealers like that kind of thing. It's a symbol even a lowlife can understand."

It is easier to talk to him as a colleague, two professionals on safe ground. I remember that was part of it, too.

"Was there evidence of drugs?"

"No, but what are the two reasons a female would be out on

Santa Monica Boulevard at five in the morning? Dealing crack or turning tricks."

"A typically sexist assumption."

"That's me."

"No shit."

"This Gutiérrez woman keeps bugging us, swears the victim was related to Ana Grey in the big FBI and that she has proof."

"What kind of proof?"

"*Yo no se* but the thought ambled across my cocked-up brain that if Alvarado was dealing and the bad guys were pissed enough to blow her away, and if they know you're a fed . . . Who the fuck knows, there could be some kind of fallout."

"I appreciate the concern."

Now I can clearly hear him taking a toke. On the exhale, "Relax, Ana. You'll be happy to know I'm boffing the lady lieutenant over on homicide."

What was I afraid of?

John Roth hadn't stopped calling until I threatened a court order. A few weeks later I found a blood-soaked tampon hanging from the doorway in my living room—a symbol even a lowlife could understand that John was seeing another woman. I never confronted him, never had proof, but changed the locks and stopped dating men.

"I'm happy for you both."

■　　■　　■

You couldn't walk or even step on the balconies of the apartment building where Violeta Alvarado lived in North Hollywood; they are purely decorative, as if a dozen grates of phony wrought iron and some Spanish-looking lamps could transform an orange stucco box into a hacienda. The building is typical West Coast tenement housing, a cockeyed design of stucco trapezoids overhanging an open carport, so that everybody's windows open into everybody else's and a central courtyard is created that magnifies and echoes every sound. Someone has wedged a bicycle between his window and the black metal filigree. Needless to say it is on the second floor—otherwise, the bicycle would have been picked clean through the bars like a skeleton.

Nobody is around this Monday morning. I am buzzed into the lobby through some warped metal doors and pass underneath a hanging sculpture that looks like the innards of a pipe organ, skipping the elevator because who knows what is lurking inside, trudging up two flights of metal stairs.

The apartment smells like roach spray and fish cooked in oil. The light-chocolate-colored carpet is thin and cheap and bunches up under your feet; if you don't trip on the rug, you will over the children—five or six of them running between two small rooms.

"Is this Violeta Alvarado's apartment?"

"Yes, but I am living here now." Mrs. Gutiérrez beckons me to a sofa in harshly textured pea-green plaid, the kind you would find in a twelve-dollar-an-hour motel room in Tijuana.

"Were you living with Violeta?"

"No, I had a small apartment upstairs. One room only. I called the landlord right away and asked if I could have this one."

Mrs. Gutiérrez lights a cigarette. She is buxom, with the most improbable hairstyle—dyed bright black, chopped short around the ears and teased high off the crown, then falling below her shoulders in a mantilla-like effect. She wears a yellow sleeveless dress that does not apologize for a stoutish body, the short skirt showing off bare round legs and feet with painted toenails in rubber thongs.

"So after Violeta was killed, you got her apartment." I watch for her reaction.

She nods. "I had to call right away. Lots of people wanted it." She is proud of herself for making a smart move. She is a survivor.

"Are these Violeta's children?"

"Teresa and Cristóbal are in the other room. I have a day care business. In San Salvador I was in charge of the kitchen of a very big hotel. I had a nice white house, a husband and two boys—all killed by the military."

"I'm sorry."

"I can't get that kind of a good job here. So these are the children I watch for the parents who are working."

They seem clean and healthy and occupied with one another and the few frayed dolls and beat-up blocks they have to play with. I become aware of a biting, sour smell just as Mrs. Gutiérrez rises, murmuring something in Spanish, and lifts an infant from a rickety wooden crib I hadn't noticed that was stuck in a corner.

I stay where I am while she changes the baby on a card table, taking in the Japanese prints on the wall alongside paintings of volcanos, beginning to suspect that what I am seeing is simply what there is: no addicts, no hookers, no child abuse, no scam.

Mrs. Gutiérrez props the baby up on her shoulder and gives it a few comforting pats. "I am very glad you came," she says.

"I came to tell you to stop saying Violeta Alvarado was my cousin."

The woman puts the baby back in the crib, opens a drawer in a wood-grained cardboard dresser, and removes a small black Bible stuffed with folded papers. She removes the rubber bands that hold it all together, carefully rolling them over her wrist so they won't be lost, takes out a white business card, and gives it to me.

"This is why I know it is true."

The card bears a gold seal and in discreet black type: FEDERAL BUREAU OF INVESTIGATION, Ana Grey, Special Agent, along with our Wilshire office address and phone number.

"There are a hundred ways she could have gotten my card."

Mrs. Gutiérrez points with a bronze-red nail. "Look on the other side."

Turning it over I see the words "Immigration and Naturalization Service, 300 North Los Angeles St., 213-894-2119," written in my own hand.

"You gave this to Violeta when she first came to this country."

"I honestly don't remember."

"It was seven years ago."

Mrs. Gutiérrez folds her hands over her stomach and rocks back with a satisfied nod.

It could have been that when I was a rookie agent on desk duty a young Latina came tremulously to the FBI in the big skyscraper. Possibly she couldn't speak English (animated now in imagination, a peasant girl, humble, a mass of black hair) and I slipped information on the U.S. Immigration Service to her through the slot, condescendingly, impatiently telling her to try somewhere else, too pumped up about the real challenges at the Bureau that lay ahead of me to listen or care what another confused immigrant was babbling about in Spanish, as she backed away in frustration from the double wall of bulletproof glass that protects us from the public.

The card that I hold in my hand seems to be evidence that we did once meet. I wonder if it could have happened that way, if my arrogance somehow caused a young woman to take a path that eventually led to crossfire and contorted dying.

Slipping the card into my jacket pocket, "How are we supposed to be related?"

"She told me once you are cousins through your father."

"I don't know a lot about my father's side of the family."

"I will show you."

Mrs. Gutiérrez wets her lips and shuffles through the papers, holding them at arm's length and squinting.

"This is Violeta's mother, Constanza. Probably she is your aunt."

In the snapshot a middle-aged woman is standing alone in a cleared area that seems surrounded by luxuriant overgrowth. She has shapeless black hair and there is darkness under the eyes, but she is smiling warmly. She wears a black and white dress with pale orange blossoms and no shoes and is holding a baby.

"This is the house where Violeta grew up."

It looks more like the unfinished frame of a house to me, made of bamboo sticks, cloth, and leaves with no roof or walls. There are pictures of Violeta's brothers—more alleged cousins—husking corn, and a dim shot of a parrot in a palm tree, the colors faded to a uniform, dull aqua.

I shake my head. None of it makes sense.

"The police think Violeta was involved with drugs."

"That is wrong." Mrs. Gutiérrez looks straight at me with clear brown eyes.

"They think that's why she was killed."

"The police are crazy. *I* know Violeta. She was *afraid* of the drugs. She didn't want her children to grow up with the drugs and the gangs, that is why she was saving money to go back to El Salvador. She was a good person," Mrs. Gutiérrez insists, eyes swelled now with tears. "She loved her children. In our country there was a war, but she came all the way to the United States to be shot down in the street."

She holds the cigarette under running water in the sink until it turns a sickly gray, then tosses it angrily into a metal garbage can.

"Where did she work?"

"She was a housekeeper for a lady in Santa Monica. That lady owed her a lot of money."

"What is a lot of money?"

"Maybe . . ." Mrs. Gutiérrez puts a fist on her hip and looks toward the cottage cheese ceiling. "Four hundred dollars. Violeta was very unhappy. The lady was mean and she fired her."

"Why?"

"It wasn't her fault," Mrs. Gutiérrez says sharply. "You can ask the lady. I have the address because I used to take care of the kids when Violeta worked there. Look. This is Cristóbal and Teresa."

Two children dash across the room. The little girl is maybe five, her brother three. She leads him by the hand to the refrigerator, which she tugs open after several tries, reaching for something.

"I'll get it, *corazón,*" Mrs. Gutiérrez calls. "What do you want?"

"Kool-Aid."

Suddenly the apartment is flooded with unbearably loud Latin music coming from the open carport. I move the dirty beige fiberglass curtains aside to peer at two young fellows laughing, talking loudly, carrying a ghetto blaster, and unwinding a garden hose in the direction of a 1975 Dodge Dart with most of the paint honed off. They are going to wash that piece of crap using a half hour's worth of city water in the midst of a serious drought. My neck is tensing up.

"Cristóbal? Teresa? This is Señorita Grey. A cousin of your mommy and you."

Facing me are two golden-skinned children with almond-shaped eyes holding plastic mugs in their hands. It is preposterous that they have anything to do with me. The girl, unsmiling, slides her eyes away. She is wearing pink shorts and a scrawny tie-dyed T-shirt that looks as if it might have actually survived the sixties. The boy's green army fatigue shorts are way too big for him, folded many times at the waist and pinned with a big safety pin, no shirt at all.

"Do you know where my mommy is?" he asks.

"Your mommy is in heaven," Mrs. Gutiérrez says, ruffling his thick black hair. "I told you that."

But the boy repeats his question imploringly, directly to me: "Do you know where my mommy is?"

Mrs. Gutiérrez clucks her tongue with sympathy and scoops him up in her arms. "Come here, Cris. Want to dance with me?"

She tilts her hips this way and that to the music which is shaking the floor, bouncing the boy against her body and laughing a big laugh, grinning a big grin to his tiny bewildered simper.

"Teresa! Let's dance! Let's do some *merengue.*"

The girl is standing before me, not moving, not looking exactly anywhere. Drawn to her, I kneel down until we are eye level and then without quite knowing it, brush her cheek with my hand. She drops onto all fours and crawls under the baby's crib, curling up tightly with her arms folded, face pressed against the wall.

I feel a strange, distant portentous hum—then suddenly it is upon me with tremendous force: mixed with the pounding music, waves of heat ripple through my body along with a raw, unidentified fear. Panicked, I fight the urge to follow Teresa under the crib, to be small again in a small dark place, to seek the almost immaterial tininess of a dot of a spider who can wholly disappear into the safety of a crack in the tile, because if you are that small your pain must be small too, small enough to become inconsequential and, finally, gone.

The music has been turned up, incredibly, another notch. Mrs. Gutiérrez gathers the papers and puts them back into the Bible.

Speaking with a quiet intensity that penetrates the music she says, "Take this. It was Violeta's," and presses the book into my hand.

"Even if I could get the money . . . it won't go to you. . . ." I am shouting, but Mrs. Gutiérrez has surrendered to a faraway look and slipped into a smooth sideways step, the boy on her hip too stunned by the movement and the volume to cry. "The money will go to the children. And they'll probably be put into foster care—"

I finger the worn dry leather of Violeta Alvarado's Bible, giving up, drowned out, having lost the girl to her inexpressible grief and Mrs. Gutiérrez to the dreams of the *merengue*.

FIVE

WE HAVE REASON to believe the "JAP Bandit" has struck again. This slurring appellation was bestowed by squad supervisor Duane Carter on a woman in her thirties who dresses well with lots of gold jewelry, has long manicured nails, and happens to like working the Valley. Her M.O. is to blend in with the clientele and take the tellers by surprise. We think she has about a dozen robberies to her credit, Washington Savings and Loan in Sherman Oaks being the latest.

Donnato and I respond to the 211 and get there about the same time as the local police. We are just beginning to interview the witnesses when my beeper goes off. When I call the office, Rosalind says that Duane Carter wants to see me immediately.

My message to him is basically to take a flying leap since we're in the middle of an investigation. I don't exactly speed back when we are finished three hours later, either. I am chatty. Donnato is subdued.

"After a few years on C-1 I'm going to put in for transfer to headquarters. I always wanted to live in Washington, D.C."

"Washington is shit city during the summer."

We are stuck on the 405 freeway going south, a solid motionless curve of cars in both directions between dry brown hills.

"Worse than this?"

Donnato doesn't answer. I let it go. He lives in Simi Valley in a house he had to borrow from his in-laws to finance. On a good day it is an hour's commute to Westwood; tonight he will fight the traffic going north all over again, opposite to the way we are heading now, and when he gets home at eight or nine o'clock he will spend an hour doing homework with his oldest son, who has a learning disability and is a source of constant anxiety.

Donnato married a girl from Encino fifteen years ago and stayed married to her. They were having a rough time and separated for about six months when we first became partners, but Donnato and I were new to each other and he didn't talk about it. Also Donnato is one of the most moral people I know ("I live by a code," he once said, not joking) and I think, as unhappy as he was, he refused to be disloyal to his wife. When they got back together there was general relief that the Rock of Gibraltar was still standing and, as if to make a statement about their marriage, shortly thereafter Rochelle and Mike won their event in our annual Bakersfield to Vegas Run. Every time you go by his desk you have to look at that photo he has propped up of the two of them drenched in sweat, kissing over the damn trophy.

"Don't fuck with Duane Carter," he says finally, out of the depths of a moody silence.

"What'd I do?"

"I heard you on the phone being Miss Hey-I'm-On-A-Case. Don't tease. Carter's like a cornered rat."

"Why, because he's dying for a promotion?"

"He wanted Galloway's job—he wanted to be in charge of the entire field office. Look at it from his point of view—a Catholic from New York, no less, holding him down by the throat."

"Galloway seems to have gotten the picture pretty quick."

"Galloway's on pretty thin ice himself. He's been out here eight months, keeping low, just trying to avoid mistakes. Carter makes him nervous."

"I have nothing to worry about from Duane Carter," I say confidently. "The California First bust speaks for itself."

Donnato only grunts. I turn on the radio but he isn't interested in "Sports Connection" and turns it off, watching quietly out the window while I buck and inch along the endless choked artery, cars cars cars cars as far as you can see.

■ ■ ■

Duane Carter is in his office doing paperwork when I finally get there, feeling that whatever it is might go down a little easier if I say something halfway conciliatory:

"Sorry it took so long, the traffic was unbelievable."

"Don't I know it."

Duane is from Austin, Texas, with one of them cute accents to match. On another man that drawn-out lazy boy intonation might be charming—echoes of cowboys with hearts of gold—but on Duane it is menacing and icy, a gunman with no regard for human life. When Duane levels that slow-moving good-ole-boy stuff at you it's like he's taking his time pointing a .45 at your forehead. I would call him a sociopath but he doesn't like people.

And nobody much likes him, probably because he has no facial hair. He looks like a stunted adolescent: a fifteen-year-old with cottony pale skin, a large soft body hunched over at the shoulders. He's got a round face, straight black shiny hair—one forelock always hanging down—and his eyes are also black, impenetrable. He went to good schools, has a law degree from Georgetown, but there's still something dangerous and unpredictable about him, a backwoods brutality at odds with all the book learning.

A male agent told me Duane once confessed to having been a virgin when he got married. He says he is no longer practicing but came up through the ranks when the "Mormon mafia" ran the Los Angeles field office. They got shaken loose when a class-action discrimination suit filed on behalf of some Hispanic agents broke up the power structure and now the place looks like a poster for Brotherhood Week. That was before my time. Some of the guys enjoy hanging out with him because of his Japanese sword collection, but for a woman, walking into his office is like entering a deep freeze. I imagine the carcasses of former female agents swaying on elaborately wrought scimitar-style hooks.

"Where were you yesterday?"

I have to think. In Violeta Alvarado's apartment.

"North Hollywood."

"What you got working over there?"

"Personal business."

"On government time?"

I should just take the hit and let it pass, but I am miffed that my boss has been back two days and intentionally not said anything about the most amazing arrest of the year.

"If you look at my time card you'll see I was on duty all last Tuesday night writing up my affidavit on the California First Bank bust. I'll probably log a hundred hours on it."

Duane just sits there bouncing a tennis ball on his desk and watching me with glittering eyes.

"I looked at your time card. I looked at your affidavit too, why in hell do you think I called you back from the Valley this afternoon?"

The fear grips me. "Why?"

"You fucked up, lady."

"How?"

"You sit there and you think about it. I'm gonna take a leak and when I get back I know you'll come up with the answer because you're a bright little thing."

He leaves me paralyzed in the chair, stung by a primitive humiliation, like he is going to take a leak on me.

By the time he returns my palms are damp and I am breathing harder. "I did everything right and by the books." Then, blurting it out like a child: "It was a perfect bust."

Duane settles himself behind the desk and starts bouncing the tennis ball again.

"It would have been perfect," he answers levelly, "if you'd told anyone else what was going on."

"What are you talking about?"

"You didn't call in a 211 in progress."

I laugh. The relief is so profound I feel like taking a leak myself.

"Is that it?"

"You didn't know what was going down inside the bank."

"I had no way to know."

"Exactly right, which is why you should have called in. You placed yourself and the public in unreasonable jeopardy."

I can't help scoffing. "It turned out fine."

"It just as well could have turned to shit."

"Well, it didn't. I live right."

My arms are folded and my legs stuck out in front of me. Defiant now. Catch me if you can.

"I'm glad you're taking this lightly, Ana."

"I don't take anything lightly that has to do with my job, but I think, with respect, Duane, you're overstating the situation."

"I don't. You showed poor judgment. That's my assessment."

His use of the words "judgment" and "assessment" just about causes my heart to stop. "Judgment" is one of the categories of our semiannual performance appraisals. If he gives me poor marks in judgment, it will derail my progress in the Bureau for years.

I know what I have to do and it is as onerous and revolting as if he were actually instead of symbolically forcing me to suck his dick.

"Message received. Next time I'll call it in."

"No, Ana, I'm afraid 'sorry' doesn't cut it."

"I didn't say I was sorry. I said, Next time I will call it in."

Duane gives me a real serious look. Serious and sober, Big Daddy concerned for my best interests.

"I see you've applied for transfer to the C-1 squad."

"Correct."

"Ana, you know I believe in full disclosure . . ."

I can't wait to tell Barbara that one.

". . . so I want to let you know up front that I'm going to attach an addendum to your request."

"What kind of an addendum?"

"I'm going to say that in my opinion as your immediate supervisor you have demonstrated poor judgment and are not ready for transfer. We need to keep you close to home a little bit longer."

By now my entire body is stiff with icy cold. I can hardly bend my knees. I wonder if moving slowly like this, taking my time to stand up, makes me seem unaffected and casual.

"You can't make that call."

"I know. It's up to Special Agent in Charge Galloway."

"And his decision remains to be seen."

Duane nods almost warmly. "It remains to be seen."

I walk past the message center, collect two messages from Mrs. Gutiérrez, and continue to my desk, although the lights in the bullpen seem awfully dim and in fact there is darkness on both sides of my vision so the world narrows to what I can see directly in front of me which turns out to be my telephone, which I try repeatedly to rip out from the floor connection with both hands and although it's screwed in there tight I do manage to pop the cable from its staples all along the floorboard so that it has enough play to finally enable me to pick up the telephone and hurtle it against the wall.

Arms are around me and the smell of a man's starched shirt and suddenly I am on the stairwell with my face up against the cinder block, hands pinned behind my back.

My nose is bending. I am hyperventilating.

My hands are released. I stand still. My shoulders ache from being twisted and wrenched.

"Are you sober now?"

I nod, still facing the wall. When there is no further action from behind I turn and slump down on the metal stairs. Donnato sits next to me.

"I hope I'm the only one who witnessed that little display."

I brush my nose with my sleeve. It is scratched and bleeding. Doesn't feel broken.

"Sorry. I had to get you out of there. Didn't know if you were armed."

"Armed," I echo hoarsely, as if an assault rifle could have stopped that sweeping awful wave of darkness.

"I knew when he beeped you at the bank that Carter was getting cute. He's spent most of his career walking over bodies. Yours isn't any different. Don't take it so goddamn personally."

I lean over and put my head in my hands. I want desperately to disappear. To be that small being in a dark place, inconsequential and alone.

"Talk to me," he says, so gently that a tear actually leaks from my eye.

I shake my head silently. I don't understand these overpowering, nameless sensations. I can't seem to get control of my voice.

Someone passes us. I turn my face away. Donnato calls out very brightly, "How're ya doin'?," and the person continues to clatter down the stairs.

"Seven-year burnout," he says when they are gone.

"Is that what it is?"

"Unless you're psycho and been hiding it from me all these years."

A crooked smile: "Been trying."

"This is a new Ana Grey. What's going on?"

I can't describe it. "Pressure."

"I can dig that. Let me buy you a drink."

I am deeply ashamed of having behaved like an asshole and certainly don't want to sit around and dwell on it. If I weren't fixated on the searing humiliation of having lost control, I might have heard the tenderness in Donnato's voice.

"Thanks but it's better if I work out in the pool."

"You're too good."

"Hey, I'm perfect."

"You try to be. That's why you're throwing phones against the wall."

We are moving back toward the doorway of the stairwell. My body feels like it has been run over by a truck.

"It's not just Carter." Struggling to put a label on it: "There's some weird stuff that came up that might involve my family."

"I hope your grandfather is okay."

"Him? Healthy as a horse and knocking the hell out of golf balls in Palm Desert." It makes me feel brighter to think of Poppy in his yellow Bermuda shorts out there at seven in the morning with the other old farts—a foursome of retired policemen if you can picture that, cursing and telling racist jokes all the way down the fairway—embraced by the baking heat of the rising desert sun and the infantile pleasure of their unbroken routine.

"Poppy's got it wrapped," I tell Donnato. "No, it's these other people."

"Relatives." Donnato shakes his head. "Take 'em to Disneyland."

The wonderful simplicity of that idea makes me laugh.

"Okay now?"

I nod.

"Can you take care of it?"

"Sure."

Donnato squeezes my arm. "Good triceps." That wry, affectionate look. "Go swimming. See you tomorrow."

When I duck inside to grab my bag I notice the Bank Dick's Undercover Disguise embracing the phone in a tangled heap on the floor, the empty hanger still rocking above it.

SIX

A FEW DAYS later I slip into my car with the intention of returning a humidifier. I hadn't been too precise about changing the water so it stopped working last winter and rotted in the bedroom all spring. When I finally dumped the tank out sometime around Halloween it was evident that new life forms had sprouted inside. The store where I bought it guarantees a "lifetime warranty" so you can keep bringing in the old fishy-smelling one and exchanging it for a brand-new one, no questions asked, for the rest of your life. I know, because I already pulled this stunt last year, when the original humidifier dried up and died.

Somehow despite the excellent intention of running over to Century City and back during my lunch break, I am still sitting here in the G-ride without having turned on the engine. I have found the Bible that belonged to Violeta Alvarado thrown on the passenger seat along with a ton of papers and law books and am looking through it, suddenly disoriented in the middle of the parking lot of the Federal Building.

Slowly removing the crossed rubber bands with the same care as Mrs. Gutiérrez, I run my finger down the dense type printed in

Spanish on delicate tissuey pages and look through the faded snap-shots again, stopping at the one of Violeta's mother holding a baby. Behind them the landscape is gray green, scrubby and heartless.

I have never been to the tropics. I cannot know what life is for that woman and that baby. My past begins and ends with my grand-father—his California boyhood, his own mother's trek across this country from Kansas, his devotion to the moral duties of police work in the expansive fifties, have formed my sense of myself as a full-blooded optimistic American and, growing up, there was never any reason to question any of it.

Now I am forced to question it all as I hold a piece of paper torn from a small notebook upon which is written the name of a white woman who allegedly fired a cousin of mine who was Hispanic. The name is Claire Eberhardt. The address is on Twentieth Street, eight blocks from Poppy's old house, north of Montana, where I spent the first five years of my life, in the city of Santa Monica—a former beach town of funky bungalows and windswept Pacific views that has now become an overbuilt upscale enclave on the westernmost edge of the Los Angeles sprawl.

Even pulling out of the parking lot I hesitate, then make a de-cisive turn away from Century City and the sweet new humidifier, west down Wilshire and on to San Vicente Boulevard. These days I come to Santa Monica on Bureau business or to catch a movie at the Third Street Promenade, but north of Montana is definitely not my turf. This is the land of the newly rich where noontime joggers pass beneath scarlet-tipped coral trees on a wide grassy meridian. The Ford looks stupid next to Mercedeses and BMWs and hot Toyota Land Cruisers that have never seen a speck of mud. I take the fork onto Montana Avenue and curve past a golf course. Already the air is flooded with the scent of flowers and cool watered grass, pine and eucalyptus.

The top end of Montana Avenue could be a small nondescript residential street anywhere, but as you pass a school and start down an incline all of a sudden you are hit by a row of shops with blue awnings.

I have noticed that whenever you have awnings you have quaint.

On Montana Avenue there are lots of awnings: maroon awnings with white scallops, artsy-fartsy modernistic awnings that hang by steel cords. . . . The stores that don't have awnings make up for it with two-story glass windows and dramatic lettering, letting you know that it takes a special kind of money to shop here: a lot.

Males and females amble along carrying shopping bags or pushing baby strollers, enjoying themselves. I guess they have nothing else to do all day. Sidewalk tables are filled with folks taking a leisurely lunch under green umbrellas, watching the steady stream of traffic flow down Montana Avenue to the ocean, which you can actually see at the rise on Fifteenth Street, a flat band of blue straight ahead.

I'm kind of mesmerized, it's a different pace from the rest of the city and my old neighborhood after all, even if I could never afford to live here today. Passing the vintage Aero Theatre now wrapped in a slick retailing complex, I wonder if as a girl I ever saw a movie there, then on impulse turn up Twelfth Street looking for our old address.

There it is, just past Marguerita, beside some big pink modern construction with round windows: an old California cottage, which must have been built in the 1920s, with a pitched roof and a real estate company's For Sale sign out front. I park with the engine idling. The house is *tiny;* a modest-sized beech tree in a dry scrap of a front yard easily hides half of it. The wood siding is painted a sickly tan and the front door and trim a kind of red chocolate brown. There are two narrow glass panels on either side of the door. The only distinguishing flourish is a bit of arched wood over the entryway supported by two posts, like an open bonnet with trailing ties.

Something hits my windshield, a spiny round seedpod from a gum tree growing near the curb. I wait for some revelatory memory to hit me over the head but there is nothing, just an abandoned old house. The property next door is also for sale. It is made of white clapboard and small enough to be home for a family of field mice.

The chain-link fence that separates these two relics has been long smashed at the post, as if the neighbors had a problem backing a car out of the mouse-sized driveway.

It is curious all right. The age of the place alone makes it easy to picture Poppy as a handsome young man with blond hair and strong jaw striding out the front door in his blue policeman's uniform, my mother on the strange little side porch coming off the kitchen shelling peas in some kind of a hairdo from World War II. . . . But that's imagination, not memory.

My earliest real memory is of an event that took place fifty miles south. It was the first day of kindergarten at Peter H. Burnett Elementary School in Long Beach, 1965, when my mother said goodbye on the sidewalk and turned away, seemingly without emotion. Before that moment when she pushed me out into the world at the age of five there is only darkness and silence, but afterward I remember everything: the weak feeling in my legs as I crossed the schoolyard alone toward the sandy-colored building. The exotic art deco architecture that made it look like a castle carved from brown sugar. Inside I remember the spice of tempera paint and the fresh smell of new books and my first friend, Laura Levy, who wore two neat braids. We had sour-tasting milk in the afternoon.

Poppy, my mother, and I lived on Pine Street in an upper-middle-class neighborhood called Wrigley. Most of the homes had been built in the thirties, Craftsman or bungalow style, but ours was redbrick and brand-new. The trolley tracks ran two blocks away and it was a big deal to take the Pacific Electric Red Car into downtown Los Angeles to go to Cinerama or the May Company, a fancy department store they didn't have in Long Beach.

The Public Safety Building that housed the Long Beach Police Department, where Poppy eventually earned the rank of lieutenant, was then less than ten years old, and seemed very forward with its sea-blue glass and columns encrusted in mosaic tile. In Southern California in the sixties everything was on the upswing.

I could continue from there, a million tiny remembrances of a normal childhood in a sunny coastal town where farmers would

come to retire from the brutal winters of the Midwest; a conservative, easygoing community before developers got ahold of downtown
and surgically removed every last twitching tissue of life. My claim
to fame at Long Beach Polytechnic High School was being elected
captain of the girls' swim team. My best subjects were science and
math. The motto over the school entrance still reads, "Enter to
Learn—Go Forth to Serve," and I guess I still take it seriously.

All of that is clear; what I can't figure out is this wizened little
preconscious cottage in Santa Monica. I strain to place myself inside
its tantalizing history. What kind of little girl was I? Where were my
secret places? Did I climb the beech tree? Who lived in the house
next door? Memory does not respond. I sit there with my hands on
the steering wheel, feeling numb.

The next thing I know I am driving up a street with tall pines
and deep shade. Clearly when we lived here we lived on the modest
end of the neighborhood; as the street numbers get bigger, so do the
homes. By Twentieth Street the landscaping is lush, the flowers
sumptuous, screaming orange-red bougainvillea flopping over white
stucco walls. On every block gardening or construction work is being done by Hispanic men. Lunch trucks selling Mexican food cruise
the area along with private Westec security patrols. I am concentrating on these details to avoid a growing feeling of sadness. I know
it is coming from having seen that house, which I now wish I had
avoided. I note a uniformed maid walking a dog and try to conjure
up some cynicism but the sadness is there. Maybe I am confusing
myself with Violeta's children, it must be Teresa I am picturing hud-
dled in the skirts of a starched dress in the scrawny marigolds beside
my grandfather's house, not me. Teresa alone and crying, not me.

■ ■ ■

The Eberhardts live in a two-story contemporary Mediterranean,
bald and newly built. It has a red tile roof and two huge curved case-
ment windows looking into the first-floor living room that echo the
archway over an outsized door. A quarry tile walkway bends through

a scruffy brown lawn; a few plants edge up against the off-white walls—except for a grouping of vigorous young birch trees, the place looks dry and neglected as if after paying a million and a half dollars the owners didn't have the stamina to deal with landscaping. I guess to most people a million-and-a-half-dollar box with a few doodads is plenty.

Of course on this scale of house there is no doorbell—instead, a security system, with a square white button to push and a speaker to talk into.

"Yes?"

"Hello, my name is Ana Grey. I'm looking for Claire Eberhardt." Since this is not government business I do not identify myself as a federal agent.

"This is she."

"I'm a . . . friend . . . of Violeta Alvarado," still speaking into the microphone. "Could I talk to you?"

Pause. "Violeta . . . doesn't work here."

I stifle the urge to say, Of course not, she's dead. I am getting tired of talking to the wall.

"I know that. This will just take a minute, ma'am."

"All right. Hang on."

Silence. She's coming. Which gives me the opportunity to study the front door—four feet wide and twice as tall as normal with a crescent-shaped window over the top, dark wood, mahogany maybe with some sort of finish intentionally scratched up. Just as I am wondering why anybody would need such a huge door, it opens.

She is holding a boy about two years old who is resting his head against her bare neck.

"Peter just woke up from a nap," she explains, pivoting so I can see Peter's flushed cheek and glossy eyes. They both have shiny black hair, so dark it almost has shades of eggplant purple, the boy's in long loose curls, hers sticking out in all directions from a pink elastic band pushed up off the forehead as if she just wanted to get her bangs out of the way.

"I'm Claire." She is wearing a gray hooded sweatshirt with the sleeves cut off and baggy turquoise cotton tights meant to hide a few extra pounds. Her breasts are loose. Even with the crazy hair and padded hips she is attractive in a reckless sexual way; but her looks are a neglected afterthought, as if it is enough that she's made it from wherever she came from, she lives north of Montana. Although she seems as if she's been napping along with her son, she is wearing strawberry-red lipstick. My first impression of Claire Eberhardt is that she is as unfinished as her house.

You'd expect her to take up the doorway with ownership and conviction, but instead she is backed up inside, curved around the child, unsure. She seems to be looking at me but away at the same time.

"Sorry to barge in on you, but it's about Violeta Alvarado."

"What about her?"

"Did Ms. Alvarado work here?"

"Yes. Until about three months ago. We had to let her go."

"Why was that?"

She cocks her head in a peculiar manner as if staring down at a corner of the doormat. "It just didn't work out."

"How long was Ms. Alvarado employed here before you let her go?"

"Almost a year. Why?"

She shifts the boy to her other shoulder and faces me directly. Now I see the reason for the strange bearing: the left eye turns out slightly, enough to give an off-centered look of which she seems to be extremely self-conscious.

"I'm afraid I have some bad news."

"Bad news?"

"Violeta Alvarado was killed."

Suddenly the child seems too heavy for her. She turns and calls, *"Carmen! Por favor!"* in the worst Spanish accent you can imagine.

A tiny brown grandmother appears, right out of the Andes. She grins with gold teeth and reaches for the boy, who clings to his mother's neck. They have to pry his hands apart. He starts to wail. The grandmother, still smiling, whispers soothing words I can't understand and bears him away, still crying fiercely, arms outstretched toward his mom.

Claire Eberhardt closes her eyes to her son's distress and turns back to me, clearly shaken.

"How did it happen?"

"A drive-by shooting. About two weeks ago."

"She was shot to death?"

I nod.

She props an elbow against the doorjamb and pulls off the elastic band, running a hand through her bangs, then clamping down tightly as if she's going to pull out her hair. As it falls into place I see that actually she has a shoulder-length precision haircut and is wearing a diamond wedding band.

"Jesus fucking Christ."

Despite the diamonds and the do, this is not a lady of culture.

"Excuse me, but—Jesus Christ. She had kids."

"I know."

She stays that way, gripping her hair, staring down at her bare feet.

"I'm a nurse. I mean, I haven't worked since we moved out from Boston, but I've seen . . . ," her voice trails off, "in the ER . . . what it's like when someone is shot."

She is a nurse. I am in law enforcement. She lives in this house now, she has servants now, but maybe we are not so far apart. We both serve the public. We are both in the business of order and repair. She gazes up and for a moment I am able to hold her look in mine. One thing we share is professional knowledge; we have both seen what a young woman's body looks like after it has been decimated by bullets.

"You're her friend? It must be pretty bad for you, too."

Embarrassed because it's not as bad as it probably should be, "I'm trying to help out because of the kids. Somebody told me you owed Violeta money."

"I wouldn't know about that."

"When she left. About four hundred dollars."

"My husband took care of paying her."

"Would you like me to talk to your husband, then?"

"I would really like you . . . to just go away."

She gives me a half-assed smile as if I'm supposed to graciously understand her confusion and shock. But I don't understand, because there's something else going on here, something much deeper.

"You seem upset, Claire."

The tip of her nose is red and moist, eyes bright with tears. She shakes her head and looks up at the sky as if to contain them. "Did you ever make a really bad mistake?"

"I never make mistakes," I say. "I'm a perfect person."

She appreciates that and it opens her up. "I used to drink a lot in high school," she goes on, "I could do Southern Comfort all night long and wake up in the morning fresh as a daisy."

There's something fresh about her still. Maybe it comes from the creamy pale skin and light freckles, but she seems unguarded and direct, as if after one beer she'd tell you her whole life story and you'd be interested because there wouldn't be any crap.

"We used to party, it didn't matter with who, we used to skip school and go to Revere Beach—no matter what you did, you could get away with it. But then there's the one guy you really fall for, and he's always a mistake. Does that kind of thing ever happen to you?"

She makes me think of John Roth and I blush.

"Once or twice."

"Did you get away with it?"

I reply with a wry look. "That remains to be seen."

Suddenly her fingers form a fist and she gives the mahogany door frame a good pop. I wonder if her husband, the hapless sap who paid for the multimillion-dollar house, was the mistake she'll never get away with.

"I wouldn't hit that too hard," I advise. "They don't build houses like they used to."

She smiles. "Hey, we're in California. Isn't it all supposed to fall apart?"

I return the smile. "What else about Violeta?"

"She was a very sweet girl."

"Do you think she was involved with drugs?"

Claire Eberhardt seems shocked. "No, not at all. Never. She was straight as straight could be. A *real* Catholic." She tries to laugh. "Not like me."

"Then why did you fire her?"

In an instant the openness dries up. As direct as she can be, I see also that Claire Eberhardt can take on a stony working-class defiance. I've crossed some line of propriety and there's no going back; she's simply through talking to me.

"We just had to let her go. Excuse me. I'll be right back."

She has left the door open. I glimpse a two-story entryway with a crystal chandelier way up there in the stratosphere. And she's arguing with me over four hundred bucks?

She returns clutching a peach-colored business card and a tissue. She's apparently got herself all worked up again.

"My husband would know about the money."

I observe her critically, trying to square Mrs. Gutiérrez's description of the lady being "very mean" with what I see. There is something churning inside Claire Eberhardt, but it does not appear to be malice. It appears to be guilt.

On the verge of breaking down completely, she murmurs, "I'm so sorry," and gently closes the door. In gray script the card says, RANDALL EBERHARDT, M.D., DANA ORTHOPEDIC CLINIC, with an address on Fifteenth Street, south of Wilshire across from the hospital, ten minutes away. So she's a nurse and the sap turns out to be a doctor. Now I know how Claire Eberhardt got into the neighborhood.

■　　■　　■

The Dana Orthopedic Clinic is in its own remodeled Victorian house in the medical center of Santa Monica. The waiting room, just like the business card, is peach and gray. The receptionist has told me that without an appointment to see Dr. Eberhardt I will have to wait.

Luckily the upholstered benches—peach and gray—are orthopedically correct and it is actually relaxing to sit there and read *Glamour* magazine.

Then I get antsy. Then I get pushy. Because there is nobody else in the waiting room.

"Is the doctor in surgery?"

"No."

"Is the doctor on the premises?"

"Yes."

"Then what is the problem?"

"He's with a patient. It will just be a little longer."

We have three more rounds of this and another forty-five minutes pass. My plan is to bully the doctor into writing out a check for four hundred dollars then and there and be done with this whole business. If he balks I will threaten a lawsuit on behalf of Violeta's children. Doctors don't like lawsuits. That should end the discussion. Again I refrain from pulling out my badge and terrifying the receptionist. That would be against regulations.

An hour later the doctor is still with a patient and I feel a sudden panic about getting back before Duane Carter notices how long I have been gone. Resigned to confronting Dr. Eberhardt at another time I thank the receptionist for her tremendous help and skulk out the door around back to the alley where I have parked my government car illegally and where, I am further incensed to discover, it is being blocked by a black limousine.

I had backed the blue Ford between a telephone pole and a dumpster next to a brick wall; now this limousine has pulled up alongside, making it impossible to maneuver out. The doors of the limousine are locked and there is no driver in sight.

By holding my breath and walking on tiptoe I can squeeze in between the two vehicles and open my door about eight inches— enough to angle a shoulder inside and turn on my siren and loudspeaker.

"A black limousine, license plate JM, you are blocking the alley, you will be cited and towed . . ."

The second repeat and a couple of good *whups* from the siren brings a bulky red-faced driver in uniform running down the alley carrying a cone topped with a large spiral of ice cream.

"Hey, lady, what's your problem?"

"Just move the car."

He eyes me derisively. "Gotta get to the sale at J.C. Penney's?"

I badge him. "No. I'm with the FBI. Now move the car."

Suddenly he grins. "And I'm a state trooper. Used to be, before I sold out and went Hollywood. See that? Brothers and sisters under the skin. Tom Pauley. Glad to meet you."

He offers a stubby hand. We shake.

"Can I get you frozen yogurt?"

"No thanks."

"Here. Have this one. It's virginal. Never been licked."

"You enjoy it, Tom. I'm going to catch hell at the office." I squeeze into my car and turn the engine.

"I understand. Guess I was kind of a jerk, but you should have seen your face. I really should have let you run the license plate. That's what I do with the cops. Then it's: Tom, what can I do for you? Tom, can you get me an autograph for my wife?"

"You're a celebrity, huh?" I jam the gearshift into drive, hoping he will get the hint.

"Anybody who works for Jayne Mason automatically is."

I have to admit, he got me as he knew from experience he would; that the mention of the name is enough to stop even the most cocky cop in his tracks.

"Where is Jayne Mason—at the yogurt store?"

"Seeing the doc. That's why I had to park near the back. Sorry for the inconvenience."

He nods toward the gray door of the Dana Clinic.

"I thought she was at the Betty Ford Center."

"They sprung her."

"Cured?"

"Seems to be, but she's always had a back problem. You're not going to leak this."

"Yeah, Tom. I really care about Jayne Mason's back problems." Then, curiously, "Is her doctor named Eberhardt?"

Giving me a smile: "You know I can't release that information."

I look toward the door as the sweet odor of rotting garbage rolls toward me on the ocean breeze. "So that's why he kept me waiting two hours."

"Jeez, I'm sorry. Hanging around like that can fry your brains. I'm used to it. That's why I went and got myself some lunch."

The gray door swings open and Jayne Mason strides out. She doesn't get far before a white-coated arm grabs her by the shoulder. She tries to twist away but the arm holds tight, forcibly turning her around so she's facing a tall, solidly built man with blondish hair and aviator glasses, wearing a white lab coat.

"Is that the good doctor?"

Tom nods.

Dr. Eberhardt—a nice-looking man with the soft underchin of middle age—keeps the hand on her shoulder so she won't run away. She is wearing a red sweat suit, sneakers, and a red turban that completely covers her hair. He is taller, younger, stronger; but she is strong too—a dancer and still lithe. He is maintaining an authoritative posture, talking calmly although she seems distraught.

"The whistle blows," Tom says, tossing the uneaten yogurt into the dumpster.

He positions the limo in the middle of the alley, then, leaving it running, gets out, opens the door, and waits. She doesn't even have to look in his direction for him to know the correct moment to make his move as she finally pulls away from the doctor with an expression of willfulness so he can be right there to gracefully take her hand and guide her over the torn asphalt. As they approach I can see that her sweatshirt is decorated with a pair of kittens batting a yarn ball. It is a real yarn ball and the kittens are furry with big glittery eyelashes. They pass right in front of me. The actress's skin is dove white against the crimson knit, reflecting a brilliant smear of color in the immaculate black shine of the limousine door; she is her own annunciation, creating in this smelly alley a moment of startling vivacity that could not have been outdone by a hundred performing troubadours dressed in gold.

The limousine pulls away. Dr. Eberhardt is gone, the gray steel door sprung shut. I wonder if the doctor's wife knows how intimate her husband is with his famous patient; how he kept his hand on her shoulder the whole time and how, although she was angry, she did not move away as long as she felt his touch.

I pull out of the alley, picturing Claire Eberhardt leaning against the other side of the mahogany door of their home, innocent of this, crying a river of penitent tears over a poor Salvadoran house-keeper.

PART TWO

DESERT CLARITY

SEVEN

IN THE DESERT everything is clear.

It doesn't hit until you are two hours out of Los Angeles, past the tangled hell of downtown and the protracted ugliness of San Bernardino, beyond the world's biggest freeway interchange where the 605 meets the 10 in swooping parabolic ribbons of concrete. It starts somewhere out there when the shoulders of the road turn to white sand and there are no more sky-blue town-house colonies popping up in the distant wasteland; when the air, thinned of pollutants, becomes light and transparent and you can see amazing details like rockfalls on the slopes of snow-topped mountains miles away.

Slowing down off the freeway, suddenly quiet enough to hear your very tires chewing over feathers of sand blown across the off-ramp, as the setting sun shoots every tiny needle of every single cactus with scarlet backlight, it hits. Desert clarity. The absence of motion, pressure, traffic, and people. A mysterious monochromatic landscape speckled with life. Your body settles down. The air feels spiritual—that is, filled with spirits that a tacky little town can't restrain. Rolling down the gamy main street of Desert Hot Springs you want to shout just to hear how your own voice would sound as a loose uninhibited coyote wail instead of the tight pissed-off squeak with which you usually address your fellow man.

Poppy's condominium is no great shakes for what it cost, set up on a ridge looking west over an empty shopping center with a Thrifty Drug and a Vons market, a KFC and video rental store, all new construction—clean black asphalt without a tire mark and spindly palms in redwood boxes. Carrying groceries to my car (if I don't buy my own supplies, I wind up drinking Seagram's at night and gagging on All-Bran in the morning), I enjoy the mild breeze and calculate that by the time the town grows big enough to actually support this overblown supermarket Poppy will be dead and I can sell his condo for a nice piece of change.

I know I am fooling myself with that kind of thinking. We buried my mother when I was fourteen, my grandmother was gone before I was one year old. One more trip to Eternal Valley Memorial Park would finally cut me loose from the already thin thread of kinship like rusty shears operating in the hands of one of those gnarly sisters of fate. It wouldn't be a clean easy cut, not at all, but a slow severing with lots of fray and lots of pain. I can see my fingers stretching up last minute to catch the end of the line so I won't fall into space, because without my Poppy I don't know who I would be.

In fact, when I really look at our family, it becomes as clear as the lucidity of cactus spikes revealed by the blood-red sun that three generations of females have lived our lives not as free individuals but in relation to this one man.

Grandma Elizabeth was a policeman's wife in a small seaside town in the 1950s—what choice did she have? When she died, my mother, aside from working as a receptionist in a dentist's office, took over the solemn duty of caring for Poppy, preparing Koenigsberger Klops, his favorite veal and pork meatballs (when he worked the night shift, she woke up at five in the morning to warm them up for him in the oven). These past ten years it has been my turn (drawing the line at Koenigsberger Klops). We talk on the phone several times a week, I drive out to see him at least once a month. First thing in the morning Poppy is in my thoughts, sometimes with a fearsome rush of anxiety that he has died during the night, although I know he is independent and strong as a horse. When I have a question, his voice tells me what to do. When I screw up, his voice punishes me. I may be a hotshot federal agent who carries a gun and a pair of handcuffs (they're light, you can throw them in the bottom of your purse trash) but my self-worth is still measured by my grandfather's rules. From childhood he was my standard and my mother's standard and I have always believed as innocently and completely in the rightness of Poppy as I do the American flag.

I am here for an overnight visit to wish him a belated seventieth birthday, but questions about my supposed cousin Violeta Alvarado and my father and the lost Latino side of the family are definitely percolating in the back of my mind, so that when I approach the tan steel door loaded with groceries, a birthday cake, and a duffel bag and hear barking from within, I am not pleased.

Sure enough it's Moby Dick, one of Poppy's whacked-out desert pals, and his friendly pack of killer Akita dogs, which he raises in a shack out there in the wilderness, illegally crossing purebreds with German shepherds to create these hulking muscular monsters with mottled gray fur and curling tails and schizophrenic personalities, just like his. Bikers and police officers with families buy them for five hundred dollars apiece.

"Freeze! It's the FBI!" laughs Moby Dick, opening the door. I give him a wincing smile. His enormous bouncing belly is almost covered by a black T-shirt that says Fuck Dieting.

The television is on, beer cans on the coffee table.

"It's about the dogs."

"No problem." He drags them out to the balcony by their collars and slides the heavy glass doors shut, shouting, "Commissioner! Your little girl's here!"

I put the stuff in the kitchen. Poppy keeps a neat place. The dish drainer is empty. One box of Keebler's crackers on the counter. Inside the refrigerator everything is low salt, low cholesterol—except for Bloody Mary mix and two New York steaks. At least Moby Dick isn't staying for dinner.

"Annie!" He is there in the doorway wearing nothing but a white towel at the waist, vain as ever, showing off his extraordinary tanned barrel chest and weight-lifter's ropy arms.

Even though he is seventy, hugging him bare-chested is an experience in maleness that brings back Sunday afternoons at the YMCA on Long Beach Boulevard, the reward for sustaining a perfect freestyle for fifty yards being holding my cheek to that strong upper quadrant—the compact pectorals, cool feel of chlorine-scented skin, dark furry hair surrounding a useless nipple, fascinating turkey folds under the chin, hard shoulders beneath my small naked feet as he magically lifted me out of the water to dive over his gleaming wet head. I didn't have a father to teach me to swim; I had Poppy.

"Happy birthday. You're looking great."

"Not bad for seven decades on this earth. What're you drinking?"

"Brought my own." I slip a bottle out of a bag.

"White wine?" He shakes his head. "That's the L.A. crowd." Grabbing a handful of ice, "Hope you still eat red meat."

"I eat it and I fuck it." Beating him to the punch.

He cracks a can of 7UP. "Easy on the language."

"Sorry. I wouldn't want to offend Moby Dick."

"Is that how Feebees talk?"—derisive cop term for FBI agents—"I thought they were educated bastards."

I laugh. Here we go. "We try to be tough. Almost as tough as you."

∎   ∎   ∎

Poppy sits in a chair near the balcony wearing nothing but the towel, legs crossed demurely, drinking Seven and Sevens until long after it is dark and the relentless air conditioning has given me a chill. The dogs are still out there. From time to time they nose against the glass near his feet like canine spirits conjured up by the original Agua Caliente Indians.

I admit that the other reason I drove out to the desert was to tell all the details of my perfect bust at California First Bank to Poppy in person. How I was alone. How I staked the guy out and made the right moves and cuffed him with no assistance. How my brilliant interview technique led the suspect to confess to six other robberies. How it was so good it was pure sex.

I am always offering Poppy things like that. Accomplishments. Gifts. His reaction is usually noncommittal, with the implication that it really isn't good enough, although he did attend my graduation from Quantico in his lieutenant's full-dress uniform, and he did cry. Still I keep coming back, hoping that what I've done will be better, that it will please Poppy at last.

Moby Dick is a more appreciative audience and I find myself playing to him. He follows the action as if it were a *Police Academy* cartoon (which he watches religiously in the shack on Saturday mornings), stomping his huge Jordans and shouting "Right on!" Poppy's only reaction is to tell about the time *he,* as a rookie patrol officer, cornered a murder suspect alone on the footpath near the Santa Monica Pier and chased him onto the beach. It was Saturday in July, crowded as hell, the suspect dove into the ocean and was never seen again.

"Wow, Commissioner, that's a story," Moby Dick tells my grandfather reverentially.

"What else happened when you were a rookie? When we lived north of Montana?"

"Well, we had the famous Hungry Thief," Poppy grins, settling back with his drink. "Broke into a market, stole a thousand bucks, left two half-eaten knockwurst sandwiches."

Moby Dick laughs, a whistling snort up the nose.

"I went past the old house on Twelfth Street," I put in casually. "Trying to remember what it was like. Did you and Mom and I ever live there with my father?"

"*I'll* tell you something that happened," Poppy says suddenly, eyes bright, blatantly ignoring my question. "I had you down at the station one time when all of a sudden we hear this god-awful racket and we run outside to see what the hell it is, and goddamn, a military helicopter is making a landing right in the parking lot."

Moby Dick asks, "What for?"

"For John Fitzgerald Kennedy."

Poppy nods to our dumbfounded silence. "The President wasn't actually on board, but at that time he used to make quite a lot of trips out to L.A.—*they said* to see his brother-in-law Peter Lawford at the beach, but actually it was so he could keep on sticking Marilyn Monroe, so the Secret Service was checking out where to land the presidential helicopter and I guess they thought the Santa Monica police station would be pretty secure, the stupid bastards, boy did they fuck up in Dallas."

Moby Dick says, "Amazing."

Poppy chuckles. "They had these guys painting lines on the parking lot, they had it all marked off with chalk, then this goddamn huge thing lands and blows it all away."

"Did I see the helicopter?"

"You?" Poppy looks at me, surprised to remember I am part of the story. "You were a little girl, you were scared of all the noise and the hullabaloo. Held on to my hand like there was no tomorrow."

I remember none of this. It is the oddest sensation to hear a description about yourself when you can't remember any of it, like having sex and feeling nothing.

"Is it true President Kennedy had an affair with Jayne Mason?"

"Great legs," Poppy croons, again ignoring my question. "They used to call her Little Miss Sunshine, of course that's when she was a kid. She grew into some looker. The guys had a picture of her up in the station. I saw Jayne Mason maybe ten years ago in Vegas. Beautiful voice, really something. The way she sings makes you cry." He pats a finger against his eye as if I wouldn't believe him. "Those are my songs."

Moby Dick interrupts my grandfather's reverie with an urgent bulletin: "I'm only laying this on you because I hope and pray the FBI could do something about it but I'm warning you right now that when the shit goes down, I'm gone. I'm invisible. Okay?"

It turns out he's heard there are satanic sacrifices of children taking place at Frank Sinatra's compound in Palm Springs.

By this time I have killed the bottle. We forget about the steaks, work our way through two Domino's pizzas and the birthday cake. "Let's go down to the Escapade," suggests Moby Dick.

In my present state it sounds like a lot of fun: "You mean that place with the twin girl saxophone players?"

"Those dolls were in their sixties at least," Poppy corrects me.

"All I remember is drinking Salty Dogs and dancing with a retired locksmith," I say.

"He's dead. Sorry, golf tomorrow, seven a.m."

"It's a rough life, Commissioner."

Poppy slips on a polo shirt and khaki slacks and we all go down to walk the beasts. It is midnight and the air must still be seventy degrees. The moon is high, crumpled, yellow as an old dead tooth. Moby Dick loads the animals into his van, which is spray-painted black and gray, and mercifully drives away.

We take a circuitous route through the complex just to breathe the night air. I suddenly decide that it is too late to start rooting around the family tree. I still feel stung by Poppy's refusal to acknowledge the question about my father and don't want to bring it up again. Besides, I'm tired. He's tired. I have to get up at five to drive back to L.A. and be on duty by eight. Another time. Maybe over the phone. But my voice is talking anyway:

"Do I have a cousin named Violeta Alvarado?"

"Not to my knowledge. Not with a name like that."

"On dad's side of the family."

"Who is dad?" Genuinely puzzled.

"My father. Miguel Sanchez. Or Sandoval. Nobody ever told me which."

Jesus, what is this? Just saying the name out loud, seeing him tense, and a cold chill passes through my body. Through the warm cozy alcoholic shroud I am suddenly alert. I am scared.

"We don't know a lot about that son of a bitch, do we?"

"We must know something. Was he from El Salvador?"

"Somewhere."

"What was he like?"

"He was a common laborer. What do you care?"

"I'm curious."

"Forget about it."

Almost thirty years old and still afraid to make Poppy angry.

"Some people have shown up claiming to be relatives."

"What do they want?"

Making it simple: "Money."

"You know what I would tell them, whoever they are—get lost."

"You didn't like him because he was Hispanic?"

"I have nothing against Hispanics. I was pissed off because he knocked up my daughter." He says this easily. Authoritatively. As the one in charge of history. "Then the son of a bitch walks away. Abandons her—and you. Why would you care about a guy who left? I'm the one who raised you."

"I know that, Poppy." I take his hand. "Would you rather he stuck around?"

"No. I didn't want her to have anything to do with him."

"What did she think?"

Poppy makes a little snuffle. A warning. "Didn't matter what she thought. She was eighteen years old."

"Why didn't she ever marry again?"

"She was busy raising you."

"But she was pretty. Did she go on dates?"

"I didn't encourage dating."

"Why not?"

"She was too young."

I laugh. "Young? She lived with you until she died at the age of thirty-eight."

Unexpectedly he puts his arm around me. "You getting this from the L.A. crowd?"

"Getting what?"

"This multicultural bullshit."

I grin with slow deep amusement. "Poppy . . . I think maybe I am the epitome of multiculturality."

As has been said of the Ayatollah Khomeini: he doesn't get irony.

"Like hell you are. You're an American and if you're not proud of it then one of us has fucked up beyond belief."

He goes behind a palm tree to take a leak.

I call after him, "The house on Twelfth Street is for sale."

"I'm surprised it's still standing."

"Who lived in the little white place next door?"

"Swedish family. Everyone in the neighborhood was German or Swede. What I remember about them is I was working nights and they had a dog that barked its head off all day long so I couldn't get any sleep."

Alone, I sit on a curb with my arms around my knees. I am getting a headache from the gummy pizzas and the saccharine cake and too much wine and I really don't like it in the parking lot anymore. Although the sky is jammed with glittering stars, down here it is very, very dark and the lights spotting the parked cars are too weak. A constant dry wind rakes the palm fronds, rattling them with a sound like the snapping of cellophane. I am wearing cutoffs and a sleeveless denim top and I feel vulnerable. My gun is in my bag upstairs. Just around the corner from these last silent buildings is open desert. Black space.

My heart is beating fast. I keep hearing dogs. No, now I can identify them as coyotes, laughing like a bunch of lunatics out there in the darkness. The parking lot looks strange. Did that fat asshole put LSD in my drink? I am walking home with Juanita Flores. She is wearing a sleeveless lilac-colored cotton dress trimmed with red rickrack and she is older than I am, maybe eight years old. She has stolen a tablet of white paper from school for the novel she is writing about a pair of sisters who live in a haunted house and she is asking me to steal some stamps from my mother's bureau drawer so she can send it in to be published. She seems to be lonely and never supervised and I don't know where she lives. We met in the playground at Roosevelt Elementary School and she drew me into her vivid world of fantasy, often wandering up to Twelfth Street on her own to find me and continue our games.

In this memory I am seeing in the black and white of the parking lot, a mongrel named Wilson gets out of the yard of the brick house next door and confronts us in the middle of the street, snarling and snapping. We are terrified to go on. Juanita begins to whimper. I know I must save her. I drag her back to my house.

"Wilson's out! Juanita can't go home!"

My policeman grandfather will take care of this. He comes out of the bathroom holding a rolled newspaper, big, blocking what little light there is in the narrow corridor to the kitchen.

"She can't stay here."

"But Wilson—"

"I don't want a little spic girl in my house."

I watch dumbly as he escorts my friend to the front door and out. Parting the white lace curtains that cover the narrow windows on either side of the door I see Juanita Flores alone, immobilized by humiliation and fear. The barking dog is ahead. A closed door is behind. Slowly a yellow stream trickles from beneath the lilac dress, puddling on our doorstep.

But I am safe. I am not thrown out. Even though I have heard the boy who was my father referred to as "the Mexican," that was far away and doesn't count and I am not a little spic girl like Juanita Flores. In the cool darkness I look up at my grandfather, grateful for his love. From that moment on, I want to be just like him.

EIGHT

IT IS KYLE VERNON'S IDEA for everyone to contribute to a potluck lunch once a month. A serious student of French cooking and connoisseur of fine wines, Kyle once conned three of us from the office into taking a class in pizza making in the private kitchen of some schmancy chef up in the Hollywood Hills. I sat on a bamboo stool and drank the free Chianti Classico and made wise-ass remarks. Kyle was in ecstasy. He just didn't want the excitement to end. The Brentwood housewives went home with special pizza baking stones and dried oregano still on the vine; I went home with no illusions about rolling out the dough for the man in my life.

This month Kyle shows off with a couple of French apple pies for which the apples have been cut so thin he must have used a razor. The slices are arranged in perfect concentric circles on a layer of custard and covered with a coating of orange jelly that he identifies as apricot glaze.

"Geez, Kyle," I say, "why didn't you just go to a bakery? You could have saved a lot of work."

"Ana, it's people like you who wrecked the Pietà."

"Pietà," I muse just to get him going, "isn't that some kind of a Middle East sandwich?"

73

Barbara baked lasagne and Rosalind brought a tuna casserole. Duane Carter's contribution, needless to say, is Texas chili so bitter and hot it makes you sweat. Frank Chang's mother made Chinese raviolis and I plunk down a family-size container of Chicken Mc-Nuggets.

Kyle looks pained. "I'm not even sure we should allow that semi–food product on this beautiful table."

"Hey, I don't have a *wife* to go shopping for me."

"Who's talking wives? I went to Ranch Market and personally inspected each and every piece of fruit that went into those tarts."

"That's because you're a compulsive maniac who should be treated."

"What about Barbara? What about Rosalind?" Kyle goes on. "Do *they* have wives? Or do they put their best effort forward for their squad?"

"*He* has a wife." I point dramatically to Donnato, who looks up from prying the lid off a giant blue plastic bowl filled with lettuce and topped off with slices of carrots and radishes that are in turn carefully overlaid with rings of red onion and green pepper to create a virtual kaleidoscope of vegetables.

"Admit it, Donnato. Your *wife* made that salad."

"The evidence is compelling. I've never known a man who could use Tupperware," Barbara remarks in her dry way. "The airlock seal is beyond them."

Donnato unscrews the lid from a fresh bottle of blue cheese dressing and dumps the entire thing in a pile into the bowl. "Guilty as charged. Chain me to the wall and beat me."

"Very tempting," I whisper, reaching past him for the Chinese raviolis, which I know from experience are the best thing out there.

At first he doesn't seem to react. His eyes are on the black plastic tongs he is using to toss the salad; the tongs from the utility drawer in the harvest gold kitchen in the tract house in the Simi Valley, where the daisy pot holders match the daisy towels and the metal canisters lined up by size are lettered Sugar, Spice, Everything Nice.

Finally, after giving it a lot of thought, Donnato calls my bluff: "If you're into that sort of thing I know a leather bar up on the Strip."

"And I bet you're a regular customer."

Still deadpan: "We've been partners for three years but how much do you really know about me, Ana?"

I laugh. "I can see you in a lot of things, Donnato, but somehow leather is not one of them."

"What's so funny?" Barbara wants to know.

"Donnato in a black leather girdle."

Donnato's mouth has taken on a funny pull, a hint of a smile beneath the beard.

"I can see *you*," he says. "Annie Oakley in black lace."

Barbara elbows my ribs conspicuously and fires something back at him which I am not hearing. His eyes touch mine for half a moment—*Annie Oakley in black lace?*—then he turns away and I find myself unexpectedly flushed from the groin like a teenager.

Back in the bullpen a phone is ringing.

"I'll get it." Rosalind automatically puts her plate down.

"No—it's mine." I can see the light flashing on my desk across the room.

The moment I hear Mrs. Gutiérrez's voice the sexy little high evaporates as my stomach contracts into an anxious knot.

"Everybody is sick," she is telling me. "All the children have the runny nose and Cristóbal is hot."

"Does he need to see a doctor?"

"I don't think so. I think he gonna get better in a day. I just give him soup."

I am watching the group behind the glass partition of the lunchroom. Donnato is listening along with everyone else to Duane Carter holding forth. Even with his slumped shoulders Duane is tallest. He says something that makes everyone laugh.

"Did you get the money from Mrs. Claire? I was waiting to hear."

"No. I didn't. I talked to her, but . . . I didn't get anywhere."

"How can I take care of the children with no money?"

"I don't know, Mrs. Gutiérrez."

While I am standing there, Henry Caravetti, a mailroom clerk with muscular dystrophy, rolls by in his electric wheelchair and puts a bundle of envelopes into my tray. I give him a thumbs-up. His pale lips stretch into a wobbly smile as he removes one frozen hand from the controls, jerks it up toward the ceiling to return my gesture, and travels on.

"These children are your family," Mrs. Gutiérrez spits angrily, "but you feel nothing. Lady, I am sorry for you."

She hangs up. I sit there motionless, feeling attacked from within and without. Suddenly it all turns to anger and I slam through desk drawers, purse, and the pockets of my jacket, finding the peach and gray card from the Dana Orthopedic Clinic squashed on the bottom of my blue canvas briefcase along with some warped throat lozenges. Once again I fight the impulse to identify myself as an FBI agent in order to cut through the standard receptionist bullshit but I do use the words "very urgent" and "legal matter," which finally get me through to Dr. Eberhardt.

"I'm sorry—who are you again?"

I tell him that I am a cousin of their late housekeeper, Violeta. It sounds odd but I stick with it.

"Apparently you still owed her money when she left your employ."

Cold: "She was paid."

"She told a friend you still owed her approximately four hundred dollars."

"That's crazy. I wouldn't rip off a housemaid."

"Let's short-circuit this." I feel guilty and deeply conflicted and he is a doctor living in a million-and-a-half-dollar house with a crystal chandelier. "Her children have nobody to take care of them, okay? May I suggest out of common decency, as her last employer, you make a contribution to their welfare?"

"Hold it, Ms. Grey," he says, making a big deal out of *Ms.* "I fired Violeta. Do you want to know why? Instead of watching *my* children, which she was paid very well to do, she was inside gabbing with another housekeeper. Because of her negligence my four-year-old daughter fell into a pool and almost drowned."

Subdued: "I didn't know about that."

"No, you didn't know, but here you are making insulting accusations."

"Still," pressing forward despite shaky ground, "her children need help."

"How about help from a government agency? I pay fifty-one percent of my income to the government, which is supposed to take care of people like Violeta. People, by the way, who aren't even American citizens."

Another burst of laughter from the lunchroom.

There is a pause as if he's thinking about it, then Dr. Eberhardt blows an exasperated breath into the phone. "If she claims I owed her money I'll write out a check just to close the books."

I thank him and tell him to send it directly to Mrs. Gutiérrez.

"Violeta behaved negligently, but what happened to her was senseless and outrageous, and I feel for the kids. Just don't ever come to me again."

I sink into the chair, nodding triumphantly toward the Bank Dick's Undercover Disguise as if it should congratulate me for solving the problem of Teresa and Cristóbal. It doesn't wave or hold its sleeves up in a clasp of victory, however, and a darkening shadow edges my relief. The doctor's description of Violeta's negligence does not square with his wife's reaction to my questions. Claire Eberhardt shut down, saying only, "We had to let Violeta go, it didn't work out." If a maid let my kid almost drown in a pool I'd feel a right to be a bit more critical. My impression of her at the door wavers and finally becomes clear: Claire Eberhardt was behaving like the classic suspect with something of her own to hide.

As if to sort things out, I absently start going through my mail. That is when I find the official letter from Special Agent in Charge (SAC) Robert Galloway, who has reviewed my request for transfer to the Kidnapping and Extortion Squad. He has denied that request, citing an "unfavorable addendum" from my supervisor, Duane Carter.

I return to the lunchroom and stand there empty-handed while people tuck into neat slices of Kyle's French apple tarts and Duane

Carter tells a story about a fifteenth-century *katana* sword worth hundreds of thousands of dollars. Harder than steel we make today, it is still incredibly delicate. Touch it and your fingerprint will ruin the surface. Breathe on it and it will begin to rust in thirty minutes, Duane says.

The men wow and the females in the room start to clean up.

I say to Barbara: "Duane fucked me."

"What now?"

"Request for transfer denied."

"Damn." She folds her arms and sinks into the word. *"Damn."*

Our voices are low. My jaw is clenched with the effort of not giving in to a rage that is steadily building out of control.

Barbara leans over to pick up a dish off the table. "This is discrimination."

Looking past her I see the smudgy glass window plastered with notices of softball games and scuba diving trips, wavery white shapes of anonymous people passing in the hall. Sometimes I so desire the comforting of a mother.

"If it is discrimination it's going to stop right now."

Ignoring her look of caution I step toward Duane Carter and square off with him right there at the potluck lunch.

"Hey, Duane."

"Ana?"

"The SAC denied my request for transfer." The talk quiets. "Your unfavorable addendum had a big influence on his decision."

Duane glances at the members of the squad who have caught the drift and suppresses a smile.

"I'm sorry it didn't work out."

"Are you really sorry, Duane?"

"Of course he's sorry," says Donnato from out of nowhere. "Now he's got to put up with you for seven more years," giving our supervisor a sideways cock of the head as if commiserating on how difficult and challenging it is to manage women on any level in this world today. I hate it when Donnato mediates for Duane, even though he does it because he thinks he's protecting me.

"I guess I can put up with her," Duane jokes.

"If you force me to continue to work on your squad, Duane, I promise you this: only one of us is going to be left standing."

Donnato's smile fades into a look of appalled disgust, as if I have just wandered out into the middle of a firefight like some rank rookie amateur while he and every other smart veteran is well under cover and intends to stay there. Nothing I can do for you now, he is telling me with a shudder, the only question remaining is whether he will hang around to watch me get blown away.

But instead of letting loose with everything he's got, Duane surprises everyone by pulling up a chair and straddling it so he and I are actually eyeball to eyeball and I can observe the fine texture of his porcelain-white skin and the few short dark hairs that lie flat beneath his lower lip, wondering if he even shaves.

"Why don't you like me?"

It is meant to be disarming and of course it is, this roll-up-the-sleeves honesty undertaken in public, Duane's attempt to make me look like the bad guy, my aggressiveness turned ugly in the face of his genuine hurt. I know Barbara doesn't buy it and neither does Donnato, but they leave the room anyway, along with most everyone else who suddenly has to get back to their desks.

"I could ask you the same question."

"But that's just it. I don't dislike you, Ana. If I'm tough with you it's because you can take it. And maybe also, frankly, because you need it. You do tend to carry a chip."

"So you denied my transfer for my own good."

Duane isn't interested in sarcasm from me. He is concentrating on following the line of his sincerity, which is an effort.

"When the time comes, you'll take off like a bat out of hell and nobody'll stop you. But there's no need to be in such a hurry. Christ, you're not even thirty yet, are you?"

I have been leaning my butt against the edge of one of the brown lunchroom tables. I am wearing a short black skirt, black tights and heels and it makes me feel sexy and insouciant to be lounging there, arms crossed, fingering the soft sleeves of the white sweater I wore for the potluck lunch, the one with the lacy almost see-through bodice. Duane Carter is looking at me with a neutral kind of innocence like an adolescent boy who has quit setting fires for the day and is on his knees playing with a toy car collection like when he was six.

"The fact remains that I made a perfect bust out there at California First Bank and I deserve to be rewarded for it, not punished."

"I'm trying to explain this is not about punishment—"

"Sure it is. You're punishing me because I'm female."

He squeezes his eyes shut and laughs out loud. "I hope you don't really believe that."

"Yes, I do, and I'm going to bring an EEOC lawsuit charging sex discrimination against you and the Bureau to prove it."

Duane gets to his feet and tosses the chair aside. His hands are deep in his pockets, feeling for those stolen matches or whatever his source of destructive psychic power. The innocence is gone and black fire rages once again in his eyes. That didn't take long.

■　　■　　■

Ever since that class action suit on behalf of Hispanic agents, the FBI has been under scrutiny; another lawsuit filed by some black agents also received wide attention. I know very well the powers that be within the Bureau will not tolerate accusations of discrimination against the Los Angeles field office.

It turns out, after a couple of conversations with the advocacy lawyers, that I have a very good case. So good that on the eve of the filing deadline, Special Agent in Charge Robert Galloway calls both Duane and me to his office for a special meeting.

I have never been inside Galloway's corner office, with the wide-open view of downtown Los Angeles and the better carpeting and new butterscotch plaid furniture.

"I had to go back to the start of this thing to try and get somewhere," Galloway begins in his Brooklyn accent, "and I can see where each of you has a particular point of view."

Galloway worked the organized crime division of our New York office for eighteen years yet there isn't a strand of gray on his head of thick wavy black Irish hair. He always wears a turtleneck—his trademark—never a shirt and tie, no matter what the occasion or weather, giving rise to rumors of tracheotomies and bullet wounds and cancer scars. . . . But he still smokes cigars so either he's got a death wish or, like the rest of us, he holds out for being a maverick in his own way.

It is ten thirty and below us the blocky low cityscape of Los Angeles is lit by a dazzling milky white haze that will burn off to clear skies and seventy-five degrees by noon. By coincidence Duane and I are both wearing navy blue suits with white shirts, which makes us look like a pair of airline reservation clerks.

On the coffee table there are souvenirs of Galloway's days in New York City, including a model of the Statue of Liberty and a four-inch oval brass seal of NYPD Detective Division.

Galloway picks it up and worries it in his hand. I ask what it's for.

"It's a belt buckle. They couldn't afford to give me the whole belt."

He refers to a file on his lap. He has come around the desk, management style, positioning himself near us to show we are all equal, comfortably sitting with legs crossed, an unlit cigar between his teeth.

"Going back to this bust at the bank . . . it looks like Ana did quite a noteworthy thing. She ascertained there was a felony in progress, single-handedly isolated and subdued the subject so that he could be arrested without incident by LAPD. . . . And then"—he shakes his head and laughs—"the schmuck turns out to be good for six other robberies!"

He laughs and laughs. He laughs until he coughs and turns red in the face.

Duane Carter is not even smiling. He is leveling that eerie killer look at Galloway. I remember Donnato telling me about their rivalry and feel a chill, wondering if Galloway feels it, too.

"Special Agent Grey failed to call for backup assistance, thereby endangering herself and the public," says Duane.

Galloway wipes his eyes. "You're right. Calling in a 211 in progress would have been the approved procedure."

His arm is dropped over the side of the chair but he's still holding the heavy belt buckle, fingering it with implacable cool. They are locked on to each other now.

"He's right on a technicality." I am swinging my leg impatiently. "He's not right to deny me a transfer because—"

"I said at the beginning that you both have a point," Galloway interrupts sharply. "Stop pouting, Ana, it'll give you worry lines and you're much too young and pretty."

He raises his eyebrows, daring me to call him on it. Instead I take a cue from his own behavior and laugh. More of a snort, actually, but at least I'm not pouting.

"I'm going to allow Duane's addendum to stand."

Meaning it will be a part of my personal file forever. Other people down the line will read it, not know the facts, and assume I screwed up. The unfairness of it propels me to my feet.

"That is just plain wrong!"

"Nobody says you have to agree."

"I don't agree. I disagree in the strongest terms and I'm certain the EEOC will back me up."

I stop breathlessly. The power has shifted with dizzying speed. Now they're both watching me, secure in their chairs, while I'm stamping my foot in the middle of the room.

The worst of it is Duane Carter looking at me with *pity.*

"Well, if you'd calm down and cool out," Galloway continues, "I'll tell you the rest of my decision."

I back down into the chair.

"I'm going to let the addendum stand . . . but I am also going to approve Ana's request for transfer."

"Excuse me," says Duane, "but ain't that just the teensiest bit disingenuous? How can you do both?"

"I'm approving Ana's transfer on a contingency basis. If after a trial period it looks like she can handle it, then we'll go ahead and move her up to Kidnapping and Extortion."

"What a complete pile of steaming horseshit."

In my opinion it is a masterly compromise.

"What's the contingency?" I ask eagerly.

Galloway gets up and goes back to the desk, puts the half-chewed cigar in an ashtray with two other soggy butts.

"I'm going to put you on a drug case. See how you do."

I'm leaning forward in my chair ready to jump up and sprint for it, whatever it is.

"This came to me through the Director's office. It's what they call 'high profile.' "

I can't tell if Galloway is smiling because he's giving me a gift or because he finds the words "high profile" particularly amusing, worthy of an ironic twist. In the meantime, Duane's face is turning so dark it is almost the color of his navy blue suit.

"Jayne Mason is alleging that her physician got her addicted to prescription drugs."

There is a moment of stupefied silence. We were expecting Colombians, Mexicans, Crips, and Bloods.

"You'd have to be on Mars not to know Jayne Mason was in and out of the Betty Ford Center," Galloway continues. "Well, now she claims she's an addict because of this shyster M.D. named Eberhardt."

Duane: "What's the Bureau's jurisdiction?"

"She claims the drugs he gave her came from Mexico." Galloway tosses a file at me.

"Mighty thin," observes Duane.

"Look at Title 18 of the Federal Code, Drug Abuse Prevention, or maybe 21, Wrongful Distribution."

I am speechless.

I know perfectly well that I am obligated to tell the Special Agent in Charge immediately of my conflict of interest concerning this case. That my alleged cousin, who died under mysterious circumstances, worked for this very Dr. Eberhardt.

"Sounds like a case of medical fraud to me," Duane persists, "which would put it under the jurisdiction of the White Collar Crime Squad, am I wrong?"

"Like I said before," Galloway repeats sternly, "this came from the Director's office."

He has made the political significance clear to both of us.

"I will handle it with discretion."

"Fuck discretion," Galloway grunts. "Just get to the fucking bottom of this so I can appear halfway fucking intelligent."

We file out. Duane is already through the doorway when Galloway touches my shoulder lightly. I turn. The cigar is back in his mouth.

"There's no reason to file that lawsuit now, am I right?"

"I think you've been very fair."

"Glad to hear it."

Duane is waiting for me in the hall.

"Prestige case," I say, tossing my hair.

"Dog case," he replies with a great big happy smile and strolls away.

It doesn't matter what Duane Carter thinks, this is my chance to advance a dozen squares on the achievement chart or even rocket off the chart—Jayne Mason, it *has* to be big—and the fact that I have prior knowledge of the players involved has pivoted in my mind from being a conflict of interest to an incredible advantage.

I am thinking about that day in the alley behind the orthopedic office when I saw Jayne Mason and the accused doctor together. She was dressed in red, breaking out of his grasp, striding toward the limousine. Now I remember something else. A fanciful detail. The doctor had been holding a rose. A yellow rose on a long stem. After the limo disappeared, he tossed the rose into the trash and the heavy door snapped shut behind him.

THE FIRST STEP is to assemble all the information on Randall Eberhardt, M.D., that currently exists on the hard disk and magnetic tape archives of the world.

I run his name through our in-house computer, which will turn up previous arrests anywhere on the globe and discover there are none. I check with the California Department of Motor Vehicles for citations of reckless driving, driving under the influence, or speeding, which are, again, negative. I subpoena the records and obtain a printout from the telephone company of toll calls made from both the medical office and the residence on Twentieth Street, looking for a pattern that would point to a drug connection, but all I learn is that the Eberhardts still make a lot of calls to friends and relations in Boston.

Our huge revolving "dead files" downstairs are records of every complaint we have received by a citizen over the phone or transom, and a thorough check by two of the brighter clerks yields nothing. The California Medical Licensing Board tells me no charges have been filed by any other patient regarding Dr. Eberhardt. They confirm that he graduated from Harvard University and Harvard Medical School and completed an internship and residency in orthopedic medicine at New England Deaconess Hospital. He was born in Cambridge, Massachusetts, and graduated from Buckingham, Browne and Nichols, an upper-class prep school.

I contact our Boston field office and request a deep background check, emphasizing this is an urgent, high-profile case that came to us through the Director. The road back to Boston feels promising. Whatever the cause of Eberhardt's deviation it must have been in evidence before the move to California. Maybe there's a pattern. I put in a request for travel to the East Coast just in case.

All of that in place, I allow myself to return to the question of Dr. Eberhardt's housekeeper and what I alone know about her. I have been keeping the envelope containing Violeta Alvarado's meager archive in a desk drawer and sometimes find myself looking through it: a Bible, a few snapshots that tell of a journey to America, autopsy photos documenting a violent death. I have heard her described as a hard worker and loving mother and have seen her children, real enough. She might turn out to be a cousin of mine after all, but my job is to sweep all that sentimentality aside and look at the facts. The more closely I look the more convinced I become that LAPD Detective Sergeant John Roth's theory has a strong possibility of being correct: that Violeta Alvarado was involved with drugs— perhaps on behalf of her former employer, Dr. Randall Eberhardt.

My work often requires me to make this type of construction, a model of human behavior, like the origami polyhedron that hangs on a string off Special Agent Michelle Nishimura's desk lamp. I have watched her make the most amazing things out of paper, complex folds executed in sequence, the pure logic of the design giving strength to the most fragile of materials.

I have bounced my little spheroid, the possibility of Violeta Alvarado's connection to the Jayne Mason case, off the mental wall a couple of hundred times and it still holds up, which gives me the nerve to call John Roth again.

It takes a few days for him to phone back because he is working undercover. His attitude is maddeningly the same:

"Why the fuck should I do you a favor?"

"Do yourself a favor and close a homicide for once."

"Why break my record?"

"Did you get the autopsy report yet?"

"No."

"So what's the status of the case?"

"It's in the 'Who Cares?' file, as in, 'Who cares about a dead Mexican?'"

Something is blowing far away, not even visible on the horizon, detectable only in a subtle shift of atmosphere, from dry to humid, say, as aspen leaves flutter in the first omen of change. . . . And a strange quieting of the usual roar so that one note can be heard over and over, sultry and urgent.

My voice drops to a level warning. "She was from El Salvador and she had kids."

"So do a million other dead Mexicans."

"You asshole."

He laughs with a wild stoned hysterical edge.

"It's your own brilliant deduction, John. She was out on Santa Monica Boulevard at five in the morning. She was killed in a drive-by that looks pretty deliberate. Her hands were blown away, which means a hit."

"Pretty good."

"She was working for a doctor who's been accused by Jayne Mason of overprescribing medication. She could have been a street connection for him. I'm asking you to reopen the case."

"I've got a few other things going."

"This is major."

"So is my hard-on."

I bite my lip. I need this badly.

"John. Cut me some slack here, okay?"

I wonder if the vulnerability is as obvious to him as it is mortifying to me.

■　　■　　■

"A doctor who overprescribes narcotics is like a fireman who sets fires," Barbara declares. "One sick puppy."

"Not necessarily. It could be very calculating."

"You mean blackmail and extortion?"

We have met over the copy machine and are walking together down the hall.

"Or he could be getting kickbacks from a pharmacy or an insurance company, but I checked out his bank accounts and credit cards and he's solid."

"Then it's not about money, it's about power." Barbara's eyes are bright with conjecture. "Can you imagine what it would be like for some boring straight doctor to have Jayne Mason under his total control?"

"Doctors are control freaks," I agree, starting to make sense out of it.

"How could you even perform an *examination* on a woman like that?"

"I'll let you know. I'm going out to Malibu this afternoon."

Barbara punches herself in the chest and doubles up in a paroxysm of envy.

"Don't worry," I assure her as she continues to pant wordlessly, "I promise to get Jayne Mason's lingerie closet on microfilm."

■   ■   ■

I swing out of the tunnel at Ocean Avenue onto the Pacific Coast Highway and the sun hits me whap off the water, tall corridors of air suddenly open and unobstructed. Even the palm trees are tiny, way up there on top of the palisade, as I shoot along a narrow roadway with cars rushing at me sixty miles an hour in the opposite direction, no divider. I'm reeling from a sudden sense of space, distracted by surfer-dotted silver waves, RVs jammed crazily along the narrow shoulder, a continual jumble of low-slung houses with their backs up right against the road, thinking it must be death to turn into one of those precarious garages. The ocean chews at the shore on the left, and looking at the huge gouging claw marks that mud slides have taken from the hillside to the right, I remember boulders rolling onto the road during last year's killer winter storms. The order of the world steadily uncoils as I head north, skimming the very edge of the continent like a top in dizzy balance between sanity and the unknown.

Just past Pepperdine University I leave all the crap behind—the Spanish-style malls and the beach traffic. The road narrows and becomes pastoral, horse ranches reaching up into the Santa Monica Mountains, spectacular vistas of the Pacific to the west with an occasional glimpse of surf curling up to a cove half hidden below rocky cliffs.

Arroyo Road comes up quickly, marked by a thin, weathered sign. After a hairy left turn across the highway I find myself on a dirt lane canopied by shaggy giant eucalyptus trees obviously planted a very long time ago. It is surprising how much land can be secreted away between the highway and the sea. A flimsy corral fence made of pipe runs along a meadow of high golden grass where two Appaloosa horses are grazing. I wonder about security. The road curves through the pasture into a clump of sequoias.

There is a gatehouse but it is empty and the white armature is up, so I breeze through to Foxtail Ranch, acres of coastal woodlands with a private beach that Jayne Mason bought in the seventies for two million dollars, now worth easily ten times that much.

Five or six vehicles are parked in a small gravel area, workmen's light trucks, the JM limousine, and a creamy new Cadillac with gold detailing that must belong to Mason's personal manager, Magda Stockman, who (I have been told) will be present with her client today.

Thick foliage obscures most of the house. The entrance is nothing more than a door in an unglamorous white wall next to a garage.

A young man with lustrous shoulder-length brown hair answers my ring. Some men with long hair look like greaseballs and some look like jungle sex gods—like this one, with his muscular shoulders, alert animal eyes, faded swimming trunks, magenta polo shirt, and bare feet.

"My name is Jan. How was the traffic?"

"Better than Westwood."

"It's a hassle coming out but once you get here most people are glad they made the trip."

I follow Jan through a courtyard, keeping my eyes on his powerful ankles (forget the calves, I won't even go into the calves), which are embraced by a pair of woven Guatemalan ankle bracelets. I like the way the tan goes all the way between his toes—long, prehensile toes you can easily picture curled around the edge of a surfboard or, okay, the rails of a brass bed.

"You like it out at the beach, Jan?"

"Oh, yeah. I used to be a windsurfing instructor."

"Don't tell me Jayne Mason is into windsurfing."

"No, she's not," he answers seriously.

"What do you do for Ms. Mason?" trying to keep a straight face.

"I'm her assistant."

The Hollywood term for secretary. So Jayne Mason walked down to the beach one morning and picked up a hot young surfer to adorn the house and open her mail. His absolute lack of imagination makes me believe he is her secretary and nothing more. Everything he says is delivered with just enough energy to sound personal when it is actually by rote, like a bellhop in a good hotel. He isn't interested in me. He doesn't bother to meet my eyes. He is interested in his body and how he will look posed against the bar at McGinty's tonight. I take note of these things because I have noticed that people generally hire assistants who are like themselves.

We continue around a corner where I am immediately hit by the sense of an old pool—the dense smell of chlorine and wet concrete—and sure enough, to my left is an oval-shaped swimming pool about forty feet long with a turquoise tile bottom. Nearby are two redwood chaise longues with green and yellow floral cushions, and, on the ground beside them, a Frisbee. The water looks funky and not very inviting, even to a water rat like me. I imagine the only people who use this pool are Jayne Mason's grandchildren. Barbara told me she has five, from three marriages.

We enter a huge den with fake beams and a bright shamrock

green carpet where I am suddenly jolted to find myself face-to-face with Jayne Mason, wearing an evening gown and a big smile and holding a bouquet.

After a stunned moment I realize it is only a life-size cutout but the presence is unsettling.

"Can I get you something? Coffee? Perrier?"

"Coffee would be great."

"Decaf or regular?"

"Highest octane."

"You got it," Jan says without smiling, and leaves.

There are large deep brown swivel chairs that look like barrels and several coffee tables inlaid with stained-glass designs of maidens and doves and suns and moons. A prominent wet bar is stocked with everything from Glenfiddich scotch to French crème de cassis and plastered with layers of memorabilia.

Welcome to Café Jayne Mason. There are comic strips and caricatures and photographs of her taken with every conceivable celebrity including the last five presidents of the United States, as well as framed tabloid articles with amusing headlines speculating about her exploits. In the very center of the bar stands an enormous arrangement of fresh yellow roses in a crystal vase.

The odd thing is, the dates on the newspapers stop in 1974.

Now I understand the room. Why the brown louvered shutters are closed. Why the furniture, despite its grand scale and spotless upkeep, seems worn, and the air feels closed in and damp. This is a seventies house that has not been changed in twenty years. This room was designed for smoking dope and drinking alcohol and flirting and fucking and hiding from the California sun. It is a stage set for the kind of hedonistic pleasure that was taken in a certain style during a certain age and preserved intact so Jayne Mason can revisit that lusty image of herself whenever she steps through the doorway.

I pace the room, trying to get a feel for how recently it has been used and for what. No ashtrays. No wastebaskets. The fieldstone fireplace has been swept clean. But right above it, so poorly hung that it angles out from the wall as if about to tumble, is an utterly astonishing painting. A seascape of sailboats racing across translucent blue-green water stirred by wind, so alive that it actually radiates light, too alive for the boundaries of its heavy gilded frame, the outdated room, the movie star's sterile home.

Seeing such a thing in real life is a shock. I stare with longing into the passionately felt world of the canvas, unexpectedly moved to tears. The vitality of the painting makes everything else, including my own sad heart, seem dead.

"It was painted by Edouard Manet."

I spin around. I hadn't known there was anyone else in the room besides the cardboard cutout of Jayne Mason.

"She saw this when she was filming on Majorca. I have always encouraged her to collect art, but it does not suit her. She is only interested in acting, which is lucky for me. I am Magda Stockman, her personal manager."

She is a large woman, a size fourteen, but dressed in a black suit with braided white piping of such fine wool and style that it makes her figure look trim. She moves with a rustle—it must be lined with silk. As we shake hands several heavy gold charm bracelets on her wrist jingle like Christmas bells and I am enveloped by a sweet, rich perfume. She wears black stockings and black high-heeled pumps with two back-to-back gold Cs on the toe that even a lowlife like me recognizes as the trademark for Chanel.

"Are there paintings like this all over the house?"

"Only a few small Picassos. It is just as well. Jayne is not the kind of person who enjoys to sit by the fire and look at pictures. She must always be *in motion.*"

Magda Stockman rolls her hands over each other like a small engine so the bracelets tinkle merrily. The accent is mellow and burnished, possibly Central European. I get the impression she has been in this country a long time but cultivates the accent as part of the persona. She has broad Slavic cheekbones and moist unlined skin that seems extremely white against the black hair pulled severely off the face into a bow. She is so artfully put together that the only way to imagine her age is to guess somewhere between fifty and seventy.

"I am sorry to say that Jayne and I cannot see you today. We are having a meeting with some people out from St. Louis and it cannot be interrupted. Please to apologize to the FBI."

My back stiffens.

"This matter came to us through the Director. We were told it was urgent."

"It is of the highest urgency. But not today."

She smiles indulgently with polished red lips.

"Please take your time and relax. You are of course welcome to walk down to the beach. Ask Jan if you need anything."

Having given the United States government thirty seconds of her time, Magda Stockman hurries out, drawn by the ringing of a telephone somewhere in the house.

Jan reappears with a silver tray on which is a china coffee set patterned with strawberries—pot, cup and saucer, cream and sugar, the whole thing: service for one, like you'd see on a bed tray in one of those mail-order catalogues with hundred-dollar sheets, including a silver teaspoon on a blue cloth napkin.

He sets the tray down carefully, then runs a strong square hand through his tawny hair. "We'll call your office to reschedule."

"Jayne likes yellow roses." Figuring if everyone else is calling her Jayne I'll give it a try.

"Yes, she does."

And that's it. He leaves me with the coffee and the souvenir Manet. I have never been told quite so graciously to take a flying leap.

■　　■　　■

I walk down to the beach, what the hell, the path across the sloping lawn looks enticing, bordered by fluttering pansies in combinations of yellow, red, blue, and purple that remind me of my mother's cotton hankies flapping on the clothesline in the backyard. At the top of the cliff a sea wind powerful enough to blow the hair straight back is like an elixir drowning you with exotic promises—Hawaii is out there and China, after all—so by then there is no choice, so what if the wet air wilts the beige linen suit I wore to meet the movie star, I grip the metal chain that loops along the steep wooden stairway and make my way down a hundred vertical yards of headland rock.

Here I am sitting on Jayne Mason's private beach at three in the afternoon as the sun reflects off the sand like a mirror with just the right intensity of heat, watching the whitecaps on green water, tasting the salt in the air, no noise, nothing in the brain but wind, no other humans or their works within view, utterly alone, thinking I would cheerfully commit a capital crime in order to have something like this, when a man climbs unsteadily over the rocks adjoining the next cove. For a moment he is a black silhouette against the brilliant screen of light and I think he must be a fan of Jayne Mason or a tabloid photographer trying the marine approach to her property. I get off the weathered wooden chest I am perched upon, my hand hovering instinctively near the weapon under my jacket.

As he lumbers closer I realize it is Tom Pauley, the limousine driver.

And that he is completely naked.

"Tom," I call out to warn him, "it's Ana Grey, FBI. We met in the alley, remember?"

"Sure do." He continues walking until he is standing right next to me. "Gorgeous day." Unconcerned, he opens the chest. Inside is a tangle of old netting, some clothes, folded towels, and a red cooler. Inside the cooler is fresh ice and some brown bottles of Mexican beer and fruit sodas and half of a shrink-wrapped watermelon.

"Jeez, Tom. We have to stop meeting like this."

He grins. His lips are sunburned and chapped. Shoulders padded with fat. A pale distended belly. The usual dangle. And a pair of bow legs the color of boiled Santa Barbara shrimp.

"Have a beer."

"I'll take a black currant–boysenberry."

"What are you doing here?"

"I was invited."

"By who?"

"Your boss."

"Someone under investigation?"

"Could be."

"Someone on staff?"

"Yes, Tom. We know all about that scam you're running."

He smiles and raises his eyebrows over the Dos Equis.

"Got me."

"You can run but you cannot hide."

We stand there looking out to the ocean and I'm the one who feels like an idiot because I'm dressed, don't ask me why.

The tide is coming in faster now. The boulders Tom climbed over are almost totally obscured by foamy surf, which makes it harder for a second figure, a woman, to make her way around the jutting cliff, clear the rocks, cross the sand, and join us.

"Meet Maureen."

Also naked.

Maureen is a very thin redhead, too thin, as if she's got an eating disorder. She has bony arms and flaccid thighs, two small mounds with flat nipples for breasts, but great hair. Ropes of terrific red hair whipping around in the quickening breeze.

Maureen takes Tom's hand and says nothing. I guess she's shy. She reaches for a denim shirt inside the locker but instead of putting it on—as I hope she will—spreads it out and lies down.

Tom grabs a towel and sits cross-legged next to her, his middle-aged form like a big pile of pearly white Crisco beside her delicate nymphette body. One meaty hand tips the bottle of beer to his mouth while the other smooths Maureen's young freckled forehead.

"You two look like you want some privacy."

"No, no. We're just on a break."

"This is how they take coffee breaks in Malibu?"

"Whenever possible," Tom grins.

"You both work for Jayne Mason?"

"Maureen does her clothes."

"I have a friend named Barbara who, due to a tragic childhood deprivation, is obsessed about Jayne Mason and where she gets her clothes."

Maureen shrugs her bare shoulders. "She takes them."

"What do you mean, takes them? From a store?"

"From the studio." Maureen keeps her face to the sun, speaking without opening her eyes. "She'll be like talking to a grip or someone, doing her Greta Garbo imitation, and I'm backing the car up to the dressing room and carrying out boxes of stuff."

"What kind of stuff?"

"The stuff she wore in the movie. I guess it's kind of like hers anyway."

"Does this behavior have anything to do with the drug problem?"

"That's over. She gave up drugs," Maureen tells me in a solemn voice. "Big time."

Tom rolls over and props up his head on an elbow.

"They all steal from the studio, Ana. Standard operating procedure."

"Someone will go, Where did you get that dress? And she'll go, Oh, it's from my personal designer, Luc de France, when it's really from Twentieth Century–Fox. I love Jayne." Maureen smiles into the infrared rays.

I realize this girl can't be more than twenty years old with about as many brain cells.

"How long have you been working for Jayne?"

"I don't know. Maybe a year?"

"Isn't that fast to be given such a big responsibility? Don't they have union rules?"

"Maureen's an assistant," Tom explains. "There's someone else—or actually a few people—in charge of, you know—"

"Designing, buying, fitting," Maureen chants like a child at her lessons, "con-ceptualizing." She waits. Her eyebrows frown. "I don't really want to do clothes."

"No?" I drain the bottle.

"I have a great idea for a screenplay."

"Little Maureen's big dreams." Tom strokes her hair affectionately.

"*Maaagda* thinks it's a good idea." She opens her eyes just wide enough to glare at Tom.

He smiles placatingly. I toss the bottle back into the cooler.

"Why don't you stay and join us?" he offers.

"Join you in what?"

"Whatever."

I look out at the ocean one more time. The waves are six feet high now, heavy and forbidding.

"In another life. Nice to meet you, Maureen."

I walk back to the cliff, grab hold of the chain, and hoist myself up the stairs.

When I get to the top, just a touch out of breath, I am startled to meet Jan, who is standing on the head of the promontory, wearing the upper half of a wet suit, hair streaming back over the shoulders in a stiff wind. He is looking at the ocean through a pair of high-powered binoculars.

"Dolphins," he explains as I pass, without taking his eyes from the glass.

Clearly he is watching the naked lovers.

TEN

JAN DOES CALL to "reschedule"—and cancel and reschedule—maybe a dozen times. I keep working on my other cases but drop everything each time Jan says his boss is ready to meet. Once I go all the way to a fancy Italian restaurant at the top of Beverly Glen only to be told by the maître d' that Miss Mason will not be able to meet me but I should go ahead and order lunch as her guest. I choose a seafood salad for $21.00 and when it comes, to my horror, a tiny naked octopus the size of a dime crawls out of the mixed greens to the edge of the plate and collapses onto the tablecloth.

"To keep the calamari extremely fresh, the chef puts them into the salad alive," the waiter explains, "and kills them with olive oil."

The next day I find a rubber octopus hanging at the end of a noose over my desk. What astonishes me is that one of them—probably Kyle—actually stopped off at a joke store and bought a rubber octopus. The merry pranksters also made photocopies of a picture of Jayne Mason and taped them on my wall: "Meet me at the Polo Lounge!" "Meet me in the bathroom." "Luv ya, baby!" "To Ana—My Dearest Friend."

It is now "absolutely set in stone," according to Jan, that I am to meet Jayne Mason in the office of her Beverly Hills attorney a week from Monday. That settled, I am able to give full attention to deep intercourse with Les, a new mechanic at Marina All-Makes. I actually enjoy having work done on the Barracuda, it's such a quixotic challenge to keep it running. Although he can't explain why the headlight is shorting out he is telling me the smart thing would be to replace the entire wiring and light bulb assembly. It will cost around $300 and we'll have to wait for parts.

I become aware that something is going on at the far side of the bullpen, a small commotion over a mildly extraordinary event, as if someone had won fifty bucks in the lottery, but I am concentrating on Les, trying to control my irritation, appealing as he was at seven a.m. this morning in a filthy flannel shirt, ponytail down the back, long blackened fingers wrapped around a white paper coffee cup, aromatic vapors and stale breath commingling in the cold air.

Maybe old Les was intimidated by the muscle car, or maybe he just had a hangover, but if he had applied a screwdriver instead of a screw job he would have seen that the headlight bulb is interchangeable with the one Chrysler uses in all its Dodge vans. You could pick the thing up for ten dollars in an auto parts store, but as I am trying to educate him the disturbance at the other end of the office has started to build and is coming toward me. Like a wave cheer in a baseball stadium people are standing up in tiers and within fifteen seconds everyone around me is on their feet.

My first thought is that we are under attack, that some nut has managed to get through the security door, but nobody's reaching for their weapon and no SWAT teams have arrived. "To be continued," I promise Les and step around my desk to crane a look, only to find the view opening up as a sea of white shirts parts for Jayne Mason, who is walking right toward me.

I don't have time to wonder what she's doing here. Frantically I rip the photocopies of her picture off the wall. Big flakes of plaster come loose and fly into my eye. I stuff everything into the trash, trying to compose myself into the serious-minded FBI agent Jayne Mason has come to see. Then I realize a rubber octopus is hanging over my desk.

I glance down the aisle. I can see Magda Stockman's glossy black head above the crowd and the flash of gold earrings. She is subtly managing the flow of human energy around her client by positioning herself like a rock, keeping Mason in her lee while moving her along, protecting her from the onslaught while maintaining a benign expression and expertly scanning the room to anticipate what might be coming toward them next. Being almost six feet tall gives her the ability to see over the heads of many people.

I calculate I have ten seconds before they reach me so I grab a scissors and step onto a chair, but two desks away the entourage suddenly turns left, continues to the end of the bullpen, and disappears into Galloway's office. I climb off empty-handed, staring after them.

Immediately Barbara Sullivan is on my back like a dervish, digging her fingers into my deltoids.

"I got her autograph!"

She sticks a legal pad under my nose. A carefully legible signature has been written across an entire sheet.

Jayne Mason can turn a scrap of paper into a marquee, she can transform the day with a walk across a room. The woman is magical, and even I, a disbeliever, feel on the outs, hurt and inadequate because I am not on the other side of that door. "What is the big deal about Jayne Mason?" I mutter sourly.

"Either you get it or you don't," Barbara sighs and hurries away. "I'm calling my sisters in Chicago—they're not going to believe this."

She takes two steps, then stops herself and turns back as if suddenly surprised to see me.

"What are you doing here?"

"Trying to get my headlight fixed." I have already redialed Marina All-Makes.

Barbara's eyes grow round and horrified. *Why aren't you in Galloway's office?*

"She came to see him, not me." I offer a stiff smile.

"Are you crazy?" She snatches the phone away. "Get in there."

"Barbara, I can't just crash a meeting—"

"You're going to sit here and wait for a royal invitation?" Goofiness gone, her eyes are bright with the same fanaticism that comes over her whenever someone mentions Duane Carter's name. "It's your case, don't let them ace you out."

"Obviously this thing has kicked up to a higher level."

Barbara grips my upper arm in a very unpleasant way. "Get in there, you dumb shit."

Her reaction seems excessive, but I say, "I'm going."

She releases me. It hurts.

"Jesus Christ."

I pick up a file and a half-drunk can of cola and sashay slowly toward Galloway's closed door, lifting the uninjured arm to fluff at my hair, looking back once to find Barbara Sullivan glaring at me. The eldest of seven, she can be swift and severe. If I had a big sister like her, God knows where I'd be today, but it wouldn't be here.

■　　■　　■

As I sidle into the room, Galloway booms heartily that he was just about to buzz me.

He should have told me to bring my own chair because the place is crowded.

Jayne Mason sits alone on the butterscotch plaid sofa. I can't take my eyes off her face; naturally and perfectly formed, it radiates light just like her Manet. She is wearing a peach-colored chiffon dress with a scoop neck, long sleeves with lacy cuffs that flop over the hands, and a flounce at the knee and dyed-to-match high-heeled sandals. Maybe later she is going to a bridal shower.

Magda Stockman is to her right in the armchair and two male attorneys, who, I am told, are from a Beverly Hills law firm, perch on typing stools that have been rolled in. Galloway lugs an ungainly black leather desk chair around and motions for me to sit. It's one of those masculine "executive" numbers where the back is higher than my head, the seat swivels uncontrollably on loose bearings, and I feel like some bizarre shrunken monarch about to be dethroned by cen-trifugal force.

All this time Jayne and Magda continue a private conversation.

"It is truly astoundingly funny, it never stops," Magda is saying. "I cannot believe it will not be a huge success."

"I hear it's a four-hankie ending."

"No, it's wonderful."

"I cry all the time," says Jayne. "Why do I have to go to a movie to cry?"

"He's lovely in this picture, he's a darling person. And they are so real together."

"We're all flying back to New York on the same plane," Jayne tells her. "Isn't that cute?"

Everyone in the room has been listening politely without understanding a thing. Finally Jayne Mason acknowledges the rest of us by asking:

"Can I get some Evian water?"

"We've got sodas in the machine." Galloway nods in my direction. I raise my can.

"The sugar would send me around the bend."

"We've got regular water."

"My nutritionist would have a conniption."

Galloway is looking a bit rumpled and both attorneys have begun to search for a phone but Stockman hasn't flinched.

"The water is coming, Jay."

Again I am impressed by the dark throaty voice that seems to match the authority of her big solid body and today's olive brown suit with brass buttons and gold braiding on the sleeves, an elegant take-off on an officer's uniform (Barbara would know which designer). Her legs are stocky—peasant legs—she keeps them knees up, pressed together, in brown stockings and matching pumps with the signature Cs. The olive quilted bag with the gold chain also says CC. She is sporting more Cs than a caracara.

While there is a nervous tenseness about Mason, Stockman is nothing but composed command. Her movements are resolute and unhurried. The black hair drawn back into the bow accentuates the cheekbones and knowing Mongolian eyes.

"Really, we can get water," Galloway is going on, rattled.

"The hell with water, bring on the Scotch!" Mason cries cheerily and we laugh.

"Did you say hello to our woman FBI agent, Ana Grey?" Stockman prompts.

The movie star looks me in the eyes and extends her hand, instantly, subtly, putting me in my place. Make no mistake: we have been gathered here to serve her personal needs. I stumble out of Galloway's chair. My hand is damp. Hers is trembling.

"We've heard such good things about you," she murmurs with a smile.

It takes me by surprise. I can't imagine what the good things were or who said them to whom.

"We're very pleased to have a woman on the case," adds Stockman.

"Ana's here because she's good, not because she's female," Galloway chimes in, placing a cigar in his mouth. "Don't worry, I'm not going to light this."

"Oh, men and their cocks," Mason declares. "I told Clark Gable, why do you smoke a cigar when you're hung like an ape?"

"Jay, don't fib."

"Women don't need to smoke a big cigar or carry a gun to prove they can come."

The two attorneys giggle quietly as if they've heard this kind of thing before. Galloway catches my eye with an amused look.

"Not that we don't need to protect ourselves, that's another story," Miss Mason continues. "Tell me, Ana, do you carry a gun?"

"Yes, ma'am."

"Good," she whispers, "you can protect us from the lawyers!"

Everyone in the room is hooting and snorting as the door opens and Maureen, the formerly naked Maureen of the private beach, enters the office carrying a large bottle of Evian water.

"Sit by me, sweetie."

Jayne Mason sweeps the folds of the dress aside so Maureen can be close. She is introduced as "the very talented girl who does my wardrobe, and a dear friend."

"We've met," I respond, although from her vacant look I wonder if Maureen has a clue about when and where. She is definitely, as they say, "in her own space." Today she looks like an incarnation from another era with those extraordinary ropes of orange-red hair falling from a tortoiseshell comb, a vintage rayon dress loaded with amber necklaces and running shoes with thick socks.

"I'm sorry, this is all they had at the 7-Eleven." Maureen pulls a party pack of fifty plastic cups from a big canvas shoulder purse, plucks one out, and pours for Jayne.

Magda Stockman now addresses Galloway: "In my conversations with the Director, he assured me that we would receive your most serious attention."

"You got it," says Galloway. "Do you mind if we put this on tape?"

"I was hoping you would, so we may all have a record."

Galloway places a Panasonic microcassette player on the coffee table and presses the On button.

Magda nudges softly, "Jayne?"

Jayne Mason stands up. Her eyes blink. Her hands find each other and clasp at the diaphragm as if she is about to begin a concert.

"This man, this Dr. Eberhardt, got me addicted to painkillers."

She is moving now, turning to us occasionally, testing the swing of the skirt, adjusting her body to the space of the room.

"Of course I trusted him, I was his patient. At first the pills helped, but he kept giving me more until I couldn't live without them. I became a drug addict, I can admit that now without shame."

She lifts her chin, relaxing into the role.

"What kind of pills were they?" Galloway asks.

"Dilaudid." She glances at Stockman for reassurance, then goes on. "He said they were generic Dilaudid from Mexico, that they were cheaper that way, although he sure charged *me* a fortune."

I follow up: "Where did you get these pills from Mexico?"

She looks back to Stockman, confused. The manager answers for her smoothly: "He gave them to her in the office."

"He didn't write prescriptions?"

"Prescriptions would have been easy to trace. This guy is smart," says one of the suits.

"Not that smart," says the other. "Dispensing a controlled substance from his professional office?"

The intercom buzzes. Phone call for Miss Mason. She disappears into an adjoining office. The lawyers take the opportunity to make calls of their own. Galloway clicks off the tape recorder. We make small talk. I go to the bathroom. Fifteen minutes later we start again, Jayne Mason now poised dramatically by the window.

"Where did Dr. Eberhardt keep the Dilaudid?" I want to know specifically so when we search the office he doesn't get the jump and flush the pills.

"In the examining room in a locked cabinet. He had a shoe box filled with bottles and boxes of all sorts of pills with Spanish writing on the labels. He'd give them to me, just like that."

I think about this. Locked cabinet. Pills in a shoe box. Dr. Eberhardt sounds like a reckless fool. What I saw that moment in the alley behind his office was just the opposite: a man in his prime with everything ahead of him, very much in control. It was she who was out of control that day.

There are more interruptions—Miss Mason would like some yogurt to tide her over until luncheon but it has to be nonfat and it has to be honey nut crunch, until finally I've had it.

"Ms. Mason, with respect, can we cut to the chase?"

Galloway rolls his eyes. The two lawyers freeze on their stools as if a bolt of electricity has just shot up their butts, but Miss Mason and Ms. Stockman exchange a chuckle.

"I told you she was terrific," the manager assures the actress. To Galloway, "Please tell your secretary Miss Mason will not be taking any more calls," and nods toward her client to begin.

"I was doing a picture at Fox, a spy thriller kind of thing, and it was the scene after the cocktail party where they throw a bomb through the embassy window. . . . And I was dancing with Sean— what a love!—who plays my husband, the ambassador who gets killed. . . . We were rehearsing for the camera, dancing in front of the most beautiful marble fireplace, when I'm supposed to hear gun-fire in the distance and break out of his arms—well, I took one step and suddenly my ankle went out and Sean tried to catch me but I fell right on top of my leg, all twisted. The floor was hard as blazes. What kind of floor was that, Maureen?"

"Teak."

"Right onto the teakwood floor."

"And you went to see Dr. Eberhardt?"

"They packed my leg in ice and put me in a limo and Maureen and I took off down Pico at about a hundred miles an hour, right, sweetie?"

"I felt sick at my stomach the whole time," Maureen says in a soft, sweet voice. "For you. Because you were in such pain."

"Thank you, darling." Jayne squeezes her hand.

"Were you already Dr. Eberhardt's patient?" I ask.

"That's where fate steps in. Actually I'd never met Dr. Eber-hardt. They wanted to send me to Cedars but I insisted on going all the way to Santa Monica to see Dr. Dana, a dear, dear old friend I've known for years. My driver was calling ahead on the car phone when they told him Dr. Dana had recently retired to Maui and this young Dr. Eberhardt from Boston was taking his place. By that time we were halfway there and I was in such agony and so mad at Dr. Dana for leaving me that I couldn't think about anything else."

"How was Dr. Eberhardt's examination?" Galloway wants to know. "Would you say it was thorough and professional?"

"As a medical man, he's absolutely wonderful. Very smart. Very well educated. And charming. He was moving my hip around and it hurt like hell and I said, 'I'm really a big chicken, I can't take pain,' and Dr. Eberhardt said, 'Don't kid me. I saw you kick that gunslinger in the balls!' Well, he made me laugh and I knew I was under his spell."

"What was the diagnosis?"

"Troco-something bursitis of the hip. And I tore some cartilage in my knee."

"What was the treatment?"

She turns to Maureen. "You were in the room. What did he say?"

"Rest, ice, and physical therapy."

I wait a moment. There is silence except for the faint whirring of the tape recorder.

"No pills?"

"What?"

"Dr. Eberhardt did not prescribe any pills for your bursitis of the hip at that time?"

Jayne Mason gives up her ownership of the room to sit on the edge of the coffee table and bend toward me until her face is about ten inches from mine. She smells of citrus and vanilla.

"I'll be very honest with you," she says. "He would not have given me those pills if I didn't ask for them."

"You asked for the pills?"

"Yes." Her skin, even up close, is flawless. The aquamarine eyes are rimmed with green and unnaturally shining with large black pupils. "He gave me the pills because I told him I had to go back to work that afternoon." She is speaking slowly and deliberately. She wants me to buy this—her bare-faced, up-close, not-ashamed-of-anything honesty.

"You mean so you could work on the movie, even though you were injured?"

"I've had a lot of problems in the last three years, Ana," speaking intimately now as if we did in fact meet in that fancy restaurant up on Beverly Glen, two rich ladies sharing lunch while baby octopuses commit suicide off our plates. "I've been through two agents, I'm being sued by a so-called producer—I can't tell you how difficult it's been. I owe a lump-sum payment on a third mortgage to the bank—"

"Jay, let's stay on track," Stockman warns.

"This *is* the track. This is *why* he gave me the *pills*. I owe the bank five hundred thousand dollars. If I don't pay it, I will lose my house in Malibu. I *had* to finish that picture—and believe me"—she stands restlessly—"it was a piece of crap."

She frowns, thinking about the crappy picture, pouring Evian water while everybody waits.

"So I made a deal with Dr. Eberhardt. If he would just give me the pills so I could finish work, I would do ice packs, physical therapy, whatever he wanted."

"Did he agree?"

"It was supposed to be for one time. But I was weak and he played into my weakness."

"How?"

"If I had a headache, he'd prescribe pills. Then I'd get a reaction and he'd give me something else, until I became a dependent wreck. He never said, Jayne, be a big girl and go cold turkey. He was the doctor, I put myself in his hands. Finally I got into the Dilaudid and it became a chemical addiction beyond my control. The bottom line is I needed Dr. Eberhardt and his pills to get through the day."

"Did you sleep with Dr. Eberhardt, Ms. Mason?"

"Absolutely not."

"Did he ever send you roses?"

"I sent *him* roses," she laughs. "I send everybody yellow roses, it's my way of saying thank you. And he did fix my hip."

"You must understand this man has destroyed her career," Stockman intones. "Who will hire a known drug addict to make a movie? All this negative publicity has made her uninsurable and without insurance she cannot be employed to act. She has no source of income, and due to some unbelievably incompetent money management, Jayne Mason is in a serious financial crisis."

Stockman fixes those knowing eyes on me—wolf eyes, when you look carefully, with that same predatory calm.

"But she has decided not to be a victim anymore. As a woman, you understand what courage that takes."

Considering what I'm going through with Duane Carter, it hits home. "I've fought my battles."

"We all have."

Gee, I kind of like the feeling of the men in the room being excluded for once.

"Ana, I know you are going to make a difference—not only to

Jayne, but to other women who don't have the resources to stand up to exploitation."

Stockman is as skilled a performer as her client, and I'm ashamed to say I fall for it. The flattery—of me, of each other—is finally as dizzying as the narcotic perfume of yellow roses and in an anodyne haze I promise to do my best.

As Galloway escorts everyone out, I compliment Miss Mason on her peach chiffon dress.

"Don't you love it? It's by Luc de France, my personal designer."

"I've heard of him." I smile at Maureen, who is still holding Mason's hand like a child. There is nothing in her look to acknowledge the joke. But then, there is precious little there at all.

■　　■　　■

Two days later the Boston field office comes through with the gold. As a result of their deep background check they located a former patient, Claudia Van Hoven, who claims Dr. Eberhardt got her addicted to prescription drugs, exactly like Jayne Mason.

I am perched at an angle on Donnato's desk so I don't have to look at the picture of him and his wife.

"You know how long it takes to get approval for travel—but Galloway told me to get on a plane for Boston *tomorrow* and come back with Van Hoven's testimony against the doctor. An hour with Jayne Mason and he's like a puppy dog rolling on his back with his paws in the air. Get her anything. Do anything."

Donnato's looking through the latest stats on bank robberies in Orange County. They're up.

"Want some advice about Boston?"

I'm always eager for his expertise. "Tell me."

"They have the best meatball subs in the world."

I shake my head restlessly. "Galloway is treating me differently now that I'm working Hollywood."

"This has nothing to do with Hollywood," Donnato observes.

"Come on—if Joe Schmo called the FBI and said some doctor

gave him too many Percodans, you think I'd be flying off to Boston on a background check?"

"It's politics," he explains patiently, "Magda Stockman is a major contributor to the Republican party. She hangs out at the Annenbergs. She was one of the 'private citizens' who paid for the renovation of the White House under Reagan, don't you remember? Oh, that's right, you were twelve."

"Still, when a person like Jayne Mason—"

Donnato interrupts, "Jayne Mason is another dippy actress and, believe me, Galloway would never roll over for a pretty face." He holds up a hand to stop my protest. "Magda Stockman is the power player."

He shakes his head sadly and goes back to the printout. "You ought to be reading *The New Republic* instead of *Engine Grease World.*"

"I like engine grease. You should give it a try."

He pretends not to hear.

I laugh and slip off the desk. "I feel sorry for you, Donnato. Who will you have to abuse while I'm gone?"

"Only myself."

■   ■   ■

This is wild. I get to go home early to pack for an eight a.m. plane to fly to a city where I have never been, on my own case, with no supervision except the SAC himself. My head is humming with what I need to bring and what the moves will be once I get there.

At this hour the lobby of the Federal Building is filled with great blocks of brownish yellow afternoon light but the press of humans has not slowed since I arrived this morning. The same impatient crowd waits to move through metal detectors monitored by two excruciatingly thorough security guards, and outside the line to get a passport seems longer and, if possible, slower.

The lobby is a place of crossroads where the course of each of the thousands converging from all parts of the world cannot be logged, but they have this in common: desperation and a seething frustration with the bureaucracy of the United States government, a combustible anxiety that makes me always stay alert when crossing these marble floors.

Maybe it's that alertness, or perhaps a sixth sense when it comes to John Roth, that warns me he is close a split second before he calls out, "Ana."

Yes, I'd caught the figure leaning against a wall, and known it was John despite the dirty hair down to the shoulders, raggy beard, and ripped jeans. The posture, the hungry gaze, cause my alarm system to shriek.

"You look good," he says with a smirk.

"You look like Serpico."

"Undercover narcotics. I like to run with the vermin."

His shirt, missing a button, is open at the navel. The belly is concave, jeans hanging low.

"The fox guarding the chickens?"

"You're looking at Mr. Straight."

I nod. He looks like hell.

"Are you staking me out?"

"Just waiting. Indulging in a little fantasy."

He takes a step toward me. I take a step back.

"I've got something for you."

"Try it and I'll bust you so fast—"

"No," he interrupts, "it's that Alvarado homicide."

I stop my backpedaling but maintain a good eight feet between us.

"I went back on the street and tracked down that kid, Rat, the one who witnessed the drive-by. Turns out he was able to ID the car."

"What jogged his memory?"

"He's a male prostitute, I threaten to bust his ass, so he comes around. Turns out it was a gang hit but Alvarado was not the intended victim. A dope deal was going down a few feet from the bus stop. One of the suspects was marked by the Bloods. They missed. Ms. Alvarado happened to be in the wrong place at the wrong time."

"You're sure?"

"The kid is good."

"What about the hands? Or did they blow them away just for kicks?"

"The autopsy report says amputation of the hands resulted from the victim attempting to protect herself from the bullets."

He brings his arms up and crosses them over his face.

I can see it now, all too clearly. A car swings around the corner. *Pop-pop-pop* and street people with experience duck for cover. Violeta Alvarado, out there alone in the middle of the night, who knows why—but *innocent,* she was *innocent*—is struck over and over again. She tries to fend off the hits but they come with astonishing force and so unbelievably fast. . . .

"There's no connection between Alvarado being killed and her working for the doctor. She just got caught in the crossfire. Happens every day."

I say nothing.

"I did this because I thought that might mean something to you."

The autopsy photos flip through my mind like a grisly pinup calendar.

"It won't help on your case, but at least now you know your cousin was clean."

I'm thinking of the way her little girl hid under the crib. And the boy, with his lost dark eyes.

"She *was* your cousin, right?"

I have not answered John for several moments. Now I cross the marble one square at a time, deliberately walking toward him until we are face-to-face.

"Yes, John. She was my cousin."

In acknowledging this I find I have gained something. Relief. Confidence. I can stand here, this close, and hold the look of a man I have long dreaded in a frank, new way. I can see new things, like the fear in John Roth.

"Take it easy on yourself." I touch his shoulder. "And thanks."

"Hey," he says, shaky, off guard, "I'm not a total fuckup."

We look at each other one last moment, then I take off, out of the building and into the parking garage at a fast clip. My teeth are all gummed up from the two colas I had to get through the afternoon and I can't stand wearing these tight panty hose one more minute. Inside the car I wrestle them off. Much better. I turn on the engine and back out, on my way to crucify Dr. Randall Eberhardt.

ELEVEN

BOSTON IS a massive traffic jam just like Los Angeles except here the cars are crammed together even more tightly, pushing through tiny, twisting, illogical roads that used to be cow paths.

Or maybe it's just that I have arrived during rush hour in the middle of a spring sleet storm.

I am stuck on the ramp leading out of Logan Airport, watching the wipers of the rented Taurus sweep away crescents of slush. Through the momentary clear spots I strain impatiently to make out the road to Boston, to Randall Eberhardt's past, which I had felt all along was going to be promising. But all I can see in the darkening evening are dazzlingly lit billboards for the New England Aquarium and Prince Spaghetti Sauce.

I am wrestling with the heater to get it to stop fogging up the windows. I have been waiting forty minutes to enter the Sumner Tunnel, watching hunks of soft ice picked up by the windshield wipers and carried lazily upward then sliding down into long melting peninsulas. If I were working the case with Donnato we'd be making jokes about this freaky weather, cozy in the warmth of the car like a pair of lovers sneaking away for the weekend; even the thought makes me burn with embarrassment as the traffic suddenly lurches forward.

The tunnel itself is no erotic experience but a narrow, claustrophobic gas chamber at the end of which is an incomprehensible tangle of overpasses that trick me into a blind detour through a neighborhood of weathered three-decker houses dominated by huge oil tanks. I get back on the overpass, panic when I see signs for Cape Cod and get off again, only to find myself in Chinatown. Finally I pull into a gas station and call Special Agent Lester "Wild Bill" Walker at the Boston field office, who tells me to stay put. He's there in twenty minutes, climbing out of a green government car, a big man wrapped in raincoat and knit wool cap, coming toward me through the silvery falling globs of ice illuminated by my headlights like some kind of Eskimo dream bear. As I roll down the window he extends a gloved hand, the most welcome hand I ever shook, and that one gesture—my bare palm in his leathery paw—makes it clear how unprepared I really am for this trip.

"Where are you staying?"

"The Sheraton."

"Follow me."

He gets back in his car and we drive out of there. In a few minutes we are somewhere deep inside the business district, an untouched pocket of downtown where every building is not a skyscraper or cutesy renovated warehouse but an old brick factory or granite-faced office building. You can easily imagine, a hundred years ago, Portuguese fishermen selling haddock from pushcarts and scriveners arriving before dawn to calculate the earnings of great banks and behind those huge mullioned windows Irish girls stuffing mattresses in flurries of goose down. Commerce thrived along this crooked lane as it will tomorrow morning and for the next one hundred years, but tonight the street is utterly empty, utterly dark, except for the misty rose-colored light of sodium vapor street lamps coming through the freezing rain.

"This ain't the Sheraton, Wild Bill."

We have parked a block apart and met on a street corner. I am keeping a hand on my purse, inside of which is the .357 Magnum.

"Thought we'd get something to eat," he says.

The street is deserted and pitch black. Not an open liquor store. Not a lighted coffee shop.

After the long flight and the insane drive through the butt end of Boston, I am thoroughly disoriented except for one thing: I am here to nail Randall Eberhardt.

"I don't have time for sight-seeing."

But Lester is already striding ahead. He opens a door. Now I notice a smoky storefront window with people moving behind it. We enter warmth and cigarette smoke and a noise level equal to a commodities exchange.

It is a large bare room with a big old mahogany bar, dusty brass fans, a wall of mirrors that reflects the downtown crowd. Briefcases are lined up beneath laden coatracks. Everybody—male and female—is wearing a suit. I take off my raincoat and hang it on a peg. In my navy blues with the skirt primly brushing the top of the knee I look like every other female attorney and stockbroker there. I like the feeling. The convivial talk, the good, clean smell of whiskey make me feel very present, ironically more present than in my usual life in Los Angeles, where it takes all your energy just to stay on the grid. But there is another difference: in Los Angeles I live with the feeling of constantly being judged. Here nobody is watching. The relief is so profound that after five minutes of standing among this crowd of friendly strangers, my neck starts to relax all by itself, miraculously as loose and easy as a newborn babe's.

Lester buys us Bloody Marys and we shout at each other until an overweight woman with pocked cheeks and teased yellow hair takes him by the arm, kisses him on the lips, and leads us to a table, upon which are a pair of plain salt and pepper shakers, an ashtray, and a bottle of Tabasco sauce. We both switch to vodka martinis and are immediately presented with a platter of freshly shucked clams. I decide to forget about jet lag.

Lester is an old warhorse who's been around since Hoover, which is why they assigned him to this case. He's through chasing gangsters. A background check on a Harvard doctor is just his speed. On an assignment like that you can stay loaded all afternoon. I realize when he's on to a second vodka martini before we have seen menus that the reason he likes this place is not the authentic pressed tin ceiling but that it is far enough from Government Center so no agents are likely to come here and he can self-destruct in peace.

Red faced, it seems an effort for him to reach across his beefy chest to an inner pocket of a moss green plaid wool jacket and re-move two sheets of folded paper.

"Think I've got what you need here. . . ." Smoothing them with shaky hands. "This Van Hoven gal."

He pauses to lick his lips and take a kiss of vodka; yes, they are close friends.

"Everybody else says the same thing about Eberhardt—nice guy, smart, good athlete, good doc, that sort of crap. But this Van Hoven gal really has a hard-on for him. Says he ruined her life."

"Is she good?"

"She's a music student, plays the violin for chrissake."

He gives me a strained smile: "Come on, Ana. I wouldn't have drug you all the way to Boston if I didn't think she was good."

"I've got a lot riding, that's all."

"I've been doing this for a number of years, Ana. Don't worry. I won't let you down."

I think of his big hand rescuing me from the freezing night.

"Anything on your computer about Eberhardt?"

"Criminal checks negative. No malpractice suits. A regular boy scout. In fact in 1985 the guy flew on a mercy mission to some damn famine in Africa."

"Oh, shit."

"Doesn't mean he didn't turn into an asshole," Walker suggests encouragingly.

"Any background on his wife? Could she be tied up in this? Pushing drugs, spending his money?"

"What I got on his wife is that she's a nurse. That's how they got together, over at the New England Deaconess Hospital. Both local kids, grew up here. Except he's Cambridge upper-crust WASP and she's shanty Irish, no offense."

"Why should I be offended?"

"Sometimes I put my foot in it. Thought you might be Irish."

"No . . . but a lot of people think so."

"Armenian?"

"Spanish, actually." I feel myself blush. "Half and half."

"A Spanish señorita. Or," continuing at his courtliest, "shall I call you señora?"

"Señorita."

He nods. For no reason at all, we toast.

When the waiter appears, Wild Bill tells him, "The señorita will have fish and chips," which makes me cross my arms on the table, lay my head down, and laugh.

■　■　■

We are very drunk. The air is clear but a sheet of ice has formed on top of the sidewalk. We grip each other's arms as we slide toward our cars. I am feeling a lot of affection for Wild Bill, dyed black hair and all. It takes me a while to maneuver out of the parking space, and when I do I discover that the road has glassed over as well. The green car is waiting for me at the corner of the deserted street, red taillights wreathed in white steamy exhaust. I smash right into it.

Wild Bill climbs out. "This is a government vehicle!" His arms fly up and back down to his sides. Then he shakes his head and skates back inside, slams the door, and we begin our slide across Boston. It feels like I am going sideways. There are wrecks at every intersection. The AM radio blasts an old Rod Stewart song, "Maggie May," out the open windows and the heater is turned up to broil. I am reckless. I know nothing about this city except that it is complex beyond imagining. There are millions of beds in this city like cocoons in a butterfly colony and inside each one is a unique individual with a unique history about to be born or replicate itself or die except for me: I don't have a bed, I think with boozy self-pity, skidding to a lopsided stop at a light on a corner before a row of darkened redbrick town houses. Behind one drawn parchment shade there is a warm light. Maybe there, in a room I will never see, in a city I know nothing about, a mother is awake nursing a child and the child is at peace.

Certainly not my mother, and not me. She was there, in the house, but vague. *What the hell was she doing?* I demand to know in the middle of Commonwealth Avenue. The question arises, righteous and crystal clear. *Why don't I remember being held by my mother or soothed by her, why was I always alone in my room, listening to her cry?* Because she didn't want to have me, comes the self-righteous response. She was a teenager and pregnant and her lowlife boyfriend split. She was weak and couldn't cope with having a half-breed brat. Only Poppy was strong enough to love me.

When we get to the Prudential Center, Walker waves his gloved fist out the window of the now battered and bruised government vehicle and heads off. I plunge into some mammoth underground garage and rise up again carrying my suitcase to a lobby like every other in America, then rise even further to a room with a stunning view of the city, hard white lights and provocative red ones; sitting down at a desk, inebriated, reaching for the phone instinctively, unreasonably, selfishly, from unutterable loneliness for the only one who loved me, dialing 8 for long distance and then the number where my grandfather lies asleep in the icy cold bedroom of the condominium in Desert Hot Springs, California, longing to wake him from his deep stillness and bring him back to me, but the phone rings emptily many times and I cannot.

I force myself to drink three glasses of water and strip down to my underpants before sinking into the thick soft mattress where I pull the sheet, blanket, and heavy bedspread over my shoulders and dream about the helicopter.

I am outside the Santa Monica police station holding my grandfather's big warm hand. Everything is colored red by sunset light, like looking through the orange wrapper of a Charms lollypop. The President's helicopter is landing in a storm of fine orange chalk, its huge belly pressing down on us—I am terrified that we are going to be crushed. The chopper touches down and JFK climbs out, floating along the steps, not waving, very sober, something is wrong. He is wearing a dark suit. His face is dead white and his head is mangled by bloody gunshot wounds. He is a walking corpse.

Beneath the heavy coverings I wake up frozen stiff, mummified by fear. The dream is not about JFK. It is about my father, bloodied and dead.

■   ■   ■

Wild Bill Walker and I are sharing a bench in a playground on the northwest corner of the Cambridge Commons. It is hard to tell which direction is northwest at nine in the morning with a hangover. I circled the park several times until sighting a big galoof sitting alone, looking like a bum with his big raincoat and cap, and realized that must be him. As we waited there under leaden overcast skies I began to envy that cap and the heavy black shoes with thick gum soles.

Claudia Van Hoven had insisted on meeting here instead of her place or anywhere else. She told Wild Bill she has a tiny apartment and her husband, a graduate student, works at night, sleeps during the day. With the baby, she told him, it's hard enough.

The playing fields are bald stretches of half-frozen mud. I turn my face into a wet wind. We have now been waiting almost an hour and a half during which I have heard every detail of Wild Bill's radiation treatments for prostate cancer five years ago.

Finally I stand restlessly. "This is fucked."

"She'll show."

"Let's go to her house."

We are already through the iron gate of the park when I look back and see a slight woman in a long dark coat with a trailing red scarf wheel a stroller across the puddles and into the playground.

"That's the lady," Walker says with relief. "Told you she was good."

We approach and shake hands all around. Claudia Van Hoven smiles brightly. She is younger than I am, early twenties, young enough to have smooth uncrinkled skin around the eyes.

"Have you been waiting long?"

I glance at Wild Bill, who I know would say nothing.

"We got here at nine," I tell her.

Claudia looks worried. "What time is it now?" She checks her watch and makes a pained frown, as if just realizing she had lost something. "I'm sorry. I don't know how that happened."

"My daughter has four kids, all boys," Wild Bill says with a cornball wink. "Sometimes she loses entire days at a time." He takes her elbow and eases her down on the bench, going on about his grandsons and getting her to talk about her baby. I'm starting to admire his style.

"What will happen to Dr. Eberhardt?" Claudia wants to know.

"He could lose his license to practice medicine," Walker tells her gravely. "He could go to jail."

She closes her eyes for a moment then looks off into the distance through gold-rimmed glasses; small, old-fashioned oval frames like they wore to sign the Constitution. She is bareheaded. The wind blows her straight shiny brown hair. It must look pretty when she bends to play the violin.

"Do you want to see him go to jail?" I ask.

"The angry woman inside me does." She gives us a reassuring smile. "Not to worry—I won't let her interfere."

She has an artsy way of talking but seems sincere.

"Tell us how you became a patient of Dr. Eberhardt."

She doesn't balk at the tape recorder. She explains how three years ago last March she was crossing the street to go to a concert at the Gardner Museum when a kid in a Datsun Z nipped around the corner and bounced her off the windshield twenty feet into the air. She spent six weeks in the hospital in a body cast. Dr. Eberhardt was the senior orthopedist.

"He talked to me a lot. I was trapped in this cast and he talked to me, for which I was grateful."

A tear forms and she wipes her eye. I am thrilled by the emotion. Save it for the witness stand, baby.

"I was worried I would never play again. He sat with me . . . and he promised I would. . . ."

Walker fishes out a pocket-sized pack of Kleenex and gives her one.

"I don't know how long I was on medication in the hospital, but it was all those months afterward that he kept giving me pills."

"What kind of pills, Claudia?"

"Dilaudid. Valium. Halcion when I couldn't sleep. I was so doped up I couldn't even listen to music anymore."

"Were you able to go back to the violin?"

Claudia shakes her head. "She died."

"Who died?"

"The musician inside of me." She is pushing the stroller back and forth in short strokes. "I kept telling Dr. Eberhardt she was dying."

"What did he say?"

"He told me to be patient, that the healing process takes a long time, and gave me more pills."

The crown of her head and the nap of the brown wool coat along her shoulders glisten with the first tentative drops of rain. The stroller cover is all the way down over the baby, who I assume is asleep since I have not heard or seen it. I can't feel my fingers or toes. Walker writes in a small spiral pad.

"How long did this go on with Eberhardt?" he asks.

"For a year after I got out of the hospital. Then Allan came along and told me I should stay away from him, that he wasn't good for me, he wasn't telling me the truth."

"Allan is your husband?"

"My helper." A dreamy smile invades the tears. "My dear friend."

"Did Dr. Eberhardt write prescriptions?"

"Yes, he did."

"Where did you get the prescriptions filled?"

"Bay Pharmacy on Mass Ave."

"Great."

Walker says, "I'll check it out," and makes a note.

"Were you addicted?" I ask. "Meaning that you couldn't stop taking the pills if you wanted to?"

"Yes."

I fix her right in the eyes. "Then how did you stop?"

"Allan helped me. That's what he was there for."

"Claudia, why do you think Dr. Eberhardt prescribed these drugs if he knew they could be dangerous?"

"I was depressed. My injuries weren't healing. Maybe he thought I would make trouble for him." She stands. "I'd better get the baby home."

"It's getting cold," Walker agrees, a Boston euphemism for the onset of hypothermia.

"We'll be coming back in a few weeks to take your deposition," I tell her, walking toward the gate on numb wet stubs of feet. "And then we might ask you to fly to California at government expense to testify against Dr. Eberhardt. Would you agree to that?"

"The angry woman inside me can't wait to get on the airplane," Claudia says with a smile.

I turn off the tape recorder and smile back. "Bring her along."

■   ■   ■

Walker and I are running for a phone booth in Harvard Square. Because they have made the Square a pedestrian mall and closed it to traffic, our cars are double-parked three blocks away. Hordes of students and homeless people seem intent on getting in our way. My plane leaves in a matter of hours and I still need to see Eberhardt's former supervisor at the hospital.

"Too risky," Walker is huffing. "Why I ruled it out in the first place. He'll just get on the horn and tell your boy you're onto him."

"I'll take the chance."

"It's foolish when we've got that Van Hoven gal all sewn up."

"She's not sewn up until we confirm her story."

"Let's get out to the airport, get something to eat." Walker is plainly ready to quit. After all, it is past noon and we haven't had our first Bloody Mary of the day.

A middle-aged woman has set down a canvas tote that says Save the Trees in front of a pay phone. I grab the receiver off the hook before she can remove her gloves, fiercely turning on Walker at the same time: "I've got to come back with something hard or they'll skin me alive, do you understand?"

Dr. Alfred Narayan, chief of staff of orthopedics, will be glad to speak with us but is scheduled for surgery in forty-five minutes. No problem. We dash back to our cars and Wild Bill ably demonstrates how he got his name, leading me with red bubble flashing on a wild charge down Memorial Drive, across the Boston University bridge to Longwood Avenue. I have noticed horseshoe tracks embedded in the sidewalks of Boston at various spots where Paul Revere passed on his famous ride; well, they should have tire tracks to commemorate ours.

Dr. Narayan is waiting for us at the nurses' station of the cardiac care unit: tall, aquiline, black curly hair cropped close, warm brown eyes, and pale brown skin. He is wearing a red silk tie beneath the starched white lab coat. The accent is not Indian but educated Oxford and he smells like lilacs during a wet English spring.

"This must be a serious business to send federal agents," he says over his shoulder, leading us past gurneys and IV stands to the end of a hall.

There is no time for pleasantries.

"When Dr. Eberhardt was on staff, did he prescribe a lot of drugs?"

"Only what was called for."

"Did he ever overprescribe?"

"Of course not."

Walker: "Did you notice any drugs missing during the time he was employed?"

"No. We've never had a problem."

The doctor looks back and forth at us, astonished by this line of questioning. Walker gives me a lugubrious shrug and turns toward the window where an electric trolley is passing beneath empty trees.

"Do you recall a patient named Claudia Van Hoven?" Dr. Narayan shakes his elegant head. "Three years ago," I prompt anxiously, "she was hit by a car. Dr. Eberhardt took care of her."

"I can pull the record."

"That would be terrific."

"You seem distressed," he says with kindness. "Why not just ask me what you really wish to know?"

What I really wish to know is whether Dr. Narayan will leave his wife and fourteen children and live with me in South Kensington, but instead: "Was there anything in Randall Eberhardt's behavior to lead you to believe he might have been exploiting patients?"

" 'Exploiting' them?"

"Overprescribing drugs. Getting them hooked. Especially women. Making them dependent on him as a doctor."

"Completely absurd."

"Why? Health care fraud is a multibillion-dollar industry."

"Randall Eberhardt is a talented, dedicated physician, sought after and respected. His work is impeccable, I'll vouch for it personally. If you don't believe me, have one of your own experts evaluate his charts."

"Did he have any financial problems?"

"My God, the man comes from old Cambridge money. I can't imagine it, no."

Walker, seeing that I'm coming up empty and eager to get to the airport bar: "Thanks, doctor. We have a plane to catch."

Desperate now: "What about his marriage?"

We are walking back down the corridor. Some poor person with rolling eyes is wheeled past us, wired and tubed.

"His wife, Claire, was a cardiac nurse on this ward. Their liaison was certainly the talk of the town at the time, but beyond that I'm out of my depth. Look—I'm being paged." He calls to one of the RNs in green scrubs working a computer at the nurses' station, "Kathy Donovan! Come talk to these people."

Kathy Donovan sticks a pencil behind her ear and gets off the stool. She is what you would politely call "ample," big bosom, big behind, walks like a Marine.

"Kathy knew Randall and Claire Eberhardt very well. Don't hesitate if there's anything else I can do." Narayan shakes hands briskly and is off.

"How do you know the Eberhardts?"

"Claire and I grew up on the same block, two houses apart," says Kathy Donovan in a husky voice. The Boston accent is blunt and unapologetic—"Claih," "apaht." "I was a bridesmaid at her wedding. Who are you?"

"FBI."

She laughs uneasily. "What'd they do? Not pay their taxes?"

"Routine check," Walker answers, baring his yellow teeth with a phony smile. He is really suffering from withdrawal now.

"We'd like to talk to you."

"I'm on 'til four. I could meet you after."

That means I will miss my plane and have to catch a later flight or spend another night in Boston, neither of which I should do without authorization. But nobody is watching so I go with my gut.

"Fine. We'll meet you after work."

"Where?"

"Someplace we can get a meatball sub."

■　■　■

As soon as we leave the hospital Walker peels off, claiming to be going back to the office to start checking for duplicate records of the prescriptions Claudia Van Hoven had filled at the Bay Pharmacy, but I am certain he ducked into the nearest sports bar and is still there.

I have some time, so I explore the area. You can see that a lot of professionals live around the hospital complex. I follow Huntington Avenue past fashionable old apartment houses—one like a Tudor mansion a block long, another with a fantastic Renaissance gingerbread roof—the people so conservative in their corduroys and backpacks and skirts down to the calf, the streets so clean and fancy-Dan it's almost laughable to the dulled-out California eye, a cliché of the comfortable highbrow life, what do they do all day, go to the Boston Symphony? However, when I turn east on Massachusetts Avenue, according to Kathy's directions, things change fast. I sit up and pay attention. Suddenly the income level has dropped like a plane catching wind shear, plummeting into poverty in the space of ten seconds.

The larger stores are all boarded up or barricaded by heavy gates, leaving Mom and Pop bodegas the only ones still open for business. Men sit in groups with their backs against the buildings or huddle in doorways of redbrick row houses scarred with graffiti. I look straight ahead because I don't want to be a witness to a drug deal.

Suddenly figures are ahead of me. At thirty miles an hour I have to slam on the brakes. Two black teenage girls have picked this moment to waltz across the street against a red light, moving as slowly as humanly possible, close enough to my car to languorously run their long curved fingernails painted Day-Glo purple over the hood, challenging me through the windshield with burning eyes. I put my face in neutral and keep both hands on the wheel, although I know precisely where my weapon is on the right side of my belt and how long it will take to draw it.

I wait them out, aware of the screams of multiple sirens crisscrossing the neighborhood. Finally the girls realize I will not take the bait and run the rest of the way across the street, dodging speeding cars. I drive on but now I am alert and it stays with me all along Columbia Road, past torched buildings and vacant lots and the occasional graceful private residences, relics of a lost time, everything tarnished by a murky haze. The sky is a dirty white, lit from behind as if through a scrim. Here there is no long spring sunset. Instead, as the raw afternoon drains toward night, it seems that all the color is being sucked out of the world until the streetscape looks like a photo printed in metallic grays, the working-class enclave of Savin Hill perched on a rise over Dorchester Bay reduced now to silver faces of shingled homes with dead black window eyes, and tangles of tree branches in burned-out brown, only the signs of neighborhood bars lighting up the monotonous dusk with the promise of cherry red.

I park in front of St. Paul's Church across from the Three Greeks Submarine Shop. A cold wind whips off the water. Ten blocks away the churches are storefronts with hand-lettered signs in Spanish; here they are Gothic brick but their rooflines are swayed as if their backs had finally been broken. I can see by the old ladies in shapeless coats and kerchiefs pulling empty shopping carts, and the ten-year-old American cars rotting away with salt, that this is a hard-working but tired place depleted by the endless Massachusetts recession, attacked by hostile neighbors, backed up against the bay with nowhere to go. It holds on only because its roots go very deep. Incidents of domestic violence must be through the roof.

Nurse Kathy is waiting for me inside the Three Greeks, smoking a cigarette and reading a paperback of poetry by Robert Frost. She has changed from hospital greens into denim and looks like a female truck driver.

"I had to look in on my mother and father," she tells me first thing. "Make sure they get their dinner."

"You live with your parents?"

"They own their own house and they're getting on. Frankly, they're too old to move."

She stubs the cigarette out in a gold paper ashtray and looks at me. Just looks. The place is overly warm and smells of yeast. I shrug out of my raincoat.

"So, Kathy," I say pleasantly, figuring I'd better try to establish some kind of a rapport, "what do you like about being a cardiac nurse?"

"It's intense. You're on your toes. You have to make decisions quick, like if someone has ventricular tachycardia you have to decide whether to give them a precordial thump."

She is showing off. The Robert Frost book is part of it. She is trying to say that she is really a smart, sensitive person trapped inside a toad's body. Now she is giving me that toad look again. Sly. Unblinking. Hostile.

"Was Claire Eberhardt a good cardiac nurse?"

"Very good." She nods slowly. "She could take the pressure. She liked the adrenaline rush. Nice with the patients, a good care provider. But she was feisty. She'd argue with the doctors."

"About what?"

"Medication. Whatever. If she thought the patient wasn't getting what he needed. We get to know the patients a lot better than the doctors."

"Did she argue with Dr. Eberhardt?"

"Why should she argue with him? He was taking her to California."

"Is that the reason she got married?"

"I dunno." Nurse Kathy laughs. "Seems like a good reason to me. Want to get something to eat?"

Donnato was right. The Boston Italian meatball sub made by a Greek in an Irish neighborhood is a unique experience. There is something special about the way the red sauce dissolves the bun into a spongelike mass and something exciting about the pursuit of the meatball when it drops out onto the paper plate, forcing you to get up and go to the counter for a fork with orange grease running down your chin, twenty napkins glued to your fingertips. I vow to bring one back on the plane and force him to eat it during a squad meeting.

"My parents' house is around the corner from here." Kathy settles back with a paper cup of black coffee and another Parliament. "Claire's folks still live two houses away."

"You two were best friends?"

"I wouldn't say best. She hung out with the cheerleaders, with those freckles and that cute body. I hung with the nerds, obviously. But we went through a lot. We both grew up very Irish. Oppressively Irish. I even took a course in the sociology of drinking—I could discuss that deeply, if you're interested," she says with bitter irony.

"Sure."

But she shakes it off. "Claire and I were both the first ones in our families to go to college. Then nursing school. There was never even a consideration that we could go to medical school."

"But she got out."

Kathy takes a long draw on the cigarette. "She got out."

"And you hate her fucking guts."

"I don't hate her fucking guts," she says, unnerved. "I wish her the best of luck out on the coast."

I let her sit with her anger for a moment. Then,

"What if I told you Randall Eberhardt has been accused of overprescribing narcotics?"

Kathy answers quickly, unthinkingly, "I wouldn't believe it."

"No?"

"No. Randall's a good guy."

"You don't think he might have changed out in California? Life in the fast lane?"

"Randall's the type of person who is very happy with himself. Why would he change? Unless there was a money problem or something unforeseen. Or someone's setting him up."

"So maybe the person who changed was Claire."

"What do you mean?"

"Maybe she wanted the fast life."

"The thing Claire Eberhardt wants out of life is a good lay," spits Kathy Donovan before she can stop herself. "In high school she was the first to lose her virginity."

I nod, returning the bitchy sneer. "There's always one."

"She wasn't actually a tramp. She had a boyfriend, Warren Speca. He's out on the coast now, too."

"In Los Angeles?"

"Pretty close to there. The girls in the neighborhood threw her a going-away party. We gave her Warren Speca's phone number in—what?—*Venice,* California?"

"That's right."

"I wrote it on a prescription. 'Rx for horniness—Call Warren Speca.' She died. She turned beet red."

"She still had the hots for Warren?"

"Oh, I don't know about that. They weren't in contact after high school. For a long time nobody knew where Warren was. He was into some stuff"—this time she catches herself—"I shouldn't tell you about. Anyway, my mother was talking to his mother and it turns out he's an electrical contractor in this place called *Venice,* California. I mean it was a joke—the only person Claire ever heard of in California was her old high school boyfriend. I thought it was a hoot."

I agree with her and force a smile, making sure to get the correct spelling of Warren Speca's name. We have balled up our plates and napkins and tossed our cans of Diet Slice into the trash. I've got Donnato's meatball sub triple-wrapped in aluminum foil inside a waxed paper bag. I thank Nurse Kathy for her help and move toward the door. If I leave now and don't get lost I can make the last plane.

"So what's it like in California?" she asks as we hit the night air.

"Great. You can wear a T-shirt in December. Are you thinking of coming out?"

I hand her my card. She studies it, intrigued.

"Who knows." She pockets the card and looks at me for the first time in an unguarded way. "I promised myself next year I'm moving out to my own place in Quincy."

■   ■   ■

I have noticed that violence happens very fast, faster than the way they stage it in movies, faster than you'd think of it in your imagination.

Moments after leaving Nurse Kathy, I am at a traffic light at Cushing Avenue. I look down for half a second, checking the map for the fastest way to the airport, and am rear-ended with enough force to throw me almost to the steering wheel before the seat belt locks. A moment later the front-seat passenger window explodes and I am smacked so hard on the shoulder by a brick that my arm goes numb.

Gloved hands reach quickly through the shattered glass and grab my purse off the passenger seat.

"Suck my dick!" howls a male voice, then he and the purse are gone.

I get out of the car with my hand on my weapon but the late-model Oldsmobile that whacked me is already disappearing into the night. I can't make out the plates. I stand there in the intersection in a daze like any other victim, flexing my tingling right hand. I take off the raincoat and shake out shards of broken glass, picking them out of my hair. The lady two cars back pulls out and takes off, she wants no part of this. My federal ID and plane ticket are in the blue canvas attaché case in the trunk and thank God they didn't take Donnato's meatball sub. I get back in and toss the brick into the backseat. I am shaking like a dog. The pain is tightening my shoulder muscles into a spasm and my back does not feel great. I slam the car into gear and, swearing steadily, kick it up to fifty miles an hour as cold air pours in through the busted window, not stopping for traffic lights or asshole pedestrians, focused on only one thing: *Get me out of this depressing fucking place and onto a plane for Los Angeles,* knowing that Claire Eberhardt, leaving Savin Hill, was thinking the very same thing.

Forty minutes later, as I gimp toward the open door of the plane, I think again of Claire Eberhardt, possibly hurrying down this very same ramp, the toddler asleep on her shoulder, the little girl holding her hand. She believes she is escaping those dead-end streets, but instead arrives in California with the phone number of an old high school boyfriend written out like a prescription, a gift from the gals in the neighborhood. I begin to wonder if Warren Speca was the "wrong guy" she was talking about in the doorway, and if so, how many times she made the same "really bad" mistake.

If they had wanted to destroy her for saving herself and starting another life, they couldn't have found a better way. That innocuous slip of paper was like a time bomb placed on the airplane. My buddies on the Inter-Agency Task Force Against Terrorism have come up with some pretty hardened amoral killers. But they are amateurs compared to the terrorists who operate with skillful deadly accuracy among our own friends; and, as I am soon to find out, within our own families.

PART THREE
TRAVELTOWN

TWELVE

THE VISIBILITY over Los Angeles is a million miles, the air so smooth I feel as though I am gliding home in an armchair, one of those heavy green damask armchairs from the thirties with fringe along the bottom, sailing over the crystalline city of Oz.

The Russian immigrant cabdriver tells me, "They predict a socko storm," which must be some lunatic misinterpretation of English because there can't be rain so late in the season, especially on a night so clear. We are driving up Lincoln Boulevard with all the windows open. It is midnight and I should lie back and dream, but my mind is ready for the start of the day, churning with a catalogue of urgent tasks, from calling the credit card companies to checking up on Wild Bill.

The cab lets me off at the main entrance to Ocean View Estates, where I borrow twenty bucks for the fare from the night guard, Dominico, who has been here as long as I have. Carrying the overnight duffel, the blue attaché on the good shoulder, I walk the familiar maze of pathways to Tahiti Gardens.

The ritual is always the same: I'm glad to be home but instantly crave fresh air, opening the glass doors to welcome a humid breeze and the calming view of legions of sailboats peacefully moored under bright white spotlights.

Even after such a brief absence, my bedroom seems unfamiliar, a hotel with a few pieces of institutional furniture scrupulously dusted, on view for the next occupant; nothing personal or telling except a trace of White Linen perfume and an antique handmade quilt that covers the double bed.

If I were trapped in a fire and could save one thing, it would be this quilt. It belonged to my great-grandmother, Poppy's mother, Grace, who was born in Kansas in 1890 and drove all the way to California in a Model T. The design is made of tiny hexagons in pale floral prints and you can plainly see the topstitching in coarse white cotton thread. The fabrics must have come from ladies' house dresses and kitchen curtains that hung in farmhouses lit by kerosene lamps.

I remove my clothing, which smells like the inside of an airplane, and lie naked on this quilt, wondering about the circle of women who made it, imagining their fingers working all around the hem, callused fingers, lean hard fingers, joining scraps of fabric in weak yellow light; as long as they kept working they could hold in their hands the sweet connection of female companionship. *Where is my connection?*

I am thirsting for fresh orange juice. I am back in Los Angeles, back to the feeling of being watched, maybe by a camera mounted on a crane up there in the shadows of the ceiling, looking down at me on the bed. *I should call Poppy.* Outside the wind is nudging the brass chimes hanging off the balcony, sounding them like tiny warning-bell buoys for tiny distant boats. The camera is moving closer, a slow spiral ending with the pupil of my eye.

Why is there part of me that is always afraid?

I am drifting in the center of all those tiny hexagons. Is it Boston time or California time? Is it my empty body or Claire Eberhardt's hungry body or Violeta Alvarado's, cremated to ash?

Those mysterious faded aqua snapshots of her life are never far from my mind: brothers lined up in a solemn semicircle, Grandma

Constanza holding a baby, the parrot. What would it be like to grow up in a house without walls? To sleep on a bamboo mat on bare ground, through a dry season of parched dust and a wet season of steamy rain—to live in a house that is open to it all?

Suppose I made the trip to El Salvador and located the Alvarado encampment? If I walked through that landscape, past male cousins stripping the kernels off dried corn with their fingers, females grinding it in a *molino*, patting the mixture into flat circles and baking them on a stone, if I finally came to Constanza and called her name, would she look up from the wood cooking fire at this strange foreign relative and panic . . . or would she simply go on making tortillas, not at all surprised to see me, or to hear the news she has feared since the day her daughter left for America?

■ ■ ■

I awake to rain needling the windows, turn over in the bed and reach for the TV remote. My shoulder is feeling better but my lower back is stiff and sore. Channel 9 unfolds on the screen. A strong Pacific cold front is driving sleet and showers along the entire West Coast of the United States. It is thirty degrees in San Francisco, hailstorms during the night. There will be two feet of new snow in Nevada by tomorrow and more storm systems are backed up over the ocean like airplanes at LAX. When I hear there is flash flooding in Palm Springs, I grab the phone and hit two digits for Poppy's number, which I have stored on speed dialing.

"Poppy? How're you doing? Staying dry?"

"I just spent a night in the hospital."

"What happened?"

My grandfather has never been hospitalized in his life. He must have sliced his finger on one of those old-fashioned double-edged razors he has always used along with menthol shaving cream.

"Up around the eleventh hole I had a pain in my gut. They panicked and called an ambulance."

"Jesus Christ, Poppy."

"Well it was just a goddamn waste of time. They kept me overnight, couldn't find anything wrong."

"It must have been the night I called you," I gush apologetically, "I was out of town on an investigation, and nobody picked up the phone. I feel terrible that you went through all that alone—"

But he interrupts, "What was so important at four in the morning?"

"I was lonely." I laugh to take the edge off it, but when he doesn't answer I feel compelled to explain to the silence. "I was drunk."

There is a pause, then, "You're a jerk."

"Thanks, Poppy."

His voice is strong, mine is shrunken and weak.

"Do you have a drinking problem?"

"No, I do not have a drinking problem."

"Then don't be a jerk, especially on the job."

His belligerence triggers a sulky rage: "Nobody else seems to think I'm a jerk. They gave me a case that involves Jayne Mason."

"What's the case?"

"She alleges a physician got her hooked on painkillers he obtained from Mexico."

"Did you get to meet Jayne Mason?"

"Interviewed her at length."

"What was she like?"

"The woman of your dreams, Poppy."

"We'd get along."

They probably would. "It's a prestige case. Came to us through the Director. That's why I was in Boston."

"You'd better bust your boiler on it."

"What do you think I'm doing?"

"And not be a jerk."

No use. You can't win. By the end of the conversation with Poppy I am spent. I sit on the edge of the bed naked and shivering, drenched with guilt because I got angry with him, chastising myself for not being there when he went into the hospital, worried about what these abdominal pains could portend . . . and filled with a new, inarticulate dread as icy as the cold rain.

■   ■   ■

I down three Tylenols and some instant oatmeal, pull on jeans and knee-high rubber boots, zip up the parka, tighten the hood, and slosh through the flooded walkways to the freezing cold garage where the Barracuda, standing in six inches of water, refuses to start.

"Stay home," Rosalind tells me over the phone. "They're asking federal employees to stay home unless they're essential to their department."

"That lets me out."

She puts me on hold, then comes back on. "Except for you, Ana dear." She continues, lowering her voice, "Special Agent in Charge Galloway just walked by. He wants you in here."

An hour later Donnato inches his car along the narrow service road outside my balcony and honks. He must have badged the guard to get inside the complex. The downpour is so intense that just running out from the lobby completely saturates my jacket.

I jump inside and slam the door.

"So the Barracuda finally died."

"She didn't die, she just didn't want to get her tires wet."

"Why do you drive that wreck?"

"It's romantic."

"For the same money you could have gotten a cherry old Mustang."

"Everybody drives Mustangs. Nobody drives a Barracuda with a scarlet paint job like some old floozy."

"This is why I worry about you." He hands me hot coffee in a paper cup. Suddenly I am hungry all over again.

"It smells like a bakery in here."

"I got you Zen muffins."

"You did?"

Zen muffins are huge heavy balls of blueberries and fiber that are sometimes the only thing I eat for lunch. It takes an effort to find them and I am touched. The inviting scent of coffee, the fogged windows and the rain outside, our wet overclothes—the way he won't exactly look at me—slams me hard with the same illicit longing I had sitting in the car waiting to enter the tunnel in Boston, of Donnato and I as real lovers, each moment together part of the continuous invention of our own special world.

But in the next instant I am slammed hard the other way by the impossibility, the "jerkiness" of it, as Poppy would say.

"I should leave town more often," I observe with wry sadness.

"Yeah, I miss your butt now that you're on this glamour assignment."

"Let's face it: I am glamorous."

He looks over. "Especially with that hood."

I unzip it self-consciously. "I brought you back a meatball sub from Boston but left it on the kitchen counter."

"Very thoughtful." He is distracted now, backing out carefully, brushing the dark leathery leaves of holly bushes bright with rain. "I came to warn you Galloway is out for blood."

"Whose? Mine?"

"Somebody's." We are at the entrance to the complex, facing an out-of-control blinking red traffic light. Five or six cars are stopped uncertainly, gray water up to their hubcaps. "I hope you got good stuff in Boston on that doctor."

"It's good," I say with confidence, picturing Claudia Van Hoven's touching tears in the park.

"It better be better than good. It better be excellent."

"It's superlative," I snap, annoyed. "It's the best fucking evidence any FBI agent ever came up with in the history of the world. Why does Galloway have a hair across, anyway?"

"He's upset about the Cuban thing—where the young girl died?"

I stare at the rain. The Cuban thing was a major fuckup by agents in our field office; a public relations fiasco that won't go away.

"I'm screwed."

Donnato plows ahead through the flooded intersection.

Robert Galloway has made a career of being tougher than the tough guys. He has played chicken with Mafia dons. He has gone nose to nose against the ugliest teamsters in Kennedy Airport, worked deep undercover in the heroin trade along the piers of Manhattan. During his last years as an organized-crime specialist, he was forced to move his family from Brooklyn to Pennsylvania because of death threats against them. Finally the separation from his teenage kids became too much and he reluctantly accepted the promotion to Los Angeles, although he remains a purebred New Yorker who, I suspect, still believes we're a bunch of nuts and fruits out here.

Galloway is an action man not suited to lying, which doesn't make him the best choice to deal with the press. Instead of sleazing his way through the Cuban thing like any other bureaucrat would have done without a second thought, Galloway feels compelled to actually answer the question, which is the following:

Why did the FBI fail to save a twenty-four-year-old former beauty queen from Iowa from being stabbed to death thirty times with an eight-inch kitchen knife by her Cuban drug-dealing boyfriend when their Hollywood apartment was under twenty-four-hour surveillance by us and the entire crime, blow by blow, scream by terrified scream, is recorded on our magnetic audiotape?

"Galloway had a press conference yesterday. It did not go well."

We are rocketing up in the elevator and I'm leaving that warm glow in my stomach from the coffee and the muffin somewhere down around the fourth floor.

"He told them the truth? That nobody was listening to the surveillance?"

"Yes."

"Unbelievable."

"It was a personal embarrassment for Galloway, after that big speech he made to the Bar Association about 'the war on drugs will be won or lost in L.A.' "

"I guess we know the outcome."

"You can bet the Duane Carters of the world are nipping at Galloway's heels like a pack of Dobermans. Still," Donnato shrugs, "I was saying to Pumpkin in the shower this morning, nobody can expect us to actively monitor every case every minute of the day."

Silence between us as we cross the corridor.

"Married fifteen years and you still take showers together?"

Donnato gives me one of those endearingly painful smiles.

"She was gargling at the sink, okay?"

We punch in our codes and enter the Agents Only door.

"Gee, I kind of liked picturing you all soapy and slippery."

"Don't get your hopes up," Donnato tells me.

■　■　■

Duane Carter's door is open. He and two other guys are tossing a Nerf ball into a basket.

"How was Boston?" Duane calls.

I'm not about to say I got ripped off at a stoplight by some punk. "Super!" I give a big grin and the thumbs-up sign. He returns the smile like we're best buddies.

I barely sit down at my desk when the phone rings. It is Jayne Mason.

"They've got a photograph of my tits."

"Who does?"

"*National Enquirer, Ladies' Home Journal,* how do I know who?"

Hearing that familiar voice speaking directly and intimately into my ear is like seeing her suddenly appear in the bullpen—as jolting a shock as the human body can bear.

"How did they get the photograph, Ms. Mason?"

"Yesterday, if you recall, was a stunning day before it started raining like hell, and I was sunbathing in the buff by the pool when a helicopter passes overhead. I know exactly what they were after."

"Were there any markings on the helicopter?"

"It said KTLA."

"That's a television station."

"Of course it is."

"So it's your belief that KTLA was taking nude pictures for the six o'clock news?"

"Please respect my intelligence." I hear ice clinking in a glass. "All these cameramen freelance on the side. On their way to cover a traffic jam they fly over the home of some perfectly innocent actress and point their sneaky little zoom lens and imagine they can make an easy ten thousand dollars."

I let out a whistle, mocking and low. "Really? That much?"

"For the right pair."

I have to admit that now she's got me thinking about her breasts. Is she embarrassed because they're old and withered, or pissed off because they're perky and firm and *worth* ten grand?

"I want the FBI involved."

"We're a federal agency, we only investigate federal crimes. We have no jurisdiction over something like this. I suggest you contact the local police."

"But you're my FBI agent."

"Actually, I'm employed by the United States government, ma'am."

"Oh, get off your high horse!" she says with a great deal of irritation and hangs up.

Next thing I know, Galloway, wearing a scarlet turtleneck, papers flying out of his hands, cigar askew between his teeth, grabs my arm, pulls me out of the chair, and steers me into his office.

"What have you got on the Mason case that's so goddamn good?"

Oh, boy.

"I've got a former patient of Dr. Eberhardt, Claudia Van Hoven, who claims he overprescribed painkillers and got her hooked on them exactly like Jayne Mason."

"Will she testify?"

"Yes."

"Let's go for a warrant."

He is reaching for the phone to call the U.S. District Attorney's office.

"I think we should wait."

"Why?"

It is a hard moment. Galloway is champing at the bit. It would be easy to allow him to place the call and set a hundred wheels in motion, and lie back and take the strokes for doing my part, having completed the mission in Boston . . . but it would not be responsible. If he's going to be muddled by emotion, then I'm the one who has to keep that clear head. We can't both be running off half-cocked like my poor bank robber, Dennis Hill, tearing through the parking lot with a fistful of cash and a starter pistol, red-eyed and strung out, desperate to stay ahead of the demons.

"I don't think we should go for a warrant without a full background check on the patient."

"When will we have it?"

"I'm waiting for a call from the Boston field office."

Galloway lets go of the phone. Behind him torrents of rain cascade down the steamy windows.

"I know you really want this case."

"Jayne Mason is not a case. Jayne Mason is a goddamn complex political situation waiting to explode just like the Cuban thing."

He reaches toward the coffee table, gestures in frustration.

"Where's your lucky belt buckle?"

"Gone."

Instead he grabs the remote, points it at a TV on the credenza, and savagely pushes the button.

In perfect synchronicity with his mood the local news is showing live helicopter coverage of a fifty-foot camper being swept out of a flooded trailer park and carried along by the deluge, smashing apart against a railroad bridge, the pieces washing out to sea. We both stare with fascination at the slow inevitable destruction.

Then Galloway gets out of the chair restlessly. "The Director is on my ass. The press is on my ass. The district attorney calls me at home—"

"Jayne Mason's calling here."

"What for?"

"She wants us to do something about helicopters flying over her property."

This causes Galloway to almost twitch himself right out of his skin.

"We've got to resolve this thing before it gets out of control." He picks up a handful of yellow messages. "This morning alone I got three phone calls from Mason's personal manager."

"I hear she carries a lot of personal influence."

Galloway grimaces. A thin whistle escapes through his back teeth.

"You don't know the half of it and neither do I."

"What's the half you do know?"

"I was briefed on Magda Stockman by, let's say, an official source in the Administration when we got the case. She's one tough cookie. Came over to this country from Hungary during the revolt in 1957, got a job in Macy's Herald Square selling lipstick, had a knack for it, went on her own, ran a snooty beauty shop up on Madison, met some famous Broadway actress and became her manager."

"Where's the political influence?"

Galloway mouths the cigar. "That came from ratting on her old Communist buddies to interested folks in Washington."

"You mean she wasn't escaping from the Communists—"

Galloway nods. "She was one of them. A party member. But more than that, an opportunist."

"So she came to America—"

"Greener pastures."

Now we are nodding together.

"Isn't it great?" Galloway grins like a carnivore. "I've got the darling of the Republicans on my back on top of all this other crap with the Cuban thing."

"The Bureau's looking at hard times."

Suddenly he has stopped listening, absorbed by an anchor-woman on the TV screen wearing a low-cut electric blue suit with a lacy camisole peeking out underneath.

"There's a lesson to be learned," he muses. I politely wait to hear it: "Hollywood."

I nod soberly.

Galloway turns from the television set, his face composed.

"Maybe I should put someone else on the Mason case."

Icy fear goes through me. "Why? I'm handling it."

He hesitates. "I wish the hell you didn't remind me of my four-teen-year-old daughter."

"I'm not your fourteen-year-old daughter. And don't worry—I won't get pregnant."

Galloway laughs. Or at least his tight shoulders heave up and down in a fair imitation. He'll ride with me. For the moment.

"What else do you have cooking on this doc? What other sources can be approached and remain confidential? Neighbors who can't stand the guy, disgruntled employees, the gardener, the mail-man, a love affair, what?"

"If it's there, I'll find it."

They have gone back to live coverage of the storm. A lone fire-man is stranded in a flat plane of green water, holding on to a post with one hand, a walkie-talkie in the other.

"I want hard evidence by the end of next week. If he's guilty, let's put him away," Galloway grunts.

"Done."

His eyes go back to the man trapped in water up to his chest.

"Poor bastard."

"Don't worry. The chopper's going to pull him out."

But Galloway does not look convinced.

THIRTEEN

I GO BACK to my desk and have a long conversation with the Bank Dick's Undercover Disguise, arguing that it is imperative to first complete the background check on Claudia Van Hoven to be certain she will make a sound witness. To this end, I leave an urgent message at the Boston field office for Wild Bill.

Following up on Galloway's idea to look for someone close to the doctor who would be motivated to talk, I go through the file again and come to the printouts subpoenaed from the phone company. During a period of several months a whole lot of calls from the Eberhardt home were made to a local 454 number listed as belonging to Theodora Feign. After highlighting them with a marker it becomes graphically clear that Ms. Feign is linked to the Eberhardt household in some way: for one week alone there are twenty pink lines.

The Bank Dick's Undercover Disguise and I are working on the same wavelength. We agree that since the calls were placed from the residence during the day they were most likely made by the wife, maybe to a girlfriend, maybe her only friend in California, someone the displaced nurse from Boston could unload on about how lonely she is over in the contemporary Mediterranean on Twentieth Street.

Theodora Feign could be the kind of source Galloway is looking for. But if I call her cold, she could easily turn around and tell bosom buddy Claire the FBI has been asking questions about her husband, thereby blowing the entire operation and busting me back to desk duty.

To be safe, I should talk to someone who has knowledge of Theodora Feign's relationship with the Eberhardts. Who would know?

It was obvious from cruising the streets that there was a dual society north of Montana, upper-middle-class whites and working-class Hispanics living in parallel worlds. While the white women are absent you can see the housekeepers gathered on shady corners of those lush residential streets with crowds of strollers and babies, gossiping in Spanish like there's no tomorrow, and it's a safe bet, I explain to the Bank Dick's Undercover Disguise, that the gossip has to do with the white women and how much they pay and how they run their households and who has an unhappy marriage and who is good friends with whom.

If Theodora Feign were close to Claire Eberhardt, there's a good chance her housekeeper, Violeta Alvarado, would have known, and maybe Violeta talked about it with *her* good friend, the older woman in the building who was also from El Salvador and baby-sat for her kids; a *comadre* who understood and cared.

I dial Mrs. Gutiérrez's number and say I have questions concerning my cousin. What kind of questions? she wants to know. Oh, about her life, how she came to America. Pleased that I am showing interest in my *family*, Mrs. Gutiérrez agrees to meet on Sunday.

Of course that stuff about Violeta is a lie, what I'm really after is information on her employer. Hanging up I glance smugly at the Bank Dick's Undercover Disguise, but sense disapproval: it knows I am lying only to myself.

■　■　■

Sunday afternoon we get a break in the rain and although it is overcast and fifty degrees I grab the opportunity to put the top down on the Barracuda, bundling up in boots, a leather bomber jacket, aviator sunglasses, and a Dodgers cap turned backward. When I pull up in front of Violeta Alvarado's apartment building, Mrs. Gutiérrez is already waiting out front with Teresa and Cristóbal.

The children barely murmur a response when I say hello. I thought they'd get a kick out of riding in the convertible but they say nothing. The wind whips their glossy black hair but their faces remain blank.

Mrs. Gutiérrez and I exchange a few words in the front seat about whether it will rain again tomorrow. As I accelerate down Sunset Boulevard she clutches a large white pocketbook to her bosom, cupping the other hand over her ear as if to stop her lacquered hairdo from blowing.

What now? Do I try my few words of Spanish to get a conversation going? Put on a Latino station? Would they enjoy that or be insulted? Finally the uneasy silence is more than I can take and I shove in an old Springsteen tape, withdrawing to my own space—my car, my Sunday, my music—for the twenty minutes it takes to get on the freeway and off again at Traveltown in Griffith Park.

The damp, smoggy air on the other side of the Hollywood Hills smells like cigar smoke and old rust. Despite the uncertain weather the parking lot is half full. We pass beneath some frail eucalyptus trees and through the gate, finding ourselves at a tiny railway station where a tiny steam-driven train has just rolled in.

"Do they want to go for a ride?" I ask Mrs. Gutiérrez.

Teresa shakes her head no. Her brother simply holds her hand. He is wearing a new Ninja Turtle sweat suit.

I notice some outdoor tables. "Are they hungry?"

"They have lunch but maybe they like to eat."

We make an unlikely contingent, me in my leather and baseball cap, Mrs. Gutiérrez who is wearing turquoise flowered leggings and a big red sweater the size of a barrel, and the two orphans.

I buy nachos and microwaved hot dogs. We are surrounded by birthday parties, mostly Hispanic. Teresa and Cristóbal eat slowly and carefully, as if they had been taught to appreciate each bite, staring at the wrapped presents, a piñata hoisted into a tree, a portable grill laden with smoking pieces of marinated meat and long whole scallions, releasing the aroma of roasted garlic and lime. Each group seems to include ten or twenty family members, good humored and relaxed. The birthday cakes are elaborate, store bought. Teresa is watching without envy. Without any discernible emotion at all.

"*Mamá!*" Cristóbal suddenly exclaims, excited, pointing.

"He think that lady look like his mother." Mrs. Gutiérrez strokes his head. "*Pobrecito.*"

A pretty young woman, who might in fact resemble a reconstruction of the decimated corpse I saw in the autopsy photos, is holding a baby while unwrapping aluminum foil from a tray of fruit. She laughs and nuzzles the baby, who grips the wavy black hair that falls to her waist.

"Does Cristóbal understand . . . ?" I find it hard to finish.

"He know his mommy isn't coming back."

Cristóbal tugs at his sister's arm. She continues to chew uninterestedly as if he were pointing out a passing bus.

"Do you remember if Violeta ever talked about a friend of Mrs. Eberhardt's named Theodora Feign?"

"You mean Mrs. Teddy?"

"Could be."

"Oh yes, Mrs. Claire and Mrs. Teddy were very close. And Mrs. Teddy's housekeeper, Reyna, was also close with Violeta."

"So the four of them got along."

"Not so much anymore."

"No?"

"Mrs. Teddy is very mad with Mrs. Claire."

"Why is that?"

"I don't know, but Violeta was sad that she didn't get to see Reyna anymore. And the two little girls liked to play together."

"What happened? Did Teddy and Claire have a fight?"

"Oh, yes. They don't talk to each other anymore."

This is good news. It means I can approach Theodora Feign with confidence. As far as I'm concerned, the afternoon is over. I get up and stretch my back, staring idly at a dense rose garden sprinkled

Did you knw that

by a few light drops of rain. Returning to Mrs. Gutiérrez I inquire politely,

, "Did Dr. Eberhardt send you that check?"

"Yes, he do, and I buy new clothes for the children." She nods proudly toward Cristóbal's bright green sweats. "Then I write to the grandmother to ask what she want to do. Maybe she come here, maybe the children will go back to El Salvador and live with her and their big brother."

"Violeta had another child?"

"Yes, you saw him in the pictures. The baby that the grandmother is holding, that is Violeta's oldest son. She left him to come to this country."

"How could she leave a little baby?"

"To make a better life," Mrs. Gutiérrez explains with an ironic lift of the eyebrows. "She work to send money home to take care of the son and the grandmother. Inside"—she taps her heart—"she miss her mommy."

She clicks her purse open, discharging the scent of face powder, and removes a fat roll of folded tissues.

"Now the boy must be eight or nine years old. He doesn't even know he lost his mommy yet."

There is nothing between us but a gentle splatter of raindrops—on our hair, the bench, on a hundred fading roses.

Mrs. Gutiérrez bends her head forward and presses two tissues against the corners of her eyes. It is as if Grief himself has taken a seat between us on the cold concrete and put his mossy arms around both of our shoulders. I can feel the weight of the children's loss. My own heart tightens with the same bereavement, the kind that bubbles up from time to time and overwhelms you in an instant. Within myself it remains mysterious, an underground spring without a source.

"It was Violeta's dream for the family to be together."

"Were Teresa and Cristóbal born in this country?"

"Yes," says Mrs. Gutiérrez. "The father left."

She sniffs and snaps the pocketbook shut.

"If they were born here, they are American citizens, wards of the U.S. government. That means the government will take care of them."

Mrs. Gutiérrez is as immovable as the poured cement table. "That is wrong."

"It's not up to us. It's the law."

"The law is wrong."

I take a sip of sugary lemonade. I don't want to get into an emotional argument. I am an agent of the federal government—obviously I believe that society has the obligation and compassion to care for those of us who are lost, or damaged like Teresa, with the face of a pupilless angel carved in stone. The drizzle has passed, the burn of the sun presses through a thick layer of cloud. I can see it is painful for her just to be sitting here outside her secret places in the apartment, alone and unprotected in the dull glare of this world.

"When is your birthday, Teresa?"

She looks at Mrs. Gutiérrez and says nothing.

"Come on, you must know your birthday."

She whispers a date.

"What would you like for your birthday?"

"I would like a bed," Teresa answers without hesitation.

"Don't you have a bed? Where do you sleep?"

"Under the kitchen table."

I look away, squinting into the brightening distance, thinking that although these sunglasses are supposed to afford the best UV protection, the lenses are not nearly dark enough—not dark enough at all.

Teresa's eyes are on her empty plate.

"Want another hot dog?"

She nods. I buy two of everything the lousy little snack bar has: popcorn, ice cream sandwiches, tortilla chips, and watch the children work their way through it all.

"Tell them to go and play."

Mrs. Gutiérrez repeats my request in Spanish, but the children do not move. There's not a hell of a lot to do in Traveltown if you are not part of a big exuberant family on a picnic. I wish I'd known that when I picked it from the front pages of the phone book. You can run through a transportation museum housed in a dark old barn and see a horse-drawn fire engine from 1902 or climb on engines of defunct trains like iron behemoths sunk into the mud. Teresa and Cristóbal don't want to do anything. They cling to Mrs. Gutiérrez's hands, squat down, and wrap their arms around her chubby knees.

"Tell them to play," I repeat with an edge.

She speaks more sharply and they drag reluctantly toward the trains.

"If the family cannot be located, Teresa and Cristóbal will have to go into foster care," I tell her, speaking slowly, with absolute level conviction, as clearly and emotionlessly as possible, the way you advise a criminal of his rights. "I will notify the proper agencies myself."

Mrs. Gutiérrez takes a sharp breath and covers her mouth with both hands. Her broad square nails are earth-red, three or four dime-store rings on pudgy fingers.

"I love these children!" she cries. "I thought you gonna help."

"We have to do what's right."

"What is right?" Mrs. Gutiérrez asks. "Violeta wanted to make a better life. To make money in America to send back to her child. She was only eighteen years old. She got on a bus from Mexico City to Tijuana and she was raped by the men on that bus, each in his turn, right there on the floor. Is that right?"

"That's why we have the law."

"She just left a baby. Her breasts were full of milk. The law means nothing."

Cristóbal and Teresa have been screwing around behind the bench and finally Mrs. Gutiérrez can't stand it anymore. She gets off to see what they're up to, then comes back dragging Cristóbal by the arm.

"This lady is the police," she says smartly, presenting him to me. "Show her what you did."

Cristóbal refuses to look up. Mrs. Gutiérrez yanks his hand out of his pocket. He is clutching a plastic car worth about sixty-nine cents.

"From the birthday party over there." She shakes him roughly. "Little thief."

She glares at me. Since I know what's best for the children, obviously I will take care of this.

I lead him across the plaza. "We can't take things that aren't ours," I explain gently.

We come upon a broken piñata, some candy, and a few small toys left scattered on the damp grass.

I march him up to the father of the birthday party. "Cristóbal took this, but he knows it isn't right and he wants to give it back."

The boy remains rigid, the car in his hand at his side.

"It's okay, let him keep it," the man says.

Cristóbal breaks from me and tears back to his sister.

"Thank you," I say desperately. "Thank you very much."

I mean it. I am tense, and despite the rawness of the air, drenched with sweat. I didn't want to take away his wretched little car. I don't want to be here at all, but I have promised the children of my cousin, motherless and fatherless and sunk in unhappiness, maimed by malnutrition of the soul, an afternoon in Traveltown. And the pony rides are yet ahead.

FOURTEEN

DURING THE NIGHT another storm blows in. Monday morning the sky is white, the light is brown as I head toward Teddy Feign's house through dense unrelenting curtains of rain. I choose not to detour past the Eberhardt residence on Twentieth Street or Poppy's old place on Twelfth, sticking to the main thoroughfare, San Vicente Boulevard, where it is slow going, dodging around stalled cars and palm fronds that have been blown into the road. Several delicate coral trees have been completely upended, roots clawing the air, finished.

I take a right at the light on Seventh Street heading for Santa Monica Canyon. Going down the hill the wimp-ass government Ford loses traction and skids for several long seconds, lurching to a stop just short of a traffic sign, with two wheels stuck in the mud. I fight to maneuver back onto the road but the strength in my arms isn't enough and my hands slip painfully along the steering wheel. I sit there, steaming. If I have to call a tow truck it will be an embarrassment and a huge waste of time. Just then the back of my neck prickles up. Something is approaching fast from behind. Instead of slowing down a Range Rover speeds past, intentionally swerving through a puddle and spraying the windows with a noisy mix of pebbles and water the color of bile. The driver, wearing a baseball cap, never looks back.

A rock gets caught in the wipers and etches a half circle across the glass with a chilling nails-on-chalkboard scratch. Enraged, I blast it loose with a plume of bright blue windshield cleaner and jam on the gearshift.

Easing back and forth between first and second gear, concentrating on nothing but the whining tires, I rock the Ford gently in the soup, straining for that first touch of friction, nursing it, feeling the tires finally catch and heave up onto the pavement, scooting across the curve into the canyon, cursing the Range Rover all the way. Only on the Westside would someone driving a forty-five-thousand-dollar vehicle feel the need to go out of their way to kick mud in your face.

Santa Monica Canyon is a tiny valley between the elevated flatlands north of Montana and the southern bluff of the Pacific Palisades, two miles from the Eberhardt residence. At sea level and only blocks from the beach, its mouth is open to constantly flowing ocean breezes that become trapped between the canyon walls, creating a microclimate of uncommonly clear sun, deep shade, and fresh salt-kissed air. It has become an exclusive neighborhood for attorneys and people in television, but the most extravagant home is the one built by Teddy and Andrew Feign up against the hillside at the end of San Lorenzo Street.

It is an enormous Tudor mansion, half timbered with ashlar veneer of brown gray, an ivy-covered arch over the driveway. It has twin pent roofs, three large medieval chimneys, and diamond-shaped panes of glass in tall bay windows that make you think Snow White herself is about to flow out the door. In fact, if you don't look at the Guadalupe palms across the street, the house gives a pretty good impression of Leicestershire, England, on a rainy day.

Opening a wrought-iron gate, I follow a flagstone path that has now become a running stream. Teddy Feign appears in short order, an attractive slender woman wearing high yellow boots and holding a mop. When I explain that I am from the Federal Bureau of Investigation and have questions about some acquaintances of hers, Dr.

and Mrs. Eberhardt, her eyes brighten and she beckons me in. Like the driver of the Range Rover she appears more than willing to take a swing through the mud, if only for the opportunity of slinging it at somebody else.

I follow into the kitchen.

"Do you believe this? Could you die?"

We are splashing through a half inch of water that covers the oak floor. The somewhat amusing source of this minor flood is a utility closet where rainwater is pouring in through the light switches and cascading in shiny sheets down the walls. A young girl wearing a white pants uniform is methodically moving everything that was in the closet to another room. Brooms, a vacuum cleaner, piles of wet rags, detergents, flowerpots, tennis racquets, and a slide projector are piled on the counter as she retrieves them one by one.

Whereas the girl moves with deliberate slowness, her boss is going at a couple of thousand rpms.

"I've seen this movie, thank you very much, I don't need to see it again."

She swipes at the water, slams a bucket with futility against the wall.

"Last year during the storms we had a mud slide. At three in the morning that whole mountain came roaring down, I thought we were all going to die."

Through generous windows, past a brick barbecue area and planters crammed with impatiens, I can see a hill bandaged by a sheet of concrete.

"It tore through here like a bulldozer, took off the whole back of the house. We just finished remodeling the kitchen a month ago. I am absolutely beside myself. *Where is Dirk?*"

While mopping at the water she picks up a radio phone and angrily demands that Dirk, apparently the contractor, be beeped, carphoned, lassoed, or otherwise delivered to her door immediately.

I don't dream about kitchens, but if I did, this would be the one. Teddy Feign, still yakking fiercely into the mouthpiece, gestures for me to sit on a comfortable stool, which even has a backrest, at an island with two stainless steel sinks set in about fourteen acres of polished green marble. The room is so large you can hear the air rushing past tiers of glossy white cabinets. You can tell it is a brand-new kitchen by the scent of fresh paint and the hot white clarity of the recessed lighting—the bulbs haven't been there long enough to get filmed over with cooking grease.

She hangs up and drums short perfect nails manicured in clear polish on the edge of the marble. (If you're going to use clear, why get a manicure?)

"Coffee," she decides. "Now. You?"

"Great. How well do you know the Eberhardts?"

"I was their *spirit guide* to the mysteries of the West Coast."

She wiggles her fingers and makes a mocking spirit face.

"They had just moved here, they knew nobody. I introduced them, I had them for dinner, I made an open invitation to play on my tennis court, I even said they could use my pro *for free*—"

The woman can get out more words per second than rounds off an AK-47.

"I referred patients to Randall, let their kids swim in my pool, although that didn't work out very well—"

"I heard there was an accident."

Her version is uncharacteristically succinct: "Laura fell in, I wasn't home, she was fine."

Then she pauses to tick off the rest of her kindnesses:

"And I tried but did not succeed in getting Claire out of those plaid flannel shirts of hers from L.L. Bean."

"So you know them pretty well."

"Intimately. Before they dropped me, but that's another story."

She opens cabinet doors, assembling cups, coffee, and measuring spoons in rapid succession.

"I understand there's been some antagonism between you and Mrs. Eberhardt."

"How would you know that?"

"It wasn't hard to find out."

She regards me curiously and pushes the glasses up on her

nose. They have heavy black frames like some dorky engineer would have worn in the fifties, but on her fair delicate face they look exceedingly hip. Although she must be close to forty her dishwaterblond hair is cut in a rock 'n' roll shag. She is wearing a black cashmere sweater and tight black crushed velvet leggings. The only accent to break up all this basic black is a pair of round diamond stud earrings with stones the size of raisins.

"Would you say the Eberhardts are under financial pressure?"

"Sports injuries? Are you kidding? Randall's practice is huge."

"Is he a big spender?"

She snorts. "He drives an Acura."

"Have you ever seen him take drugs?"

"Never."

"Has he ever offered drugs to you?"

"I don't do drugs."

"Maybe he wrote a prescription for you or your husband for some sleeping pills as a favor."

"Never happened."

"Tell me about his character. Would you say he's one of these doctors on an ego trip?"

"Randall?"

She laughs and pulls the levers on a big polished copper contraption for making cappuccino like they have in restaurants.

"The first time I met Randall Eberhardt he was running down the street wearing nothing but a pair of sweatpants, waving a frozen pork chop."

Steam spits from the machine and she flinches away, murmuring, "Thing is out to kill me." Then, back in control of her coffeemaker: "I'd gone over to take Claire out to lunch and I was just getting out of my car when I saw a good-looking man with a very nice chest running down the street after a dog that had shown up in their backyard, some pathetic little runt Randall called a 'homeless dog,' because it had that empty look in the eyes you see in homeless people. It wouldn't get close enough even to be fed and eventually it just ran away. Here was this lady he didn't know from Adam getting out of a Mercedes in an Armani suit and here he was in grungy sweats running after a stray dog, not at all embarrassed, and I thought, What a lovely guy."

The machine rattles and a rich intense aroma pours out along with dark coffee into two large white cups.

"In fact I can't imagine what Randall could have done to interest the FBI."

"You tell me."

"Gee, maybe he smoked dope in the sixties."

I give her a goofy smile.

"You were close to his wife until she dropped you, you said. What was that about?"

Teddy Feign frowns. She's not getting what she wants from me but she's in this, she'll play it out a little longer.

"The first time I met Claire was in *that closet*. It was leaking then just like it's leaking now." She points accusingly with a spoon coated with foamy milk.

"After the mud came down it was still raining and we had to get plastic over the hill to keep it from completely burying the house. We needed *bodies*. It was six in the morning. I had Reyna call everybody we knew, including everybody in my daughter's preschool class."

Teddy Feign walks across the slick oak flooring in her rubber boots and sets the steaming cups on the counter.

"Claire Eberhardt was the only one from the class who came."

Her voice quavers.

"We had my husband's relatives helping out and some *hombres* he hired on the spot in front of a hardware store, and I came back from Zucky's with lunch for everyone and I find this strange woman with long black hair in a velvet headband wearing a Fair Isle sweater, trying to sweep three inches of water out of that closet. I asked if we'd met and she told me she was one of the mothers from the preschool. We had called every one of the parents from Diedre's class. These are people we had birthday parties with and play-dates with and movies and dinners . . ." She continues with evident pain, "I didn't even know Claire Eberhardt, but she was the only one who got off their butt and came over here to help somebody else. I was so touched by that, I lost it. I started to cry. She's a nurse, she can be very comforting. So we sat here and ate hot pastrami sandwiches and became friends."

I sip the coffee, light and sweet.

"I really tried to help Claire. She was lost out here. Her husband was making money and she didn't know what to do with it. I told her to get a housekeeper and not be so chained to the kids. But the truth is, she was chained to Randall. Totally dependent on him. Nurse and doctor, over and out."

"Did she follow your advice?"

"Oh, drop dead, I was her best friend, she called me ten times a day! Our housekeepers were friends, our kids played together— but I'm so mad at her now."

"Why?"

"She just stopped calling. A cold shot out of the blue, right after Dee-Dee's fourth birthday. Suddenly she started making up excuses and stood me up four times in a row. Remember in seventh grade when your best friend stopped talking to you for no reason? That's how it felt, and it hurt."

"Did you ask what was going on?"

"She said she was busy." Teddy Feign shakes her head. *I'm busy. I gave up my Saturday to take her shopping. She buys all this great stuff at Neiman's, takes everything back. Why bother?"

Teddy Feign rests her chin on her hand like a teenager, still stung by the rejection.

"Claire was stuck back in Massachusetts. Randall thrived in California."

"Why is that?"

"Both his parents are doctors." She raises her eyebrows. Do I get it? "We're talking major pressure. Randall comes off low-key, but he is driven. I mean, look: they've been out here less than two years and already he's one of the top orthopods in the city."

The door swings open. Teddy Feign is so wound up she startles in her own kitchen.

A little girl bursts in.

"This is Diedre. Watch the water, honey."

Diedre is wearing a pair of overalls and Minnie Mouse boots, and has a sassy chin-length haircut, along with a pint-sized sense of entitlement.

"Pleased to meet you," she chirps with her chin in the air and I think, When she's fifteen, Teddy Feign doesn't have a chance.

Diedre is followed by an older woman.

"Reyna says we can play in the puddles," the girl announces.

"Hey, that'll be fun," cries Teddy Feign, jiggling her daughter into a smile. She introduces me to Reyna, who shakes my hand. Plump, maybe sixty years old, Reyna is clearly a cut above the other housekeepers. She speaks without an accent and wears a tan belted dress with low matching heels, tinted brown hair, and fashionable glasses in gold frames.

"It's almost stopped raining and Dee-Dee is tired of playing in her room."

"Good idea."

I like Reyna's stately competence. I like the way she strokes Dee-Dee's hair.

"Take a pair of my boots," Teddy Feign offers. "Reyna and I have the same size feet!" She says this with a bright grin, as if that miraculous connection bridges all the gaps between them.

Reyna is matter-of-fact. "Thank you. Come on, Dee-Dee, let's see which pair of Mommy's boots Reyna can wear."

She takes the child by the hand and helps her slide off her mother's lap, leaving us with a polite smile.

I am glad my cousin had a friend like Reyna in America.

The rain has lightened to a fine mist with just enough force to put a slant into it. The air is saturated with humidity and outside the deep green foliage is motionless, drooping straight down with the weight of the water.

The flow down the walls in the closet has abated and the maid in uniform has one more armful of wet dish towels and pot holders to clear away.

"What do you know about Dr. Eberhardt's relationship with Jayne Mason?"

"It was big news when Jayne became his client. She adored Randall, used him for every little thing. That's the reason he couldn't come to Dee-Dee's party—he had to go out to *Malibu* because *Jayne* had the flu."

"Was Claire jealous?"

"She didn't know what to make of it. Whenever Jayne called the house she'd freeze. I told her to *use the connection,* but she didn't know how. She's just not political."

The phone rings.

"Hi, doll, I'll have to call you back," Teddy Feign sings, full of cockiness, "I'm talking to the FBI."

With all the solemn authority of the Bureau, I admonish her sternly not to go around blabbing our conversation to the world.

"I'm sorry." She is immediately abashed, her fragile self-confidence fractured, "I promise I won't."

Embarrassed, she opens a drawer and pulls out an accordion-file envelope.

"Now I've got to get that electrician back to fix the lights in the closet *again.*" Pulling out a card: "Here it is: Warren Speca."

"Why do I know that name?"

"Claire gave him to me. They went to high school together back in Boston. He worked with Dirk on the remodel." Suddenly indignant about the unanswered phone call, *"Where is Dirk?"*

Now I recall Kathy Donovan telling me about Claire's old boyfriend, how they'd given her his number out in Venice as a joke. So this is the second time Warren Speca's name has come up in connection to Claire Eberhardt. One of the skills you learn at the academy is how to memorize an address off a card, upside down.

Outside we can see Diedre piling wet sand on the sliding pond of a redwood play structure while Reyna watches from under an umbrella, wearing a pair of knee-high riding boots.

"When I told her to take my boots I didn't mean my four-hundred-dollar Ralph Laurens, Jesus Christ." Teddy Feign sighs. Then, despairing of the water damage to her pristine walls and newly sanded floors, "What am I supposed to do?"

"Wait for Dirk."

■   ■   ■

The route back along San Vicente is blocked by fallen trees. An emergency crew is diverting cars along the residential streets. I follow a long line of traffic moving slowly past Poppy's old house on Twelfth.

The For Sale sign is still out front and the place looks even more shrunken and forlorn in the rain. This time I don't stop, but a memory comes with me.

I am on my knees on the hardwood floor of the living room. It is a dark Saturday morning and I can see the rain through the lace curtains on the narrow windows on either side of the front door. Yesterday I was five minutes late coming home from school and my grandfather is punishing me by forcing me to kneel in front of the television with the set turned off so I cannot watch my favorite programs. My mother comes and goes past the doorway but says nothing. I stare at the empty green screen. My knees ache. They have been pressing against the hard wood for a long time.

Suddenly I am pulling in to the garage at Bureau headquarters in Westwood. I don't know how I got there or how, in the dry safety of the car, my cheeks became so wet.

FIFTEEN

IN LOS ANGELES there are seven days out of the year that are so spectacular you feel lucky to be alive . . . and to own a convertible that is running again.

The days come after a rain or a fierce blow by the Santa Ana winds has blasted all the muck out of the basin. On those days you understand why eighty years ago they could shoot movies here all year round—because every morning they woke up to a world already lit with desert clarity. The natural light was so pure and abundant it could reveal every orange tree in a distant grove or every close-up nuance in an actor's face.

Today is one of those seven days. I leave the government car and take the Barracuda so I can hit the freeway with the top down. Looking inland you can see snow-capped peaks sixty miles away; sailing west every discrete fold in the Santa Monica Mountains is visible, every window in the towers of Century City shines. The sky is filled with the rare sight of white and charcoal clouds thick enough to cast rippling shadows across a sparkling metropolis newly born.

I am exhilarated also by the news from Wild Bill Walker that he has finally "gotten past a tangle of red tape" and gained access to the prescriptions that Randall Eberhardt wrote for the accident victim Claudia Van Hoven. He had to subpoena the records, but he said the pharmacy was going through their computer files right now and promised to fax me copies immediately. I am pleasantly inflated by the image of myself laying hard evidence on Galloway's desk before his deadline of the end of the week. Another faultless performance by Ana Grey.

I could sit in the office and stare at the fax machine or get out into the air, so I decide to spring myself on Warren Speca, who has not been returning my phone messages, to see if he has inside knowledge of the activities of his old high school girlfriend and her doctor husband. If not, I'll take a walk on Venice beach and look at the ocean.

Speca Electrical operates out of a bungalow on one of the canal streets. Nurse Kathy back in Savin Hill, Massachusetts, would be amazed to see that there really are canals in Venice, California. There used to be bridges and gondolas as well and an opera house that was meant to bring culture to the wild Pacific edge of America, part of Abbot Kinney's sweetly literal idea that if you built a town that looked like the Italian Renaissance, a Renaissance would occur.

God knows dreams die hard every day out here on the frontier but Venice was one of our saddest losses; although The Pike amusement park in Long Beach went down to shorefront developers, Venice was a much grander idea. But the canals were poorly engineered, either from ignorance or greed (it didn't say in *The History of Our State of California,* which I had to read in Poly), and almost immediately the sea began to reclaim them. Abbot Kinney's waterways to culture filled steadily with silt until they became standing pools of stagnant waste and were declared a health hazard in the twenties and covered over with asphalt.

Warren Speca's tiny yellow house is perched at the edge of one of the remaining canals. Today the water is filmed with a rainbow slick of oil and the banks are swarming with ducks, the grass bleached white from their droppings. Across the way is a spate of expensive condominiums, but on the canal side a row of bungalows that must have been built in Abbot Kinney's day has resisted development. Judging from the deteriorating wood and peeling paint and oddball toys and rusty garden equipment scattered across the backyards, they must be rentals owned by one stubborn or crazy landlord. Like Speca's cottage, they all have security bars covering the windows and doors, which detracts considerably from the vintage charm.

I follow the sounds of an easy-listening radio station to the driveway, where a Toyota 4x4 is humming and a man in worn jeans and cowboy boots is loading up the last of his toolboxes and slamming the door.

"Mr. Speca? Could I talk with you a minute? My name is Ana Grey, I'm with the FBI." I show him my identification.

He turns the engine off. As he's climbing out of the cab, he looks beyond my shoulder at something behind me that has suddenly caught his eye. I spin reflexively, expecting a gang-banger from the Shoreline Crips.

"Is that a 1971 Plymouth Barracuda?" he says, walking right past me.

"Actually it's a 1970." We are standing in the street as he inspects the car.

"Nice paint job. Is it yours?"

"Yes, it's mine."

He doesn't seem surprised or make anything out of it. "What've you got there, a 440 four barrel?"

"I looked for a six-pack but I couldn't get air conditioning. Tell me you're into 'cudas." .

Warren Speca goes to his truck and comes back with the latest issue of *Hemmings Motor News.* I can't help it. My heart jumps.

"My favorite bedside reading." He thumbs it so I can see all the turned-down pages.

"Mine, too."

"Think of all we'd have to talk about in bed." He runs a gaze across my chest and meets my eyes with an amused and frankly randy look. "What do you get for mileage?"

"Thirteen. But that's not why you own one of these cars."

"I dig it." He digs it all right. He has prematurely gray hair in a military buzz cut and soft full lips with a sensual curve to them. Weathered cheeks, eyes buried in sun creases. It's those lips, like Paul Newman's in *Sweet Bird of Youth,* that have allowed him to get away with what he's been getting away with since high school; lips that whisper an insistent invitation to meet with them and break all the rules.

"Pretty good maintenance?"

"Not too much goes wrong. The alternator failed during the rain. The battery dies on you, things like that."

"But I bet it'll do the quarter mile in the fourteen-second bracket."

"I've had it up to a hundred on the freeway at night."

Warren Speca is fingering the red leather on the driver's seat. "Naughty girl."

"It was a high-speed chase through five counties ending in a four-way shoot-out, you know how it is."

He smiles. "Like that TV cop—what was his name—drove a car like this?"

"Mannix."

"Was it exactly like yours?"

"Exactly."

Warren Speca looks at me and then at the car, nodding slowly. "I am truly impressed."

"Well, *I'm* impressed," I chatter on, believing that I've got him heading down that garden path. "You're the only one I've ever met who knew that Mannix drove a Barracuda."

"I used to watch a lot of television in the sixties. Used to do a lot of other things, too."

"You and Claire Eberhardt?"

His eyes stay steady. "What about Claire?"

"When you guys went to high school together, I can see you two drinking beer, smoking whatever, spacing out watching TV. . . ."

His hands go into his front pockets. "All right. What the fuck is going on?"

I knew he'd come on like this sooner or later, so I just stay smooth.

"We have no interest in what went on before. We want to know if you're in contact with her now."

"Why?"

"Routine background check on the Eberhardts."

He waits a moment, looking for something in my face. Apparently I give it to him because he says, "I don't think so," and walks down the driveway back to his truck.

"What's the problem?" I find myself going after him.

"No problem. I don't have to talk to you, so have a nice day."

He backs the Toyota out.

"By the way"—he leans from the window—"Mannix drove a *Hemi* 'cuda."

"I knew that," I say, cheeks burning.

He ticks a finger back and forth reproachfully and heads off down the street.

■　　■　　■

I know I will get Warren Speca. He can't just challenge me and drive away.

I go back over the notes I took with Nurse Kathy in the submarine shop. She said Speca was "into some stuff" she wouldn't tell me about. I swivel up to the computer and run the criminal checks. Before I can take another sip of foul end-of-the-day coffee all the information I need comes up neatly on the screen.

I wait until nine o'clock that night to catch him at home. He picks up the phone with a dull, unguarded "hullo."

"Hello, Warren. It's Ana Grey with the FBI."

"I knew you'd call."

"You did?"

"You want to ask me out on a date."

Instantaneously discarding several other possible responses: "Actually I'm calling about your State of California conviction for possession of marijuana and cocaine with intent to distribute."

"Ancient history . . . but what about it?"

"I'll bet when you applied for your state contractor's license you left out the fact that you are a convicted felon."

There is a pause, then, "I don't get it, Ana. Why are you threatening me?"

"I want to talk to you about Claire Eberhardt."

"I'll talk to you if I can have an attorney present."

"Of course you can have an attorney present—" I am bluffing, the last thing I want is some lawyer getting on the horn to the Eberhardt's lawyer. "But this isn't about you, Warren, it's about Claire and her husband."

"I've got nothing against Randall," he says with dark defensiveness.

"Most people think Randall Eberhardt is a solid citizen, but I get the feeling you know differently."

Warren Speca agrees to meet me in the bar on top of the Huntley Hotel in Santa Monica the following afternoon.

■　■　■

The only way to get to Toppers bar is to ride the exterior elevator that climbs up the side of the hotel like a glass slug. Two nineteen-year-old secretaries are giggling and covering their eyes as the machinery shakes and whines and we rise slowly above palm trees and rooftops to a dreamlike suspension twenty stories above the ocean. I don't like it too much, either.

The doors open and I find myself in a Mexican cantina of white-washed stucco edged with indigo blue. Above two curved doorways it says in faded pink paint, "Acapulco" and "Santa Cruz"—one leads to a restaurant with pink tablecloths, the other to a bar covered by a bamboo roof. Warren Speca is sitting at the bar sipping a drink and wearing a big Mexican sombrero covered with tiny round mirrors.

A bartender with a dark moustache and slicked-back hair can't hold it in anymore and just cracks up.

"*Está loco.*" He nods toward Warren, who grins boyishly, the string dangling below his chin.

"What's in that drink?" I ask.

"Nothing. Soda water. I just wanted to get in the mood."

"For what? A bullfight?"

Warren slings the hat to the bartender, who hangs it back on a hook, still chuckling.

We take a window table in the cocktail lounge with a view of white and beige buildings with red and orange roofs stretching all the way to the tree line north of Montana.

The waitress brings me a nonalcoholic margarita over lime-scented crushed ice in a stemmed glass as big as a soup bowl.

"I'm out here in California minding my own business when I get a call from this lady Teddy Feign whose house got creamed by a mud slide."

"She's got more work for you. She's going to call."

"That's cool. So she says Claire Eberhardt recommended me, an old friend from high school. I don't actually grok to the fact that Claire might be out here on the West Coast, I figure it's some damn thing through our mothers. If you think Jewish mothers are bad, you don't know the Irish and Italians. You're not Jewish, are you?"

For a moment I'm stopped by a surge of anxiety, but I push through it: "My father was from El Salvador, my mother was American."

It's out on the table and it's not so bad.

"This turns out to be a major job and Mrs. Feign is pressuring me to finish so I start working weekends. She has this gigantic birthday party for her kid and a hundred of their closest friends, and I'm outside screwing with the circuit breaker when these two French doors suddenly pop open and Claire Eberhardt comes flying out. I mean *flying*. They were dummy doors that were never supposed to be used, but what did Claire know. So she goes flying into a ditch and I help her up and it's Claire McCarthy from Savin Hill. She's put on a little weight but there's no doubt about it. She's so embarrassed and fucked up she doesn't recognize me—truthfully, it's been fifteen years—so I let her go.

"Later on, I walk into the kitchen and there she is looking out the window at the party like a wallflower—and Claire was never a wallflower—tears streaming down her face. She sees me and tries to cover it up.

" 'Claire McCarthy,' I say. 'What've you been up to? Tell me you don't recognize me.'

"Finally she gets it. 'I couldn't figure out what you were doing here, she says, then I remembered I gave Teddy your number. Why didn't you say something outside when I was doing my Chevy Chase routine?'

" 'Didn't want to embarrass you.'

" 'I must have looked like an idiot.'

"I go, 'No, you only looked scared.'

"So then I ask about her parents who are major alcoholics and we start talking and I tell her I'm in the program now, I don't drink, which blows her mind, and to cheer her up I point out this fat guy out there at the party wearing running shorts and a sweatshirt who's worth sixty million dollars.

" 'Thinks up one TV show, now he's worth sixty million. Go over there and rub against him, maybe it'll brush off.'

" 'You rub against him,' she says.

" 'I tried but he wasn't interested. Hey, for sixty million I'd do just about anything.'

" 'No, you wouldn't.'

" 'You're right. I wouldn't. What do I care? It's only money.'

"But Claire's staring at all those people again and getting teary, feeling pathetic about herself because her daughter's already part of the crowd and Claire knows she will never fit in.

" 'That's my daughter, Laura. She's best friends with the birthday girl. She loves California.'

"There's this huge fancy birthday cake on the counter, so I take my finger"—he demonstrates on the edge of the cocktail table—"and wipe it all around the edge, and rub the chocolate frosting into my gums and I say to Claire, 'You can't take these people seriously.'

"She looks at me and picks off one of the flowers from the cake and puts it into her mouth and I know right then and there we're going to sleep together."

■   ■   ■

"Did you and Claire Eberhardt sleep together?"

"Two and three times a week. Mostly in my place, although once we made it in her husband's bed. I thought for about thirty seconds she was actually going to leave him for me."

He smiles ruefully.

"Was she in love with you?"

Warren Speca folds his arms and tips back in the chair with bare knees apart, squinting toward the haze moving in over the sea. He's come from work and is still wearing beat-up shorts, heavy boots, and crew socks.

"The thing she loved most about me—unfortunately—was when we'd lie around afterward and talk about the old neighborhood. She'd get into these memories, did I remember what she was like when she was twelve, that sort of crap. Of course the sex was pretty good too."

I can't help knowing that it was.

"She hated it out here. People like Teddy Feign scared the shit out of her, but she felt a lot of pressure to be like them. She was glad for an excuse not to hang out with Teddy anymore. She had a much better time with me," he adds, with a teasing grin.

"So where was all this pressure coming from?"

"Dr. Randall, where else? I always thought the guy was a snob. Here was his wife drying up inside and he's out playing Doctor to the Stars."

"With Jayne Mason?"

"Dig this: he had a pass for the security gate, a key to the front door, and Jayne Mason used to pick him up from his office in her limousine and take him around to charity dinners and the movies."

"Were they having an affair?"

"No, just for the hell of it. She gave him the key for emergency house calls."

"Why Randall?"

"Who knows. Because she felt like it and he was star-struck, like any dope just in from the boonies. For a doctor, I've got to tell you, he wasn't very smart. I've done a lot of work for movie stars. It doesn't take many brain cells to figure out all they want to do is use you."

"So you think Jayne Mason was using Randall Eberhardt."

"Using him how?"

"To get drugs."

"No, to me it was just the opposite. He was trying to get her *off* drugs. I'll tell you something."

He swirls the sugar in a second iced tea.

"Claire came to that birthday party alone, right, and met me and the rest is history. The reason why Randall wasn't there and couldn't come was because he had to go out to Malibu to take care of Jayne Mason, who supposedly had a cold."

He leans forward and taps a finger on the Mexican tile inlaid in the tabletop.

"Claire told me later when he got out there he found Jayne Mason lying in bed, completely naked, covered with her own feces and vomit."

He taps each word for emphasis: *her own feces and vomit.*

"It's a good thing he had that key because she'd almost OD'd on downers. That's when he checked her into the Betty Ford Center."

I think about it.

"Then where did she get the drugs?"

He shrugs. "She must have a street connection somewhere."

I nod. It's a good guess, an educated guess you might say. But if Randall Eberhardt weren't supplying Jayne Mason with narcotics, why is she going after the doctor now, as if her life depends on it?

■   ■   ■

To the west a gray mist has blended the ocean with the sky, creating a curtain of fog. The surf looks mild and green in the late afternoon light, playful, benign. Bicycle wheels spinning along the bike path, tiny as gears in a watch, throw off faint metallic sparks of light.

"Are you still seeing Claire?"

"It ended a couple of months ago when she decided she was still in love with Randall. No surprise. She could never let go, she clings to him like a life raft."

"How did it end between you two?"

He rubs a knuckle across his short hair.

"Pretty bad. She was at my place, late getting home, she calls Teddy Feign's because Laura was over there playing with their little girl. . . ." He sighs. "And she finds out over the phone that Laura's fallen into the pool and almost bought the farm."

I've put the pen down and stopped taking notes. My heart is beating faster because I know from his dread tone of voice—and because I shouldn't be here in Claire Eberhardt's place, feeling what she must have been feeling sitting across from this hunk Warren Speca—that we are about to make an abrupt turn onto a dangerous track.

"We jump into my truck and race over to Teddy's house. Claire's saying the Our Father all the way. Teddy wasn't home at the time. The housekeepers already called 911 and the street was jammed with paramedics and cop cars. You don't want to ever come home to that. Claire gets out of the truck and almost faints into the arms of this black woman cop. I don't go into the house—what am I doing there, right?—but Claire comes back out to tell me Laura's all right, she never even lost consciousness. Turns out it was the house-keeper's fault."

"Which housekeeper?"

"I forget her name."

"Was it Violeta?"

"Yeah. Violeta."

I feel a dull thud in the chest, the way you do when you hear something bad about someone you have come to like.

"Did you know Violeta?"

"Uh-uh. I think I ran into her once, when I showed up at Claire's."

"When was that?"

"One time toward the end. We didn't see each other for a month after the thing with Laura, then Claire told me it was over."

"Why? Guilty conscience?"

"Yeah, she thought it was all her fault, but also she claimed going through it with Randall brought them together." He makes a wry sideways frown. "What can I tell you? The thrill was gone."

He flicks the empty glass forward with thumb and forefinger.

"This is the first place I took her when we started being together."

We wait for the elevator in front of a large antique mirror in a wooden frame painted with roses. Warren Speca has put on a baseball cap that says Warner Bros. Studios. I look at us in the mirror. The bartender is slipping a pot of chili into the steam tray in preparation for happy hour. The elevator arrives, empty. We step inside.

"The first time we kissed was right here."

We stand in silence as the capsule shimmies and starts its descent, the way they stood, close together, awkward and lusting.

If he surprised me with a kiss the way he first kissed Claire Eberhardt, I know it would be just a brush, a tease, nothing you could take offense about, the way it was for her: a token from an old friend, remembrance of the days in high school when they weren't afraid of what they didn't know, when they rushed headlong into it all—a summer night in a moving car and all the windows down, intoxicated by the syrupy vapor of Southern Comfort and the jumbled weedy smells of a pitch-dark country road. The headlights off, blind, picking up speed.

SIXTEEN

THE NEXT DAY I get some disturbing information from Boston.

"Bay Pharmacy searched their records back to 1985 and the only prescriptions filled by Claudia Van Hoven were for an eye infection and some female problems," Wild Bill says casually over the phone. "Even so they weren't written by Randall Eberhardt."

"Maybe she went to another drugstore and didn't remember the name right."

"I'm checking into that now, little señorita."

Suddenly I'm not buying Wild Bill's jocularity. The breathless quality of his voice betrays fear, which is instantly communicated to me in a rush of adrenaline.

"We're in trouble, aren't we?"

"Not by a long shot."

"Yes, we are." The panic mounts quickly. "She was lying to us out there in the park."

"Now that doesn't make any sense at all." The more he tries to be reassuring, the more I know the ship is sinking fast. "Why would she make up something like that?"

"I don't know, I don't know, but we've got to find some other substantiation to her claim that Eberhardt overprescribed. Otherwise we have no corroborating witness."

"I hear what you're telling me."

"Did you pull her hospital records?"

"Haven't had a moment—"

"I'll do it," I say abruptly, cutting him off with the touch of a button.

Four minutes later I am talking to Dr. Narayan, Randall Eberhardt's former boss at New England Deaconess Hospital. He says he will pull Van Hoven's chart by the afternoon and his lovely measured English accent is filled with promise. In my experience even the most educated people find it a turn-on to ride posse with the FBI.

The Bureau requires us to pass physical fitness tests every six months and you get three hours a week built into your schedule for exercise, so it isn't goofing off for me to walk across the parking lot to the Westwood Community Recreation Center on Sepulveda and do a twenty-two-minute mile in the public pool. I am so wired there is nothing else but to hurtle myself down a tunnel of water as fast as I can, focusing on the big cross on the opposite wall, taking pleasure in the neat flip turn and the rhythm of the push-off and the glide and the power that comes from those abdominals I've been crunching every night; today I have power to spare and even welcome the challenge of the lady in the orange bathing suit paddling down the center of the fast lane, which adds another 10 percent of effort to the workout.

I return to the office with wet hair and all cylinders firing smoothly. After a good swim I am loose enough to cope with anything, which is fortunate because Rosalind has a message waiting for me to call Dr. Narayan in Boston.

"Claudia Van Hoven was treated here for fractures and trauma sustained in an automobile accident," the doctor tells me enthusiastically. "Before that she had a long history of psychiatric treatment for all sorts of illness from depression to schizophrenia until finally she was hospitalized at Ridgeview Institute in Georgia and accurately diagnosed with dissociative identity disorder, which we used to call multiple personality disorder."

"Hold it. You're telling me she's one of those people who takes on different voices and personalities?"

"Right."

"Isn't that kind of far out?"

"Dissociative identity disorder is probably more common than you realize. It's a mechanism for the psyche to avoid trauma by literally becoming another person. In Ms. Van Hoven's case it seems to have begun in early adolescence, stemming from sexual abuse by a neighbor. From the looks of this record," he goes on, "twenty-three separate personalities have been documented in the patient, including an aggressive male named Allan."

"She said Allan was her helper."

"Yes, some patients refer to certain alters as 'helpers'—that is, helping personalities. Did you notice any switching when you talked to her?"

"Switching?"

"Did you actually see her become somebody else through a change in voice pattern or physical attitude—"

"Jesus, no." A chill goes through me.

"Interesting."

Struggling to get back to understandable reality, "Can we believe what she told us about Dr. Eberhardt?"

"That would be tricky."

"But she seemed totally rational. She was intelligent and shy—said she played the violin."

"That was probably her personality named Becky."

"*Becky!* What is this—the Twilight Zone? Look, she had a husband and a baby. She was wheeling a stroller."

"Did you actually see the baby?"

"No. But it was starting to rain," as if that explains anything.

Dr. Narayan's tone is gentle. "I'm sorry to tell you that I doubt very much if there even was a baby in that carriage."

The idea that she was out there in the cold pretending to be taking care of a baby—and that I bought it—leaves me awed. Finally:

"In your professional opinion, given her condition, is there any way Claudia Van Hoven could make a credible witness in a court of law?"

"Ultimately? Not a chance."

I hang up the phone and take my head in my hands, hoping to crush my temples together into an unrecognizable mass. The sleeves and chest of the Bank Dick's Undercover Disguise hanging on the coatrack nearby are puffed out and stiff as if filled with expanding hot air.

I have no corroborating witness.

And Galloway is expecting results tomorrow.

I could whine to my boss that I had been guaranteed the Van Hoven gal was good, but that the old drunk in Boston screwed up by not checking her out. As angry as I am right now, I can't bring myself to give up Wild Bill. A letter of censure would only jeopardize his retirement and besides it would not solve my problem, which is to present hard evidence of Randall Eberhardt's guilt.

For a long time I sit there with my mind scrambling like a rat inside a wall pawing with needle nails. I make notes, I make charts, but I can't see how to make a case against the doctor. All we have is an actress's unconfirmed story. Then the phone rings and it is Jayne Mason herself.

She is the last person I want to talk to. I'm not interested in helicopters flying over her property, or maybe this time it's a late garbage collection she wants me to fix.

Surprisingly, she is totally contrite. She needs to talk to me but doesn't want to go into it further on the telephone, may we meet?

Since, the last time, it took about a month to arrange a meeting and then she showed up a week early and at a completely different location, I am somewhat grouchy and suspicious of the entire venture, but she promises her car will pick me up in front of the Federal Building at 4:45 that afternoon, and it does.

■　■　■

It quickens the heartbeat to walk past the crowd to a shiny black limousine waiting just for me. Heads turn. I feel giddy and a dufus grin has plastered itself across my face.

Tom Pauley opens the door with a knowing nod. It's not like climbing into a car, it's like entering a room, a room that smells of lipstick and fine leather, with pearly white panels of light glowing around the edges, a chrome shelf holding crystal decanters with silver tags around their necks—Whiskey, Rye, Gin. I can stretch out my legs and still be miles away from the state-of-the-art console with built-in TV, VCR, CD player, and tape deck, above which a sheet of dark glass separates us from the driver. There are two telephones, a fax, and even a clip-on holder for what looks like a long test tube that holds one yellow rose. As we leave the curb a row of glasses tinkles against a mirrored backlight and a pile of scripts slides across a miniature kilim rug, spreading itself out like a fan.

"Thank you for coming, Ana, dear."

Jayne Mason, fully made up with Parisian red lips and dark shadowed eyes, hair pinned up in a twist, briefly puts her hand on mine, then turns back toward the window with a pensive stare. She is wearing hot pink silky trousers with white heels and a hot pink silk T-shirt underneath a white blazer with the sleeves pushed up. There is a multitude of gold bangles on each wrist and around her neck a pearl choker with some sort of sparkly thing hanging off (it's hard to see in the soft light). She looks like she means business, in a Palm Springs sort of way. Sitting so close I can catch her body scent—like a lingerie drawer spiced by a clove sachet.

It is easy to picture how Randall Eberhardt was drawn into this sultry female womb, accompanying Miss Mason to exclusive fund-raiser dinners, wheeling around town in a private bubble, protected by one-way tinted glass. As I observe a group of office workers waiting for a light to change on Wilshire Boulevard, I realize that the ability to see people when they can't see you is usually reserved for us law enforcement types; what a thrill it must have been for the doctor to share the privilege.

Then Jayne Mason begins to sing. Her head is still turned away from me and the voice is musing and low, as if I weren't there:

"In the wee small hours of the morning / While the whole wide world is fast asleep . . ."

So this is what all the attention and fussing is about, why people put up with the silliness and the excess, why Magda Stockman has chosen to place her body between Jayne Mason and the rest of the world, why someone like my grandfather could actually be moved by a performance: this gift.

I steady myself as the limousine rocks gently around a corner, listening to Jayne Mason's voice, unadulterated and flawless; for this moment, one of the elite.

. . .

We enter the Century City Shopping Center by some VIP entrance I never knew existed, parking behind another limousine, this one a double stretch in white. Jayne Mason puts on big dark glasses and fits a pale straw fedora over her French twist.

"Forgive me. I have to check one thing," she says as Pauley comes around to open the door.

So I get out and follow. On the escalator I say, "If I'd known we were coming here, I would have brought my humidifier," which of course makes no sense to her but she isn't interested anyway, eyes on the widening bright space above us.

Once we hit solid ground she's off like a smart missile weaving through the crowd toward a predetermined target. I have to quicken my pace to keep up. I've never seen a woman move so effortlessly in high heels. She is fixed dead ahead and pays no attention to the stares that come her way, shedding them off like raindrops from a nose cone. The nice thing about Century City is that it is an open-air mall and you get sunshine and updrafts and outdoor food stalls and guys selling cappuccino from wooden carts—but all of that goes by in a zip. The target is Bullock's.

She pulls the chrome handles on the glass doors and strides across the cosmetics department on the first floor.

I guess she's looking for a certain type of perfume because we make the circuit in about thirty seconds, past brass-trimmed counters, beautifully made-up salesgirls, customers, glossily lit displays, collections of fancy bottles, the two of us reflected in mirrored posts—she in vivid white and pink, me in khakis and a blazer—and gone. Overly sweet hot air envelops us and disperses in an instant as she hits the glass doors again and we're back out on the sidewalk.

"I guess they didn't have it."

"No."

"Want to try somewhere else?"

"If it's not at Bullock's, it's nowheresville," she says despondently.

We pass a chocolate shop and a place that sells dishes, keeping up the sprint.

"What did you want to talk about?"

"I *did* want to talk but now I'm not in the mood, are you?" she asks intimately, as if we're on a shopping spree and maybe we should have some tea and rest our feet.

"Actually, yeah, I'm ready to talk anytime. It's my job."

We're passing a complex of movie theaters.

"Have you seen *Days of Thunder*?" she asks.

"Not yet, but I like Tom Cruise."

A modest crowd is lining up to buy tickets for the early bird shows. Without another word, Jayne Mason walks ahead of everyone, shows the cashier some kind of card, gets two tickets with no exchange of cash, and we're off on another escalator up to the lobby.

This is definitely a left turn in the proceedings.

"I'm not sure I can do this—"

"Oh screw that," she says. "Let's go look at Tom Cruise."

So we do. We actually do. We sit there and eat popcorn, Jayne Mason and me. It's my kind of movie, full of bravado, and I enjoy it tremendously.

" 'Live fast, die young, and leave a good-looking corpse,' " Jayne Mason observes as we step out of the theater. "That was my line in a picture I made with Stewart Granger. Now *he* was a dreamboat."

It is dark. Small white lights entwined in the trees and colorful banners flying off the Food Market create a carnival effect. People sit under yellow umbrellas eating teriyaki and kebabs and cheeseburgers at outside tables with their jackets buttoned up on this cool early summer evening, shoppers whisk by with floating white sacks. I feel flushed with the excitement of being on a first date: I like this person. I want to know more.

"Let's eat. Someplace wonderful," Jayne decides, and I acquiesce happily, enjoying the extraordinary experience of walking beside a world-famous movie star and the secret pleasure of knowing we are going back to a VIP entrance where we will get into a private limousine and be driven across the city to someplace wonderful.

. . .

We pull up at an Italian restaurant with a modest neon sign and a small green canopy. Tom Pauley gives a wry salute as we leave him back at the car. What a job. No wonder he's down at the beach whenever possible. Inside there's a cozy bar hung with clusters of half-size Chianti bottles and a huge photo of JFK. The walls are covered with movie posters and head shots of Lucille Ball, Don Rickles, and President Eisenhower, among others. I don't see Jayne Mason in the crowd.

A slump-shouldered gentleman in a worn tuxedo says, "Good to see you again, Miss Mason," and leads us into the main room, which is awash in soft orange-red light. The sweeping curved banquettes are orange-red and an assortment of ginger-jar lamps with linen shades have orange-red bulbs. Most of the tables are empty and white napkins are standing up throughout the restaurant like a herd of rabbit ears.

We pass a display case filled with models of trucks and pictures of that same slump-shouldered gentleman, thirty years younger, with the Pope. We pass two geezers complaining about losing at Santa Anita, and a decked-out blonde with some sleazeball type talking real estate deals. The waiters seem too old and depressed to notice their famous customer, but then I recognize an actor from a cop show and figure this must be a Hollywood hangout, the real thing.

"I've never had good luck with men and so I've always had to fend for myself," Jayne says suddenly.

We are sharing an appetizer of fried zucchini, which, truthfully, they do better at T.G.I. Fridays. Jayne is drinking vermouth and I'm enjoying my 7UP and the clown art on the walls.

"My third husband, the used car king, was the final straw. He treated me like a piece of dirt under his feet. I used to wonder why the manicurist came out of his office wiping her lips."

She pours us each more water from a small ceramic pitcher in the shape of a rooster head, which is the signature piece of the restaurant.

"He was the one who spent all my money. We were divorced in 1959. What else could a gal from Oklahoma do, flat broke with two children to support, except sing and dance her little heart out? So I did dinner theater, regional theater, hotel bars, any gig I could get, from Vegas to Palm Beach to Poophead, Iowa, and back. I did that for years, then I met Maggie Stockman."

"She's a smart lady."

"She has no life," Jayne says. "Her clients are her life." Mason points the broken end of a bread stick at me. "She is an angel sent from heaven. Excuse me."

On her way to the ladies' room she passes a husband and wife wearing formal clothes. It is amusing to watch them trying to say, "That's Jayne Mason," without moving their lips.

She returns with fresh lipstick and Magda Stockman still on her mind.

"Maggie was the one who told me I should do drama. She convinced Joe Papp to take a risk with *A Doll's House* and it changed my life, not only because it was wildly successful, but because it changed my thinking about myself."

"You knew you were good."

"I knew I was an actress. I left Ninety-first Street, rented a house in the Hollywood Hills, and within three years I won my first Oscar. You see, it's all about self-image. We can't let anyone take that away from us."

A mumbling waiter brings two plates of Manicotti Dolly Parton. I had stared at the menu, confused by the Shrimp Angeli Mickey Rourke and the Chicken Dabney Coleman, and decided to get whatever she was getting.

"I'm sure you've heard terrible things about me—that I'm late on the set, that I'm drunk or high or rude, but let me tell you, *the crew loves me."* She drains the drink and says it again, *"The crew loves me,"* with too much emphasis and I wonder if the cocktail is already getting to her.

"I'm having a wonderful time," I say as we dig into our fat creamy noodles, "but what does this have to do with Randall Eberhardt?"

She folds her hands on the tablecloth so the bangles splay out with a golden splash. "This is why I am so passionate about bringing this man to justice. Despite everything I have learned, I am still a sucker for the male animal, and Randall Eberhardt took advantage of me all over again. I've worked too hard."

She accepts another vermouth. "I'm sure you're too smart to fall for that kind of thing."

"Not necessarily."

"How do you handle men?"

"I avoid them at all costs."

Jayne throws back her head and laughs. "Oh my *dear,* we don't want to do *that.*"

"It works."

She regards me quizzically, then hunches her shoulders in the white cotton jacket and works for a while on the Veal Johnny Carson.

"My third husband, the used car king, once secretly filmed us making love. Not many people know that. Do you have any idea how hard it is to find someone you can trust?"

"Yes, I do."

"Magda's the only one who's stood by me all these years. Thank God for her and my children and grandchildren. I've had a rough time of it, but I still believe in romance."

She catches the indulgence in my smile.

"I'll bet you think it's silly to wear all this makeup. I don't do it for men, I do it for myself. I wake up in the morning and look in the mirror and keep *putting it on* and *putting it on* until I see *something* looking back."

She laughs and I laugh with her, although trying to follow the increasing zigzag of her conversation has lost me.

"I did a musical directed by Vincente Minnelli. It was a Technicolor extravaganza and in one scene I wore a fox cape. Well, Mr. Minnelli had it sent to New York and dyed to match my eyes. Why? Because it was *romantic.*"

"I think I saw that one."

"Louis B. Mayer always told me his philosophy was to make beautiful pictures about beautiful people," she goes on with great sweep. "We all need romance, even you, Ana, dear. You are a serious young woman—I could see that right away—but there's a part of you that needs to blossom."

She is leaning over the table, fixing me with misty green-blue eyes. The pupils are dark and wide and wondering in the caressing orange-red sunset light.

"Give yourself the magic, Ana."

It is as if she has seen through to my soul, seen what was missing, and supplied it. I feel myself touched and melting. I nod. I want to say, Thank you.

Tom Pauley is holding the car door open as we exit the restaurant.

"Did you enjoy dinner?"

"Lovely, Tom," says Jayne with an edge.

Inside the limousine, she explains, "Now when I talk about romance, I don't necessarily mean between a sixty-year-old driver and a twenty-one-year-old wardrobe girl, not that I think there's anything *inherently* wrong, God knows John Barrymore was old enough to have been my grandfather at the time, but I do feel protective about my people and I'm afraid these two are heading for disaster."

"So Tom and Maureen are an item," confirming what I'd seen on the beach.

"Yes, but all is not well in the castle," Jayne sighs, "all is not well."

Pauley pulls the limousine into traffic.

"Take this." She hands me a rooster water pitcher she has evidently just filched from the restaurant under my very eyes. "To remember the evening."

I take it. It seems a harmless, endearing gesture. After the movie and the manicotti and the veal and the cheesecake and espresso, I feel cozy and content as a pet cat, stretching out and yawning unself-consciously, hoping Jayne Mason will start singing again.

Like Randall Eberhardt, I have totally lost my bearings.

■　　■　　■

Barbara looks up I enter her office carrying a large heavy glass containing two dozen yellow roses.

"For me? Are we getting engaged?"

I put the vase down.

"From Jayne Mason. On my desk this morning."

"Why?"

"Because I'm such an understanding person."

"You?"

"She said so in her note: 'Thank you for being understanding.' We went to the movies and dinner and she told me her philosophy of life."

Barbara's fair face flushes red. "You had dinner with Jayne Mason?"

"Just the two of us. She likes me." I sit down and cross my feet up on her desk.

"A once-in-a-lifetime experience," Barbara murmurs enviously.

"It was pretty amazing," I admit, still basking in the warmth of the limousine. " 'Live fast, die young, and leave a good-looking corpse.' She said that in one of her movies. I told her, Hey, Jayne baby, you're talking about *me!*"

"What else did she say about her philosophy of life?"

Barbara has stopped fingering the yellow petals. Her smile is tentative.

"Oh, she told a lot of great old Hollywood stories. You would have loved it. Like the time this guy had a fox cape dyed to match her eyes—"

"Who did?"

"Liza Minnelli's father."

"Vincente Minnelli? The director?" she asks incredulously.

"Yeah, she was doing a picture with him and he sent this fur to New York to be dyed . . . What's wrong?"

Barbara's mouth is tight and her exhilaration has drained to pale concern.

"That was Norma Shearer in *Marie Antoinette*."

"Can't be."

"It was one of the most excessive movies ever made. They spent a fortune on period antique furniture and incredible costumes and the wardrobe designer, Gilbert Adrian, even had a fox cape custom-dyed to match Norma Shearer's eyes. The punchline is, to save money they wound up shooting the movie in black-and-white. It's a famous story."

"But Jayne Mason said it happened to her."

"It didn't."

"Maybe she got mixed up."

"And that line about 'Live fast, die young'? That was John Derek in *Knock on Any Door* with Humphrey Bogart."

"Are you sure?"

"I'm sure."

I know it is futile to question the recall and accuracy of the Human Computer. I think of the rooster carafe and the intimate moment just for me. My feet drop off the desk and onto the floor.

"What's the matter?"

"She just takes things."

I don't know why this should be so upsetting and bewildering.

"Maybe she was acting."

"Uh-uh."

"Maybe she's crazy."

"She's not."

Barbara is dismayed. Even the Human Computer can't process this.

"I don't understand. These are *facts*. She openly lied. What unbelievable arrogance."

But I have processed it all too quickly.

"She's lying about the whole damn thing."

"The doctor?"

I nod. I think I'm going to cry.

"Check him out," Barbara advises softly. "You have to. For Galloway. One more time."

SEVENTEEN

I TRACK DOWN Donnato in the public cafeteria on the first floor of the building. He is sitting behind a pillar where nobody can find him, finishing a piece of blueberry pie and reading the *Wall Street Journal*.

"I'm between a rock and a hard place, Donnato." I tell him my troubles and eat the piece of crust he has left on the plate. "I need something for Galloway. I can't go back and say the trip to Boston was a bust and I've been chasing my tail ever since. I've got to find out for myself if the doctor is dirty."

An Indian woman in a yellow silk tunic edges to the table beside us and wearily sets down a tray. Another civil servant trying to make it to the next three-day weekend.

"It's time to check out the source. I think I should go undercover. Put on a wire, get in there as a patient, ask the doctor for painkillers and see if he'll give them to me."

"Why didn't you go to a wire before?"

"I never had the evidence to get Galloway to approve an undercover assignment."

"You still don't."

"Right. But I'm going to do it anyway."

"Without approval?"

I nod, swallowing down the anxiety that is rising in my throat like acid vomitus.

"I know this is a little out of bounds—"

"Way out of bounds."

"Will you partner up with me? Monitor the wire?"

"On a maverick operation? What if it goes bust?"

"It can't go bust, it's too simple. You and I have each done this routine a thousand times."

Donnato rubs his beard upward against the grain in that impatient way of his when he wants to be done with an annoying thought.

"It's a risk."

"A controlled risk."

Donnato shakes his head. "Not my thing."

"I understand." I feel hot and foolish and suddenly lost. "That's okay. I'll use a microcassette in my purse."

Donnato drains the last of his lemonade.

"Pumpkin started law school, did I tell you?"

"Good for her."

"I was hoping she'd wait until Jeremy's settled in high school, but that's two more years."

"Is he having a tough time?"

"Working with a tutor, but with attention deficit disorder, which is the latest thing they say he's got, it's an ongoing process. Rochelle didn't want to wait."

He stands and dumps his garbage. The public cafeteria smells of hot dogs sitting in greasy water. We walk past a table of government co-workers: a Japanese clerk using chopsticks to eat food she brought from home in a plastic box, two white males in shirtsleeves, and a Filipino girl with a fake Gucci bag. What on earth do they have to say to one another?

When we get to the door, he opens it for me.

"I'll partner up," he says.

I look at him with gratitude but his eyes are focused across the plaza, where members of a film crew are setting up folding canvas chairs and dragging cables through the shrubbery, fitting a big ungainly camera onto a tripod and unpacking black cases filled with lighting equipment. A crowd of workers from the Federal Building is gawking at some television actress whose mane of blond hair looks familiar. I can see that if she were Jayne Mason it would cause a serious disturbance. We head straight through until a kid with a walkie-talkie stops us and makes us go around to the side doors. I don't like being bossed around by civilians and I resent like hell being called "Madame."

You're supposed to get used to film crews shooting on location in Los Angeles, it's good for the local economy and some people think it's a thrill, but to me it's nothing but a pain in the ass, all these self-important types taking over our plaza like they own it because—let's face it—movie people are special, they are above life.

Meanwhile, down here in the public cafeteria, we are all the same.

■   ■   ■

The cubicle where you check out surveillance equipment is in the southeast corner of the garage behind an unmarked door.

I hate going there because the clerk running it has a terrible purple birthmark across half his face and compensates by being unbearably helpful, nodding and making little bows over every transaction. He's got a pocket-size TV tuned to the soaps and three postcards pinned to the wall that people sent him from vacations, and he stays down there all day in his dark orderly little warren, tape recorders and cameras neatly numbered and stowed on metal shelving. Filling out the forms in duplicate, you know that if there is an anteroom to hell this is it, and if there is a keeper who suffers for eternity this poor guy with the birthmark must be he, or maybe your discomfort is appropriate for the act you are about to commit, the threshold you are about to cross: spying on citizens, recording their most intimate acts.

I finesse an appointment with Dr. Eberhardt by pleading with the receptionist that I have incapacitating back pain from a recent car accident in which I was rear-ended, thinking of the incident in

Boston that still gives me a twinge after a hard set of butterfly. She asks who referred me and for one appalling moment I don't have an answer. Then:

"I overheard two women in the gym talking about Dr. Eberhardt. They said he's the best."

"We think so," the girl responds warmly.

I tell her my name is Amanda Griffin and she gives me an appointment for 9:45 the next day.

■   ■   ■

From the pile of clothes on the floor in the back of my closet I dig out a pleated gray skirt and cranberry silk blouse, dating from my early days as an agent when I thought the way to get ahead was by dressing smart. After a few undercover assignments where you had to sit in a car on stakeout for ten hours at a stretch I abandoned my suits and heels and started wearing whatever I felt like to work, discovering it was a lot more fun to be one of the boys than an uptight corporate girl. In my jewelry box I find a string of plump fake pearls and in an overstuffed bathroom drawer an old tube of wine red lipstick. It's kind of a kick, like getting dressed for a play, with the same nervousness. I look in the mirror and the word that comes reflecting back is "straight." I am pleased with the transformation. It fits Amanda Griffin, who, I have decided, is a legal secretary.

I am swinging a long lost imitation-lizard bag over my shoulder and my keys are in my hand when the phone rings. It is Poppy.

"I can't talk, I'm on a case, the Jayne Mason thing."

"I need five minutes of your time."

"Can I call you back later?"

As usual my assertions are meaningless.

"I want you to go to the bank on Wilshire, what's it called—"

"Security National?"

I put my keys down on the counter but they are still contained in my clenched fist.

"And get some papers out of my safe-deposit box."

I force myself to expel the breath I have been holding in frustration.

"I want my birth certificate, my will, everything that's in there, clean it out."

"Okay."

"We've got a fight on our hands, Annie."

Boiling with impatience now, I can just imagine Poppy engaged in a lawsuit with some neighbor who doesn't like the way he lets his Buick slop over into two parking spaces.

"Can we talk about this later?"

"The doctor says I've come down with cancer, but I told him it's bullshit."

Some kind of ice-cold chemical flushes through my bowels.

"What do you mean, 'cancer'?"

"Oh I found some bumps in my neck when I was shaving."

My fist unclenches. The keys have left deep marks in the flesh of my palm.

"It sounds serious."

"Uh-uh. Not to worry. This is not the one that takes me down."

I suddenly have to go to the bathroom. I have to be in Santa Monica in ten minutes.

"I'll drive out and see you as soon as I can."

"No need. I'm fine. Just put the papers in the mail. Nothing's going to happen to me. Go rescue my gal Jayne from the bad guys."

■　　■　　■

Donnato parks at a meter in front of the Dana Orthopedic Clinic.

He opens a briefcase. Inside is a Nagra tape recorder hooked up to a radio receiver. I place the radio transmitter inside the shoulder bag.

"What's your cover?"

"Amanda Griffin. She's a legal secretary who lives in Mar Vista with her two cats." My voice sounds oddly flat.

"Keep it simple," Donnato admonishes, twisting the plug into his ear. "And whatever you do—don't entrap the bastard. Talk into your handbag."

I hum into the radio receiver and the needles on the Nagra jump. Without another word I get out of the car and cross the sidewalk and walk up the steps to Dr. Eberhardt's office.

I barely have a chance to settle against those curved peach and gray benches when a young woman in a white lab coat opens a door, calling softly, "Amanda Griffin?"

She shows me to an examining room. A cotton gown is folded on the table.

"Take everything off except your panties. Put the gown on with the opening in back. Dr. Eberhardt will be just a few minutes."

She leaves. I place the bag with the radio transmitter on a chair close to the examining table.

I start taking off my clothes, then realize that I am not wearing panties beneath the carefully chosen daytime sheer neutral panty hose and that I must face the doctor, the criminal suspect of this investigation, totally naked.

Clutching the gown around myself uneasily, I pad barefoot across the spotless linoleum and start looking through cabinets and drawers. I find several shelves filled with a drug called Naprosyn— "Successful management of arthritis," it says on the cartons—gauze, towels, child-size smocks printed with dinosaurs. All the cabinets are open except for the lower one near the window, which is locked just as Jayne Mason described. My heartbeat increases with the possibility that inside are shoe boxes full of Mexican narcotics.

A knock on the door. I quickly sit in a chair as the doctor comes in.

"Amanda Griffin? I'm Dr. Eberhardt." A smile, a dry handshake, eyes on Amanda Griffin's empty chart. "You had a car accident and your back is giving you pain."

I have seen the subject only that one time across the alley. He is bigger than I remembered but somehow softer too, wearing not a starched white lab coat but loose short-sleeved green hospital scrubs revealing well-developed biceps. His sandy-colored hair is expensively styled and he wears steel-rimmed reading glasses low on the nose. Soft and helpless inside the gown, I shrink from the sense of privilege that emanates from Randall Eberhardt, in his physical assurance and in the firm sense of medical authority that is sealed for the world by the crest on his Harvard class ring.

He casually hops up on the examining table and crosses his feet in big puffy blue paper boots. Peering affably over the glasses, he asks, "How fast were you going when you were hit?"

"I was going nowhere. Some punk rear-ended me when I was stopped for a light. On Cushing Avenue. It happened in Boston."

"I'm from Boston," he says. "I know all about Massachusetts drivers."

He writes on the chart. I watch the muscles in his smooth tan forearms.

"You're in great shape," says Amanda Griffin, who is a bit of a dork. "Do they pump iron in Boston?"

"Not like here. I have to work out for two reasons: to practice orthopedics and keep up with my kids."

"They keep you running, don't they?"

"My little girl is a climber. I swear she's part monkey. You come home and she's sitting on top of the piano. You should see her balancing on the edge of the play structure with the seven-year-olds, it gives me arrhythmia. And quickly her baby brother is following in her footsteps. Were you looking up in the rearview mirror when you were hit?"

"No, I was looking down, trying to read a map."

"Probably saved your neck from getting whiplash."

"I don't have kids, I'm not even married," volunteers Amanda.

"Kids give you perspective on what's important."

"What's important, doctor?"

"The *only* thing that's important to me is my wife and children."

"And making a lot of money helps."

"I like making money," Randall Eberhardt admits with easy candor, rubbing the side of his nose. "But I don't care about 'stuff,' which means in this town people look at you like you're some other life form."

"I know. You've got all those film stars showing off all over the place."

"I actually enjoy entertainment people. I'm basically a boring uncreative jock, so I find them fascinating."

I can see why Jayne Mason liked to take Randall Eberhardt around in her limousine. In the still close smog of Los Angeles he is an impertinent gust of a crisp New England fall. And cute, too.

He continues to ask questions, writing down Amanda Griffin's answers with a Mont Blanc pen held between large powerful fingers. There is no gray in his hair; he carries his age and stress in deep brown bags beneath his eyes. It is now my job to discover what other darkness might be hidden there.

"I need some painkillers, Dr. Eberhardt. My back is killing me, I can't sleep."

He puts the chart down and climbs off the table.

"Let's take a look."

I get up and stand in the middle of the floor.

Our voices are being transmitted to Donnato's ear and simultaneously onto magnetic recording tape, a manipulated dialogue that will be studied later as if it were scientific fact.

But the tape cannot document the illicit thrill of his warm, firm fingertips as I stand naked before him, turning as requested so he may part the gown, so my vulnerable bare back may be exposed and spine examined by his intelligent hands slowly, curiously, piece by piece. Can a healer locate the site of one's pain just by touch? Perhaps Dr. Eberhardt will discover mine. Not Amanda Griffin's, but Ana Grey's. It must be there in the bones, only to be read.

I am staring at the striped aqua wallpaper. My Poppy was examined in a medical room like this, a professionally designed environment meant to be dim and soothing to the patient who is being told the bumps in his neck are cancerous, while the desert sun hurtles itself against the tinted window like a fireball from hell.

Randall Eberhardt's thumbs are pressing the trigger points along the top ridge of the pelvis and around the curve of the hips expertly, knowingly, putting my mind into a trance. *Does it hurt when I do this? Yes. No.* Playing along the tendons of the back of the neck, chin falling forward, the medicine man touches my naked body while Donnato listens in the car, like having two lovers at the same time, one man caressing you while the other man watches.

He puts his hands around my waist and tells me to bend over and touch my toes. The gown falls away and my bare buttocks are pushed up toward him and exposed. Gently he gathers the edges and holds them closed. Sweat falls from my armpits to the floor in large audible drops.

On the table now, lying flat, he is holding my foot with instructions to press against his hand. My fingers tear the tissue paper beneath me, telling him how much it hurts, everything hurts, I am breathless.

A memory comes of a time once before when I was this vulnerable and defenseless. I am in the backyard of Poppy's house on Twelfth Street. It is night and I can't see very well except when headlights rake through the cracks in the wooden fence as cars pass in the alley. I am again between two males, both of whom love me and want to possess me. One is my young immigrant father and the other is Poppy.

They argue in loud voices. They pull my arms in opposite directions. My father wins and holds me to his chest in the most forceful sense memory of him I have ever experienced. My arms are wrapped around his neck and my legs are around his slight waist and I am clinging to him with my entire being. I want my father at this moment, as I lie here as a patient, now. The yearning is so intense that it burns through my most present emotion, which I thought was sadness concerning Poppy's diagnosis. As the sadness dissolves I can see it has been nothing but a curtain to mask my true sentiment about my grandfather, a feeling that hurtles at me now like that comet from hell smashing through the tinted window glass: I wish Poppy were dead.

The thought propels me off the table and sends me reaching for my clothes.

"What is it, Amanda?"

"I feel much better. Whatever you did to my back, it worked."

"I don't think I'm that much of a genius."

I am hooking on my bra at top speed under the gown. Dr. Eberhardt has one hand on the doorknob. He's uncomfortable watching me dress.

"See me in my consulting room."

"I don't think I need to, thanks."

He frowns, worried.

"Something's going on here. Let's talk about it."

My first clear thought: he's found us out. And then, oh, God, this is all on tape.

"I was really in shock after the accident but just talking about it helped."

Randall Eberhardt is standing close enough to show his concern and far enough away to give me space. His brown eyes have lost their academic preoccupation and are communicating sincerity and calm.

"Your back looks fine. Your muscle tone is excellent. You don't need X rays or physical therapy or any of that stuff. I'll bet you can beat this thing by yourself."

"But the pain comes back at night." I am doing my job like a robot broken into pieces still making meaningless sounds.

"Try aspirin and hot baths."

I have pulled on all my clothes except the panty hose, which I have jammed into the shoulder bag. I am wearing a wool skirt with no underpants and bare feet in heels.

"Is that all you can give me?"

"Amanda, if you are having a problem with drugs, I would like to refer you to a clinic."

■　　■　　■

I climb back into the car.

"Let's go."

Donnato takes his time rewinding the tape.

"That was the worst performance by an undercover operative I have ever witnessed."

"So I won't win the Academy Award, let's go."

"I want you to hear yourself."

"No"—I close the lid of the briefcase—"thanks."

Still Donnato doesn't start the car.

"He made you by the end of it."

"No way."

"He knew you were not a patient, that you were looking for drugs. That wasn't the plan." Donnato's voice is rising in an unsettling way.

"It doesn't matter."

"I've seen you perform some pretty reckless acts lately. I've seen you try to destroy your telephone—"

"Donnato—"

"I've seen you get into a pointless fight with Duane Carter and then threaten a lawsuit that could totally jeopardize your career, and now, after you drag me into it, you abort an undercover assignment."

"An *unauthorized* undercover assignment."

"Even better."

"That's why you're mad. I dragged you out here and now you're all . . . nervous."

"I am not nervous, Ana. I have concerns about your stability."

I am quiet. I take two deep breaths. "Just before I came here I found out my grandfather has cancer. I know it shouldn't make a difference on a case, but it did and I'm sorry."

"Is he going to be okay?"

"You know Poppy. He'll beat it."

"Good."

But still Donnato does not start the car.

"I'm concerned that you're over the edge emotionally. It comes from being hypervigilant and eating soup at midnight and not having a life. If it's too much, be a grown-up and get help. That's what Harvey McGinnis is there for," he says, referring to the shrink the Bureau keeps on retainer for agents who have gone around the bend.

"Harvey McGinnis wears a skirt," I retort. He does, he puts on a kilt for Christmas and for funerals when he gets to play the bagpipes.

"I care about you and you are being a wise ass." His cheeks are flushed, he is furious. "If you wig out again, I will have to notify Duane Carter that you should be evaluated as to your ability to carry a weapon."

"That's ridiculous."

"I don't think so."

"I found out what I needed to know, so just lighten up."

Finally he turns the engine and we drive. Neither of us says anything more all the way back to Westwood.

I am glad he doesn't know about the locked cabinet. Now the only way to bust into it would be with a court order.

But I don't need a court order. I don't need to look inside the cabinet, I don't even need the taped conversation to support the findings of my investigation.

Because I knew, from the moment he laid his doctor's healing hands on me, that Randall Eberhardt is innocent.

EIGHTEEN

I PUT ON the navy blue suit and go to see Galloway.

"I have been unable to substantiate Jayne Mason's claims against Dr. Randall Eberhardt."

Galloway has the blinds closed against the early afternoon glare. He is sitting stock-still, one elbow resting on the arm of the chair, two fingers propped up on the side of his head with a tense look as if he's got a killer headache.

"Keep going."

"A deep background check on the doctor turned up negative. A current investigation proved negative."

"Keep going."

His sullen passivity is unnerving.

"There is no evidence of illegal narcotics, of a Mexican connection, previous infractions, or other patients with the same complaint. All we have is Jayne Mason's story, which remains unconfirmed. She has also been found to lie about facts concerning her own life, which casts doubts on her character. And"—I pause—"I have reason to believe she stole your belt buckle."

"Now you're blowing my mind."

"Sorry."

Galloway delicately shifts the heavy weight of his head to two fingers of the opposite hand. "What about that lady back in Boston?"

"She . . . didn't turn out to be good."

I am suddenly mumbling as if my lips were shot up with Novocain, so Galloway asks me to repeat what I said and I have to say it twice.

"Since Jayne Mason's allegations against her physician have been investigated," I continue, "and no evidence of criminality has been found, I recommend that we drop the case. I'm sorry. That's not what you want to hear."

"Stop being so sorry."

"I took it as far as it goes."

Then there is silence.

"Let me ask you something." His eyelids lower like a drowsy crocodile. "If the doc is clean, why is Mason going after his balls?"

"I don't know."

"He fucking her?"

"I don't think so. I think she's just . . ."

"Nuts?"

"No, an actress and a known drug addict."

He nods with understanding. He knows an addict is an addict and it doesn't matter if she's paid five million dollars a picture; like Dennis Hill on cocaine and Wild Bill Walker on booze and John Roth in bed, her existence is simply about feeding an insatiable maw.

"She needs the power."

Galloway only grunts.

"I'm writing a report but I thought you'd want to know the results ASAP because of the . . . political situation."

After a moment Galloway stands, smooths his hair with both hands, and tugs back and forth on the belt of his slacks like an old man trying to get his undershorts to lie right after a long sit.

"I'll take care of it."

He seems refreshed. Out of the uneasiness. Resolved.

He even tells me I did a good job.

When I relate the play-by-play of the meeting to Barbara she gives me a high five, certain I will be getting my promotion to the Kidnapping and Extortion Squad by the end of the month.

■　　■　　■

But an hour later I receive a phone call from Magda Stockman.

"I have just spoken with Mr. Galloway and I am quite upset. Why did you close this case?"

"There wasn't a shred of evidence to indict the doctor."

"Not enough evidence? We gave you times, dates, dosages—"

"I'm sure you know it takes more than one person's accusations to make a case in court."

"There is something here that is not right."

"I was the chief investigator and I'm satisfied the case should be closed."

"I am not satisfied in the least."

"That's your privilege."

Stockman has refrained from raising her voice, still speaking in a deep monotone of authority, the Henry Kissinger of personal managers: "We feel enormously let down by you, Ana."

"We do?"

"We believed that as a woman you would understand the deeper issues."

"As a woman"—I am spitting mad and having a hard time censoring myself from being slanderous—"I think you and your client haven't got a clue about the deeper issues."

But she just rolls on in that smooth, inevitable tone:

"We must prevent Dr. Eberhardt from doing this again. Jayne wanted to keep everything quiet and discreet but the time has passed for discretion. I'm going to recommend that my client file a lawsuit against Dr. Eberhardt today and you can be certain the whole world will know about it tomorrow. I hope you don't get caught in the crossfire, Ana. I wouldn't want that to happen to someone as bright and promising as you."

When I hang up, the Bank Dick's Undercover Disguise gives Magda Stockman the finger. Hey, it wasn't me.

. . .

The next day I am awakened at five a.m. by the beating of my own heart. I lie on my stomach, face in the pillow, my whole body vibrating to a bass percussion as if listening to a pair of kettledrums through stereo headphones.

With the Mason case on ice I had decided I would leave work early and go over to the bank, get the papers from Poppy's safe-deposit box, and be on the freeway heading out to Desert Hot Springs before the traffic. It is going to be a long and stressful day, I rationalize, maybe that is why I woke myself up so painfully prematurely, to get ready.

But I am in such an edgy state that the only possible thing to do right now is to swim. I figure I can make the 5:30 a.m. workout run by the Southern California Aquatics Masters at the Santa Monica College pool. Believe it or not, fifty people show up regularly before dawn. You can swim to compete or to stay in shape or just because you are terrified that you are losing control of your own thoughts.

I bundle up in sweats and swing the Barracuda out onto Washington Boulevard. It is still dark and maybe fifty degrees and riding the empty streets matches my restless mood. I change in the unheated locker room, listening to the chatter of some UCLA students for whom this first swim of the day is just a warm-up for their friendship. They will breakfast together and meet later tonight to run a 5K. Alone, I stalk outside into the chill. The lights are on in the huge outdoor pool, all the swimmers gathered at the wall in Day Glo–colored caps, a bright vivid Kodacolor against the white steam rising off the surface into an indigo sky.

Then we are ten lanes of synchronized elbows and feet, neat masses of churning water chugging back and forth to a rhythm set by the coach. I am part of the pattern and nothing more, two swimmers behind the leader, five seconds apart, four laps in ninety seconds repeated six times and on to the next set. Halfway through the workout my mind gives up and accepts the beat. The panic subsides, at least for an hour.

I return to my apartment to take a hot shower and grab some things for the trip out to the desert and already there are two messages on my answering machine from the dispatcher, saying that Special Agent in Charge Galloway is looking for me.

Now the pounding of my heart makes sense. It is as if my body woke up this morning knowing the Mason case was not over yet.

Forty minutes later my hair is still wet and I've still got owl eyes from the imprint of the goggles as I hurry breathlessly into Galloway's office. He had been calling my machine from his car and was tied up in traffic, so I get to stare out the window at the full-blown bright day for twenty long minutes until he strides inside, closing the door with a slam. He is clenching a dead cigar in his teeth and his arms are full of newspapers which he tosses at me all at once.

I fumble through the headlines:

JAYNE MASON SUES DOCTOR; MALPRACTICE CITED

"MY DR. MADE ME AN ADDICT"—JAYNE MASON

"I AM A VICTIM," SAYS JAYNE MASON IN DRUG-RELATED SUIT

JAYNE MASON ALLEGES DOCTOR PRESCRIBED NARCOTICS; FBI INVOLVED

I have just a moment to absorb the impact like a quick jab to the solar plexus when he grabs a chair and pushes it up close to me, leaning forward so our knees almost touch. I recoil slowly against the sofa.

"The case is reopened."

"Because of the publicity?"

"You bet because of the publicity. I was on the phone with Washington past eleven last night. The Mason case is now a top story and it's going to be played in the media like the National Anthem."

"But we completed our investigation."

"Apparently it wasn't thorough enough."

"Yesterday you thought it was fine."

"I said *apparently*. It might have been good for us but it wasn't good for them." He jerks his head toward the window, indicating the entire civilian world.

"You know that stuff in the paper is a bunch of junk. It was planted by Magda Stockman."

"That's right. But I have to answer to the Director."

"You're going to reopen the case just for show?"

"Let's say it was a good investigation, but it didn't go far enough."

"How much farther can we go?"

"Undercover."

I blurt out. "We already went undercover."

"When was this?"

"You may not remember."

My forefinger is picking at a cuticle. Galloway is looking at me with the superior penetration of a law enforcement officer about to snag a suspect in an irrevocable lie.

"Help my memory, Ana."

"I went undercover to see if the doctor would give me illegal drugs. He didn't. In fact, he suggested I go to a clinic."

"You did this without authorization?"

"Correct."

"Who else was involved?"

"Nobody," I lie. "I had a microcassette in my purse."

I know my face is scarlet.

Galloway shakes his head in exasperation.

"Jesus Christ, Ana, all we need is to be sued for entrapment."

"I'm sorry."

"You realize I have to put a memo in your file."

"That's okay. My file is starting to look like target practice."

Galloway stares at me.

"If you want me to manufacture something against the doctor, I'll do it." I meet his eyes.

"You'll be out on your ass."

"Then tell me what you want."

Galloway stands up. "What do I want? What do I *want*?"

He spreads both hands in the air as if grabbing something ineffable, then rubs the tips of his fingers together as if it had just flown away.

"I see my mistake. Back in New York you and the media are family. Maybe not with every local bozo, but you and the TV news director and the cop shop reporter—you're working opposite sides of the street, but after hours you're going to meet in the same joint in Chinatown and eat egg foo yung. Out here nobody knows anybody, everything's a national story because Los Angeles is the capital of the world, and everybody's an adversary because they're only going to be around five minutes, so they've got five minutes to score. It's different . . ." He seems to be searching for the right word.

"It's Hollywood."

"What do I want?" He grabs one of the newspapers and holds it up in a crumpled bunch. "You see all this bullshit publicity of hers? I want to fight fire with fire. I want hot publicity for the Bureau on the same scale. Fanfare, visibility, the whole nine yards. I want the public to see we are doing our job."

"The doctor may have been suckered in," I say quietly. "Maybe she got him to write a prescription or two, but I'm telling you he's clean."

"Then let him come clean in lights. In lights across the fucking sky and we'll be fucking out of it."

I am sorry, more sorry than I could have ever imagined, that Galloway, for all his New York smarts, turns out to be a wimp like everybody else.

. . .

I call Poppy and Moby Dick answers the phone.

"What are you doing there?"

"I drove your grandpa for his treatment. He's back now. He's taking a nap."

"What kind of treatment?"

"Radiation therapy."

Hearing words of any sophistication coming from those beer-sucking lips causes you to sit up and make sure you're still tuned to the right channel, but these words are truly terrifying, because they mean that even Moby Dick has been forced to learn a new vocabulary concerning my grandfather—the vocabulary of serious illness.

"Tell him I'll be there soon, I'm just wrapping up a case. How's he doing?"

"A little wiped but bad as ever. You know the Commissioner."

■ ■ ■

Under the best of circumstances, a search and seizure takes a week to push through but I am empowered by fear. Aside from the excruciating pressure from Galloway I know I must go out and take control of Poppy's situation as soon as possible, so I heave myself against the bureaucracy the way you would bench-press twenty pounds more than you were ever capable of before, on the exhale and praying for a miracle.

I bully and beg. Little by little we build momentum. I get the title report back in a record six hours. It confirms that the converted Victorian on Fifteenth Street is owned by the Dana Orthopedic Clinic, Inc., of which Randall Eberhardt is chairman of the board. I go in person to the Federal Building on Los Angeles Street and hassle with the forfeiture attorneys, leaving with the paperwork in hand that the U.S. Attorney's office needs to issue a warrant and writ of entry, which will enable me to walk into Dr. Randall Eberhardt's office and take possession of all evidence in clear view on behalf of the federal government.

Twenty-four hours later—*fanfare and visibility*— six burly federal marshals wearing bright orange raid vests converge on the doctor's office as if it were a crack house in East L.A., accompanied by—*the whole nine yards*—a caravan of reporters and photographers and minicam crews from the local and national news who were leaked the information by our press relations department.

I have it on videotape, me leading the charge, Randall Eberhardt coming out to the reception area after his nurse has told him something unpleasant is going on.

"Good morning. I am Special Agent Ana Grey with the FBI. We have a seizure warrant for your office."

The doctor looks at me quizzically.

"Don't I know you? Did I ever see you as a patient?"

"It's possible. May we come in?"

"No, you may not come in."

"I have a warrant, sir."

"What does that mean?"

"It means that the contents of these offices are now the property of the United States government."

A search and seizure is generally the end of the line for the bad guys, because it means you have finally come around to collect the evidence that will indict them. They also don't like it because someone is taking away their toys and they are used to being the one who take from others. They'll rant and shout and deny or point their weapons or try to escape or break down and cry, but you rarely see a subject retain his dignity the way Dr. Eberhardt did that morning.

"Is this a result of the outrageous charges made by Jayne Mason against me in the press?"

"I can't discuss an ongoing investigation."

"I'd like to know," he says evenly. "Just for my own personal sense of the absurd."

"Maybe you would like to call your attorney."

"Maybe so. I've never been in the center of a media circus before." He picks up the phone but lowers it again without dialing when he sees the marshals heading for the examining rooms.

"Wait a minute, I have patients back there!"

I march past him like an S.S. commandant leading the infantry and Dr. Eberhardt's confidence gives way to horror as he realizes these indifferent thugs are truly going to invade his world, the world of medicine, like Nazis tramping through the great libraries of

Poland and burning them to the ground, a thousand years of reason perishing in the flames. Dread rises as Dr. Eberhardt begins to understand that reason won't protect him here; a lifetime spent puzzling out the exquisite logic of the bones can also be obliterated by a single senseless act.

"There's a locked cabinet back there," I say.

All of us have assembled in the examination room where I once posed as a patient. It is crowded now with the federal marshals, Eberhardt in the white lab coat, and two thunderstruck nurses.

"May we have the keys?"

He nods and one of the nurses hands them to me.

It is close and hot with too much breathing. I reach toward the lock like an observer outside my own drama, hoping that in the next moment I will be proven wrong and lose all credibility at the Bureau, that Jayne Mason will be vindicated and the shelves will be stuffed with narcotics—not because I want to see Eberhardt suffer, but at least then all this destruction would be for a reason.

"Why do you keep this cabinet locked, sir?"

"I do a lot of work with children who have disorders of the spine." Randall Eberhardt licks his lips as if they have suddenly become dry. "You know how kids get into everything."

There is silent tense anticipation in the room as the door swings open. Inside is a collection of tiny teddy bears.

"My patients give them to me. I used to keep them on display but they started disappearing. Then some kid would get upset because his special bear wasn't there on his next visit."

In front of everyone I must examine the teddy bears as solemnly as I would any evidence. Alone, I think I would have banged my head against the door. There must be a hundred little cutesy figures of every conceivable material—clay, calico, metal, origami, even homemade teddies of pink cotton balls with wiggly plastic eyes.

I run a flashlight over the inside of the cabinet, feeling for false compartments as if I am firmly in charge here, then get up from my knees. "Let's get started."

As the marshals pack medical equipment and records into cardboard cartons, Dr. Eberhardt shoulders his way down the hall toward the sound of hammering.

He opens the front door, appalled to find that a locksmith is already changing the locks and another guy is nailing up a sign over the dove gray paint that says "Property of the U.S. Marshals." Then, suddenly, he is confronted by a sea of cameras and questions shouted about charges by the actress Jayne Mason that illegal narcotics were dispensed from these offices, and that's when the shock sets in.

He turns back pale and disoriented.

"This isn't really happening to me." His eyes are watery and enlarged.

I take his arm and steer him away with pity, remembering that he once put a compassionate hand on me, guiding him to a quiet corner of the waiting room, where he slumps into a peach and gray chair with a look of dissociation that comes from being deeply violated, when the only way to escape the torture of humiliation is for the body and mind to shut down; a look of passive despair I have seen before in victims of rape.

THE FOUR ROADS

NINETEEN

THE SECURITY NATIONAL BANK building on Wilshire where Poppy opened a savings account as a young Santa Monica police officer is now the Ishimaru Bank of California. It must have gone through several face-lifts since the sixties, but all the changes have added up to nothing more than a box made of beige bricks, inside and out.

I imagine the vault is exactly the same as when Poppy first deposited his important papers. You don't move vaults around when you remodel. I'll bet every day for the past thirty years the time lock has clicked at 8:45 a.m. and the manager has spun the wheel, grunting and pulling the door open with both hands, leaving it ajar for the public to marvel at six inches of layered steel. It's still impressive, the way a mausoleum is impressive; the way you know, from the weight of the granite stones sealed together with mathematical precision, that inside this place nothing will change, ever.

A quiet pensive black woman with her hair pulled back into a ponytail and long crystal earrings checks my signature against a card and unlocks an interior gate. We pass through a massive doorway inlaid with a checkerboard pattern of brass and chrome to a small room lined with burnished gray doors on hinges. I hand her my key. She puts a blue heeled shoe on a stool to reach up and unlock number 638. Behind her is a sign that says "Emergency Ventilation" with a set of instructions. She steps down from the stool and places an oblong box on a desk inside a tiny cubicle with a door I can close for privacy, leaving me alone in the dead air.

I am stilled by a sense of dreadful sadness and it takes many moments to force myself to lift the long metal lid.

I had expected there would be nothing except the will rattling around in a cold empty box, but it is filled with an assortment of household stuff like a drawer casually pulled from a sideboard.

On top of the pile is a yellowed clipping from the *Santa Monica Evening Outlook* dated September 12, 1962. The headline reads, "'MEANEST THIEF' FEELS PANGS OF CONSCIENCE." The article tells the story of a partially paralyzed baseball fan who was carried to his seat by friends to watch the "exciting game" in Dodger Stadium. He left his wheelchair at the top of the aisle and it vanished. After some publicity, it turned up days later just a few blocks from the Santa Monica police station with the following note:

> I am that meanest of mean thieves who stole your wheelchair. I would like to offer an explanation if there can possibly be one. Yes, we did it as a practical joke, but I honestly thought the chair belonged to Walter O'Malley and was put there for an emergency. I still realize this offers nothing but a very low sense of humor.
>
> I hope if at all possible you may find it in your heart to forgive me. I think I will have learned a great lesson from this "joke" that backfired. I am really not that sarcastic of an individual and hope that both you and God will forgive me for this prank.
> Sorry

Accompanying the article is a photograph of Poppy with one hand on the recovered wheelchair. He looks young and vigorous with his crew cut and dark uniform. You can see the outline of the nightstick and the Smith & Wesson .38 on his belt. The caption explains:

> PARALYZED MAN'S WHEELCHAIR, stolen while its owner watched last week's game between Dodgers and Giants at Chavez Ravine, is inspected by Santa Monica patrolman Everett Morgan Grey. The owner has been offered a new chair by a rental firm.

What a poignant relic of a time when Santa Monica was a sleepy undiscovered seaside town and thieves had consciences and somebody thought that having your photograph in the local newspaper was an event of such importance that they entombed it in the bank.

Digging underneath my grandfather's moment of glory I find silver dollars worn to the color of pewter and Kennedy fifty-cent pieces wrapped in tissue, still as shiny as new. There is also a series E savings bond from 1960 with the face value of $100 made out to me, a brown photograph with a white scalloped edge of my mother as a baby being held by her parents, my grandfather's Last Will and Testament (naming me as the beneficiary of his estate), along with his birth certificate, my grandmother's birth certificate and social security card, insurance policies from 1955, a small notebook embossed *Your Child's Medical History* with a record of my childhood immunizations written in my mother's hand, a spiral note pad containing a ledger of household expenses for the year 1967, and, inside an envelope, my grandmother's gold wedding ring and a brooch with amber stones. Loose in the box are a small gold heart with an enameled pansy, some costume bracelets, and a thin string of real pearls that were given to my mother on her sixteenth birthday.

I touch these things and for a few moments my mother comes back to me, her quilted cotton apron, where I would sometimes be permitted to lay my head, woven with splatters of batter and oil, the residue of a hundred meals and a thousand washings—it was like inhaling the essence of comfort. I suddenly remember that her nylons smelled of tannin and autumn leaves, drying on the towel rack in the bathroom with the salmon and black tiles, and at her dressing table in the front bedroom where she kept her rings in a glass ashtray, my God, she used Chanel No. 5. Furniture polish. Meat loaf with green peppers. She wore wool skirts and see-through white blouses with tiny round buttons and demure ruffles when she worked as a receptionist for Dr. Brady, but what you saw underneath was the stern construction of slip straps. They were short-sleeved blouses that revealed the pale fleshy undersides of her upper arms, which now in this stagnant closet I recall with foolish tenderness.

She worked until noon on Saturdays and often she and I would take the Atlantic Boulevard bus past those mysterious landmarks of childhood—Peg's for Perms, Bardlow Top Shop with a painting of a 1964 Mustang on a revolving oval—to a one-story dental building across the street from the Long Beach Mortuary, where I would spend three hours in a tiny back room, kitchen cum laboratory, waiting while she typed on the IBM and answered the phone, reading Superman comics and finding the hidden pictures in office copies of *Highlights for Children*—*"Fun with a Purpose."* Mother would freeze those tiny cans of Mott's apple juice and I'd eat my American cheese sandwich and suck out the icy slush with a straw, looking through huge dusty textbooks with close-up photographs of malformed gums. The place smelled like ether.

But when it was over we'd get back on the bus and continue downtown, where she would pay her bills at the electric and gas company offices, then continue on to Buffum's and Sears and the tedious business of keeping up a household: getting extra keys made, buying shower curtains and aluminum pots, Mother asking my opinion about every tiny purchase because she could never make up her mind. The worst was Lerner's, where I remember many excruciating hours playing beneath racks of blouses while she dawdled and agonized.

If I was lucky we'd end up in Woolworth's or Kress, where I'd wander the flat wooden tables, drawn to cheap beach souvenirs like plastic wallets with photos of palm trees or figurines made of seashells, but what I lusted after most—and was never allowed to possess—were the medals of St. Christopher, which they kept in a locked glass case because every kid in Southern California wanted "a Christopher" like the coolest surfers wore.

I suddenly have the sense of sitting at the lunch counter in Woolworth's spooning a black-and-white ice cream soda while Mother had cinnamon toast and coffee, sharing a guilty pleasure because it was just an hour until dinnertime. My mother rarely indulged either of us, maybe because in a way it would mean robbing Poppy of something, but those Saturday afternoons did provide an indulgence—being alone with her, away from my grandfather, which I now realize was the underlying reason we were so dumbly, unknowingly, happy.

Because at the other end of the bus ride, after carrying those heavy shopping bags past an oil rig that pumped day and night in a fenced lot in the middle of the neighborhood, we'd inevitably arrive at the one-eyed redbrick house on Pine Street. I saw it that way as a child because a loquat bush hid one of the two front windows and the other seemed to stare from between gray shutters with glassy spite.

The house was new when Poppy bought it, the only one on the street made of brick. It was buttoned up, closed off like a bunker, with a square green lawn mowed to anal uniformity, no ornamentation except a black mailbox on a post. One innovation of the sixties was a bright yellow all-electric kitchen with a clock built into the stove that of course ran on Poppy's time: *"Ask your grandfather what he wants for dinner . . ." "We'll eat when Poppy's ready . . ."* Looking at the household ledger in the spiral notebook, I discover that for our two rooms in my grandfather's spartan home, my mother paid rent, $54.67 a month.

I miss her then, I want those freckled arms around me, I want our bond, broken not only by her death but by a mysterious invisibility during my young childhood, to be healed. But how? Instead of coming close, I feel her fading away from me again, eclipsed as always by Poppy.

What was her shadowy life compared to the scary, exciting visits to police headquarters in the bold blue glass building on Broadway? Poppy would steer me through busy offices where everyone thought I was cute, then, if there were no prisoners, through the actual jail with its terrifying steel toilets. Waiting outside for him, I'd call out to his buddies by name as they climbed into their squad cars, running my fingers over a big brass plaque near the lobby, a bas-relief of a policeman sheltering a boy and girl, "Lest We Forget"—Long Beach Police Officers Association, with a kind of preadolescent sexual thrill.

Poppy took me trick-or-treating, Mother stayed home. He took me body surfing in the breakers off Shoreline Drive, bullying me to get up and do it again no matter how many times the waves sent me sprawling—where was she? Timid, passive, afraid, self-effacing until dissolving into a ninety-pound cadaver before my eyes. In the end her skin was actually green and she didn't have the strength to roll over in the hospital bed, lying on her side facing away from me, one arm struggling to rise above the collapsed curve of her hip, one word, my name, spoken as I entwined those dry brittle fingers in mine at age fourteen.

And yet she is not completely gone and yet . . . perhaps I really did mean something to her. Who else would have saved the document I now hold in my hand, and for what purpose other than some- day her daughter might find it, shoved way in the back of a safe-deposit box inside an unused birthday card inside an envelope? It is her marriage certificate, stamped by the City of Las Vegas, August 3, 1964. It states that on this day, Miguel Sanchez and Gwen Grey, my father and mother, were married.

I stare at it with only one wish: that the black woman with the ponytail will dig her blue heels into the beige carpeting and push that steel door closed and give the big brass wheel a good strong spin, sealing me and what I now know into a dark airless crypt, where secrets are buried precisely so nothing will change, forever.

■   ■   ■

When Poppy doesn't answer my ring at the door I use my key. I find him sitting out on the balcony with eyes closed, face to the late afternoon sun. He looks the same. He is wearing his usual tan slacks and yellow polo shirt open at the neck, bare feet in flip-flops crossed up on a small plastic table. His square rugged hands—reddish and hairy with age—are clasped on his chest. His chin is sunk forward and he is snoring.

Even now another ancient admonition stops me from waking him up, *"Grandfather needs his sleep."* I turn back into the condominium and start picking up coffee cups and glasses and carrying them into the kitchen. A few yellowish curds have collected on the brown Rubbermaid mat in the bottom of the sink near the wooden dishwashing stick with the soft cotton head Poppy has been using for years. I see those red soapy hands rinsing bacon and scrambled eggs off green melamine plates and a wave of revulsion as powerful as the Long Beach surf almost doubles me over. The cups chatter as I place them on the counter and walk back into the sun.

"Poppy. I'm here. Wake up."

He opens his eyes and smiles. "The woman of the hour."

I am cold. "Why do you say that?"

"You busted that sleazy doctor who was harassing Jayne Mason."

"Something like that."

"Hell, it's all over the news. I've got it right here."

He swings his feet off the small table and stands. Steadily, I notice.

I follow him through the sliding glass doors into the cool darkness of the living room. Sun spots are still swimming in my vision as he picks up a sheaf of newspapers and magazines from the top of the television.

"You're a celebrity."

But there is nothing congratulatory in the flat tone of his voice. He holds my eyes before handing me the papers and behind the handsome mask of strong nose and weathered cheeks is a baby-faced pout of envy.

Of course I am nowhere near a celebrity. I receive no personal mention in Poppy's collection of articles from the *Los Angeles Times,* *USA Today* and the local Palm Springs rag. The FBI is said to be only peripherally involved. The big story is the million-dollar malpractice lawsuit being brought against "the sports injury doctor to the stars" by "movie queen" Jayne Mason with plenty of spicy comments from "superpower personal manager" Magda Stockman. The big graphic that has played in all the media is a split-screen image of Mason on one side and Eberhardt on the other. She looks beautiful and vulnerable, he looks hunched over and guilty.

"You don't usually show much interest in my cases."

"This one is different, it's my gal, Jayne. That doc deserves to hang. What can I get you?"

"Water."

"Good idea. Dry today."

He goes into the kitchen, I remain standing. When he returns with two glasses I drop the manila envelope I have been holding onto the coffee table.

"I got the documents from the safe-deposit box."

"You didn't have to make a trip. The U.S. mail would have been more than adequate."

Is he deliberately undercutting me today, not thanking me for my effort, not acknowledging my accomplishments, or have these subtle put-downs and manipulations been going on for years? I can feel the tendrils of rage coiling around my throat, threatening to choke me off. I have to reach up and forcibly pry them apart to keep breathing.

"I made the trip to show my concern for you, Poppy." I let the angry sarcasm hang there but he doesn't hear it.

"I'm fine."

"Are you?"

"Well, the radiation makes me drowsy and chemotherapy ain't no day at the beach, but we'll take that on when it comes."

"What exactly is the diagnosis?"

"They call it a lymphoma."

"What's your doctor's name, I'd like to speak to him or her."

"No need for it."

"You can't go through this alone."

"I've got friends in the complex. Lots of ladies want to look in on me."

"Don't screw with me, Poppy." My finger is jabbing into the space that separates us across the living room. "I need to know your doctor's name."

"All right."

Having won that bout, I spit a breath out between my teeth. I am still standing. He is sitting on the sofa with his legs crossed and eyes unfocused, a bleak inward repose as if I weren't there.

I sit down in an armchair but it is too deep to get my feet firmly on the floor and too far from Poppy to force him to look at me. I try to drag it closer but the legs get tangled in the matted shag of the rug.

For a moment I am frozen like a diver at the edge of the board. As a child I would clutch, looking down at the water so far away. Once, when a line of kids behind me started hooting because I couldn't jump off and I couldn't step back, a lifeguard had to walk out, pick me up under the arms, and drop me into the pool like a slab of stone. She's there now, the healthy well-muscled self taking firm hold of the shivering frightened self at last.

"When I was going through the safe-deposit box I found some things. Some jewelry, which I kept, and a marriage certificate between my father and Mom. You never told me they were married."

"Who was married?"

"Miguel Sanchez and Gwen Grey. Do the names sound familiar?"

"What are you getting at?"

"I've been thinking about this for the last two and a half hours, driving out from L.A. I've had a lot of time to go over it again and again and again. And I've come to the conclusion that you and Mom have lied to me about my father and my heritage and who I am and where I come from my entire life."

At the end of it my voice betrays me by going weak.

"I told you to forget about that son of a bitch," Poppy snaps. His eyes look black in the triangular shadow that cuts across the room. "He left you and your mother, can't you get that through your head?"

"Apparently he didn't leave because they ran away and got married. Maybe you didn't know about it."

Bitterly, "I knew about it."

"Why did they wait until four years after I was born?"

We are facing each other squarely now. Poppy is alert and still as a snake.

"Let me take a wild guess." I am feeling an enormous pressure in my chest, a miserable kind of total body ache. "You threatened my father and behaved like a raving bigot until finally you chased him away."

"I'm the one who raised you!" Poppy shouts, causing me to flinch. "Damn you to hell."

I say it again in a stronger voice, matching his: "My father left because you chased him away."

"He was a lowlife beaner who knocked up my daughter, then this guy"—he pauses to shake his head and almost laugh—"keeps coming back and coming back . . . for five fucking years. Then he marries her against my wishes and that was the last fucking straw."

"Maybe," I suggest, "he fucking loved her."

"You watch your tongue or I'll give you the back of my hand."

"And maybe . . . she fucking loved him."

We stare at each other. I do not apologize and I do not back off.

"Let's get it clear now, Poppy, because the sun is going down. Who was Miguel Sanchez?"

Glaring silence.

"Was he from El Salvador?"

"That was the story."

"So he wasn't Mexican."

"What's the difference?"

"How could Miguel Sanchez and Gwen Grey have possibly met in 1958?"

"She was stupid enough to let him sweet-talk her over at Patton's pharmacy on Montana."

"What was an itinerant worker doing in a drugstore on Montana Avenue? Buying hand cream?"

"His line to Gwen was that he was taking night courses in management at the high school."

"So now he's not a migrant laborer, he's a Ph.D."

"I'm the *one* who raised you." His fist comes down on the padded arm of the sofa and bounces up.

"You stole me from my parents."

"What's the matter with you? Have you been smoking crack?"

I stand up with disgust.

"Your mother was a naïve silly girl and your father was trash. You think I wanted a little spic baby in the house—"

"Stop."

"But you turned out to be more white than brown."

"So you kept the half-breed bastard."

"It was your grandmother's idea, then she passed away. Now I was stuck with the two of you. You think your mother could have managed on her own?"

"She would have gone with my father and had a life, and I would have had my parents."

"All you needed was me."

I can only stare at him incredulously.

"You're as naïve as your mother," he explodes suddenly. "I *had* to send him away. He would have ruined your lives."

"So you forced him to leave and made sure he'd never come back."

"That part was out of my hands. The dumb son of a bitch got himself killed."

I am silent. "How was he killed?"

"I told you he was a migrant worker. He talked back to the fore-man one time too many, got into a fight, and got the shit beat out of him, that's all."

"Why didn't anyone tell me?"

"Your mother was devastated," he continues in a tight voice. "She never wanted you to know. She just couldn't see that side of him, that he was a hotheaded arrogant bastard."

"Where was he buried?"

Poppy scowls. "Who knows, probably in some bean field some-where. They sure didn't send him home with military honors."

"Why are you telling me this now?"

"Because I'm sick and tired of taking the blame."

A chill passes through me, then something adjusts in my body like a joint that's been out of whack for a few decades and subtly shifts back into place. I realize that I had always known my father was dead and that he had been killed violently. I have carried an image of him dying with blood on his face—I've dreamed it several times—so somebody must have told me or I must have overheard.

"Nobody's blaming you."

"Like hell."

"Look," I say softly, trying to be conciliatory, "give me the name of your doctor."

"Next to the bed, but what's the big deal?"

He picks up a magazine and lies down on the sofa. The shadow cuts across his body like a guillotine. He puts a pillow behind his neck to prop up his head and the sunset light, that amber light of nightmares, catches the worn blue eyes, which are looking at me now over the top of the page with uncensored hate.

I have nowhere to go so I go into the bedroom. The brown curtains are drawn, the maroon cover on the bed pulled tight. On the bedside table there are several new prescription bottles, a shoehorn, keys, and a bill with the name and address of an oncologist in Palm Springs. When I pick it up, I understand why my grandfather doesn't want me to talk to the doctor. It means acknowledging that the famous omnipotent powerful Everett Morgan Grey, patrol officer, rescuer of children, protector of the superior race, is mortal.

Under "diagnosis" the doctor wrote, "Aggressive B-cell lymphoma." Special Agent Charles González, a nice man who worked the White Collar Crime Squad, was diagnosed with the same thing. I will be granted the shameful wish that came hurtling out of my subconscious as I lay beneath Randall Eberhardt's hand: Poppy will be dead in a year.

TWENTY

SINCE WORKING the Mason case I have not been in touch with the guys on the Bank Robbery Squad, stranded out here in no-man's-land waiting for my transfer, and now that I need someone to talk to, nobody is around. I wander through the bullpen like a lost soul, stopping at everybody's empty desk, until realizing it is the last Friday of the month and they must be having their potluck lunch. I purge the vending machine of all its vanilla creme sandwiches to have something to contribute, but nobody is in the lunchroom, either. I figure they must have gone out to a restaurant until I notice a bunch of people are crowded into the small conference room with the lights out.

Peeking through the blinds I see it's them all right, Kyle, Frank, Barbara, Rosalind, Donnato, and Duane sitting around the table with piles of goodies on paper plates. But instead of jokes and lively conversation everyone is turned intently toward the television where a videotape is playing of Ana Grey striding up the steps of the Dana Orthopedic Clinic followed by a half dozen federal marshals in orange raid vests. I had lent Barbara a cassette of the Eberhardt arrest given to me by one of the TV stations, not expecting her to make it the afternoon's feature presentation.

When I open the door, they are surprised to see me in person.

"Take notes, guys. This is how it's done."

I unload my handfuls of vanilla creme cookies, then sit beside Barbara and pick a strawberry off her plate.

"Have some lunch," offers Rosalind.

"I'm okay."

"I didn't think you'd mind," Barbara says of the tape.

"Hell no, I just hope you charged admission."

We watch a close-up of Randall Eberhardt's distraught face as I brush past him and the camera follows us down the hall. You'd think my buddies would cheer me on like they did the morning after I made that California First bust, but instead there is an uncomfortable tension in the viewing room, the way I guess it has to be when someone leaves a group and the group goes on without her.

"This will be very good for you, Ana. You look like a leader," Barbara observes.

"Not like I'm about to wig out?" I turn in Donnato's direction but he is back in the shadows sipping coffee. His silence is nagging. It seems like a long time since the potluck when he was fooling around, calling me Annie Oakley in black lace.

"No," says Barbara, "it looks like you're in control of a tight situation."

"Pardon me," chuckles Duane. "But this is not the invasion of Normandy, they're enterin' a doctor's office, what's he gonna do, zap 'em with his X-ray machine?"

Frank and Kyle give a couple of halfhearted guffaws.

"The media was there and Galloway made *her* point person," Barbara answers crisply. "That's significant."

"Why so?"

"People around here are finally realizing that women can do the job."

Another silence. Nobody wants to get into that.

"Duane thinks it's a dog case," I explain.

"There is no case," says Duane. "Galloway and the Director are jerking each other off."

"You're jealous," Barbara fairly purrs, fingering the pearl around her neck.

"Show me a case. What evidence was recovered from the search and seizure?"

Although I am pleased to see Duane irritated, I have to admit to everyone that we found nothing in the office to implicate the doctor and, in fact, the Assistant U.S. Attorney is scrambling to figure out if there's anything to charge him with at all.

"See what I mean? Another pathetic dog-and-pony show."

"In today's world of media events and photo opportunities everything's for show," Kyle says slowly and reasonably. "Ana did what was required for the six o'clock news. It's a dirty job but someone's got to do it."

The tape is over. Rosalind gets up and turns on the lights.

Duane Carter spreads his scrawny knees and leans his chair way back on its rear legs.

"I'd be scared shitless if I were you. The case is still open and you've got *nada*—"

Luckily I'm already there. I'd been thinking about Mason's behavior when she came to our office and that night over dinner. The dilated pupils, the shaky hands, the discordant energy when she returned from the rest room had been working the back of my mind.

"We know Mason's an abuser," I cut in sharply, trying not to look at the aggressive display of crotch. "I'm running criminal checks on everyone on her staff. She's doing drugs again and she's getting them from somewhere."

Duane suddenly tips the chair forward. Its front feet land with a snap. "Don't you get it? They're pulling your chain just to keep the pretty lady happy."

"To keep her manager happy." Donnato sends me a piercing look that says *I warned you about this weeks ago but you insist on screwing yourself up.* "She has friends in high places."

This seems to make Duane happy. "You'll be riding robbery again in a week and I, for one, can't wait to welcome you back."

He saunters out. Kyle shakes his head.

"Don't say it," Barbara warns.

All I do is give his empty chair a tiny little nudge with my toe.

"I'm a big girl now."

Donnato slides the Tupperware bowl and the pair of black salad tongs into a shopping bag.

"Keep at it," he tells me with about the same personal interest he would show in the guy mopping the men's room floor.

I follow him out. He shoves the bag under his desk and looks up, not entirely pleased to find me standing above him.

"So how is Rochelle doing in law school?"

"She loves it."

"But?"

"It's an adjustment."

"Sounds like more than that."

He sighs impatiently. "It's hard on everyone, okay? Suddenly she's not around for the kids—I'm supposed to jump in and be Superdad, but how do I do that when I'm here until eight o'clock at night?"

"So who made the salad?" I say kiddingly.

"I did, that's how bad it is." He starts to twirl a silver letter opener around on his desk. "Law school is good for her. She should have done it a long time ago."

However, one flick of a forefinger and the thing spins like a knife-sharp Ninja star.

I hesitate.

"You know Duane could be right. The Mason case could fall apart and I'll be back riding with you, giving you a hard time, could you stand it?"

In the nanosecond it takes him to decide what to say, all hope dies.

"They've got me partnered with Joe Positano now."

"Who is Joe Positano?"

"Rookie transferred from Atlanta. He would have been at lunch but he couldn't wait to get his California driver's license, poor ignorant son of a bitch."

"That could change."

"What could?"

"Joe Positano. If I came back."

Again, the killer pause.

"Who knows?" Donnato says emptily, reaching for his shoulder holster and pulling his weapon out of a locked desk drawer. I feel awful.

"Are you still mad at me because of the undercover thing?"

Donnato puts his sport jacket on over the shoulder holster.

Abruptly, "No." Then, relenting, "So what are you going to do?"

For a moment I hold his look.

"Return a humidifier," I say.

There is nothing more. He gives me a laconic wave good-bye, and we separate.

■   ■   ■

I am sitting on a bench in the Century City Shopping Center finishing a Butter Brittle Bar from See's Candies, a treat I used to sneak after school, and feeling depressed about every element in my life except the fact that at my feet is a new humidifier inside a glossy box tied up with string, so I will no longer wake up with a sore throat those Santa Ana mornings when the humidity is zero.

Small comfort.

The conversation I had with Poppy's doctor was bleak. We are looking at months of increasing debilitation and pain. He advised me to take it one day at a time, which in a situation like this is all the human spirit can bear. And although I've tried not to focus on it, hearing about my father has brought that particular sorrow close enough to the surface to be almost audible, the whisper of water inside a cave.

I miss my squad and I miss Donnato. Our innocent, comfortable flirtation is over and things with the other guys will never be the same. It all started when I went after that bank robber on my own and worsened when I went off on the Eberhardt case. Is this what I get for following my ambitions like some fool greyhound let loose on a track? While everyone else has left the park, I'm still tearing after a fake rabbit.

In no mood to go back to the office, I pick up my package and wander past the shops, taking in the bright afternoon air, wishing I could think of something else to buy that would make me feel better. All I can come up with is a fanny pack.

I figure they might have one at Bullock's, so I push the glass doors open and plod across the cosmetics department, asphyxiating on that cloying powdery smell, disoriented by the play of glossy white and gold surfaces reflected in the mirrored posts. It's a hell of a heart-stopper to run right into Jayne Mason.

Not the real Jayne Mason but a life-size cardboard cutout, the same one I had seen in the den in Malibu, where she was wearing an evening gown and holding a bouquet. That one must have been the mock-up, because now there is printing across the bouquet that reads Introducing Yellow Rose Cosmetics by Jayne Mason.

A girl with immaculate makeup wearing a white lab coat with a fresh yellow rose pinned over the breast sees me staring.

"We're having a special on Jayne Mason's new cosmetics. With every twenty-dollar purchase you get a tote bag."

I am struck dumb. An entire counter is stacked with samples of lipsticks, mascara, eye pencils, powder, blush, nail polish. The bright silver and yellow packaging features Jayne Mason's signature, the same careful round lettering she wrote on Barbara's legal pad that day in the office. The amazing thing is this elaborate and sophisticated display seems to have sprung up out of nowhere. It wasn't here when Jayne Mason made her sweep of the cosmetics department. I realize now she had been checking to see if the line was in the store, disappointed when it was not.

And all this didn't just spring out of nowhere.

"Who makes the actual stuff?"

"It's by Giselle."

I see now we are at the Giselle counter and Yellow Rose is a subdivision. Their perennial product lines, Youth Bud and Moonglow—which even I used as a teenager—are displayed around the corner. So Jayne Mason has become a spokesperson for a major cosmetics company; a deal worth millions of dollars that had to have been in place long before she met Randall Eberhardt—an arrangement she and her manager would likely go to great lengths to protect.

"Would you like a makeover, compliments of Jayne Mason?" the girl asks sweetly.

She indicates a stool beside the smiling cutout of Jayne.

I emit a high-pitched giggle that seems to go on for a long time. The girl blinks and takes a step back.

"She's already done me, thanks."

■　■　■

Even at four p.m. the bar at the Beverly Wilshire Hotel is crowded with an international mix of people bartering for goods and services, including a pair of young call girls doing business with some well-tailored Japanese. Somehow Jerry Connell and I recognize each other across the bazaar; I make him for the most nervous man in the room.

"I am not a happy camper," he says as we shoulder our way through.

"Rocky flight from St. Louis?"

"Next time call before you call, okay? Say: Hi, this is Ana Grey from the FBI. I'm going to give you a cardiac arrest in about thirty seconds, just wanted you to know."

He shakes his head and grins. Fair-haired with appealing blue eyes, he's wearing one of those ultrafashionable suits that look retro and futuro at the same time—a subtle gray houndstooth with skinny lapels. I sneak a touch as I guide him to the last empty table: heavenly cashmere.

We both order Perrier. Connell is anxious and intense, talking compulsively.

"This is scary. Giselle is a tremendously important account. They've only been with our ad agency three years, and so far we've had just one slice of their business, but we've done well enough with the Moonglow line for them to take a flier on Yellow Rose."

"Your agency came up with the idea to use Jayne Mason?"

"It was Magda Stockman's idea. Have you met her?"

He squeezes the life out of the lemon wedge floating in his glass.

"I know Ms. Stockman."

"She called out of nowhere, said she was Jayne Mason's personal manager, were we interested in developing a line of cosmetics for Giselle using Jayne as a spokesperson. She flew out, made a very smart presentation, and the client bought it."

"How was the deal structured?"

Jerry Connell can't sit still. His knees are thumping up and down, fingers drumming the table. Now he's fingering his string-bean leather tie.

"It's a partnership arrangement between Jayne Mason and Giselle. They manufacture the cosmetics."

"And Jayne—"

"She's required to do some commercials, point-of-purchase displays, print ads, and one or two speaking engagements. It amounts to about a week of her time."

"How much does she get paid?"

"I can't tell you that . . ." He grinds at the lemon wedge with the ball end of a cocktail stick. "But it's in the high seven figures."

"For one week's work."

"We like to think of it as a lifetime's worth of public recognition."

"You're in a pretty business," I say.

"Almost as pretty as yours."

He looks at me sideways. The agitation subsides. Jerry Connell is a polished, educated salesman with a lot at stake and now he is going to make his pitch:

"So you called, Special Agent Ana Grey, and I took the next flight out of St. Louis. In order to do that, I had to give up my haircut with Sal. Do you know how hard it is to get an appointment with that guy?"

"Your hair looks okay."

"I have to protect my client. Tell me what's going on. Do I have a major problem here?"

"I don't know yet. When did Jayne Mason sign the contract with Giselle?"

"Two years ago. It takes time to gear these things up."

"So the deal was in place when she went into the Betty Ford Center?"

"It was."

Remembering Magda Stockman's impassioned speech about how all the publicity around Jayne's drug problem had irrevocably damaged her career, "Didn't that worry you?"

"We were assured the thing was treatable and it would be handled with discretion."

"But it wound up on the cover of *People* magazine."

"Any time you go with a celebrity endorsement there's a measure of risk. They're unpredictable. They're human."

"But didn't it bother your client that their spokesperson was a drug addict?"

"It wasn't like she was mainlining heroin. This fancy doctor got her hooked. I think there was sympathy in the executive ranks." He smiles engagingly. "Who hasn't done a little Xanax to get through the day?"

I put my hands flat on the table and lock into his eyes.

"Did Magda Stockman make the statement to you that Jayne Mason's addiction was the doctor's fault?"

"Yes, and she said not to worry, he was being prosecuted for it." Jerry Connell stares at me. "Isn't he?"

"Not until we can find something to prosecute him for."

He starts fiddling with the tie like it was a piccolo.

"Whatever. As far as my client is concerned, at this point it probably doesn't matter." He's talking to himself. "The public perception is such that . . ."

He trails off, looking into the distance, calculating the public perception.

"Well," he concludes, "Giselle is protected."

"How is that?"

"Worst-case scenario: Mason is in breach of her contract. We pull the product, we sue, bam-boom."

He slaps the table two times and seems ready to get back on the plane.

"I don't understand. How would she be in breach?"

"We have a morals clause."

"Show me."

■ ■ ■

Although it is almost eight o'clock at night in St. Louis the lights are burning at the advertising agency of Connell and Burgess. Somebody back there sends a copy of the morals clause in Jayne Mason's contract through the hotel fax. I read it line by line as it feeds off the machine:

M. MORALS. If Spokesperson should, prior to or during the term hereof or thereafter, fail, refuse or neglect to govern Spokesperson's conduct with due regard to social conventions and public morals and decency, or commit any act which brings Spokesperson into public disrepute, scandal, contempt or ridicule or which shocks, insults or offends a substantial portion or group of the community or reflects unfavorably on Spokesperson or Manufacturer, then Manufacturer may, in addition to and without prejudice to any other remedy of any kind or nature set forth herein, terminate this Agreement at any time after the occurrence of any such event.

I thank Jerry Connell and shake his hand, folding the thin paper and tucking it carefully into an inner pocket of my blue briefcase.

TWENTY-ONE

WHEN I ARRIVE at the office the following day I find Duane Carter sitting in my seat playing with my surfer troll doll, the one wearing a Walkman with fuchsia hair standing up straight.

"Stop fondling my troll."

Duane grins.

"Get out of my chair."

"That's no way to address your supervisor."

I drop the blue canvas briefcase onto the desk for emphasis. Unfortunately the force of the concussion causes my sunglasses to slip off my nose but I make a great save and continue to glower at Duane.

"You're not my supervisor, now move."

"I wouldn't bet on it. Catch this."

He pushes the Calendar section of today's *Los Angeles Times* at me. The whole top half of the page is taken up with a giant photograph of Jayne Mason sitting in her den looking vulnerable and funky and oh-so-real in a denim shirt and loose curls, huge eyes with no makeup, like she just came down from a breakfast of skim milk and toast to share her darkest troubles with you, the reader.

I have to stand there while Duane quotes from the article about how Jayne first became sensitized to victims of corrupt doctors who overprescribe narcotics in her therapy group at the Betty Ford Center. How as a result of the publicity surrounding the lawsuit, the investigation of Dr. Eberhardt has escalated to include the California Medical Licensing Board, which has suspended his license to practice medicine. Although the FBI continues to neither confirm nor deny its own investigation, it is bringing a supervisor who specializes in health care industry fraud out from headquarters in Washington, D.C., to review the situation.

"You're off the case, gal."

"Don't believe what you read in the papers," I reply coolly.

"Some of his colleagues at the hospital say your buddy Eberhardt was subject to bouts of depression."

"Under all that stress, who wouldn't be?"

"They say he's a superachiever, always pushing for perfection, the type who can't handle failure. Goes back to his Harvard Med School days. How does the media find out stuff we don't?"

He enjoys my discomfort.

Looking down, I catch a paragraph stating that Dr. Eberhardt "remains sequestered in his north of Montana home" and is not available for comment on the advice of legal counsel. I can picture him and Claire quivering behind that huge door.

Duane stands up and hands me the paper. "It was a good shot. You've had a couple of good shots lately, but like I tried to explain before, you've still got some work to accomplish before you move on."

"And how did *you* move on, Duane?" I am heaving rapidly, spitting resentment so it is hard to articulate the words. "I've been in for seven years, you've been in for eight. Tell me the secret of how you got so far ahead."

He takes his time answering and when he's ready he moves the black forelock aside, patting it down on the top of his head with pale fingertips like he's sticking it there with glue.

"I made a deal with the Devil." The look in his dark eyes is enigmatic. "When I was a teenager I wanted to get out of Travis County and have success at an early age, and one day I told that to the Devil, and here I am."

"Really? And what did you trade with the Devil for your success?"

"That's between him and me," Duane answers without smiling and leaves.

I sit there for some time, awed by the realization that he was 100 percent serious.

When I switch on my computer the little box next to Mail is blinking, so I call it up and there are the results of the criminal checks I was running on everyone I could find who works, advises, profits, eats, sleeps, or plays within a hundred-mile radius of Jayne Mason. Everyone is clean enough, except for the limousine driver, Tom Pauley, who got into a little trouble with stolen goods when he was a state cop and had to leave the force.

I remove the morals clause from the zippered compartment of the blue briefcase, grab a printout of the report on Pauley, and run down to the SAC's office.

■   ■   ■

Galloway gets up from behind the desk and comes toward me, gesturing apologetically with a cigar. "Sorry you had to read about it in the paper."

"So it's true? I'm off the case?"

"The Director saw Jayne Mason crying her eyes out on *Donahue* and went ballistic. He wants more firepower in terms of the media. It has nothing to do with you."

I am silent.

"I'm putting in for your transfer to C-1. Congratulations."

He waits for my reaction. When there is none he bends his knees, so he can hunch over and squint at me in the eyes.

"Am I crazy or were you all over me to get that transfer?"

"Right now a transfer is beside the point."

I show him the fax and explain that because of this morals

clause, scandalous conduct—like being a dope addict—could have jeopardized a multimillion-dollar contract. I tell him my belief that Mason was lying all along about Randall Eberhardt's culpability.

But Galloway is not impressed with my beliefs.

"They brought in the big gun from Washington, let him handle it." He's standing up again, arm around my shoulder as he walks me to the door. "You did a good job with what you had."

"Okay, you don't like the morals clause—" I ball it up and toss it into the trash and flourish the printout under his nose. "How about this: new lead. Jayne Mason's driver was busted for trading in stolen goods when he was a state cop."

Galloway raises his eyebrows. "Stop the presses."

"We know Mason is an abuser. I'm going to squeeze this guy and find out the real supplier, then I'm going to bust her for possession."

"Holy shit."

Galloway's hand flies off my shoulder like it was a red hot frying pan.

"Ana, we're getting off the track."

"What if I can prove possession and trading in illegal substances on the part of Jayne Mason?"

Exasperated, "That is not the direction *anyone* wants to go."

"I know, but—"

Galloway stops me with a finger to his lips. He speaks softly and slowly, bouncing the finger to the rhythm of his words like a nursery rhyme: "Let us remember the suspect in this investigation is still *Randall Eberhardt*. Now listen carefully and tell me the answer: How will this help our prosecution of the *suspect*?"

"Maybe it clears him," I say.

■ ■ ■

It turns out that, despite whatever trouble "in the castle" between Tom Pauley and Maureen, during off-hours they have been living together in her rented apartment in Pacific Palisades, a comfortable suburban townlet just across the canyon from Santa Monica. Despite the mini-malling of the main drag, it still feels like the fifties up here—families and ranch houses—which is why Maureen's place is so unusual.

The house is on a winding street, behind a large sliding gate. I walk down stone steps to the sound of trickling water; an artificial stream pools in a stone basin covered by water lilies and populated by real live burping frogs. Straight ahead is a small wooden deck overgrown with magenta bougainvillea, a white wrought-iron table, and chairs overlooking the misty curve of Will Rogers Beach, the bluish mountains, and the silver ocean all the way out to Point Dume. The vista is priceless.

Although there are houses cheek to jowl along the street, in this glorious spot there is nothing but silence and wind through the flowers. It makes you hunger for Cheddar cheese and salty crackers and bourbon, watching the sunset on the deck. Turning back toward the house the view is equally charmed: gabled roofs, gingerbread trim, a Hansel and Gretel hideaway.

The door, carved of soft wood with Balinese figures entwined in dance, is slightly open. I knock, get no response, and walk inside.

"Hello? Tom? It's Ana Grey."

Nothing.

I pass a bedroom with rumpled sheets on a four-poster bed and clothes strewn over a worn Oriental rug. The air smells of sandalwood and sex. There is a dressing table loaded with antique perfume bottles, half of them knocked over and smashed. The closets are open and so are the drawers. Straw hats, dolls, and shawls are scattered everywhere as if picked up and tossed off their window seat. It looks like Tom and Maureen were robbed.

I become more certain when I enter the ransacked kitchen. A pot is turning scorched and black, all the water boiled away, the burner still lit. I turn off the flame, crunching over a box of dried spaghetti spilled across the floor. Someone hurtled a bottle of apple juice against the wall. Someone else was throwing cans. I hear a soft moan coming from another room. The adrenaline goes up, weapon comes out.

I move quietly down a hall that is decorated with ominous-looking African masks to a living room with two windows of dia-mond-patterned glass opening to an ocean view. There are more masks, dolls with staring eyes and perfect china faces, secondhand sofas stuffed with pillows covered with chintz. A mobile of glass prisms in the window catches the sharp afternoon sun, spinning bars of colors over everything.

And in the middle of the dizzying rainbows, planted stock-still on those bowed naked sunburned legs, is Tom Pauley, wearing noth-ing but a white T-shirt, slowly masturbating.

He rolls his eyes toward me, red-rimmed. I catch the sheen of white stubble along an unshaven jaw.

"Ana," he mumbles mournfully, "help me out."

His thumb and forefinger move down the enlarged red-blue penis with a glistening drop of semen at the head. I reach over and grab a woolly afghan off a rocking chair and toss it to him.

"Jesus, Tom, cover it up."

He holds the blanket in front of himself, sinks bare-assed onto the sofa, and starts to cry.

"What went on here?"

"We had a fight."

"Where is Maureen?"

"Gone."

Tom is bent over double, holding his head in his hands.

"Is she okay?"

He nods.

"You didn't sock her black and blue, throw her over the cliff?"

"I wouldn't do that. I love her, Ana." He lifts his face to me. The puffy features are melted together, streaming with self-pity. "God, I'm a fat old fart."

I holster the weapon and sit down to give him time to compose himself. The sofa is hard as a rock. It must be stuffed with horsehair or some other perverse material.

"Interesting house."

"It was built in the sixties by a movie set designer."

He takes a big breath, draws his thumbs across his eyes.

"Any connection to Jayne Mason?"

"No, Maureen's been living here for years, long before she met Jayne."

"How is Jayne? She must be busy, running from one talk show to another defending victims' rights."

"I couldn't care less about Jayne Mason right now."

"She cares a lot about you and Maureen. She was worried something like this might happen. She told me that night on our date."

"Jayne tries, but she could never understand my feelings for Maureen."

"Let's talk about you. Want a glass of water?"

He shakes his head.

"Okay, let's have a conversation about truck drivers who are allegedly robbed in remote areas of the California desert and a state cop who shows up on the scene and fakes a report so the goods can be fenced and resold, what do you think?"

He wipes his nose with the bottom of his T-shirt. "In the past."

"Does Jayne know about your past?"

"Jayne thinks I'm the greatest thing since chocolate syrup."

"Where does she get her drugs, Tom?"

He stands up, holding the blanket around his waist.

"No way, Ana."

"Jayne thinks you're a chocolate ice cream soda, but Maureen thinks you're a big pile of shit."

Getting upset again, "Leave me alone."

I stand also. "Not a problem. I'll ask your young friend for her opinion, which at this moment is not very high. I can see why you like little girls but, no offense, Tom, what do they see in you?"

A blush is growing beneath the white stubble.

"After trying to kill you with a box of spaghetti, I'm sure she'll be thrilled to tell me how you supply Dilaudid and Dexedrine and Valium and cocaine and all the rest of it to Jayne Mason."

"I have nothing to do with that."

"But you know who does."

His jaw tightens. His lips compress. The apartment suddenly seems very small, the doll faces fetishes, the Hansel and Gretel house a closed-in obsession.

"It must have been fun while it lasted, you and Lolita with the fourteen-year-old tits."

"Go to hell."

"New plan: you get dressed and we cruise over to Westwood."

"What for?"

"The Bureau has a keen interest in this case and I'm sure this hotshot specialist from Washington would like to talk to someone who has intimate knowledge of what goes on in Jayne Mason's house, maybe go over a little of your own past history."

The rainbows spin over us.

"It's not me."

"Okay." I let out a big, benevolent sigh like I'm finally letting him off the hook. Gently, compassionately, "Why don't you put on some clothes?"

He picks up a pair of sweats from the couch, slips them on, and plops back down with a righteous look, rubbing the sweat from his temples.

"We know it's Dr. Eberhardt," I say, as if confiding a professional secret. "We've already busted his ass."

Tom Pauley shakes his head, sneering. "That's exactly the reason I hated the feds when I was a state cop. You guys are so fucking arrogant and so fucking wrong."

I can see he's got a bone to pick, so I hand him a great big turkey thigh: "We believe that we have an airtight case against the doctor."

"*He's* the one who wanted Jayne *in* Betty Ford, for Christ sake," Tom blurts out. "Magda Stockman tried to keep her out."

"I don't believe that."

"Yeah, well I was there."

"Bullshit."

Now he's on the moral defensive, red-faced and indignant: "Jayne almost offed herself with downers, okay? The doc comes out to Malibu and sees this and suddenly he gets it: the lady is an addict. He goes to her manager, who's obviously the one who runs her life, and says, 'We've got to help this lady get off drugs or she's going to die.' Magda says, 'I'll do everything I can to help.'

"Jayne throws up for two days, she's sick as a dog, they send me out at eleven o'clock at night to get some kind of goddamn tea. I have to drive all the way to Culver City to find an all-night health food store, and when I get back I hear them going at it in the den."

"Fighting?"

"Jayne's into that helpless little-girl thing, whining that she has to go to Betty Ford like the doctor says. Magda tells her"—imitating the throaty accent—" 'He only wants your money, Jay. Nobody loves you as much as I do.' "

"Magda was trying to save the contract with the cosmetics company."

"Magda was trying to control Jayne, period. She heard from Maureen that Jayne was getting close to this doctor and it freaked her out. Who do you think convinced Jayne to cut the guy off at the knees?"

"All roads lead to Magda."

"While Jayne was seeing the doctor, she tried to go straight but she was a mess—crying jags, migraines, panic attacks. Finally she went back to Maureen. Maureen didn't want the responsibility so—you're right—she took it to Magda."

Finally the dynamic of that overwrought household becomes clear, but I want it from Pauley.

"Maureen didn't want responsibility for what? Sorry if I'm being dense."

"For getting Jayne high," he exclaims with frustration.

There is silence. Rainbows turn slowly in the dust-laden air. Realizing what he has said, Pauley's face crumples but stops short of tears.

"Maureen is Jayne Mason's street connection," I supply softly. "That's why she's kept around as a 'wardrobe girl.' "

"She's a cokehead," Pauley says in a deep, choked voice. "As if you couldn't tell. Magda had her on a golden string."

"Paid for her habit?"

"You'll never get Magda. That's the beauty of it."

I desperately wish I were wearing a wire.

"Unless you turn witness. Against Magda and Maureen."

He doesn't answer. The face is hardening now, the eyes two cold ovals of red.

"Let's say in exchange for immunity from prosecution for any part you might have played in the sale or consumption of narcotics."

"Jesus, Ana, that is total crap."

"We need your testimony."

He thinks it over. After a moment, he slowly assents by nodding his head.

Just to make sure, "If you love her, why give her up?"

He seems different now, set, a grown-up man who realizes this is the last moment he may have to regain any control over the rest of his life.

"When you came out to the house," he asks, "did you ever meet Jan, the brainless beach bum?"

The windsurfing instructor with the righteous calves who was watching them that day on the beach through a pair of binoculars.

"I remember Jan."

"Maureen was fucking him the whole time."

Tom Pauley sweeps a pair of undershorts up off the floor in an angry arc and stalks toward the bedroom.

■   ■   ■

Maureen huddles in the interrogation room bawling like a baby.

"I can help you," Galloway is saying softly. "We can get you through this terrible situation, or do you want to wait until your lawyer gets here?" he adds, because the tape is running.

"This is going to kill my dad."

Galloway hands her a tissue. I let him go for it. My job is to sit there with my legs crossed, projecting female sympathy.

"The best thing you can do for your dad is take care of yourself, Maureen. You haven't been doing a very good job of that, have you?"

Maureen shakes her head. She's so clogged up with tears she can hardly breathe. The wan cheeks are raspberry red.

"Tell us where you bought the pills."

"I can't."

"Are you afraid of the dealers?"

She nods, pushing at the wet hair across her eyes.

"You have good reason. They're bad people. But see"—here Galloway sighs like the problem is really his—"if you don't give them up, you'll go to jail and they'll be out on the street doing business as usual. Is that fair?"

"It's my own fault."

I nod encouragingly.

"That's true and eventually you'll have to deal with that. But right now you can help yourself if you assist our agents in nailing these bastards."

She's silent.

"They took advantage of you. And Jayne."

Shredding the tissue into snow.

"She said she'd take care of me," Maureen whispers with her eyes down, "if anything ever happened."

Galloway opens his arms and looks around the room. His eyes pop wide. "So where is she? You tried. You used your one phone call to get through to Jayne Mason so she could trot over here—where is she?"

"Her secretary said she's in France," Maureen answers in a high voice, "because she's got this new makeup coming out."

"And if she was around the corner? Maureen. Look at me." Galloway touches her gently under the chin. "If she was around the corner, honey, would she walk into this office and admit that she's a drug addict and she used you like a slave to get what she needs? Or do you think she'd deny it and employ her influence to stay out of Maureen's little mess? You know Jayne Mason better than anyone. Tell me. Will she protect you like you're protecting her?"

You can almost hear the small bones breaking. Maureen takes three or four choppy breaths. The rage is spent, the grief begins. She weeps quietly into two open hands realizing how profoundly she's been betrayed.

When I leave the room, I run smack into Donnato.

"We got Mason's supplier. It's the wardrobe girl."

"Congratulations."

"Look."

Special Agent Jim Kelly is striding toward the interrogation room. Jim is supervisor of the Drug Squad.

"She's going to give up her street connections."

"This could turn into a nice little narcotics bust," Donnato murmurs wonderingly.

"That's because I'm terrific." I punch Donnato in the arm and laugh. "And now Galloway's got something for the Director."

"Not what they expected."

"Better than they expected. I have to hand it to Galloway, he's willing to go after Jayne Mason on possession. It's a political hotcake, but talk about publicity for the Bureau."

"You'll close the bar at Bora-Bora tonight."

"Want to partner up?"

Donnato smiles at me for the first time in weeks. "I've got dinner, homework, and a science project on electromagnets."

Rosalind comes up to where we are talking. She's wearing that peculiar look again.

"Santa Monica P.D. on the phone for Ana. You weren't at your desk. I figured I'd best come after you."

I speak to an earnest young officer named Brandt who tells me Dr. Randall Eberhardt is dead. Since the deceased has been under investigation by the FBI, he thought I might be interested in coming down to Twentieth Street to have a look, as a courtesy, in the interest of promoting interagency cooperation.

TWENTY-TWO

THE NEW CONTEMPORARY two-story Mediterranean in the exclusive neighborhood north of Montana, five bedrooms, five and a half baths, gourmet kitchen, et cetera, is now skirted by yellow tape marking it as a crime scene.

Three Santa Monica police cruisers and an ambulance are parked at the curb. There isn't a big crowd—maybe twenty-five neighbors, joggers, housekeepers with babies in strollers—because it is only 2:35 in the afternoon on a Wednesday.

I recognize a Metro reporter from the *Los Angeles Times* and there's a kid from *The Outlook,* a streamlined edition of the same *Santa Monica Evening Outlook* that ran a photograph of my grandfather and a stolen wheelchair almost thirty years ago. The two crime reporters are scouts for the media, like a pair of ants roaming your countertop; next time you look, it will be swarming.

I badge the cop at the door and walk inside. From the number of people and their intensity, I know something bad is waiting at the top of the stairs. A Santa Monica police detective is on the phone yelling about the delay in picking up the body. I heard on the radio driving over that there was a four-car collision with fatalities on the 405, so the coroner's office is probably all backed up.

I walk up the steps, past a ficus tree, toward the crystal chandelier so out of reach. I am stopped again by a cop.

"Where is it?"

"The bathroom."

Your knees go weak but you go ahead anyway, knowing that what you will see will be awful. Randall Eberhardt made sure it would be as awful as possible.

First I see the metal gas tank rolling back and forth on the silver travertine marble floor. A plastic tube attached to the tank leads over the side of the oversize spa tub. You have to walk right up and lean over to see that the tubing leads to a hole in a plastic bag which he placed over his head. The face has turned blue from cyanosis, a small amount of vomit adheres the purple lips to the inside of the bag. The well-muscled naked body, also a bluish pallor, floats in eight inches of clear water. The gas tank rolls with an empty ringing sound on the cold marble as the body subtly shifts in the water. Lined up neatly around the outside of the tub are children's bath toys—yellow rubber ducks and red pails with holes for pouring—all of it lit incongruously by warm afternoon sunlight streaming innocently through the bathroom window.

The crime scene guys are putting their triangular markers next to all the relevant objects: the small tank marked Nitrogen, the empty bottle of Valium—a prescription with Claire Eberhardt's name on it—near the sink. The forensic photographer asks me to step aside so they can get the wide-angle view. I look at Randall Eberhardt's nakedness floating in its marble sepulchre and it seems to be the effigy of all of our nakednesses—Violeta Alvarado's, mine, Tom's, and Maureen's—and I am ashamed to be the one who has survived to look at it, the way I was ashamed to see my cousin in death. Then, suddenly, I am overwhelmed by an inconsolable heartbreak, as if that underground source of my own grief had split rock and geysered a thousand feet into the air.

I stumble back down the stairs and spot the new widow alone in the living room.

I sit on the sofa beside her and introduce myself as Special Agent Ana Grey.

"Have we met?"

Lying, "No."

Her legs are crossed, ankles hooked around each other, arms holding herself entwined around the waist of her white tennis skirt.

"The police think it's a suicide, but that isn't true." She snorts and kicks her twisted legs. "Randall would never kill himself."

"What do you think happened?"

"Somebody murdered him and made it look like suicide."

She is tearless, indignant, but looking down in that peculiar walleyed way.

"Terrible things have been happening to us. He's been falsely accused, he's been hounded, his professional reputation has been attacked. If somebody could do that to us for no reason, none at all, couldn't they do this?"

"The police will complete a full investigation and an autopsy. Then you'll know."

She shakes her head. "They'll cover it up."

Her reaction is not uncommon in families where there has been a self-inflicted death. Denial. Paranoia. She can't let go of it. Of course she can't.

"If my husband were going to kill himself he would have used a gun." One hand has gotten loose from her waist and is flapping side to side. "He just bought a gun because of all the robberies in the neighborhood. Doesn't that make more sense?"

She is so encouraged by the logic of her theory that I let her believe in it for a while.

"He must have been murdered because otherwise he would have used a gun. Will the FBI get involved in that part of it?"

"I don't think so, ma'am."

"But he didn't kill himself!"

Gently and firmly, "It looks a lot like he did."

She stares at me a long time as if her ability to speak has become unplugged.

On the coffee table in front of us is a tennis racquet and white sweater and a pile of mail which she must have dropped coming in. On the cover of a catalogue from Saks Fifth Avenue is a picture of

Jayne Mason's face surrounded by yellow petals and the words "Jayne Mason Introduces Yellow Rose Cosmetics. Meet the star in person at our Beverly Hills store."

There is the image of Jayne Mason's perfect dewy face emerging from a pool covered with yellow blossoms.

Superimpose: Randall Eberhardt's dead blue face inside a plastic bag . . . and what do you get?

"I'm very sorry for your loss." I get up and walk out.

At the far corner of the bright street, Laura and the little Chilean grandmother are coming toward the house. Laura is riding a tricycle, the housekeeper pushing the baby in a stroller. Startled to see the police, the housekeeper puts her hand out to stop the child but she is already pedaling as fast as she can toward all the excitement, a look of anticipation on her simple face.

I too was five years old that night in Santa Monica when my father left forever. I turn around and thread my way back through the curious crowd, unlocking the door to the G-ride and wondering if, like me, Laura will teach herself to forget this day and everything that goes with it, and how long that kind of forgetting can last.

■　■　■

Once the freeways clear the drive out to Simi Valley only takes forty-five minutes, especially when you're doing a steady seventy-five miles an hour. It is ten at night. The top is down on the Barracuda and I don't care anymore.

Donnato's house is one of a hundred in some new development, tract houses of the nineties with round windows that are supposed to make them look interesting. The only interesting thing about Simi Valley is the way it is backed up against the mountains, the very last finger-scrapes of the Los Angeles sprawl clawing its way north—you can't get any farther from urban downtown. A lot of people still keep animals out here—horse people and breeders of Abyssinian cats who like to believe in their own freedom.

Donnato's house looks cozy and domestic with the lights on and the garage doors closed for the night. I walk up and press the chimes.

His wife opens the door. She is very attractive. A scuba instructor. Smart. Going to law school. But I don't care.

"Hi, Rochelle. Sorry to bother you."

"Ana! What's the matter?"

"Small emergency. Is Mike in?"

"Sure. Can I get you anything?"

"No, but thanks."

The air conditioning is on. The place has that plastic closed-in smell of new carpeting and new kitchen cabinets with cheap veneer.

Donnato comes downstairs quickly.

"Galloway's calling everybody in."

Donnato catches my eyes and holds them and sees the entreaty, and I believe his decision to go with me right then, to acquiesce to whatever crazy need has driven me out there, is the single most tender thing anyone has ever done for me.

"I'll go up and change." He's wearing sweats.

"You don't have to. It's a stakeout in Inglewood, not a dinner-dance," I say in a suddenly hoarse voice.

Donnato takes his gun belt from a locked box in the closet and grabs a heavy parka. His wife kisses him.

"Be careful, sweetie."

"Always."

We head out the door. "Nice to see you, Ana, except for the circumstances."

I smile and wave.

We are outside. The door closes. We climb into the Barracuda.

I screech away from the curb with unnecessary violence. Donnato has shrugged into the parka and placed the gun down on the floor near his feet. He knows perfectly well there is no stakeout.

"She set the doctor up in order to sell lipstick."

I don't say anything else until we have driven through all the blinking red traffic lights of the dark empty town and taken the first freeway on-ramp. We're heading west, that's all I know.

"Jayne Mason is hospitalized at the Betty Ford Center for drug addiction. It's all over the press. She's got a secret multitrillion-dollar contract with a major cosmetics company but they're getting nervous—who's going to buy makeup from a drug addict? The deal is worth ten times more than anything she can make in the movies and she's desperate for cash. Somebody's going to take the fall for her addiction and it's going to be Dr. Randall Eberhardt because he's stupid and naïve and just got off the boat."

Donnato sits there with his arms folded, a cyclone of cold wind blowing his hair straight back.

"That bitch manager is behind it." I slam my fist on the steering wheel.

"Hard to prove."

"I don't care. With all the shit we're getting from the wardrobe girl, I'm going to bust Jayne Mason, nail her on possession, Jesus Christ, who knows, maybe the family can sue for wrongful death."

"You're doing ninety."

"He couldn't take the humiliation. Offed himself with nitrogen gas. You know how? Very smart. The guy was smart. Hooks it up to a plastic bag, puts the bag over his head. He's a doctor so he knows the buildup of carbon dioxide inside the bag would cause a panic reaction and there's a good chance he'd pull it off in spite of himself— so he keeps on pumping nitrogen in there to displace the CO_2, that way he can keep on breathing until there's no oxygen left. A little Valium to relax, a nice warm bath, death by asphyxiation."

I pull off the freeway, fishtailing on the dusty shoulder, and brake to a stop. I don't even shut off the engine, but jam the gearshift into park and reach for Donnato, sinking my fingers into the downy shoulders of his parka, pulling him toward me, trying to swallow his mouth.

We get out. We secure our weapons in the trunk. We are on a pitch-black road next to a pitch-black field somewhere on the outskirts of Oxnard.

We walk into the field over small dry gullies.

"What do they grow here?"

"Strawberries."

We spread out a wool blanket from the days when I had Jake and Jasmine, two calicos, and, believe it or not, the smell of old cat piss can be terribly sad.

We can't get close enough we can't go deep enough we can't connect with enough bare skin. It is freezing out there, we are naked and shivering inside our jackets, frantic in the midnight darkness as if there is no other hunger.

Donnato is above, I am crushing a handful of bleeding strawberries against his clenched teeth, he is deep inside me, holding me up under the shoulder blades so my head is hanging back and my hair is dragging in the dirt, when the helicopter passes not very far above us, slicing the air with vicious pulsing whips. I open my eyes to see the shape of its belly, I know it is a military transport because we are close to Point Mugu, but it doesn't matter, I have passed through the realm of the rational into the amber twilight of my dreams. The roar hurts our ears and resonates inside our chest cavities and I am gripped by a primal fear, the way I was afraid of the chopper landing outside the Santa Monica police department, afraid of its raw male power which would soon overwhelm me. I wrap my legs around Donnato and scream his name into the howling abyss.

TWENTY-THREE

I WAKE UP ALONE in my bed at noon the following day, immediately seized by the same anxious fear. It was just past dawn when I pulled into the garage at the Marina and incredibly I was still obsessing about trying to make the morning swim workout at the college when my hands pulled the quilt over my head and my brain finally shut off.

Now my eyes are dry and burning and there is an awful pressure in my chest. Disoriented, I lurch into the living room and dial voice mail at the office in order to focus on what appointments I have blown for the day. There are several messages, including one from Carl Monte, a social worker calling about Teresa and Cristóbal Alvarado. With everything going on, it takes me by surprise but I call Mr. Monte's office right back. They promise to beep him.

There is no message from Mike Donnato, but what did I expect?

I don't know what I expected. I eat a grilled cheese sandwich and stir some cocoa powder into a glass of low-fat milk, staring dully at the billowing afternoon light outside the balcony. It has been a long time since I had sex and it is raw and sore down there, not your most romantic feeling. All I want to do is to sit in a hot bath.

I have noticed there is never any bubble bath around when you need it.

So I pull a bottle of dish detergent from underneath the kitchen sink and shoot a long stream of it into the tub, making mountains of sparkly white froth. I refill the bath with hot water three times until my skin is pink and tingly and the mirrors are all steamed up. I make a crown of foam on top of my head and put two silly mounds over my breasts like I used to do as a little girl, a bubble necklace and what the hell, a bubble beard, speculating on where Donnato is right now and if he is feeling as loose and full of wonderment as I. How will we be in the office? Will we see each other again? For the first time I can remember I have no control over what will happen next.

But that sublime balance on the razor's edge of uncertainty lasts just a moment before I am suddenly flushed with violent panic. The memory of the dark belly of the helicopter bearing down on us in the strawberry field fills my head with terrible clamor and I almost vomit into the tub.

The phone rings and my heart convulses. Suddenly transformed to a female in a 1950s comedy (Jayne Mason could have played this role), I jump out, dripping suds, grab a towel, and spring for the phone, hoping to hear the voice of my beau.

It is Carl Monte.

"I'm a case worker at Children and Family Services," he explains. "What is your relationship to the Alvarado children?"

"A distant cousin of their mother."

"Do you know they are living with Mrs. Sofía Gutiérrez?"

"Yes, she's been taking care of them since their mother was killed."

"But she is not a blood relation?"

"No."

"Does that make you the closest relative?"

"There are a grandmother, aunts, and uncles living in El Salvador."

"I need to tell you that if the children continue to live in this country, they will have to be placed in foster care."

"What happened?"

"LAPD was called because a neighbor complained about a loud television. The investigating officers found two unsupervised minors in the apartment and contacted us."

I am dressing as we talk. "Are the kids all right?"

"They're in good health, but we don't consider Mrs. Gutiérrez a suitable guardian. For one thing her household income does not meet our standard. For another, it's the law. Children can't just live with any stranger who picks them up."

I pull on jeans and socks. I understand the law.

"Unless you'd like to take them in yourself, Ms. Grey."

"*Me?*" A shock goes through my chest. I look around the Marina apartment. "I couldn't."

"Then we will place Teresa and Cristóbal in an appropriate foster care setting."

"For how long?"

"That depends. We're always looking for a legal adoption."

"What're the chances?"

"There's hope for the little one. The older girl has some emotional problems that might make her less desirable."

"You mean they wouldn't be adopted together?"

"Not necessarily."

"Well, Mr. Monte, that bites the big one."

He doesn't miss a beat, asking calmly if I'd like to be informed where the children are placed. I say okay.

"For the moment we've allowed them to live with Mrs. Gutiérrez with home inspections twice a week, but she's having a hard time understanding. She seems to hold you in high regard because you work for the FBI—"

I guffaw.

"So I was hoping you could explain this to her. Might make it easier for the children."

Sure, I'll talk to Mrs. Gutiérrez. Anything to avoid the office today.

■   ■   ■

They call it El Piojillo—a few square blocks around MacArthur Park that is not so much a flea market as another continent grafted between the Wilshire District and downtown L.A. What used to be a fashionable address for wealthy whites, where old people from a nearby nursing home could rest their wheelchairs in the shade of an elegant park, is now one of the most crime-infested parts of the city.

It is also a place where the size, spread, and density of the Spanish-speaking population becomes impressively clear. Streets in every direction are overflowing with crowds of Latinos threading past unlicensed vendors selling sausages, stuffed animals, cassettes of *lambada* music, running shoes, fruit smoothies, hot ears of corn. "Call Anywhere in the United States—25 Cents per Minute!" "Swap Meet!" in an old ornate movie theater. Video Hot, Winchell's, Salvadoran and Guatemalan restaurants. Drug dealers. Day laborers in straw cowboy hats waiting on a pickup corner for a few hours' work below minimum wage. On every block there is a stucco mini-mall with shoddy signage that looks as if it's been under artillery fire, and most likely has: Carnicería Latina, Excellent Beauty Salon, Chinatown Express, Popeye Fried Chicken, Librería Cristiana. Driving straight through, I reach a residential neighborhood on the outskirts of Echo Park and sigh with relief. Here, one hopes, the homicide rate doesn't kick in until after dark.

Mrs. Gutiérrez and the children are waiting in front of the address she gave me. It turns out to be a *botánica,* a storefront that sells herbs, candles, and spiritual advice, now locked with a rusted gate. We are on a small commercial street. Next door is a grocery called Tienda Alma, then a Mexican bakery and a Thai restaurant. Not incongruously, somewhere nearby a rooster is crowing.

"Today Don Roberto doesn't open until four. He is getting his apartment fumigated."

"Who is Roberto?"

"The spiritualist who will answer our questions."

"I don't have any questions, Mrs. Gutiérrez. I know what needs to be done."

Mrs. Gutiérrez gives an impatient *tch-tch*. With a dark and sorrowful look, Teresa lowers her eyes. I squat down and touch her hair.

"Your birthday's coming up. I'm working on a Barbie doll, how does that sound?"

Her whole face lights up with a beautiful smile. She looks like a different kid. Unable to express herself, she runs around in a circle of pure glee, then grabs her brother's hand and just as randomly runs into the doorway of Tienda Alma.

"She is such a pretty girl," Mrs. Gutiérrez observes. "Just like her mommy."

She is wearing lipstick and today, perhaps to visit the spiritualist, all white: an oversize white T-shirt, white leggings, and white mules. She looks the most together I have seen her.

"Mr. Monte wanted me to talk to you."

"I already tell him that I write to the grandmother to see what she want to do. I waiting to hear."

"Until the family is contacted, the children will have to be cared for."

"I caring for them."

"You leave them alone in the apartment."

"Only one time, when I have to go to the store."

"Teresa doesn't even have a bed."

"In my country we sleep on *petate* mats on the floor. What is more important—the bed or the love? Why you not understand about family?" she demands. "These kids are your family, but you don't think so. You are too Anglo."

"What's that supposed to mean?"

"Just like Mrs. Claire," Mrs. Gutiérrez goes on. "Her kind don't understand. If Mrs. Claire didn't fire Violeta from that job, the children would have a mother today."

I take a very deep breath.

"Mrs. Eberhardt fired Violeta because her daughter fell into a pool and almost drowned while Violeta was jabbering with another housekeeper and not paying attention."

Mrs. Gutiérrez shakes an angry finger.

"What you say is not the truth and a disgrace to the memory of your cousin."

"I have noticed there is always more than one truth, Mrs. Gutiérrez."

In answer she spits on the sidewalk and stalks into Tienda Alma.

The children are gathered around a cardboard Christmas tree studded with lollypops. I wander deeper inside, lured by the smell of spices. A rack holds packets of arnica, cinnamon stick, *chile pasilla,* anise, *te de yerbabuena.* There's not much stock—a few coconuts, oranges with green spots, two kinds of bananas, pineapples, and flowers. Rickety shelves are stacked with cans of guava nectar, hominy, sardines, *menudo,* and corn *masa* and old gray plastic sacks of rice and flour. The lights are off.

Mrs. Gutiérrez is pulling the children outside.

"Is it okay if I buy them a lollypop?"

She only glowers. I give them each a dollar, then notice that behind the lollypop tree is a picture of a saint laminated in plastic, resting on an overturned blue milk carton.

"What is that?"

Mrs. Gutiérrez isn't talking. A young woman comes out from around the counter.

"El Niño de Atocha."

She moves the rack aside to reveal a painting of a young boy surrounded by heavenly objects and animals. In front of him there are candles and a dish filled with loose change, small plastic cars, rubber balls, and candy.

The girl, wearing a USC sweatshirt and silver star earrings down to her shoulders, speaks without an accent.

"El Niño is a saint who comes from a lake and helps drowning people, or those who are lost. We have a festival in Guatemala where every year we take him out of the lake and parade him through the streets in a big procession."

"People leave him things?"

"For good luck."

"Why the toys?"

"Because he's a little kid. Roberto, next door, told my mother to make this for El Niño. Every other store on the street has been broken into except us."

"You go to USC?" She nods. "And you believe in this stuff?"

"My mother has faith on Roberto. I didn't used to believe, but people come to see him from Las Vegas, Texas, San Francisco. . . . He has a very great gift. They come sick and they leave calm."

I drop some change into the dish.

"Isn't that a funny place for a shrine?"

"A shrine can be anywhere. A lot of Spanish people make shrines in the place where someone has died, like in Baja, you see them along the road where people have been killed in car accidents." She moves the lollypop tree back in place. "We keep ours here so people won't steal from El Niño."

Some saint, I think, following Mrs. Gutiérrez outside.

The children have trailed the sounds of the rooster to a tiny pet store crammed with aquariums and rank with the smell of tropical fish in stagnant water. Two roosters blink suspiciously from cages on the floor.

"Are those fighting cocks?" I ask the man.

He nods. Cock fighting is illegal, but the hell with it. The children are fascinated by a pair of parakeets. Although Mrs. Gutiérrez is keeping her back to me, I lay a hand on her shoulder.

"I want to know the truth about my cousin."

The two of us step outside where the long hot afternoon sun smacks our faces with a direct hit. Mrs. Gutiérrez pats her white vinyl pocketbook several times. She is still seething.

"Your cousin was fired because she saw Mrs. Claire with a man who was not her husband."

"When was this?"

"Violeta came back from a walk with the baby and a man was with Mrs. Claire inside the door."

I remember Warren Speca telling me that he saw Violeta one time when he went over to Claire's near the end of their affair. This must have been the time.

Mrs. Gutiérrez waves a hand in disgust. "They were doing bad things."

I can see Warren Speca surprising Claire, emboldened by the fantasy that she will leave her marriage, pushing her up against the wall of her husband's house and trying to make love right there, standing up, underneath the crystal chandelier.

"Violeta came in. They were surprised but they no care. The man leave right away. Violeta is very angry. She is a religious person—"

Mrs. Gutiérrez's voice breaks. She wipes her eyes.

" 'You have a husband,' she tells Mrs. Claire. 'You sin against God.' "

The pocketbook opens and the pound-size roll of tissues comes out.

"Violeta says, 'I love your children like they are mine. I leave my own children to work for you. I no lie to you but you lie to me. You are sleeping around like a whore!' Mrs. Claire fires her on the spot."

"She was afraid Violeta would tell her husband about the affair."

"Yes." Mrs. Gutiérrez blows her nose savagely. Her manner turns cold. She is going to tell me the facts of life:

"Mrs. Claire spreads this terrible lie that it was Violeta's fault the little girl almost drowned. Violeta cannot get a job. She does not have a reference. She cannot pay the rent. Teresa has a bad ear infection and the clinic takes only cash. Violeta is terrified that she and the children will end up on the street or in a church basement with the homeless, or maybe the welfare people will take the children away. After many weeks she finds work at night, washing the laundry in a big health club in West L.A. Her children sleep in my apartment until she comes home at six in the morning. Only one night, she doesn't come home."

The crime scene photos tell the story. Violeta gets off the bus on a destitute corner before dawn, trudging past hustlers and dealers. By now the route is habitual. She's almost home, she's tired, her guard fails.

"This is why I say it was the fault of Mrs. Claire."

I remember Claire Eberhardt's overwhelming guilt the very first time I met her at the front door. She was acting like a suspect with something to hide: an illicit affair. A desperate cover-up that ended in ruin.

"Here also is the truth: the girl did fall into the pool, but it was Violeta who saved her life."

My eyebrows raise in skepticism but Mrs. Gutiérrez nods many times.

A youngish man with dyed auburn hair walks up to us and unlocks the rusted gates.

Mrs. Gutiérrez makes a small deferential bow, as if to a priest. *"Buenos días, Don Roberto."*

He returns the formal greeting, pushes the gate open, and continues inside.

Mrs. Gutiérrez speaks with breathless urgency: "The only person who knows what is best for the children is the mother. The government of the United States will *not* decide. Don Roberto will ask the spirit of Violeta. She alone will tell us what to do."

Hispanic workers are getting off buses, sending curious glances my way as they stop into Tienda Alma on their way home. Mrs. Gutiérrez has gathered the children. With a last look at the busy street bathed in setting sun, I follow the *clap-clap* of her heels into the darkened *botánica*.

■   ■   ■

Mrs. Gutiérrez, Roberto, and I sit in the back of the shop at a card table upon which is a small radio and a white candle. I wonder if we will hear Violeta's voice through the speaker. Roberto is about twenty-five years old, a homosexual with a dark complexion, a hip haircut that is partially shaved at the neck and longer on top, and a gold hoop earring. He wears a silky tan shirt and brown pants, but something is out of whack. The body is out of proportion—arms too long for a stunted torso—and he has trouble speaking. One side of the mouth seems to be paralyzed and as he struggles to explain how he got his gift, fingers rub the forehead with frustration:

"My father and grandfather did this in our village. A hundred people would stand in line at the door. I learned from the age of seven."

When it comes to spiritual advice the deal is simple: "You tell me the truth and I tell you the truth."

He lights the candle.

Despite the battle-scarred exterior, the place has clean floors and a certain order, and smells pleasantly of lavender incense. Behind old-fashioned wooden counters are shelves filled with small square half-ounce bottles of red, blue, and green oils. Floor-to-ceiling cases are filled with eight-inch glass candles, each with a picture of a saint and a promise of luck or salvation or protection.

From the ceiling hang ropes of colored beads. Near the door are packets of herbs and spices, a model made of plaster of paris of a Native American chief, and an aloe plant, colored ribbons tied in bows on its spiky leaves. A display holds rosaries, statues of cows, pendants with single eyeballs looking out of black triangles, greasy little booklets about "Red Magic" and "Green Magic," and on a revolving rack there are plastic pictures of all the saints, numbered for easy selection.

We have left Teresa and Cristóbal with the Indian chief and staring eyeballs to sit at the card table behind a partition. Behind us is a multilevel altar upon which have been placed glasses of water, candles, pots of chrysanthemums, and a dish holding three small eggs covered with colored confetti.

A lot of the reading takes place in Spanish with a few sidebars in English. Mrs. Gutiérrez talks about the situation of Violeta's children. Don Roberto listens and asks her to write out her name and her mother's maiden name on a pad. He counts up the letters in the names then deals that number of Tarot cards.

"Please think about the mother of these children, Violeta Alvarado."

She obediently closes her eyes. I stare at the radio and conjure up the photo of the parrot. Then the feeling comes to me of holding Violeta's small leather Bible in my hands; the dryness of it, like the poignant tiny body of a hummingbird I once found on my balcony.

Mrs. Gutiérrez is warned not to cross her legs or lean on the table as that would affect "the energy." She must turn over two cards, right to left. The first is *El Sol,* The Sun.

"This card means El Salvador," says Don Roberto.

The second, with a baby on it, represents America.

Yawning, he mixes the cards with great practiced sweeps and gathers them up again. He asks Mrs. Gutiérrez to pick sixteen.

"Now you must think about this person very hard."

We are silent. Mrs. Gutiérrez bends her head forward in prayer. Don Roberto whispers, "I feel her spirit is very close. Tell us, *mamá,* what is your wish concerning your two beautiful children?"

Solemnly Roberto spreads out the sixteen cards Mrs. Gutiérrez has chosen. He nods and she turns one over at random. It is the card called *El Sol.*

A chill goes through my body like a temblor.

Roberto's mouth twists with the effort of expressing what he sees. "The mother wants the children to come home to the grandmother in El Salvador."

Mrs. Gutiérrez presses both hands over her heart.

"I always know that!"

He indicates that she turn over the card right next to *El Sol.* It is The Devil. *Infierno!*

"But"—the side of the face contorts and a stutter clicks out—"El Salvador will be a living hell."

Mrs. Gutiérrez cries sharply, causing Teresa to look over anxiously from where she has been spinning the rack of saints.

"The children must stay here."

"No!"

"It is best."

She shakes her head and cries and grips Don Roberto's hands. I am unnerved by the depth of her feeling.

The young man's head twists close. "I will tell you about Violeta," he says softly and with difficulty. "She is not at peace."

All at once I know this is true, not only for Violeta but for legions of the dead. Legions of them.

"She had lighter skin than me," Don Roberto goes on. "She liked to laugh. It is not certain that the children are of the same father."

Mrs. Gutiérrez nods eagerly.

"There is another child, a lost child."

The boy in El Salvador. Hot tears are in my eyes and I'm afraid I'm going to lose it.

"And she had a very great struggle in the water."

Mrs. Gutiérrez lets go of his hands and sits up with wonder.

"Yes," she says, "in a swimming pool."

Don Roberto closes his eyes.

"Violeta is struggling in the water. Somebody is in danger. They are drowning. On the bottom of the pool Violeta sees *una bruja del mar*. A sea witch!"

Mrs. Gutiérrez gasps and a shudder goes through me.

"The witch has long white hair and blue eyes. It is a jealous witch and its hand is around the ankle of the one who is drowning, trying to pull this person deep into the water, away from all life."

Don Roberto rubs his forehead and squeezes his eyes tight.

"Violeta is very afraid, but she has a good heart."

Mrs. Gutiérrez gives a mournful sob.

"And because she has a good heart she does not leave the water but grabs the drowning person. And this time, *this one time,* the sea witch let go. The person is saved."

■   ■   ■

Mrs. Gutiérrez pays $20 for the spiritual consultation, $2 for a picture of El Niño, and $1.75 for a half ounce of red oil called Rompe Caminos, which Don Roberto says will "open up the four roads." Looking at the bottle, I see the oil is manufactured in Gardena, California.

"And you," he warns me, "if you continue to think of your cousin too much, *you will become like her.*"

I don't know if that means Salvadoran or dead, but Don Roberto recommends this remedy: Fill a container with a mixture of goat's milk, cow's milk, and coconut milk, available at Tienda Alma. Remove the petals from a white flower, add any kind of perfume I like and eggshells, ground up very fine. Step into a shower and pour the entire thing over my head. This will relax me and provide a "spiritual cleansing."

Then I am to float a white flower in a glass of water and place the water higher than my head. The top of the refrigerator is ideal. Every four days I must change the flower, but I do not throw it *down,* I throw it *up.* In this way, Violeta's spirit will rise, and if I do this for thirteen days, Violeta's spirit will rest at peace.

Still feeling unaccountably moved, I pluck a plaster saint dressed in blue robes from the shelf as a talisman, but Don Roberto refuses to sell it to me.

"You don't need this. Perform the remedy I have given. If you have faith, it will work," Don Roberto says, chopping at the words, *"like a miracle."*

Outside I offer Mrs. Gutiérrez a ride back to North Hollywood but, not wanting any favors from me, she says she prefers the bus.

"What do you think?" I ask.

She is subdued. "I have faith on Don Roberto."

"You know the children will have to go into foster care."

She nods sadly.

"Barbie and I will see you on your birthday," I promise Teresa.

She responds with that wonderful smile. "Thank you, Miss Ana."

"And, Cristóbal—I'll have something for you, too."

Still there is a tearing in my chest as I get back into the car, for what the children will go through, a merry-go-round of depleted social services until they get pregnant, get shot, or turn eighteen. But there is hope. There is me. I can make a difference. I can make sure they're treated well. I can be their advocate. I vow to talk to their teachers. Keep them out of gangs. Take them up to the FBI office, like other agents do for their kids, it really makes an impression. I'll treat them to the movies and the zoo. I'll take my young cousins to the beach.

By now I have crossed back up to Jefferson, a bleak landscape of low brick industrial buildings with curls of razor wire on the roofs, bordered by chain-link fences plastered with posters for hair braiding and discount video games. Savage graffiti—huge letters, cyclones of letters—roils across rippled metal walls. A hundred Black Muslims crowd out of a small church onto the street, deeply different from the Latinos in El Piojillo, all of them a galaxy away from the lunchtime shoppers north of Montana.

If only a bit of red oil could open up the four roads. The roads are dead, like dead nerves that no longer connect, and there are so many Violeta Alvarados, rolling around like marbles in a heartless maze.

I swing onto the freeway, thinking of the dead sidewalk on Santa Monica Boulevard where she lay watching helplessly as darkness rose from the bottom of her vision permeating everything, mouth, nose, eyes, gradually ending in the sounds of this noisy world with a grand silence.

Then she is alone in darkness and after a while she can't tell which is which—life being rolled away from her or a curtain lifted.

The pupils of her eyes jerk once, then stop.

Her body stops.

She knows she has drowned. The hands of the sea witch are wrapped around her ankles and this time she doesn't have the strength to pull away. But no—it isn't the sea witch! It is her own mother, Constanza, and she is lifting her little girl up from this terrifying lonely darkness to the safety of her shoulder where the world is secure and bright. What a relief that it is Mother, I think, passing a truck and flooring it to seventy. Mother, after all.

TWENTY-FOUR

I WISH I COULD SAY the mood in the office was radically changed by events concerning the Mason case; that people approached my desk with reverence and wonder at the turn it had taken, a Westside doctor dead by suicide, a major film star under a narcotics investigation. Maureen has given up the name of a dealer who turned out to be linked to the Mexican mafia, so one thing Jayne Mason did not fabricate was the fact that the Dilaudid came from Mexico. This is a good lead for Jim Kelly and the ladies and gents of the Drug Squad, but for the rest of the bullpen it is business as usual.

From the vantage point of my desk I make the observation that everyone's got their own problems. Each agent out there is working forty cases and in my wire basket alone there are two dozen unfinished reports on armed bank robberies. But at this moment the only response I can muster to all this savagery is to sit here patiently linking one paper clip to another.

When Henry Caravetti rolls by in the electric wheelchair delivering mail, my interest peaks but not for long. It will take weeks to process the transfer to the C-1 squad, and I will probably spend the entire time planted right here, trying to work up the nerve to talk to Mike Donnato. We have been avoiding each other for days.

It's going to be a very long paper clip chain.

The problem is . . . well, they don't have a word for it for females, but I've heard male colleagues refer to the condition as "continuous tumescence." It's a localized sensation down there that flares into acute, unbearable craving whenever I catch a glimpse of, say, the small of his back and think about slipping my hands inside the belt and slowly pulling out the tails of the sweet-smelling denim shirt, feeling the warm skin, drawing my fingertips down the spine to that place where it tapers, just above the hard curve of the buttock. I'd better get up and walk.

The Bank Dick's Undercover Disguise gives a friendly nudge. Donnato is across the room with Kyle and Frank, wearing that denim shirt, a forest green knit tie, and jeans, standing in what strikes me as a very provocative pose, hands clasped behind his head, stretching the chest and armpits open, open, open. Stumbling forward I tell myself it is perfectly reasonable to join the talk, which is almost certainly about the coming matchup in the All-Star Game, getting myself psyched by rehearsing a line I read in the sports page about San Francisco's manager, Roger Craig, and the A's manager, Tony La Russa, who is a vegetarian.

Halfway there, SAC Robert Galloway prevents this potentially sweaty encounter by intercepting and escorting me into his office. I figure I might as well use the line on him:

"You think Roger Craig will pound La Russa into a veggie burger?"

"I'll always have a sweet spot for Roger Craig," Galloway says. "He pitched the first game ever played by the Mets and had the distinction of finishing the season with ten wins and twenty-four losses."

Galloway picks up the NYPD detective belt buckle from the coffee table and hefts it in his hand, saying nothing.

I stand self-consciously in the middle of the room.

"Did Jayne mail that back to you?"

"I asked a captain back in New York to send a new one. Made me jumpy without it."

"Great, because now you're the picture of calm."

Galloway's fingers run uncertainly through his wavy black hair. Obviously something's up.

"I want you to go back and talk to the widow."

"Randall Eberhardt's widow?"

"I want you to convey the sympathy of the Bureau concerning her loss."

I want to throw a fit right there on the gold carpet.

"What am I supposed to say?"

"That we know her husband was innocent and we're going to find the real bastards."

He lowers the blinds against the morning glare.

"I'm lousy at diplomacy."

"Just go see her, woman to woman. Keep it low-key."

"Why do I have to do this?"

"Because it's good for the image of the Bureau . . . and because it happens to be the right thing."

He sits in the executive chair and studies the closed blinds. This is his way of taking responsibility for the grotesque raid on the medical office that may or may not have contributed to Randall Eberhardt taking his own life. Suicide is a mystery, we will never know; although I am deeply touched and admire Galloway's humanity, I wish like hell he would write his own damn condolence card.

■   ■   ■

I wait until dark, in order to make the visit seem after hours, "low-key." Boy do I not want to do this. The idea of offering sympathy to a woman who first cheats on her husband, then blackballs an innocent housekeeper for finding out, is absolutely loathsome. I plan to deliver the words and leave. Heading down San Vicente, I am pricked by just the slightest compulsion to drive by Poppy's old place on Twelfth Street one last time, and I give in to the feeling completely, relishing the luxury of even the briefest detour.

But when I pull up to the house it is very strange: the lights are on and someone is walking back and forth inside.

I park at the curb and walk up the concrete path past the beech tree to the entryway, where I pause to fit my hand into the curve of the door handle, testing the sense memory, resting my thumb on the old latch which has been worn to a green patina. Reading Lock, it says. The round doorbell crusted over with brown paint doesn't work but the door is unlocked.

I step inside to a small square room with oak flooring and a cast-iron register for gas heat. Immediately a rosy-cheeked lady wearing a blue blazer, with white hair in a long swinging braid, emerges from the kitchen extending her hand.

"Hi, I'm Dina Madison, Pacific Coast Realty, how are you tonight? Wonderful starter house, don't you think?"

"It *was* a starter house. I grew up in it."

"You're kidding. If you're considering it for sentimental value, grab it quick. I just showed the property to two Korean gentlemen who want to buy the place next door and tear them both down and build two smart houses."

"What's a smart house?"

"Usually about five thousand square feet, five or six bedrooms, master suite, fireplaces, all the amenities. No backyard, but that's what you sacrifice."

"I've seen them." The Eberhardt house is one.

"I have mixed feelings myself," she agrees, reacting to my tone. "I've heard them called anti-architecture. They're too big for the lot and can be ugly as sin, but they sell in the millions of dollars, um-hum. People are always looking for new."

The previous owners left an artificial tree.

"So you grew up here. I've been selling Santa Monica real estate probably since you were born. When I started in 1961, no new houses had been built north of Montana for ten years. People would leave their tiny California bungalows on small lots and buy a ranch house in the Pacific Palisades. They were looking for new. Montana was a funky little street, um-hum. You had the Kingsberry Market and Sully's gas station. We used to have a lot of gas stations, as far as that's concerned."

"I'd like to see the backyard."

I walk past her through a kitchen made of maple cabinets. I

can't bear to stop, to think of what happened here and what did not. A tiny Sony Watchman television plays on a chipped white tile counter.

"I take that with me everywhere," she explains. "You spend so much time sitting in empty houses."

She follows me to the back door, still talking.

"Do you remember the Chevron station on the northwest corner of Seventh and Montana? Then there was the Flying A station and of course then you had the Union 76 station at Eleventh. There was the Arco station at Fourteenth and you had another Mobil station up there . . ."

I let the screen door bang shut in the face of this eulogy over the lost gas stations of Santa Monica and walk down the steps into the backyard. A single floodlight mounted on a tall pole illuminates the faded polka dots of an umbrella set in a hole in the middle of a round table. I pull up a rickety metal chair and listen to the sound of the ocean breeze in the leaves and a child next door saying, *"Ahh-ahh-ahh."*

My eye follows a ladder going up to the green shingled roof, where a rusty old TV antenna shows against the sky, undoubtedly the same one that used to bring me *The Dick Van Dyke Show.* A car passes in the alley and I notice there is a double fence, chain link leaning against a taller one made of wood. Maybe it was cheaper to put up the chain link to support the original rather than tear it down and build an entirely new structure, tight, with no space between the redwood planks, no chance of light strobing through as it used to do at night when we lived here. The clarity of the memory startles me. Did I spend a lot of time in the backyard at night?

"You probably don't remember, but along the Palisades tract between Seventh Street and the ocean you could get a double lot for forty thousand dollars."

I turn with a start toward the diffuse shape of the real estate woman standing behind the screen door.

"They started splitting those lots in the fifties and of course Lawrence Welk built his shining white tower and now you have what I call skyscrapers. We didn't retain the respect for the Pacific Ocean that we should have, um-hum. What you see now as far as that's concerned is Santa Monica rebuilding itself for the twenty-first century."

I rise impatiently and push the door open. The real estate woman has turned toward the television on the counter, where the lead story on the local evening news concerns a small riot that occurred in Beverly Hills when Jayne Mason made an appearance at Saks Fifth Avenue to introduce her new line of makeup.

Nobody had imagined that two thousand women would line up to see her. Crowd control failed and a mob of middle-aged housewives ran amok through the cosmetics department. We're watching this ridiculous footage on a silly little miniature screen and all this lady can say is "Isn't she beautiful?" as Jayne Mason is shown throwing roses to the crowd. "She's *still* the most beautiful woman in the world." Fifteen seconds later the story ends on the solemn note that just days ago the doctor Ms. Mason had sued for overprescribing narcotics committed suicide. Again they flash that blurry hunched-over photograph of Randall Eberhardt, with the strong implication that he killed himself because he had committed health care fraud.

I am handed a sheet of paper describing the house and stating that it is priced to sell at $875,000. I ball it up and drop it into the artificial tree on my way out.

Unsettled and unhappy, I drive up to Twentieth Street and park in front of the Eberhardt residence, forcing myself to trudge up the walk. Whatever hostility I had toward Claire Eberhardt begins to fade the moment she opens the door.

She is gaunt, with dark puffy circles under the eyes. An old yellow button-down shirt hangs over the sharp bones of her shoulder blades. The cuffs are turned up, it is huge on her. Maybe it was Randall's or maybe she has lost ten pounds in the last week. Behind her the house seems empty, just a television reverberating in the background, tuned to the same local news I had just seen over on Twelfth Street. I realize she has been watching her husband being brutalized by the media all over again.

I introduce myself once more because she is obviously too

agitated to focus. When the word "FBI" penetrates, she starts to tremble.

"Why? What are you doing here?" One eye turns red and starts leaking tears. A shaking hand pats at her cheek.

"I was asked to apprise you of our investigation."

"Why me?"

"We want you to know that your husband is no longer the target. . . ."

"No longer the target?"

"He's been cleared of any wrongdoing. I hope that's of some comfort to you."

Confronted by her unresponsive devastated face, I feel like a total fool, retreating behind even more pompous language: "We are aggressively pursuing the real criminal who we hope will be brought to justice by the legal system."

She's not hearing me. She is numb, the words must be coming at her all scrambled.

"He killed himself."

"I know."

"The children are back in Boston with my folks. It's funny, my daughter really loved California. . . ."

She is actually smiling. A horrible Sardonicus grin webbed with glistening strings of tears.

". . . But now she's afraid to be in this house. That little girl was her daddy's princess."

In the examining room Dr. Eberhardt told me about his daughter, a little monkey climbing up on a piano. I remember the easy tenderness in his voice.

"I just saw Jayne Mason on the news. She looked good. She claims she never had plastic surgery and Randall said it's true. I bet she sells a lot of makeup. We always liked her in the movies, but, really, she has such an incredible voice. Even before she became a patient, we had all her albums. Brought them out from Boston."

A spasmodic grimace.

"Will you be moving back?"

She doesn't respond to the question.

"Did you know I got a call from a talk show? They want to do something on 'wives of doctors who are criminals.' "

"That's gross."

"I told them Randall was not a criminal. He didn't do anything wrong."

"We know that, Mrs. Eberhardt."

"Jayne Mason did."

Suddenly the perfume of night-blooming jasmine seems incredibly strong, embracing us both in its sickly burnt-sugar scent.

"What did Jayne Mason do that was wrong?"

Claire Eberhardt's arms wrap around her waist against a wet sea breeze. The first time we met across this threshold we shared an understanding, nurse and cop, of the way the world works. Once again those imperfect eyes hold mine.

But all she will say is "Good luck," and softly closes the door.

I walk back and get into my car and start the engine. As I am making a U-turn lights flash in the rearview mirror and I see Randall Eberhardt's bronze Acura pivoting wildly out of the driveway. Its tires bump over the curb and the brights are on. First it seems to be coming straight at me and I am momentarily blinded. Suddenly the mirror goes dark and I realize Claire Eberhardt has turned and is heading the other way, toward San Vicente Boulevard.

I swing the Barracuda around and follow her down the Seventh Street incline to Chatauqua and onto Pacific Coast Highway heading north.

I keep thinking about that immigrant Japanese woman who was so shamed by a philandering husband that she walked across the sand right here at Will Rogers Beach, through the surf and into the Pacific Ocean, carrying both her young children. The children drowned, she didn't. But Claire Eberhardt is alone in the car, maintaining a steady fifty-five miles an hour and stopping prudently at every red light. She keeps on going and I relax a little, thinking maybe she's out for a drive to let off steam, but just past Pepperdine she turns left onto Arroyo Road, which leads to Jayne Mason's property.

I am prevented from following by an entire motorcycle gang,

thirty or forty of them mounted on their Harleys and strung out over a quarter mile, zipping by on the opposite side of the road like an unending pack of maddening bees. Stalled here with the turn signal flashing, my adrenaline pumps higher and higher.

A long time ago, it seems, I was in a free-floating situation like this in the parking lot of a bank. Civilians may have been threatened, I had no way of knowing, but I chose to ride it out on arrogance and guts without calling for backup. That time I was lucky. This time I pick up the radio.

"This is signal 345," I tell the radio room at the Bureau office. "Request that you call the L.A. County Sheriff, Malibu station, and ask that they respond immediately to a possible disturbance at the Mason property on Arroyo Road. Make sure they know there's an FBI agent present who needs help."

The bikers pass and I dive across the highway, cranking the Barracuda up to fifty in second, bumping over the dirt road underneath the eucalyptus trees, along the dark empty meadow, until I see the guard gate coming up fast. Claire Eberhardt must have used her husband's pass to get through because now the armature is down. Reasoning the barrier would delay the sheriff's department, certain now that I don't have a lot of time, I duck my head and crash right through it, catapulting the wooden arm up in the air and into the brush, hoping it didn't damage the grillwork.

All of this has given Claire Eberhardt a good three-minute lead. I swerve over the gravel of the parking lot, sliding to a stop beside Magda Stockman's Cadillac. The Acura has been left with the engine running. The front door in the white wall is ajar. She must have gained admission to the house with her husband's key.

I run into the courtyard, which is underlit by just two sparse spots and wavering green lights in the pool. At the far end of the darkened patio Claire Eberhardt approaches the large figure of Magda Stockman. Stockman says something with a dismissive gesture toward the intruder, then bends over to pick up a coiled garden hose and hang it back on its hook.

I keep coming forward, calling out, "Claire!"

Someone pushes the sliding glass door open a little farther and says, "Hello out there. What's going on?"

For an instant Jayne Mason is clearly visible standing on the threshold of the lighted room.

Claire Eberhardt pulls a gun and gets off two shots. The glass blows, a triple explosion that takes place in less than two seconds.

My weapon is out and aimed at the doctor's wife.

"Police. Drop the gun."

Her head spins toward me in a shining blur of dark hair. I flinch but hold firm. My legs are planted and my arms are steady. I am going on reflex now, hundreds of hours of training enabling a bypass for the emotions clawing at the edges of my mind.

"Put the weapon down."

Magda Stockman takes a step and Claire Eberhardt whirls, jamming the gun into her chest and forcing her back against a stone planter.

"Put it down," I say steadily.

"Don't be stupid," Stockman rasps. "We have to call an ambulance."

To my right, out of peripheral vision, I see long cracks and a chunk taken out of the door. Inside the room Jayne Mason is down, sputtering and gasping and coughing up blood that splatters against long ragged fingers of glass.

"Listen to me, Claire. I've already called for backup. The authorities are coming."

"Go ahead and shoot me." Claire Eberhardt's face is distorted in the light falling softly like snow.

"You have too much to live for. Think of Laura and Peter. Peter's only one year old. Do you want them to go through life without a father and mother?"

I have taken a step closer. Her gun is still pinned against Stockman's chest.

"I have sympathy for you, Claire. I know what you went through. You can make this okay. Put yours down and I'll put mine down and we'll talk about it."

She only stares, malfunctioning.

"Think about your children, that's all you have to do."

Very slowly Claire Eberhardt bends at the waist and lets the weapon drop.

"Madness!" Stockman cries, staggering toward the house.

"You did the right thing," I tell Claire Eberhardt quickly. "Now just relax."

We hear sirens and, shortly, the clatter of police radios outside the gate. With the subject neutralized and backup on site, I can get up close. Although I holster my weapon, my hand stays on it as I approach, keeping up a patter of soothing words. The gun turns out to be a little five-shot .38 Smith & Wesson revolver, just what a panicked doctor would buy to protect his home. It's not very accurate past twenty feet. I kick it out of reach.

I put a hand on Claire's shoulder and she wilts under the touch, sinking down on the edge of the planter murmuring, "I'm sorry."

The locals take over. It's not my jurisdiction. They handcuff the suspect and take her into custody. They administer CPR and call the paramedics, who arrive with a lieutenant from the homicide division of the sheriff's department. We exchange cards and he asks that I report to the Malibu station to make a statement.

I watch from the outside, through a big hole taken out of the door by the bullets, as the paramedics cut away the blood-soaked blouse covered with shards of glass and put patches on the victim's chest in order to send the vital signs over the radio to a local ER. The beautiful face is relaxed, a normal blush going to pale, the eyes drowsily closed. One of the technicians pushes on the chest and air gurgles up through the blood. "Hemothorax," he says. The homicide lieutenant wants to know the status of the victim in order to charge the suspect. The hospital radios back that there are no vital signs. There was a lot of damage. The actress probably died within minutes of the shots being fired. The charge is murder.

The last time I am aware of Magda Stockman she is on her knees on the wet concrete, with her head down and hands clasped, weeping, "Oh my God, Jay, oh my God, Jay," and it's odd that the grievous sobs should sound exactly like my mother's. I haven't heard her voice like that, out loud, in my ears, for fifteen years. When they say her famous client is dead, Magda Stockman's forehead lowers very slowly to the ground and she stays that way for a long time, bowed down in a pose of mortification, until someone drags her to her feet.

I remember my mother crying and flush hot with fear.

It woke me up in my bed. I wandered out to the hallway and she told me to put a sweater over my pajamas because, as strange as it seemed, we were going to the Pier for ice cream. I remember there were wooden cutouts of Mary and her lamb on the wall over my bed and I even had a black woolly lamb with a music box inside that played the song.

I was clutching that lamb when I came out of the bedroom the second time, buttoned up in a sweater because I was a good and obedient little girl. There were voices and shouting in the back-yard. I couldn't find my mother so I went outside where my father and grandfather were arguing violently. My parents must have just driven in from Las Vegas, where they had gotten married, and Poppy must have been crazy with rage that this ignorant wetback dared to take his daughter, threatening him with the black policeman's night-stick, jabbing it into the air.

I got between them. My father picked me up and I held on, my legs wrapped around his waist, while Poppy tried to pull me out of his arms. They were both shouting at the same time. I fell into the grass and a car passed in the alley, spraying the yard with strips of light. In the strobing headlights, I saw. It was not some foreman in a bean field, it was my grandfather who raised his nightstick and smacked my father across the temple and around the shoulders and neck again and again until blood streaked his temples, he suddenly convulsed and collapsed and lay still.

The engine roared, the loudest sound in the universe, as I scrambled into the car parked in front of the house where my mother had been waiting for me, squirming into her lap behind the big wheel, telling her what I had seen, perhaps, or maybe unable to ut-ter a word, but whatever I said we did drive to the Pier that night, I remember how the sea wind cut through my sweater and how we sat on a bench and how, finally, she held me to her chest and cried. Whether she knew or suspected that her own father had killed her new husband, I'll never know. I wonder how he disposed of the body but after all, he was a law enforcement officer, who better to conceal a crime? Maybe he dumped it up in Topanga Canyon, maybe he delivered it to the coroner's office with a report about two drunks fighting in a Mexican bar, but Mother must have known that Miguel Sanchez left her because in some way he was defeated by Poppy's rage and then she too succumbed to Poppy and lived her life in service to him until, apparently, it was meaningless to stay alive any longer, and whatever witness I might have borne to the incident I buried, for myself and, now I see, for her.

"Ana. I'm here."

He is speaking very gently, maybe because he knows I am not at that moment on this earth. Slowly a high-pitched hum that has occluded my hearing subsides and the sounds of the waves come back, flat, regular, distant. I have been standing at the edge of the cliff.

"I was just leaving the office when you called it in. Kyle and I hauled ass out here."

"Thank you."

"We look out for our own."

I don't respond.

Mike Donnato puts his arms around me and I lean back against his chest, watching the long white line of the breaking surf against a charcoal sea.

"Are you okay?"

I shake my head no. Not okay.

"What can I do?" he asks.

I turn to him and we embrace fully, emotionally.

"I'm here for you," he whispers.

I find his eyes in the dark. They are full of questions.

Finally I say, "I can't."

"Why?"

"There's always a betrayal in it."

I pull away and don't look back. Thirty minutes later I am at the Malibu station, making my statement.

TWENTY-FIVE

SAC ROBERT GALLOWAY holds a news conference at our office to disclose the details of Jayne Mason's death. He orchestrates it carefully, making sure the coroner himself is there and the L.A. County Sheriff and that they both take the proper tone of respect for the loss of an American icon. One of those doyennes of MGM musicals whose name I never remember—the one who's eighty years old and still wears a pixie haircut—reads a statement announcing the creation of the Jayne Mason Fund for Gun Control. The press gets what it wants and treats Galloway well. He leaves the podium looking quite pleased.

Under the guise of being a law enforcement officer, Barbara Sullivan is able to attend the funeral—or at least claim a good spot alongside the security force with a clear view of the front steps of the Beverly Hills Presbyterian Church. She says the high point was seeing Sean Connery, but there were enough Hollywood celebrities in attendance to stoke the tabloids for months. As in major presidential events, the media held a lottery to determine which journalists would be admitted to the sanctuary. No cameras were allowed but, from the plethora of "insider" photographs of the rose-strewn coffin, grieving ex-husbands (including the used car king), children, and grandchildren, one may conclude that plenty of invited mourners were packing Instamatics inside those black Chanel bags.

Barbara returns from the funeral looking wan.

"I was a witness to history," she declares, busying herself hanging up the jacket of her dark gray suit, checking phone messages, and finally pouring her famous cinnamon brew into two dark blue mugs with the FBI shield.

"No wise-ass remarks?"

In better times I would tell her that her attachment to Jayne Mason is pathological, but I haven't the energy. I just shake my head.

"What's the matter with you?" she asks.

"I don't know. I just feel like crying all the time."

I shrug. Barbara's blue eyes are kind.

"It was a trauma."

"That part didn't bother me."

"Oh come on, seeing somebody get shot? You should talk to Harvey McGinnis."

"You're not the first person to suggest that."

"So?"

"I don't need a shrink."

"That's what Patty McCormack said in *The Bad Seed.*"

She sips coffee. I have no interest in mine.

"Have you been swimming?"

"No."

"At least go swimming."

"It's hard enough just to get out of bed." I stand. "Thanks for the java."

Big sister Barbara says, "This isn't good."

"I'll get through it."

Diligently I continue to work through the pile of bank robbery reports, taking refuge in the drone of it. I meet Donnato's new partner, Joe Positano, one of those wound-up gung-ho jocks with a nerdy square face and ultrashort hair who thinks he's going to save the world. I thought I'd be jealous but every time he and Donnato leave the office it's a relief, until finally Donnato corners me at the front desk.

"You've been acting like this is some kind of a high school flirtation."

"That's ridiculous." I squeeze past him. "Excuse me, I have to buy a Barbie doll."

He wraps his fingers around my neck in a relatively playful way and tugs me out the side door as if I were a wriggling puppy.

But when we're alone in the echoing stairwell the fun ends. We don't kiss, we don't even come close, in fact stand as far apart as possible, as if the air separating us had suddenly taken on the density of the atmosphere of Jupiter.

"I'm leaving Rochelle. We've been talking about it for a long time."

"Oh Jesus, Mike."

"It's going to be shit, pure shit for the kids."

He draws a sleeve across his eyes. Now mine are wet.

"Don't do this for me."

"Who said it had anything to do with you?"

I move farther away, so my back is against the rough cinderblock wall.

"I told you, I can't. Whether you're married or not."

A strange indoor wind is blowing up the stairwell creating an unsettling moan.

"So everything that's been going on is just—nothing."

Aching, "Not at all."

"Then what?"

He has asked but now averts his eyes, undefended.

"I don't believe it's possible."

"What isn't?" He gives a small laugh. "Happiness? Trust? The future of the world? What?"

Then he sees only silence.

"Got it," he says finally.

I believe the best course of action is to leave it as it is.

"If any of this between you and Rochelle was my fault, I am truly sorry."

I hurry down the stairs.

■   ■   ■

The alkies and I are all lined up in Thrifty's on Santa Monica Boulevard in North Hollywood. They're buying $3.95 pints of gin to get them through the night and I'm holding a pack of little plastic infantrymen for Cristóbal and a Barbie doll for Teresa, wishing I had the body chemistry to be able to get sloshed and like it. There's a constant pain in my chest, as if someone had buried a pickax in there, and during the most banal conversations, like this exchange with Hugo the checkout guy ("Here you go." "Thanks"), tears leak unaccountably from my eyes.

I make it through the gauntlet of street beggars blocking the way to the car and slam the door, as if to keep the vapor of their destitution out. Starting the engine, I make a resolution to leave all this behind. When I see Teresa and Cristóbal I want to be upbeat, a role model, the one who shows them the positive side, the satisfactions and achievements of working hard in this society.

Nobody answers the intercom but the lock on the lobby door is broken, so I pass under the organ-pipe sculpture up the metal stairs. It is six thirty at night and I'm hoping Mrs. Gutiérrez is at home serving a nutritious dinner, thereby not occasioning a call to Children and Family Services, but the pounding music that grows louder as I approach is stirring up an uneasy feeling.

After I knock and give it a few good kicks, the door is finally opened by a belligerent, overweight teenage boy wearing a Hawaiian shirt and smoking a cigarette.

"What's going on?" he demands.

"I'm looking for Mrs. Gutiérrez."

"She don't live here."

I block him from closing the door.

"What the fuck?"

I badge him. "FBI. Can I come in?"

There are five or six other boys sprawled around the floor playing a video game, surrounded by cigarette smoke blended with who knows what else. They look at me and their eyes slide sideways and they joke to one another in Spanish. I take an aggressive posture and keep close to the door.

"Where's the woman who lived here?"

"I told you, lady. She moved away."

"Whose apartment is this? Where are the adults?"

"It's my place," says the smallest one, wearing red mirror sunglasses and working the controls. "Actually, my mom's. She's at work. The lady who lived here went back to El Salvador."

"I need to talk to you."

"Sure."

He gets up and swaggers toward me as the others whistle and hoot, challenging him. I don't like the building sense of dare and the ear-piercing mix of technopop and video chirp is making me nuts.

"Do me a favor, take off the shades."

"What's the problem?"

"I want to see if you're straight."

Tough guy: "I'm straight."

He removes the glasses, revealing himself to be about twelve years old.

"It's very important that you tell me exactly what happened to Mrs. Gutiérrez and the children."

"Nothing happened. We live across the hall, she's friendly with my mom. One day she says she's going to El Salvador because she's taking some kids back to their parents or something—"

"To the grandmother?"

"Yeah, the grandmother. So we got the apartment and all the stuff in it for a hundred bucks."

The volcano paintings are still on the walls. The card table with its display of beer bottles intact. Teresa and Cristóbal are gone, erased.

I notice the laminated picture of El Niño de Atocha in the kitchen leaning up against the yellow tiles.

"She left that, too?"

"I guess."

"You want it?"

He shrugs. I take the picture and two stumps of votive candles. "Keep the music down."

■   ■   ■

From the apartment house it is a two-block walk past dark empty lots and wrecked cars abandoned along the curb.

The corner of Santa Monica Boulevard comes to life from the crime scene photos: a major street, a bus stop with a blue bench, a low building with bricked-in windows that turns out to be a recording studio. A few steps away a mini-mall with fast-food chicken, pizza, dry cleaners, and a huge flamingo-pink music store is jammed with vehicles waiting for parking spaces. Rush-hour traffic on the main streets is moving slowly, an unctuous flow of yellow headlights.

If I looked hard enough, I could find the bullet holes in the bench and even in the masonry wall, but I don't have the taste for it. I've been told Violeta was a religious person. Here is the congregation: young male runaways leaning into car windows hustling fifteen-dollar blow jobs. Here is the priest: a homeless schizophrenic wearing a child's baseball jacket that comes down to his elbows shuffling along, pointing fastidiously to every square in the sidewalk. Here are the stained-glass windows: broken vials of crack glittering under orange street lamps. And instead of incense we are blessed with the profanity of car exhaust.

Yet, I prop up the plastic picture of El Niño de Atocha on the sill of one of the bricked-in windows and ask him, the guardian of lakes, to bless this unlikely place where someone has drowned. I set down the candle stubs, memorials to Violeta and my father, ghosts whom I will never really know. Despite the horns and the roar of traffic like a jetway and pedestrians on every side, I close my eyes and stand there and actually pray to El Niño to keep watch over those who are lost. I pray that Teresa and Cristóbal will walk on a black sand beach where the warm water will be full of red snapper and shrimp, and that when they reach the clearing in the bush they will find an older brother who is kind and a loving grandmother waiting with open arms.

Violeta's Bible has been bumping around in my glove compartment. I finally lay it to rest on the window ledge.

A tight bitter sadness stays in my throat all the way home. When I get back to the apartment, I find Donnato's card wedged in the door. "Call me," he's written.

I don't.

■ ■ ■

Six days later the transfer to Kidnapping and Extortion comes through. Even though I know most of the guys on the squad, the first morning is tense. There are new procedures, a slew of paperwork, a different schedule, and of course a whole new section of the law to memorize.

My desk is moved to the other side of the bullpen and I say good-bye to the Bank Dick's Undercover Disguise. There's no room in the new location, so I leave it on the rack, inscribing my addition in ballpoint pen to the timeworn layers of advice: "Always make backup disks."

My first case on C-1 involves an attempt by a disgruntled employee to hold the owner of a stationery store in a garage for ransom. He escaped and ran to the house of a neighbor who called the police. The suspect is now in custody. Being low man on the totem pole, my assignment is to go back to the neighbor, who has already been interviewed twice, and verify certain facts in his statement.

The abduction took place on Sixth Street, just off La Brea. This time of day the straightest shot would be Santa Monica Boulevard, which is how I come to be passing that corner once again.

What I see causes me to veer out of traffic and park in the middle of the bus stop.

It is the stop for the same bus Violeta would have taken to work on the Westside, the one she stepped off that night, the Number 4.

Maybe she crocheted along the way, maybe she dozed—past McDonald's, Crown Books, Lou's Quickie Grill, the crimson Formosa Café, the Pussycat Theater at Genessee, the Jewish bakeries in the Fairfax district—but Violeta Alvarado always got on the Number 4 at the same place and got off the Number 4 at the same place and was unchanged by the journey. She wasn't part of the scramble. She knew who she was. She had come to America, that was her journey, and it ended here, at an intersection of dead roads, surrounded by a group of leering stoned-out creeps—misfits, night people, the forgotten, the invisible, the diseased, the disenfranchised, the damaged beyond help—at the coldest hour, just before dawn.

I know that hour of the night and I know that crossroads. I believe I have spent most of my life in that time and place, surrounded by spectres, deathly cold. The difference between us is Violeta carried hope like a simple charm, it was given to her the day she was born on a *petate* mat in the jungle, a birthright as uncomplicated as sun glancing off the leaf of a bamboo tree, and now, in the light of just such an ordinary, evanescent event, that gift has been shown to me.

I get out of the car and walk slowly, wonderingly, across the sidewalk. The haunted are gone, or at least absorbed by the larger numbers of those who are getting on with business, despite the odds. Drawing closer I see that what I'd glimpsed from the road is real: the picture of El Niño de Atocha is still standing, and furthermore, the windowsill is full of amazing objects. People have left flowers, toy cars, candies, and coins. The Bible is there, untouched. Nobody has stolen from El Niño.

In the shelter of the ledge other candles have been added: good luck candles printed with pictures of saints as I saw in the *botánica*, a fat red and green one left over from Christmas, a ragtag collection of half-burned tapers standing in juice cartons or anchored in crumpled bits of aluminum foil. All are lit. Someone has kept them lit. For the first time I can feel my mother and father inside me together, then rising together from this tender company of flames; rising up.

I don't know how long I stand there before going back to the car and picking up the radio.

"This is signal 345. Do you have signal 587 in service?"

Dispatch: "Yes, we do."

I give my location. "Could you ask him to respond?"

"Is it an emergency?"

"Not an emergency. Just a miracle."

I lean against the G-ride until Donnato pulls up ten minutes later, bubble flashing, swerving to a halt and further blocking the bus stop.

He throws the door open and hurries toward me with a worried look. I reach for his hand, in front of that doofball Joe Positano, and everybody.

ACKNOWLEDGMENTS

The author wishes to express particular gratitude to Sonny Mehta for his commitment, as a publisher, to the vision of the writer. Warm thanks also to Sarah Burnes for her insights and for staying on the case, and to Molly Friedrich, whose unstoppable enthusiasm for the manuscript made everything possible. Boz Graham of CAA and Walter Teller of Hansen, Jacobson, Teller, and Hoberman provided expert advice, and the keen editorial talent of Sandi Gelles-Cole was essential throughout.

Two dear writer friends provided more steady encouragement than anyone deserves: thank you to Robert Crais for showing the way, and to Dan Wakefield, generous of soul, for his undaunting faith, wisdom, and good fellowship—in many ways the godfather of this book.

Deep appreciation is also expressed to the comrades and conspirators who read early drafts or otherwise contributed: Deborah Aal, Michelle Abrams, Seth Freeman, Janice Forman, Lauren Grant, Nicholas Hammond, Janis Hirsch, Robert F. Iverson, M.D., Evan and David Levinson, Milena and Jorge Pardo, Gerald Petievich, Julie Waxman, Harry Winer.

ACKNOWLEDGMENTS

And to those whose courageous spirits illuminate every word: Maria Zambrano and Maria Florencia Fernandez.

An enormous debt is owed to the experts who gave freely of their time and knowledge: Carla Gates, George K. Ganaway, M.D., P.C., Matt Parker, Maria P. P. Root, Ph.D., Jane Sherwood, R.N., and the nurses on the Coronary Care Unit at New England Deaconess Hospital, and most especially Marc Taylor of Technical Associates, Inc., for sharing his expertise in forensic science.

The cooperation of the men and women of the Los Angeles field office of the Federal Bureau of Investigation added immeasurably to the veracity and heart of the novel; they embody a mix of professionalism, skill, and humanity that is truly inspiring.

Finally, the author is fortunate to have been given the enduring gifts of family: from her mother, Bernice Smith, who taught her to swim; her father, Philip H. Smith, M.D., who taught her the art of storytelling; and her brother Ronald L. Smith, whose many talents include the nurturing gift of laughter.

She has also been blessed by warmth and caring from her second family, Austin and Arthur Brayfield, and is grateful beyond measure for the joy of her children, Ben and Emma, and for the uncompromising editorial eye and steadfast support of her husband, Douglas Brayfield, whose love, strength, and tenderness have sustained both author and work.

A NOTE ON THE TYPE

This book was set in a digitized version of Caledonia, a type face
designed by W(illiam) A(ddison) Dwiggins (1880–1956) for the
Mergenthaler Linotype Company in 1939. Dwiggins chose to
call his new type face Caledonia, the Roman name for Scotland,
because it was inspired by the Scottish types cast about 1833 by
Alexander Wilson & Son, Glasgow type founders. However,
there is a calligraphic quality about Caledonia that is totally
lacking in the Wilson types.
Dwiggins referred to an even earlier type face for this "liveliness
of action"—one cut around 1790 by William Martin for the
printer William Bulmer. Caledonia has more weight than the
Martin letters, and the bottom finishing strokes (serifs) of the
letters are cut straight across, without brackets, to make sharp
angles with the upright stems, thus giving a modern-face
appearance.
Composed by ComCom, a division of Haddon Craftsmen,
Allentown, Pennsylvania. Printed and bound by The Haddon
Craftsmen, Scranton, Pennsylvania
Designed by Iris Weinstein